THE WIDOW
AND THE
Rock Star

J. THOMAS-LIKE

Copyright © 2014 J. Thomas-Like

Cover Art by James, GoOnWrite.com

Author Photo by Chasing Light Photography

All rights reserved.
First Edition: July 2014

This is a work of fiction. Any resemblance of characters to actual persons, living or dead, is purely coincidental. The author takes full responsibility for any errors and holds exclusive rights to this work. Unauthorized duplication is prohibited.

This book is licensed for your personal enjoyment only. If you would like to share this book with another person, please purchase an additional copy for each reader. Thank you for respecting the hard work of this author.

ISBN-13: 978-1500384937
ISBN-10: 1500384933

For more information:
http://www.jthomaslike.com

Dedication

For Daddy

The one person I wanted most to make proud.
It took longer than you could last, but I hope I did it.

For Nevada

It's no *Waiting for the Sunrise*,
but I think you'd like it, anyway.

Acknowledgements

To Mom, Jeff and Amy: I finally did it!

Thank you Laura for your beauty and Chris for your talent. I look forward to many more photo shoots.

Thank you to my special friends, some of whom may or may not think they resemble certain characters. You know who you are.
Please don't sue.

This never would have happened if it weren't for WRITE CLUB!

A special thank you to Natalie and Mary for going above and beyond. Jason, Brian, Philly and Matt, you were also instrumental in this particular work and I can't thank you enough. And to all the former members of WC: you gave me years of excellent critiques and generous support. If not for you, I might not have kept going.

Powerhouse Summit Members: you ROCK! I am forever grateful for your advice, guidance, and encouragement to get this book out there.

Last, but <u>NOT</u> least, my *extraordinary* husband. You believed in me from the start, encouraged me through the tough spots, was patient during the manic times, and didn't divorce me for having a crush on my male leading character.
HEY! I love ya!

Chapter 1

"Good morning and thank you for calling Glendale Bank's online technical support department. My name is Joe. How may I assist you today?"

Shit. I spit the sip of coffee I had just taken back into the cup.

"Yes, good morning! I'm having some difficulty logging in to my account. It keeps telling me the password is invalid." Grabbing a tissue, I wiped away the small drip of liquid crawling down my chin.

"Yes ma'am, I'd be happy to assist you with that. Could I have your first and last name, please?"

"Vivienne Stark." I made sure to spell it for him. I listened to Joe tap on the keyboard I couldn't see, imagining a head and two lone hands floating in space with no body. I answered all of his questions to verify my identity then waited for him to reset my password. He prompted me to log in again while he stayed on the line to make sure the new password worked.

"Success!" I smiled as the page with my financial information slowly loaded, but I could feel the grin slide off my face and my heart begin to race. Both accounts had a zero balance. What the hell? I tried to click on each one for more information, but error boxes claiming the accounts had been closed popped up on the screen, one after the other.

"Uh, Joe? All my balances are reading zero here and I'm being told my accounts are closed. Is there some problem on your end?"

"I don't have actual access to your accounts, ma'am. I would have to transfer you to customer service."

"Please do that," I muttered through clenched teeth, irritated with all the delays so far this morning. First, the password not working.

Then waiting on hold for twenty minutes for a techie. And now my accounts all saying zero and closed? *What the fuck?*

Fortunately, I didn't have to wait more than a minute before my call was answered in the order it was received. Another two minutes and there would have been hell to pay.

"Good morning and thank you for calling Glendale Bank's customer service department. My name is Maria, how may I assist you today?"

"Good morning, Maria. I'm looking at my account information online and it's saying both checking and savings are at a zero balance. I'm a little confused by that. Could you take a look please?" I did my best to remain calm and pleasant.

"Yes ma'am, I'd be happy to assist you with that. Could I have your first and last name, please?"

Rolling my eyes, I once *again* proved I was me. I waited for Marie to say there was just a computer glitch or the system was in the middle of an update. Or someone else some*where* else had made a huge mistake but that everything would be just fine.

It's a good thing I wasn't holding my breath.

"Ma'am, it shows here that all funds were withdrawn yesterday and the accounts were closed."

"*What?*" I screeched. "By whom?" *So much for calm.*

"Let me check."

More tapping that synced with my thumping heart. Sweat popped out on my upper lip.

"Anthony Lyleson closed the accounts and requested a cashier's check in the amount of $762,412.36."

"Son of a bitch!" My cardiac rhythm hit a new high while adrenaline dumped into my system, instantly giving me the shakes. My armpits burned with prickling sweat. "I thought there had to be two signers on any withdrawal requests or checks? How could he do this without my signature?"

"You aren't in California ma'am?"

"No, I'm in Michigan." I was hoping I wouldn't vomit.

"One moment please."

I began to feel lightheaded, like I was going to pass out. I leaned over in my chair, putting my head between my knees. My freshly dyed red hair surrounded my head and brushed against the floor. The faint smell of ammonia filled my nose, bringing me back to my senses. Anthony Lyleson. Tony *fucking* Lyleson. The man *I* had put in charge of my charitable foundation was a lying, thieving rat *bastard*.

"Your signature appeared on the check he presented, ma'am. I can email you an image of it to the address we have on file." Maria's lack of emotion fueled my overloaded anger circuits.

"Do it!" I snapped as I sat straight up. I sucked in my breath with the instant swooning headache that thumped my skull.

While I waited for the email to arrive, I jumped up and began pacing across the squeaky wooden floors in my dining/living area. Each creak filled my ears and mingled with the sound of blood rushing through the veins in my temples. If this didn't bring on a migraine, I didn't know what would. *What the hell was I going to do?* Three quarters of a million dollars up and gone. Poof! I blinked back a wave of furious tears as Maria spoke to me with her unaffected tone.

"If this was an unauthorized or fraudulent transaction, ma'am, I'll need to transfer you to our fraud investigation department."

"Wait!"

I wanted that email before I let Maria escape back into telephone outer space. Too late. Muzak burst through the speaker on my phone, causing me to wince. I let out a shrill scream, the tail end of which pierced the eardrum of the operator who once again thanked me for calling and asked how she could help.

Help? She could help by turning back the clock! Just then the new email bell went off and I dove back into my seat in front of the laptop. As I spoke to the fraud operator, I pulled up the attachment to be confronted with a poorly forged copy of my signature below Anthony Lyleson's on a check from The Widow's Path Foundation. Never mind the signature wasn't even close to mine, but Tony had been stupid enough to misspell my name by leaving out an "n."

I spent the rest of my morning arguing with people at the bank. Trying to convince them I hadn't authorized the embezzlement felt like an exercise in futility. I couldn't count the number of times I asked the bank officials if I would really misspell my own name. Eventually they agreed the transaction was fraudulent, but they wouldn't admit it was an error on their part or assume any responsibility whatsoever. A police report would have to be filed, an investigation conducted. My presence in California would be mandatory as soon as possible. They opened a new account on which only I was authorized. I needed to wire funds from my personal account immediately so that checks written to numerous families would not bounce. Shit, that was *all* those struggling families needed. Glendale Bank swore up and down they would honor any check that arrived before the wire transfer. They also promised under penalty of lawsuit that they would contact me directly and immediately if any of the checks looked suspicious.

I didn't hold out much hope the cops would catch Tony. He had probably left the country right after leaving the bank. How Andy Dufresne of him, ala *The Shawshank Redemption*, although Andy was a good guy and Tony was turning out to be the scourge of existence.

I also called my agent, Jake Rushmore, to let him know what was going on. He freaked out more than I did. He was more worried about the negative publicity than the money actually being missing.

"You need to get out here ASAP," he huffed over the line after spewing a string of curses.

"I know—"

"I'm serious. Get your *ass* on a plane *today*!"

"Jake, I—"

"I'll get Ariadne to book your flight. *Ari*! Get on the net, get Vivienne Stark out to Los Angeles by tonight!" He was shouting and I could picture his face growing a deeper shade of magenta by the moment.

I pursed my lips and listened to him prattle on about damage control, press releases and getting me on TV as soon as possible. Of course he wouldn't be concerned with the hundreds of widows and widowers and their families the foundation was meant to help. That would be *my* burden. *Jackass*, I thought, rather unkindly.

I held the phone away from my face and shouted his name as loudly as I could.

"Jake!"

"What?!"

"Just email me the info and I'll be there."

"Okay. Look for it shortly. Talk to you later."

Even though the thought of eating anything made me want to hurl, I went to the kitchen to find a sandwich. If my blood sugar dropped any lower, I'd be comatose before I could get out to California. I mixed up tuna and mayo, and then spread it on bread. I tried to take small bites and chew thoroughly, but the food just didn't want to go down my throat. It wasn't getting past the lump of guilt that had settled there. I tossed the sandwich aside and grabbed my phone. I called my local bank and put into motion the wire transfer of almost all of my savings. It still wasn't nearly enough, not even half of what Tony had stolen. My stomach lurched at the thought.

"War widow" wasn't the title I planned on putting on my business card of life. I reserved that spot for the word "writer." But publishing a fictionalized version of my personal tragedy forever linked me with both. *The Widow's Path* turned into my opus. Originally self-published as an e-book through Amazon, word of mouth and social media sent it skyrocketing out of the atmosphere. The publishing company offered me a contract and within six months, the book was on the New York Times Best Seller list and nominated for the National Book Award.

For something that began as a tear-stained, rambling journal entry, no one was more shocked than me when it became a success. For a dozen years, it was nothing more than a narrative of the debilitating pain in my heart. Every day I would vomit the words onto a page in an effort to purge myself of the agony. Instead of leaving it behind and moving forward, I remained in my mental shroud of mourning. A life of pain and bereavement was much easier than learning to live or love again.

The Widow and the Rock Star

Around year fourteen, I started playing around with the idea of fictionalizing it. Why not try and put it out there to help in the income department? I could change all the "I's" to "she" and "her." Give "her" a name and a happy ending. The main character could find love again and have a real life, even if I couldn't or wouldn't. I pitched the idea to my writer's group buddies and they were immediately on board. They knew the truth about me and thought my story would make a compelling read for people who'd struggled with the same issues.

When *The Widow's Path* blew up, thousands of letters and email messages poured in, mirroring my own grief and horror. All manner of survivors wrote saying the book touched them and gave them hope, even if they cried through most of it. They wanted to know how I could see what was in their hearts and minds so well. They thanked me for telling "their" story. Because I fictionalized the book, it was a closely guarded secret that it was based on my own personal experience. Only my family, friends, and Jake knew about it.

Till that point in time, I'd already indie-published a steady stream of romance/chick-lit novels at a rate that allowed me to earn a modest living outside the nine-to-five box. But *The Widow's Path* brought in the *crazy* money. Paying the bills was no longer a worry. Shopping for store brands instead of name brands was a thing of the past. Savings accounts and retirement plans were in my future for the first time in my life. Anyone outside of my inner circle probably thought my life was perfect.

Something was missing, though. I was pretty sure the universe was telling me to let go of the past, go forward, shed my widow identity and live like a normal person. It was too scary a proposition for me. Instead, I racked my brain for a way to do good and give back *without* having to put any more of myself out there than I already had. I wanted to help people and do charitable works to pay my good fortune forward. I just didn't want to be ostentatious or obvious about it.

The idea I finally got wasn't even my own. A nonprofit organization benefiting veterans approached me for an endorsement and donation about six months after the initial media explosion surrounding *The*

Widow's Path. I immediately agreed to the donation, but declined giving an endorsement. If I was going to put my name on anything, it was going to be something I controlled. Hence, The Widow's Path Foundation. Publicly, it was meant to help and support the widows, widowers and children of fallen soldiers. Personally, it was a way for me to continue to hide within the safety of widowhood and avoid real life.

I donated a third of the profits of the book to get the foundation up and running. I started making cold calls to friends, family, and anyone I had a connection to in order to keep the funds rolling in. My mom and my friends helped to organize local fundraisers, send out flyers, and with the day-to-day details of the fledgling organization. My first mistake was letting Jake take over the publicity, and things went wild. Press inquiries were nonstop. Donations poured in from all over the country when the word got out I'd started a foundation. I needed someone to take over and do all the hard work I was so unprepared for. Jake gave me a list of names to vet of reputable people who'd been in charge of large charitable organizations in the past. Tony Lyleson's name had *not* appeared on that list. It was just my bad luck he had turned up at one of the many fundraisers we held. He schmoozed me so expertly, I was hooked like a stupid walleye out of Lake St. Clair.

Within six weeks, Tony Lyleson was the front man of The Widow's Path Foundation, leaving me free to return to my life of obscurity in St. Clair Shores, Michigan. He convinced me to move the foundation to Los Angeles, where he lived, so that he could solicit the celebrity set for larger donations and glowing endorsements. He promised success for the foundation beyond anything I'd ever imagined. He spun tales of televised benefits and A-list rock stars and bands performing at them. Tony convinced me that The Widow's Path Foundation would one day be as philanthropic as The Red Cross. I was mesmerized by his charismatic passion and apparent commitment to the cause so near to my heart. I was addicted to the idea that I could finally make more of a difference in the world than by filling it with whimsical fiction *and* keep myself hidden away in the 'burb where I was born and raised. I trusted so easily, so stupidly.

Now all my dreams were as KIA as any soldier lost in any war. *Son of a bitch!*

I slammed the paper plate with my unfinished sandwich into the trash and stomped off to my bedroom, grimacing the whole way as the acid in my stomach churned into a grade-A case of heartburn. I slumped onto the edge of my bed, hanging my head in shame. I had no one to blame but myself for this mess.

Wiping my face on my sleeve, I sniffed loudly. I flopped onto my back and stared at the ceiling for a while, letting my eyes leak until the hair at my temples was soaked. Not caring how much time passed, I wondered all sorts of things that couldn't be answered in any substantive way. *How could I have been so blind? Why hadn't I checked the bank balance yesterday? Why would the bank let him present a check with a signature that clearly did not match the one on file?*

I might as well have spent time wondering why a leprechaun didn't appear at my door with a pot full of shiny gold coins. Rolling my head to the right, my eyes automatically found the urn. It was perched next to the glass-encased American flag on the shelf mounted against the wall. Bruce's battered pair of dog tags were draped over both. It didn't matter that it was seventeen years after the fact, I still felt a deep yearning for my best male friend to be at my side, instead of in pieces inside the stainless steel tube.

"What am I going to do Bruce? All I wanted to do was help people." My voice wavered in unison with my trembling bottom lip.

It wasn't as though I expected a real response, but I nearly pissed myself when the doorbell rang at the same time I stopped speaking out loud to the empty room. Startled into motion, I sprinted out of my room, down the hall and to the front door of my little shotgun ranch house. I flung the door open, a FedEx man greeting me with a smile. It faltered only slightly when he obviously saw what a mess I was. His arm stretched out to present a flat envelope.

"Vivienne Stark?" he asked, not looking me in the eye.

"Yes."

"Sign here, please."

Without even hesitating, I opened the storm door and leaned out to scribble my name in the tiny box on his digital reader. I thanked him as he bounced down the steps of my front porch and I went back inside. I tore into the envelope, curious and terrified at what could be inside. *What now?*

*****

Gripping the armrests of Seat 24E didn't help to alleviate my fear that the plane would crash on the runway in a fiery ball of destruction instead of touching down with its usual precision. If I could have walked to California, I would have. Unfortunately, I didn't have enough time for the leisurely stroll.

Instead, I left Detroit Metro airport at 5:00 p.m. on the flight Jake booked for me. When the plane finally came to a stop at the gateway and I heard the sealed door whoosh open, I began to breathe again. Normally, I'm a polite person, allowing other people to go ahead of me, holding doors for others, that kind of thing. When flying is involved, though, look out. I grabbed my carry on from the overhead and almost body checked a businessman and an old lady in order to get my ass off that plane.

Suitcase finally in hand after a twenty minute wait at the baggage carousel, I hurried through the airport and out into the humid night. I peered around. Jake assured me there would be a car waiting to take me to my hotel, kindly provided by EJR Productions, one of the largest film companies in the world. It was compliments of EJR that I was actually in California, because they were offering me a chance to sell the rights to *The Widow's Path* for the silver screen adaptation. Another company, Gleaming Bee Pictures, wanted the rights as well. It looked as though I had a bidding war on my hands.

After the embezzlement drama that morning, the last thing I expected FedEx to deliver was a formal purchase offer from a movie studio. When I'd called Jake to tell him, he was nearly convulsing with excitement because he had in his hand a similar FedEx envelope from Gleaming Bee Pictures. I wouldn't let myself wonder if things could get any screwier. I didn't want to put that kind of energy into the universe.

I spotted a tall, thin man dressed "Men In Black" style, holding a sign with my name on it. Waving my arms in the air like a maniac until he saw me, I didn't realize how nervous I'd been getting. It didn't matter that Jake had texted me to watch for a car and driver. It didn't mean they would actually *be* there. I must have sounded like an idiot when I thanked the guy five times for taking my bag. His smile was kind as he nodded while opening the door for me to hop inside. Mr. Men-in-Black's name was Marvin, and he asked if I wanted to go anywhere before the hotel. As I sunk into the soft leather seat of the Lincoln Town Car, I shook my head no and closed my eyes. The clock read a little after ten, but my body said it was the middle of the night because of the time change.

"Just the hotel, please."

"Yes ma'am."

As the car hurtled along the freeway, I whipped off a quick email to my mom back in Michigan, letting her know I'd made it safely. She told me to call her the minute I landed, but there was no way I would wake her at one a.m. She was nearing eighty, and I wasn't about to deprive her of any much deserved rest. I knew she would be on her computer checking email and Facebook while she munched on breakfast. I resigned myself to the scolding I'd surely get when I did speak to her.

Marvin delivered me safely to the Ritz Carlton and I was left speechless by the fanciness of the place. The cavernous lobby echoed with my footsteps, even though I wore an old pair of Converse Chuck Taylor high tops. Everything was spotless and sparkling. The smell of high-end cleaning solutions and fresh flowers mingled, wafting around my head.

The young woman at the counter who checked me in smiled with easy professionalism, then handed me the two plastic cards that served as keys to my room. In a scripted voice, she directed me to the elevator and asked if I needed help with my bags.

"No, that's okay; I have it." I returned her smile and wandered off in the direction she pointed.

I rode to the 12th floor, enjoying the fluttery feeling in my stomach when the car landed with a gentle jolt. I'm just an average Jane from a common suburban upbringing, but the opulence of the suite I was given blew me away. I sunk half an inch when I stepped onto the deep-pile carpeting. The striped cream and white walls were inlayed with tiny crystals. All of the furniture was pristine white and the softest leather I'd ever touched. The California king-size bed looked more inviting than winning a Pulitzer Prize for fiction. Well, almost.

As I hoisted my suitcase onto the bed, my cell phone blared "Cadillac Ranch" by Bruce Springsteen from inside my purse. I dove across the bed, grabbing it in the nick of time.

"You made it." Jake sounded relieved, as if I would back out.

"Yes, I'm here." I rolled onto my back and tried to steady my breathing.

"Get yourself some rest. The car will pick you up tomorrow morning at 6:30 a.m. sharp. After *Good Day LA*, you'll go to the NBC studios. From there, I have a reservation for us at 1:00 p.m. for lunch, and then we meet with EJR Productions at 3:00 p.m. It's going to be a busy day."

"Ya think?" I could hear him clacking away on a computer.

"There, I just emailed it to you and I'll text it, too."

"Thanks." I wasn't able to disguise my sarcasm. I had an open-ended ticket back to Michigan. Did he have to jam pack my first day in California? *Sheesh.*

"The press release went out hours ago and I've been fielding phone calls nonstop. I want to spray water before the fires even start with this embezzlement stuff." Jake sounded as tired as I felt. "The lawyer's going to want a $10,000 retainer."

The Widow and the Rock Star

"Glad I brought my checkbook," I muttered.

"What was that?"

"When do we meet with the bank and the police?" I rubbed my eyes and forehead. All the information whirling in my head was making it ache.

"The morning after next. The law firm said they would send someone. I told them we wanted a partner for all the fucking money we're going to spend with them."

I pulled myself into a sitting position and groaned when my lower back sang with a muscle threatening to winch itself out of place. *Shit, that's all I need.*

"Why are we meeting with EJR so soon?" I practically whined, then cringed. "What I mean to say is, why aren't we meeting with the lawyer, the police and the bank *first*?"

"Because the bank wouldn't schedule a meeting any sooner than that," Jake said slowly, with a little more condescension than patience. "They know they're on the hook for this but haven't figured out a way to cover their asses. And we're meeting with EJR as soon as possible because they're offering the most money at present."

"Not to mention springing for the hotel." I glanced around wondering how much this room was costing them. *I don't even want to know.* I squatted to push my suitcase under the bureau.

"That's right. Get to bed and I'll talk to you first thing in the morning."

"You aren't coming with me?" I had hoped for someone to mentally hold hands with throughout the interview process.

"No, I have some radio to do. I'll meet you at the restaurant for lunch. I texted your itinerary to Marvin."

I nodded in appreciation for all the details Jake had handled and told him how grateful I was. I might be irritated as hell to be in California at all, and furious over my current financial situation, but I never could have arranged everything as competently as he had. Well, he and his assistant Ariadne. I made a mental note to send Ari a little something for all her hard work. Jake got his 15%; he didn't need a gift.

I ended the call with Jake and plugged in my phone to charge, then set my alarm for 5:45 a.m. Worried I would hit the snooze or, God forbid, turn the damn thing off, I called the front desk to schedule a wakeup call for 6:00 a.m. Satisfied I would not oversleep and screw up the entire works, I changed into a tee-shirt and shorts and crawled into bed.

I took a deep breath and snuggled beneath the soft, cool sheets and puffy comforter, wrapping my arms around one of the fat pillows. My eyelids felt heavy as I used one of my many relaxation techniques to ease myself to sleep.

And then I laid there. *Not* sleeping.

*****

As promised, Marvin was waiting downstairs for me at 6:30 a.m. on the dot. I still wore my tee-shirt, yoga pants and black Chuck Taylors, but lugged a stylish brown silk wrap dress and simple black pumps to wear for my TV appearances. I looked like hell from my almost completely restless night. Marvin asked if I'd slept well. I only scowled at him and his amused smirk. He hadn't even shut the door when my phone yelled "text message!" It was Jake checking in to make sure I was on schedule.

R u on the road?

I replied with a "yes," then dialed my mom. She answered on the first ring.

"You should have called!" Olivia Forest admonished.

"You should have known I wouldn't." I laughed when she did. "It was after one, Mom. I was too tired."

"All right, you're forgiven. Where are you now?"

"I'm in the car on the way to the television station."

"Which one? Can I watch? Will it be live?" Mom's questions were like rapid fire.

"I don't know, I don't know, and I don't know." I shook my head and laid it on the back of the seat. "Doesn't matter. I'll be able to email you links from the network's website afterward."

"You'd better!" Mom threatened. "I'm sorry for the circumstances, but you know I love to see you on TV."

"Ugh." I groaned and smiled. Ever the proud momma. "I promise I will email you everything when I get a chance. I've got a long day ahead of me though, so don't expect it until tomorrow."

"You be careful out there." Mom's voice softened and I could hear her sigh. "When do you think you'll be back?"

"I'm really not sure, Mom. It won't be for at least a week, probably two. I could fly you out here, if you wanted."

"Hell no," she snorted. "I have no desire to see California. Send me back to London first."

I laughed out loud and opened my eyes as I felt the car slow down. Peering out the window, I could see signs for the studio.

"I told you, next spring. We'll go then, when the weather is best. Look, Mom, I have to run. We're pulling in to the parking lot now."

"All right, honey. Be careful. Just remember who you are."

Smiling, I told her I would. After I hung up, I was hit with a wave of homesickness so fierce I thought I might cry. Before the tears could form, Marvin pulled up to the studio doors and was whipping my door open to help me out.

I forgot how tired I was as I got hustled inside by a production assistant who was waiting for me. She ushered me to hair and makeup and someone gave me a cup of tremendously strong, but excellent coffee. I slipped into a chair and closed my eyes, while a pert and chatty young blond worked on my still-wet hair. I understood why Jake wanted me to be the one in the public eye: I would garner more sympathy as the cheated, single, female author than he would as my brash agent and publicist. But I still didn't like having to do it. I didn't like being the center of attention or on television. Just the thought of millions of people looking at me made feel like covering my face and crawling under the nearest convenient piece of furniture.

I couldn't deny enjoying the pampering though. The hairdresser styled my long hair in fashionable waves and then a makeup artist had me looking fresher and younger than I had in years. *If only I could figure out a way to get the pampering without having to do the interview.* When I was perfectly coiffed and made up, a production assistant took me to the "green room" where I could wait until it was my turn to go on set.

As usual, the "green room" wasn't green at all. The walls were painted sky blue, with light oak hardwood floors. There were several loveseats and a single long sofa, all covered in blue, white, and cream plaid. Along one wall was a craft services food table piled high with donuts, bagels, ten different flavors of cream cheese, granola bars, yogurt cups floating in a bowl of ice water, and three giant urns of coffee and hot water. As tempting as it was, I avoided all of it. I was afraid if I ate anything and got more nervous, I'd barf. I already knew I'd have to hit the restroom before going on for my segment, so more coffee was out of the question.

I perched on the edge of a loveseat, watching the current live segment on a huge flat-screen television. Some female actress who was up and coming, but I hadn't heard of yet, was being interviewed. Not of my era. I was at that in-between stage of life where I was too young to know all of the older celebrities, but too old to recognize the twenty-somethings. Some days this pissed me off because I didn't want to feel old. Other days I allowed myself to paddle around in a fake pool of superiority because I wasn't a slave to tabloid fodder. *Most* days I didn't think about it at all.

When my coffee was gone, I stood up and smoothed my dress and impatiently paced around the room. My nerves were beginning to wear thin and I thought I would just up and leave. Going back to an old habit of mine from high school, I started to practice my American Sign Language finger spelling, choosing all the swear words I knew.

As I was running out of expletives, the door to the green room opened. *Finally.* I looked up, expecting to see a production assistant coming for me. Instead, a group of five men barreled into the room, laughing and joking, totally oblivious that anyone was already there.

The Widow and the Rock Star

They wore jeans and tee-shirts, but the loudest one had on a weathered, black motorcycle jacket. The sleeves were pushed up on his forearms, revealing several multicolored tattoos, one of which was a golden cross covered in green serpents. It reminded me of something biblical. I didn't even get a brief glimpse of his face because the PA looking for me peeked around one of the guys and crooked her finger in my direction.

"Excuse me," I said softly, avoiding eye contact. They all towered over me like giants, hovering in the six-foot-plus range. Realizing I was trying to get through, they quieted down as I exited. Still without raising my eyes, I turned my head offering a shy smile and, "Thank you." I heard one of them say, "You're welcome." My smile got wider from the seductive lilt in his voice. I tried to see which one had spoken, but the PA was already closing the door. *Oh well.*

As I was led to a set and shown which chair to sit in, nerves exploded in my stomach. I remembered I hadn't gone to the bathroom like I should have, but it was too late now. I crossed my legs tightly as I sat and hoped I wouldn't wet myself. One of the crew attached my microphone, making me flinch. The hair and makeup women reappeared to make sure I hadn't mussed myself, eyeing me and using the tools of their trade to freshen their work. The fuzzy brush used to powder my face made me feel like sneezing, but I willed it away. The director started shouting orders and the cameras began swiveling and rolling across the stage as the return from a commercial break was counted down. I seriously thought I was going to faint, but then I saw the red lights on top of the cameras explode with color. The audience offered polite applause when the production crew held up their signs commanding it. *Suck it up, Viv.*

The host greeted me kindly and gave a 30-second introduction about me and my book, then asked me all the appropriate and expected questions. I answered with as much confidence and grace as I could muster, though I kept thinking my voice was wavering and my hands were shaking like leaves on a tree in a wind storm. Jake would later tell me I did fine, but, in the moment, I had no way of knowing whether I looked like an idiot or not.

When the questions turned to the subject of the stolen money and broke foundation, my righteous indignation was pure. I wasn't able to give a lot of information because I didn't even have it for myself, but the anger I felt came across, eliciting sympathetic looks from the host.

Finally the interview was over and I was free. To more coaxed applause, a different PA escorted me off stage and my legs went watery with relief. I was led to where my purse and other belongings waited. Some assistant had gathered and piled them on a chair just outside the green room. As I shook on my light jacket, I watched the group of men from the green room being brought to the stage. They disappeared from my sight and reappeared in a TV monitor broadcasting a view of a side stage filled with microphone stands, drums, and other various musical instruments. *Ah, a band.* I wondered which one and squinted to read the writing on the drum set. Without my glasses it was too small. I touched the arm of a passing crew member and asked him what band it was. I almost had to shout because the audience had gone wild with spontaneous and authentic applause as the men took their places.

"Static Neverland," he called over his shoulder.

Yes, I'd heard of them. I was a typical radio fan, liking the few tunes I caught in passing, but didn't own any of their music and had never seen them in concert. Not that I went to concerts anymore. I hadn't done that since my late twenties. Glancing around, I saw no one paying any attention to me, so I stayed where I was and waited for Static Neverland to begin. They played a song called "Wishbone Fantasies" that I recognized and liked, so I bobbed my head along to the beat. I wished the images on the monitor were bigger so I could see them better, but it was only a 19-inch screen and the camera was at the back end of the audience. I wondered which one of them had said, "You're welcome" in that sexy voice.

"Did you need something else, Ms. Stark?" One of the junior producers, whose name I couldn't remember, appeared at my side looking confused at my lingering presence.

"No, I just stayed for the song."

Relief flooded her face like water over Niagara Falls. I wasn't upset or needing anything, or causing trouble of any sort that could throw a wrench into her perfectly orchestrated day.

"Oh, sure, no problem," she stammered. "Thank you, again, for being on the show."

"Thanks for having me." I nodded my head at her anorexic back because she was already moving away to the next item on her agenda. Taking a deep breath, I weaved my way through the studio to the exit as I heard the band finish playing. In a moment or two I was swept away by the ever vigilant Marvin to the next anxiety-ridden event.

Chapter 2

Pepper Taylor lazily reached for the cocktail on the table beside her and took a healthy swallow. The sun's rays were hot and her body glistened with sweat after lounging by the Ritz Carlton's pool for a scant thirty minutes. As she sipped the dirty martini, she breathed deep, enjoying the scent of chlorine, suntan lotion and ocean air. Glancing over at Vivienne, she smiled. Vivienne sat cross-legged on her chaise, hidden completely beneath a large umbrella and floppy straw hat. Pepper laughed when Viv coated herself with the strongest sunscreen available, making every effort to protect her fair skin from the yellow beams. Pepper admired her friend's pale complexion — and even envied it — because it kept Vivienne looking so young, something Pepper worked very hard to do. As an aging actress/model in Hollywood, youthfulness was the key to longevity.

If only I could write like she does, Pepper thought wistfully. *I'd much rather rely on my brains than my body.*

"You look like a ghost," Pepper remarked for the fifth time, draining her glass.

Vivienne was scribbling away on a note pad, her face scrunched up with concentration. Her hand never stopped.

"A little bit of sun isn't going to kill you, you know." Pepper stuck her tongue out.

Vivienne never looked up.

"I saw that."

Pepper laughed out loud and put down her empty glass. She was so grateful to see her oldest and dearest friend. The last time they'd been in each other's physical presence, was at Bruce's funeral. Pepper had sworn she'd never set foot back in Michigan, but the horrific and devastating death of her best friend's husband was not something she could have ignored. The letters and phone calls across the years since then had been scarce, but the bond between them had never wavered.

Still, when a four-hour marathon telephone conversation would take place, Pepper was always disturbed by how much Vivienne still talked about Bruce. Over the years, she would have expected Vivienne to work through her grief and move on, but she never really did. Oh, she acted like she did, but Pepper knew better. A few carefully worded and leading questions always revealed the same facts. Vivienne had tossed her heart and soul into the grave along with Bruce. But, now that she had her bestie in her clutches in sunny California, Pepper intended to show her a good time like she'd never had before. She would do her damndest to show Vivienne that life had a *lot* more to offer.

"Let's go for a swim."

Vivienne continued to write, but eventually said, "Let me finish this thought." Three minutes later, as Pepper waited patiently, Vivienne set her pad and pen aside and shook out her hands. "Okay, let's go."

Pepper swung her legs over the side of the chair and stood up. Her long, lean body was bronzed to perfection and her honey blond hair was tied back in a bouncy ponytail. She made the slightest adjustment to her tiny bikini top, hooking her thumbs in the straps and hiking it up, causing her breasts to jiggle. Then she strode to the edge of the pool, fully aware of the glances she received from the other sunbathers. Snagging the rubber band with her fingers, she pulled her hair free and shook it out in true model fashion.

Okay, so maybe relying on my body isn't such a bad thing, Pepper admitted when she caught several pairs of male eyes staring at her.

Pepper watched as Vivienne tossed her hat on top of her abandoned notebook. She thought her friend's black, polka-dotted, one-piece bathing suit was too matronly. Vivienne had lost none of her petite cuteness from high school and yet she dressed as though she was twenty years older. She was on the small side, but her legs looked a little longer because of her shorter torso, and she had a solid C-cup on top. Pepper wanted to see Viv in a sexier suit to show off those curves, but knew it would be a hard-fought battle.

I'll have to work on that, she decided.

Sitting together with their feet dangling in the water, Pepper sighed with pleasure, in spite of the circumstances bringing Vivienne to California. Putting her arms behind her on the edge of the pool, Pepper eased herself down into the crystal clear water.

"What are we waiting for? The pool's heated for Chrissake."

Vivienne obeyed and dropped down. The water came to just below Pepper's breasts and almost to Vivienne's neck. Pepper laughed.

"Still short, I see."

"Yeah, well, there isn't much I can do about that. You'll always be the beanpole." Vivienne splashed water at her. "I love your tattoo." She pointed at the artwork on Pepper's side.

Pepper glanced down at it and smiled.

"Yeah? It's pretty old. I got it about ten years ago, but it still looks good." She ran a finger across the wings of a butterfly in flight and then across the rainbow behind it that was exploding with lots of colors.

"Did you ever get one?" she asked, peering at Vivienne's body.

"Hell no! Do you see anything on me?" Vivienne laughed. "I'm too wimpy."

Pepper grinned.

"No you're not. They can be pretty painful. Luckily, I was quite stoned when I got mine. It hurt worse the day after."

Nodding, Vivienne swam closer to get a better look at it.

"Well, it's beautiful. Just exactly what I would expect you to have. Look, I'm sorry it took me so long to get in touch. Jake's had me booked solid since I got off the plane."

"Totally okay." Pepper dog paddled in circles, enjoying the warm water lapping against her skin. "You should have called me when you got in. I could have picked you up at the airport."

"Pffft, Jake had a car waiting."

"I saw you on TV. You looked great." Pepper smiled warmly, nodding to show she meant what she said. Vivienne grimaced and shook her head.

"I looked like a troll."

"No you didn't!"

"A *broke* troll."

Pepper snorted with laughter.

"I think you did a great job." Pepper's tone was stern. "How's Mom? You know, I still get a Christmas card from her *every* year."

Vivienne rolled her eyes but there was love there.

"She's my hero. Still hustling about doing her thing. She volunteers five afternoons a week at the daycare center where she used to work, keeps up the house and yard, and has lunches and dinners with all her friends. Not to mention hanging out with me all the time."

"That's awesome. Tell her I said 'hey.'"

"Of course. She thought I'd be staying with you while I was out here."

"You could have, you know."

"I *know*, but who could pass up an all-expenses paid suite?"

"I see your point." Pepper nodded and grinned. "How did the meeting with EJR go?"

Vivienne bounced above the surface of the water to shrug her shoulders.

"Okay, I guess. It was a sales pitch for the most part. I was so tired, I kind of zoned out and let Jake handle it."

Pepper chuckled.

"As long as you didn't fall asleep in the meeting."

Vivienne returned the grin and laughed as well.

"How long do you think you'll have to be out here?" Pepper closed her eyes and tilted her face up toward the hot sun. *A while, I hope.*

"I'm not really sure. Jake has me scheduled with every flippin' TV show that's on the air and I get calls from the bank and the police constantly. I still have to meet with Gleaming Bee tomorrow, but I'm not sure of the time. I'm hoping not more than a week, but probably closer to two. I told Jake to stop smashing so much shit into one day. I can be here as long as he needs me, and I don't want to be running from sun up to sun down."

Pepper realized then just how tired Vivienne looked. There were bags under her eyes and stress lines around the corners of her mouth from frowning so much. The sparkle Pepper remembered being in Vivienne's eyes was dimmed from exhaustion and worry.

"Well, I sure hope we get more than just today out of this trip." Pepper cocked her head to the side, feeling sad for Vivienne — she wasn't able to be more excited about negotiating for the movie rights to her book because of all the chaos with the foundation.

Vivienne treaded water and then set her feet back down on the bottom of the pool.

"I promise I will do my best. We have the rest of today and tonight for sure."

Pepper nodded.

"I've got you in my clutches now, girl. Jake will have to *find* us if he expects to get you back before tomorrow." With an impish grin on her face, she bobbed up and down in the water, causing the liquid to cascade off her shoulders and breasts.

Vivienne dog paddled around in a circle, and then flipped to backstroke her way to the edge of the pool.

"I'm sorry I'm not too much fun to be around right now. I can't stop thinking about all the families I'm letting down."

"Hey!" Pepper pointed a finger at her, flicking the tip so drops of water smacked Vivienne in the face. "*You* are not letting anyone down. That scumbag Tony is the one who's fucked everyone over. He'll get caught and they'll throw his ass in jail." Pepper dunked below the surface of the water and then popped back up, smoothing her hair back with her hands.

"Yeah, but *I'm* the one who chose him. *I'm* the one who put him in charge of the entire operation. The fault ultimately lies with *me*." Vivienne dropped her face into the water, pretending to drown.

Pepper yanked her friend's head up, back into the world, and looked Vivienne in the eye.

"Look, you did what you thought was right. He snowed you, like he snowed everyone else. This is *not* your fault, Viv. Everything will be *fine*." Pepper leaned over and kissed her on the cheek.

"I hope so," Vivienne sighed, trying to smile.

Slinging an arm around her shoulders, Pepper said, "Let's go get a drink."

Pepper slumped down beneath the surface and then propelled herself through the water toward the other end of the pool. Vivienne followed as her friend climbed up the steps in the shallow end, hips swaying, her hands squeezing water out of her hair. They linked arms and strolled in tandem to a couple of stools under the shaded part of the bar.

Pepper quizzed the bartender about what the best flavored martini would be for a reformed drinker like Vivienne. The girl making drinks grinned and offered up the apple martini as the smoothest and most popular, but Vivienne opted for her standby of gin and tonic, extra lime. Pepper stuck with a repeat of her dirty martini. When it came time to pay the bill, Pepper tried to argue over it, but Vivienne had the charges added to her room account.

"You can thank EJR Productions. They're paying for everything."

"Wow!" Pepper's eyes popped open. "Pretty convenient since you're here on so much other business."

"Yeah, and because I'm broke." Vivienne offer a wry grin and Pepper returned it.

They clinked their glasses together in a mock toast. Pepper sipped and closed her eyes at how good the liquid tasted and felt running down the back of her throat, all smoothness and warmth.

"Well, I'm thrilled for you. It's not every day two studios fight over someone for the rights to her book."

Vivienne smiled and shook her head.

"I'm proud and honored, but it's all very surreal." She sipped a tiny bit of her gin. "It's a godsend in a way because whatever I make on the deal will go directly to the foundation to pay it back."

"When one door opens," Pepper said softly, putting a reassuring hand over Vivienne's. She was so proud of her friend's dedication to the cause. "What should we do tonight then? There are parties everywhere."

"Eh, I don't know. I'm not much of the party type anymore." Vivienne swirled the straw in her glass, stabbing at the piece of lime that floated amongst the ice and alcohol.

"I'm not sure if I can get us into any super A-list parties, but I'm good for a B minus. You could talk up the foundation, try to get some money out of people!" Pepper waggled her eyebrows.

"I'll think about it."

"You and your brain." Pepper shook her head and waved her hands in dismissal. "Look, I know you're upset about this whole mess, but you really need to let it go and have some fun. Get your mind off things."

"Pffft," Vivienne scoffed. "Say that when *you* lose close to a million dollars."

"*You* didn't lose the money. The foundation was robbed. It's not your fault." Pepper leaned in close to force eye contact. "Is that all that's bothering you?" Pepper always knew when Vivienne was more inside her head than in the real world, having known her since they were both five years old. From childhood, they shared an almost innate ability to understand one another like no one else.

"Nothing else is bothering me."

"Liar. You're not feeling guilty about Bruce are you?"

Vivienne bristled and shook her head.

"No, I'm not feeling *guilty*. I just miss him right now." She pushed her still-full glass away. "This whole fucking mess started on the anniversary of his death, that's all."

Pepper's face softened.

"That's all? Why didn't you *tell* me?" She reached for Vivienne's hands and squeezed them. She was pleased when Viv squeezed back.

Now isn't the time to talk about Bruce, Pepper thought. Even though he had been killed overseas almost two decades ago, Pepper knew Vivienne had never let go of her status as a war widow in spite of her protestations to the contrary. The thing she didn't know was whether or not widowhood had become a habit or an escape, or if Vivienne was too far gone to resuscitate.

"I have an idea! Let's go shopping. We could look for something sexy for you to wear!"

"Please," Vivienne snorted. "I don't think California stores cater to the short and pale." But her eyes lit up and it did not escape Pepper's notice.

"You aren't short and pale. You're fair and petite." Pepper kicked her in the shin. "If anyone could find something for you, it'd be me. What else are we going to do? Sit around here and get drunk all day?"

"Okay, okay. I'm not really the sit-around-and-get-drunk-all-day type, either." Vivienne hopped off the bar stool and put her hands on her hips. She stretched her back out and then raised her arms above her head. "Let's do it."

"Atta girl! Just *wait* till I show you my favorite stores. We're going to have a ball!" Pepper rubbed her hands together gleefully. *Nothing cheers a woman up like shopping. If I can get her spirits up, there's no telling what else I can get her to do.*

Chapter 3

The drink in my hand was really just club soda with a lime in it so I could get Pepper off my back. I was nervous enough standing in the middle of a multimillion-dollar mansion and I had no intention of getting drunk. We got to the party on Mulholland Drive about seven o'clock; the sun was still shining brightly, its rays flowing through the 12-foot windows of the great room like yellow ribbons floating across the floor. Pepper introduced me to the hosts, a twenty-something starlet of extraordinary beauty and not so extraordinary talent, and her boyfriend, a powerful Hollywood producer in his late fifties who was responsible for more than half of the highest grossing films of the last five years. He barely accorded a greeting when he didn't recognize either of us, offering only a limp handshake. On the other hand, "Lana" exuded too much warmth in her encouragement that we make ourselves at home in their "little abode."

We initially stuck together, me clinging to Pepper's arm, consumed with nervousness, having never attended a Hollywood soirée before. But we arrived on the early side, and there were few people to mingle with after the first twenty minutes. With nothing else to do but hit the poolside bar, we got ourselves drinks and stood around waiting for more people to arrive. I got bored quickly and needed to move, so I decided to sneak back inside and explore. For an hour, I wandered through the 8,000 square feet of rooms on the first floor, alternately admiring the furnishings and scratching my head at the competing design strategies. One of them appeared to love old-style Hollywood furniture and textiles, while the other preferred a more modern aesthetic. I wondered who preferred what as I ran my hand along the back of a beautiful white silk couch with wood trim, clearly inspired by the 1930s, and gazed at a modern piece of art hanging on the wall across from it.

Eventually, I returned to the outdoor patio, which looked over two acres of land stretching out behind the house. It resembled opulence straight out of a film the owner would have produced, with its lush green grass, multiple flower beds, tennis court and Olympic-sized swimming pool. At least fifty people had arrived while I wandered through the house, and they all were mingling around the tables and chairs and chaise lounges surrounding the pool. Not seeing Pepper right away, I planted myself at a corner of the bar and ordered my fake gin and tonic so I could take part in one of my favorite pastimes: people watching. I felt much safer observing the goings on than participating because I knew I didn't fit in. I might be wearing a Michael Kors dress and shoes, but my background was rooted in the blue-collar world. I knew I should be out there selling myself and the foundation, but talking about me and The Widow's Path Foundation to people as glamorous as this crowd was as foreign as ketchup on corn flakes to me.

In spite of my logical brain explaining it, my insecure mind didn't comprehend how one carefully crafted novel could lead me to an exclusive celebrity party in Los Angeles. The fictionalization of my life and grief had struck a chord, catapulting me into the literary limelight and a life of philanthropy. The "angel" intellect sang, *Yahoo! You did it! Isn't this great?* The "devil" gray matter sneered, *Are you kidding me? What are you doing here? You don't belong.* I shook my head and sipped my club soda, hoping I wouldn't sneeze as the bubbles tickled my nose.

As I watched the crowd of breathtakingly beautiful people, I thought of Bruce as the image of his dog tags and urn flooded my brain. He would have been proud of me, for sure, and would have done his best to squash that devilish voice in my head, being supportive to a fault.

Pepper's robust laugh caught my attention. I observed as she strolled from group to group, giving air kisses and half-hearted hugs, playing the game expertly with a perpetual drink in hand. She looked stylish and sexy in her skin-tight black tank dress and sparkly silver platform heels. I envied her statuesque form, wishing I were five-foot-ten, too. Instead, I barely made it over five feet and had an hourglass figure I hated. I usually loathed shopping because my bust, hips and ass were all different sizes, constantly vying for space inside regular clothes. Shopping earlier with Pepper had been a pleasure because the more expensive the clothes were, the easier it was to find a better fit, not to mention her excellent taste. Looking down, I smoothed the skirt of the metallic jacquard dress, admiring how the soft lights of the bar bounced against the golden olive fabric. It was a perfect score for me, having found it in a designer consignment shop and only paying a hundred dollars for it. The original tag read $1,495. Having a three-quarters of a million dollar debt to pay back hanging over my head would have prevented me from buying anything that expensive, not to mention the fact that I didn't spend that kind of money on myself to begin with. Then I grimaced when I shifted in my four inch, black leather, buckled ankle boots and the balls of my feet throbbed as if on fire. Pepper must have seen me because I could see her heading my way, a look of concerned determination across her face.

A smile spread across mine as I watched her approach, and was reminded of our high school days when she would drag me to all the backyard keggers. I'd stand off to the side and watch her mingle and dance and drink, having the time of her life. Pepper always was the life of the party. I never minded though, because I lived vicariously through her, being too shy and nervous to act so carefree. In my own way, I had just as much fun as she did just by watching the antics of our high school class.

I came out of my reverie as Pepper arrived at my side with a handsome, young, model-gorgeous man on her arm. She introduced him as Philippe. He was an actor/model/record producer. I could see the smirk on her face as she said it, and did my best to hide any amusement I might have been feeling. Philippe had a very thick Boston accent and was dressed in Gap jeans, a navy blue tee-shirt and light gray corduroy blazer with brown patches on the elbows. When

Pepper told him my name and background, he nodded, but peered over my shoulder to see if anyone more interesting lurked in the bushes behind me. He had the good graces to excuse himself before bolting in the direction of a gaggle of stunning young girls who were already a little more than tipsy on the champagne flowing freely.

Pepper snickered when he was gone.

"How'd ya like that one?"

"Oh he's a keeper." I rolled my eyes and fanned my face.

She grabbed my arm and pushed it down, still chuckling softly.

"You're so *bad*." I shook a finger at her.

"I know." Pepper sniffed. "You okay?"

"Yep, I'm great." I saluted and then took a drink from my glass.

"I think I see a gal over there I did some modeling with. I'll be right back." Pepper drifted off back toward the pool.

After that, every few minutes, she would haul someone else over to me and introduce them, but they weren't interested in talking about anything but themselves or their projects. Pepper would bring up the book and the foundation, which was the kiss of death. Eyes would glaze over and disinterest would settle across their faces as they slunk away, saying they saw someone they needed to speak to.

My self-worth was beginning to take a huge hit from all the rejection. Little by little, I retreated closer to the bar until I was pressed up against the farthest corner. If Pepper hadn't known I was there, she might have suspected me of bolting from the party.

I could see the consternation on Pepper's face when the people she introduced didn't find me as interesting and wonderful as she did. It made me love her all the more. After the sixth attempt, Pepper threw her hands up and teased me about being unfriendly. I played along, making grumpy faces that caused her to laugh out loud.

"Why do you do that?" she asked when she finally stopped chortling. "I'm the one who's supposed to be showing *you* a good time and you're the one making *me* laugh."

"It's a gift." I shrugged my shoulders and grinned.

"Aren't you having a good time?" She leaned in close and looked me in the eye.

"Sure!"

She caught the lie and scowled. I put up my hands in mock defense.

"My feet are killing me. The boots might be cute, but they are *not* comfortable."

Pepper snorted and raised an eyebrow at me.

"So sit down." She nodded her head at the bar stool behind me. Giving her a cheeky grin, I hopped up and crossed my legs prettily, my howling feet sighing with relief.

Two women stumbled up to the bar next to us, one with raven hair and the other with a coppery golden mane. They had their arms linked and were talking loudly about the couple hosting the party. As they both grabbed the bar for stability, they each demanded more alcohol as if it were their right instead of a gift from the hosts.

"Seriously, Viv. You need to circulate with me. I almost couldn't find you in this dark corner."

I dropped my eyes and stared at the pointed toes of my boots. I searched for the words to tell her how out of place and uncomfortable I felt. Leaning close to her, I whispered, "Everyone here is too beautiful. Too perfect. I'm intimidated. Are these the kind of parties you always go to?"

"Truth?" She touched her forehead to mine. "No. It isn't. I hardly ever do these things anymore. It took me three favors to finagle an invite to this party, and I only did it because I thought you'd have a good time and could try to talk up the foundation."

Shaking my head, I frowned.

"I'm way out of my element here."

"Bah!" She punched me in the arm and then slung hers around my shoulders. "You belong here more than anyone else, as far as I'm concerned. Look," she pointed across the yard, "there's Luke Framingham. Did you see *The Road Beyond*?"

I shook my head.

"Well, he's worth about ten million a film now. And over there is Jennifer Skarsgaard."

"She won the Oscar for best actress this year!"

"Yep. And she never lets you forget it."

Pulling me off the barstool, she drew me away from the bar and down several steps toward the pool. As we walked along the edge, she continued and I forgot about my sore feet.

"She and Luke are 'dating'," Pepper made air quotes with her fingers, "but the scuttlebutt is that it's a publicity stunt."

We passed by Jennifer and Luke as they nuzzled each other and I dropped my eyes to stare at my ragged fingernails. They never even looked in our direction.

"This party doesn't have as many big names as I thought it would, but the egos are gargantuan. I'm sure the only reason Luke and Jennifer are here is because the host is producing their next film together." Pepper sniffed, looking annoyed while smoothing the front of her dress. "I thought it might be a little better than this because of the girl who told me about it. She's been spot-on with party recommendations in the past. But none of these people even know who I am. They're only worried I might be someone important they forgot about and so they pretend to remember me."

"I'm sorry you blew your favors on me." I scanned the area, watching the crowd in their designer clothes and drinks made with alcohol that cost more than my last electric bill.

"Oh, that's all right. You're worth it." She finished her drink and set the glass on the tray of a passing waiter. "Let's get out of here."

Relief made my knees shake.

"Yes, let's."

"Unless of course you want to stay and beg for autographs," Pepper teased.

"Nuh-uh!" I dropped my glass off with another waiter just as she had done.

"Come on, then. I'll take you where the *real* fun is."

A 30-minute cab ride later and we arrived at a bar on Sunset Boulevard. Pepper paid the cabby and pulled me up to the door when I saw the sign.

"The *Relic*?" I couldn't help smirking.

"Yeah, well, what can I say? Life imitates art, right?"

"Pepper, Ljubav! We have not seen you in a while." The man at the door hollered, even though we stood right in front of him. He had to be at least six-foot-five and three hundred pounds of pure muscle. His thick Croatian accent was very sexy. Pepper threw herself into his arms and kissed each of his cheeks noisily.

"Hey babe! I've been working." She turned to me and presented me as if I were royalty. "Hank, this is my oldest and dearest friend, Vivienne Stark."

"Pleasure!" he boomed as I extended my hand. "Oh no, that will not do." He lifted me under my arms so our faces were level and pecked me on each cheek.

"How do you do!" His greeting left me breathless as he set me back on my feet with a gentleness belying his size.

"Who's playing tonight, Hank?"

"The Mini Coopers and Paper Magic."

"Excellent! What's the cover?"

"For you, Ljubav, nothing. You and your friend enjoy yourselves." He stepped aside and opened the door for us. We were immediately assaulted by loud music and the smell of beer, sweat, and a tiny hint of cigarette smoke.

"Thanks, Hank!" Pepper saluted him and then grabbed my hand to pull me inside.

The bar reminded me of the divey joints we haunted when we were seniors in high school, with our bad clothes and hair and cheap fake IDs. It was dim and smoky, in spite of the public ban in California. The outdoor patio's double doors were flung wide open, and the smoke from the people out there wafted inside. There was a band on stage and a crowd of people jumped and danced to the beat blaring from amplifiers. There were small round tables everywhere and, while many were filled with couples and trios of people, the place wasn't packed. It felt comfortable and anonymous, much more my style.

Pepper greeted the two working bartenders by name as she ushered me to the edge and gave me a stern look.

"No more club soda for you. You're going to have a real drink."

"All right." I put my hands up in surrender. "Gin and tonic, extra lime."

"I'll make it two. Go find a table."

As she got the drinks, I turned to survey the openings. I chose one close enough to the bar so she could find me, but with a good view of the stage. I liked the band that was playing, with its upbeat tempo and edgy guitar, a hard rock sound that appealed to me. I was once again feeling like a high schooler as I gave each member of the band the once over to see who was cute. Chuckling to myself, I looked up as Pepper set my drink in front of me.

"What's so funny?" she asked, as she scooted her chair closer to the table.

"I was just remembering all our time at St. Andrews Hall and The Ritz. This feels so very nostalgic. God, do you remember the time we got caught in the blind pig and we thought we were going to be arrested?"

Pepper's mouth dropped open with the shock of the memory.

"Oh shit, I'd forgotten about that. I thought for sure we were going to have to call our parents to bail us out. Thank God the cops only ticketed us."

"Good thing I worked for lawyers at the time, eh?" I snickered, remembering going to my boss in tears, begging him to represent us in court.

"What about the time I had to drive us home because you were drunk and that guy with the purple hair—"

"Jumped on the hood of my car!" I finished the thought for her, as the same memory exploded in my brain.

"That female cop was *pissed*!"

"And not even at us. She was more worried he would attack us." I could see the officer in my head, nostrils flaring and nightstick pointed at the drunken youth who thought he could catch a ride home on the hood of my Buick.

When we were finally able to stop laughing and catch our breath, Pepper leaned over to give me a one-armed hug.

"Well, I may have moved to Hollywood, girl, but I didn't leave my roots far behind. The mentality around here is a little bit on the juvenile side and reminiscent of our youth, but the music is good, the drinks are cheap and the people are *real*."

I nodded in agreement as I held onto my glass. The drink was smooth and cold, and I sipped it as I watched and listened to The Mini Coopers, the anxiety and tension from earlier in the evening completely erased. I was so much happier at The Relic than on Mulholland Drive. I forced myself to let go of my worry over the foundation for a while.

When the band finished its set, Pepper put her fingers into her mouth and let loose a whistle, piercing my eardrums. The five members filed offstage into the crowd, giving high fives and shaking hands, heading straight for the bar. The interior lights went on and some inferior music came pouring out of the speakers at a much lower volume.

"I know a couple of those guys. They wrote some music for a local commercial I did." Pepper pointed at the bass player and drummer from The Mini Coopers. I could tell she was proud of it by the casualness of her tone. I nodded and listened as she drew my attention to all the people in the crowd she knew. "These are good folks. I could probably call any one of them if I needed a favor and they'd be right there. We're all fighting the good fight to make a living out here." I liked knowing she was comfortable and safe in her life.

"I'm out and it's my turn to buy. You ready for another?" I shook my empty glass at her. Pepper's eyes widened and she nodded.

"I'll take a Red Hook this time."

I took her empty and weaved my way to the bar. Bodies were crowded against it at every point and I had to claw my way in.

Chapter 4

"Aren't you Will Foster from Static Neverland?"

I whipped my head toward the voice to my left. The girl looked way younger than 21 and had probably snuck in with a fake ID. Her makeup was too thick and her clothes were too short and tight. She was probably adorable when she looked normal, but tonight she looked like she was on the prowl. I forced myself not to smile and said, "No, but I get that a lot."

"I bet," she said. "Did you get that tattoo so people would think you're him?" She pointed to the serpent on my arm and smirked.

Crap. I hated when they were smarter than they looked. I pulled the sleeve of my jacket down to cover my arm.

"Crazy coincidence."

I turned back toward the bar, hoping she'd get the hint to take a hike. When I glanced back, she was gone. *That was a close one.*

The beer in my right hand was frigid and I switched it to the left so I could take a long satisfying swallow. It hit my throat fast, numbing everything in that fine way beer has. I almost choked as I watched Pepper Taylor saunter into the bar, along with a petite redhead. That threw me for a loop. I hadn't seen her in almost two years. *What's she doing here?* I looked away to take another drink and then she was gone, melted into the crowd. I shrugged, knowing she would find me at some point. I smiled at the thought.

I peered around the rest of The Relic, finally feeling like I was home. I saw a few familiar faces here and there, nodding when I got nodded to. I spent some time earlier on the patio, and even bummed a smoke from a buddy I hadn't seen in five years, chatting him up on his band and their status while we puffed away. It was a comfortable feeling, being in the bar where my buddies and I got our start.

The band had been on tour all over the world, and tonight was the first time I'd been able to hang out in LA in over a year. A hundred and fifty shows in twenty countries was more than we'd ever done and, if I had my way, we'd never do it again. Back in the day, before Static Neverland got signed, we were lucky to do two shows a weekend and we yearned for fame and fortune and a record contract. I was now a firm believer in the "careful what you wish for" credo. When we got all of the above, our lives changed so drastically and so fast that we almost imploded. We were headed down the path to become a statistic of too much everything all at once. Luckily, the other four guys in the band were all pretty down to earth, too, and we managed to get our shit together before we threw it all away.

When the tour finally ended and we got back to LA, we were able to crash in the house we bought together, trying to catch up on a year's worth of sleep. It took me almost two weeks to rid myself of jet lag and find the energy to get upright and conscious in a somewhat normal or meaningful way. I spent the time lounging around, watching TV, eating like a pig, and returning phone calls or emails I hadn't gotten to while on the road. Except for the brief appearance on *Good Day LA*, we had no pressing engagements or band obligations for at least three months.

I finally felt like myself and got restless for some nightlife. I opted to head out alone and decided the perfect place would be The Relic: low key, out of the way, good beer.

At first, I thought it was a mistake because I got recognized immediately. A small melee ensued with waves of girls clamoring toward me, shouting "Will! Will!" I was lucky Hank the bouncer was working. He stamped out the wildfire by pushing the girls away and shoving me into a corner of the bar. I put on my "don't fuck with me" face and soon people were ignoring me, probably thinking I was an asshole. That bothered me a little, because I'm *not* an asshole. My reputation was that of a basically regular guy who hadn't let fame go to his head. But I didn't want to be hassled, and I thought I could slip into the bar unnoticed to have a few beers and enjoy some music. Stupid me. Even ten years later, I couldn't get it through my thick head that people knew my face.

Luckily, after a while, one band would leave the stage and the crowd would thin out, only to thicken with new fans of the new band. I melted into my corner of the bar, against the wall, and I wasn't a famous rock star anymore, just another schmoe with a brew. I was able to get rid of the scowl and loosen up while the music played and the beer flowed.

Women eyed me from time to time, maybe recognizing me, maybe not, but I didn't give them a second glance. I had thought about wearing sunglasses when I left the house, but what kind of asshat wears shades in a dim bar at night? A famous rock star who wants to get recognized, not a guy who hopes to get lost in the crowd.

After two beers, I was mellowing enough to think about heading home when I saw a dainty little redhead approach the bar. She had on a dress that looked like goldish, smooth tinfoil or something, and it molded to her body in a sexy way, but not enough to make her look like a slut. And it wasn't freakishly short, like so many of the skirts and dresses on the other women in the place. I thought she might be the one who'd come in with Pepper, but I couldn't be sure. Plus, I meet so many people every freakin' day, it was hard for me to keep names and faces straight. She teetered in her high-heel boots and was having trouble getting close enough to order. She didn't look like the regular girls who haunted The Relic. She didn't have the same pushy confidence that women in LA bars had. I didn't get the "look at me, notice me, *discover me*" vibe from her. Then she got body checked right into my arm.

"Oops, I'm sorry," she said, but I could barely hear her above the noise of the crowd. She grabbed my arm before she could stumble, and my hand went instinctively to her back.

"No worries." I moved so she could touch the edge of the bar and steady herself. I caught myself staring at her because she really was oddly familiar. She was a cute little thing, so when she wasn't looking, I raised my arm and got the bartender's attention for her. I was at least a foot taller, so I got a nice peek over her shoulder and down at the slope of her chest. I smirked and considered it payback for my good deed. As soon as Kurt the bartender shuffled over to help, I turned back to the stage and tried to forget about her.

Chapter 5

I was jostled by the long-haired bass player from The Mini Coopers as he walked away from the bar. I stumbled into someone else, grabbing his arm for support. Looking up, a dazzling set of green eyes locked onto mine.

"Oops, I'm sorry!" I paused, realizing his hand was hot against the small of my back.

"No worries." His voice was smooth, melodic and vaguely familiar. He had short, dark hair, tousled with the crunchy look of gel, and he hadn't shaved. It gave him a grungy kind of appeal. He smelled like beer, leather and sweat. An image of his lips on mine flashed across my inner TV screen and I got that all-over warm feeling like just before you faint. Luckily, I didn't crumple to the floor. He was the sexiest man I had seen in a very long time. But then again, drop-dead gorgeous wasn't common where I came from. He smiled down at me and then moved aside so I could get a little closer to the bar. I turned to check on Pepper and saw her watching and beaming.

"Thanks." I nodded my head and then turned my attention to getting the bartender to notice me, filing a mental photograph of the sexy guy away in my brain for when I got back to my boring life. When I returned to the table, Pepper was saying goodbye to a woman.

"I'll give you a call, Pep."

"You do that, Gina."

When she was gone, I nudged Pepper in the arm.

"What was that about?"

"Her boyfriend hit on me at a party a couple of weeks ago. I told her and she didn't believe me, but then she caught him scamming on another woman a few days later. I was just telling her, once a cheater always a cheater. Hopefully she'll chuck the bum before she wastes too much more time on him."

"That's pretty harsh. Are you sure you should have told her anything?" I asked, worried she was poking her nose where it didn't belong.

"Harsh or not, I tell it like it is. I try not to be *deliberately* bitchy, but her guy hit on *me*. Not only is that disrespectful to me, but more so to *her* and she shouldn't have to put up with it. Besides, you know me. I'm always the one telling people the truth and getting shit on for it."

"You sound like a sexier version of Dr. Phil," I teased.

Pepper choked and then coughed with laughter.

"Did you ever think at almost forty you'd still be dealing with such high school drama?"

I shook my head and sighed, resting my chin on the back of my hand and staring into the crowd. I could see a couple arguing near the stage, their hands flying as they shouted at one another.

"No, not really. But LA is kind of like Neverland. No one here really grows up." Pepper looked a little wistful, but shook it off and sipped her beer. "What took you so long?"

"Man candy at the bar. There are quite a few good looking specimens here tonight."

Pepper nodded in agreement.

"You look hot as hell, my friend."

"Ack, no, I'm way overdressed."

"This is LA, Viv. No one is *ever* overdressed." Pepper shook her head and rolled her eyes.

Now I was having fun. People came to our table to say hello to Pepper and she introduced me to everyone. I'd never remember all the names, but the faces were friendly and they had kind words of welcome for me. Pepper even told some of them about *The Widow's Path* and the foundation. Only a few had heard of the book and no one had actually read it, but I didn't care. I was honored to have Pepper make such a big deal of it. Some of her friends even asked how they could donate to the cause. In between all the introductions, I would let my eyes travel back to the bar, searching for Mr. Man Candy. I was never able to see him for more than a second or two before the next person came to the table, or some other person across the bar would block my view.

Best of all, Pepper wasn't pressuring me to do or think or feel any more than I wanted to. My best friend could be pretty pushy, but I knew I needed it most of the time. I could never have admitted to her I sometimes wished she had talked me out of marrying Bruce when I was only nineteen. If I hadn't, my life might have been completely different. But then I might not have ever written *The Widow's Path*. Life was a tradeoff. Losing my husband at twenty-two sent me rocketing down a road that was too late to change.

Paper Magic took the stage and Pepper forced me out to dance. I never could handle my liquor, so after two drinks I was able to lose some of my inhibitions. Plus, I didn't know any of these people. Eventually I would go home, never to see them again. As we hopped and bounced our way to the dance floor, I caught a glimpse of Man Candy and I swore he was ogling Pepper. Any other person might have been disappointed, but I was used to my best friend getting all the attention. Besides, I wasn't feeling like an almost forty-year-old woman, and I certainly didn't act like it that night. Pepper said we were going to relive our youth, so I jumped on board with both feet.

Chapter 6

"I need to hit the ladies room. You okay?" Pepper asked Vivienne. Her friend's face glistened with perspiration from all the dancing. Viv was smiling and relaxed, which made Pepper feel happy.

"Yep, I'm great." Vivienne swayed in her chair to the song on the loudspeaker. "I love this song!" It was some '80s hair band tune playing over the sound system.

"Good," Pepper laughed. "I'll be right back." She left her purse on the table and then hightailed it toward the bathrooms. She looked back to see Vivienne still bobbing her head back and forth, with her eyes closed, and Pepper changed direction toward the bar. Standing on tiptoe, she scanned the faces until she found the one she wanted. Keeping an eye on Viv, Pepper strode up to a sexy, dark-haired man dressed in jeans, a white tee-shirt and black leather motorcycle jacket, who lounged against the bar nursing a Red Hook.

"Hello, Will." Pepper wedged in next to him.

"There she is!" He leaned in and kissed her on the cheek, then slipped his arm around her waist, squeezing. "I saw you come in earlier."

"Slumming tonight, are we?" She raised her left eyebrow at him.

"Come on, you know me better than that." Will gave her another, more gentle squeeze.

"I'm just kidding." Pepper threw her arms around his neck and hugged him for real and they rocked from side to side. "How have you been? I haven't seen you in *forever*."

"I've been on tour for a year. And the TV show kept me busy before that."

"Yeah, I bet! Television agrees with you. I watched every week." Pepper crossed her heart, thinking about Wednesday nights watching

Band Nation, the talent competition Will hosted. Even in the dim light, she could see the flush of pride on Will's face. Pepper snuck a peek back to the table where Vivienne waited patiently. "Seriously, it's good to see you. I'm glad you haven't forgotten the little people."

"Never." Will's face was grim. "Especially not you."

Pepper grinned but then grew solemn.

"I was sorry to hear about your breakup with Lucy."

"Don't be," Will spat. "I'm not."

"I see." Pepper searched his face, her blue eyes sparkling. "Not over her yet?"

"Oh I'm over her," Will promised. "It just pisses me off I was so blind for so long. She was just using me."

Pepper pushed out her lower lip in sympathy and shook her head.

"I tried to tell you."

"Yes, you did. And I'm sorry I didn't listen." Will turned to face her directly. "I really *am* sorry." Pepper remembered their heated conversation more than two years ago. She'd given him all the proof he needed that Lucy was scheming and cheating on him, yet Will hadn't wanted to believe any of it. She could still hear the sound of his voice when he'd told her to mind her own business and get the fuck out of his life.

"I know you are." She punched his arm lightly. "It's okay, really. I've gotten used to being the person who gets smacked in the face for telling the truth." Pepper hoped that her face wouldn't betray her words, because it wasn't something she would *ever* get used to. It broke her heart every time she was honest with someone about something they didn't want to hear and she got the brunt of their abuse. But she wouldn't stop doing it if there was a chance she could save a friend some pain.

Will nodded his head.

"You gotta stop that."

"So they tell me," Pepper sniffed. Pausing only for a moment, she leaned in close again so Will would be able to hear her. She had gotten an idea when she saw Vivienne at the bar with Will a couple of hours ago, and she was now in a position to put it in motion. It was now or never. "I'm going to cut to the chase. Are you seeing anyone?"

Will looked startled. Pepper put her hands on his chest and laughed. "Don't look like that. I'm not asking for *me*." Again, she glanced at Vivienne who seemed to be scanning the crowd for her. Pepper took Will by the arms and switched places with him so she could use him as a shield to block Vivienne's view.

Will's shoulders lowered and his eyes went back to their usual half-lidded sexiness. His easy smile also returned.

"I didn't mean to do that Pepper. It's just that you know we're better as friends."

"Yes, I'm aware."

"Then why are you asking?"

Pepper grinned wickedly and wiggled her eyebrows. Tapping a finger to her cheek, she batted her eyelashes.

"Well, you see, I have this friend—"

"Stop right there—"

"But—"

"I don't want—"

"Hear me out!" Pepper cut him off and pulled him forward so they were practically nose to nose. "I have this friend who's in town for a couple of weeks and I think you'd really like her."

Will cocked his head to the side and leaned back a little.

"If she's only here for a couple of weeks, why bother? Besides the fact that I'm not looking for a set up."

"Well, it's not really a set up, per se." Pepper's eyes lowered and she needlessly adjusted one of the straps of her dress. Her confidence in the spur-of-the-moment plan was waning. "I was thinking more of a, well, a hookup."

"What?" Will nearly dropped his beer. His mouth gaped open and he took a step away from Pepper.

"Come on, Will." Pepper tapped her foot in exasperation. "I remember, once upon a time, a guy who was good for a little fun." She twisted her hips back and forth suggestively trying to get him excited about the prospect.

"Yeah, that guy was ten years younger. You know I don't do that kind of shit anymore." Will shook his head and took a long draw on his beer, draining it. He put the empty bottle on the bar and took a long time to swallow while signaling the bartender for another. "It always ends up in the 'bloids, for Chrissake."

Pepper chewed on her bottom lip, struggling to find the words to convince her one friend that her other friend was worth a detour off the morals highway.

"At least come talk to her for a few minutes. She's really brilliant." She pushed on his chest to make him take a step backward in the hopes of moving him closer to her goal and to Vivienne.

"Pepper, don't."

"She's right over there. Tell me she's not the most gorgeous creature you've ever seen." Pepper turned him toward the tables and pointed to Vivienne, who was once again smiling and swaying with her eyes closed. Pepper held her breath while Will peered into the crowd, following her finger, hoping he would be overtaken with lust and fall into line with the spontaneous plan she had cooked up.

"I saw her earlier." Will clearly recognized Vivienne, nodding his head up and down slowly. "We bumped into each other at the bar."

"Then you know how adorable she is!" Pepper bobbed up and down, clapping her hands together with glee, not letting on that she had seen the whole thing.

Will shrugged.

"Yeah, she's cute." His answer was noncommittal and Pepper couldn't tell if he was serious or not. She put her hands on her hips and scowled.

"That's not very encouraging." She hoped he was just playing it cool, but Will was a hard read when he didn't want you to know his thoughts.

"What?" Will raised his shoulders again. "Okay, she's beautiful."

Pepper nodded approvingly, waiting for more. When he didn't give her what she wanted, Pepper waved her hand in a circular motion to prompt him.

"But?"

"She looks too smart for me. Not my type. You know I'm all about the beauty queens."

"Stick figures with fake hair and no boobs," Pepper growled. "Or fake boobs and no brains."

"Exactly." Will put his hands out. "At least I'm honest about it."

"I call bullshit," Pepper muttered, pretending to punch him in the gut. "Look, I'm not asking you to marry her. I just want her to have an experience while she's here that she'll never get back home. You've been single for a while now."

"Where's back home?"

"Michigan," Pepper answered, nibbling on her thumb and watching as Vivienne drained the last of her drink.

"What's she doing out here?"

"Long story, but she wrote a best seller and is negotiating for the movie rights. It's the most exciting thing that's ever happened to her, so I took her to one of those celebrity parties on Mulholland. It was a total bust."

"Why the hell did you do that? Those people suck." Will gave her a reproachful look.

"Tell me about it. They treated us like red-headed stepchildren."

"So you bring her here instead?" Will's tone was incredulous.

"Hey, it's what she knows. The people are real and she doesn't feel out of place." Pepper moved behind Will just as Vivienne's eyes opened and she once again looked around, this time more nervously.

"Look, I never expected to see you here tonight and the idea just popped into my head. I'm sorry I brought it up." She tried to look contrite, but knew she wasn't doing a good job of hiding her irritation at Will's refusal to cooperate.

"What book did she write?" Will asked suddenly.

"What? Oh, *The Widow's Path*." Pepper tried to think of some inducement to get Will over to the table. She had known Vivienne wasn't his type physically, but Pepper had laid bets on the way the dress hugged Viv's bust line. Will was a total breast man.

Will's eyes widened in true surprise.

"*The Widow's Path*? Are you serious? That's a *great* book." Cocking his head to the side, a look of recognition washed over his face. "I think I saw her a couple of days ago, too. She was on *Good Day LA*, right before us, wasn't she?"

Pepper mirrored his expression of shock. "Yes, she was! You've read *The Widow's Path*?" A small stab of guilt poked her in the gut.

"Of course, haven't you?"

"Not yet, but I plan to." Pepper lowered her eyes, feeling ashamed. "I'm not much of a reader." She felt like shit admitting she hadn't read Vivienne's masterpiece, but she was honest about it. It was a struggle for Pepper to sit long enough to read an issue of *People*, much less a novel.

"That's an understatement." Will laughed and lowered his head in defeat. "All right, I'll go say 'hi.' I'm *not* hooking up with her, but I admit I'd like to meet the person who wrote that book."

Chapter 7

I was feeling *really* good. I liked the music playing and the bands were great. It reminded me so much of the years Pepper and I spent hanging out in the bars in Detroit. In those days, IDs were easy to fake and we followed our favorite local bands everywhere. The Trash Brats, Happy Death Men, Rated R, Seduce. I laughed to myself remembering our teenage antics, thinking ourselves the cutest groupies out there.

The two drinks I'd had were just enough to make me feel relaxed, unlike when I was an underage drinker and getting shitfaced was the point of every night out. I kept looking around for Pepper, but she had disappeared. Not everything from the old days was different. She would often flit about, playing the socialite, leaving me to my own devices.

I didn't mind because the people watching was extremely entertaining and one of my favorite pastimes, no matter where I was. Most of the time, I would make up harmless, mostly boring stories about the people I observed. But once in a while, if I was in a devilish mood, I would turn the storytelling into judgment time. Now was one of those times. A couple to the left was arguing about how much he had to drink and if he was okay to drive home. I secretly named them Ben and Mary Jane and imagined they lived in a cramped, one-bedroom apartment. Another couple to the right was making out and needed to get a room. The girl had black roots sprouting beneath her platinum blond hair and the shortest miniskirt I had ever seen. He was covered in poorly done tattoos and was missing three of his bottom teeth, which I was lucky enough to notice whenever he would open his mouth to devour hers. They became White Trash Barbie and Wife Beater Ken. Then there was the table behind me, filled with four rowdy girls, downing their drinks as fast as they could buy more and bemoaning their single fates. The poor version of *Sex and the City*, LA style. I knew I'd feel bad in the morning for being so catty, but alcohol helped ease my conscience for the time being.

As I continued to scan the room, Pepper appeared, smiling like a Cheshire cat.

"Hey girl," she purred.

I was about to respond, when beside her I recognized Man Candy from the bar. My mouth made a circle of surprise. I tried to speak, but all I managed was some sort of squeak. My stomach dropped to my shoes and all the saliva on my tongue dried up faster than a vacuum seal.

"Will, this is my good friend Vivienne Stark. Viv, this is Will Foster. I've known him for years." Pepper unlinked her arm from his, stepping aside so Will could move in front of her chair. His hand was reaching for mine but I just stared dumbly at him until Pepper prodded me. My right hand shot out like I was going to punch him in the stomach. Pepper grabbed a chair from another table and pulled it up to ours. Will squeezed my hand while sliding into her seat.

"Nice to meet you, Vivienne." Did he hold onto my hand longer than necessary? I shook my head a little to try and clear my thoughts, attempting a natural smile. *What's wrong with me?*

"Nice to meet you, Will." My voice came out smoother than I thought it would.

"Do you need another drink?"

"Yes!" Pepper cried, as I declined. "I'll get it!" She popped back up, nearly upending the chair she'd just retrieved and bolted to the bar like her dress was on fire. I couldn't help but laugh. Pepper's abrupt departure made him smile too. I couldn't remember ever having seen a face so handsome before, and the hairs on my arms actually danced in time with the music thumping through the speakers as I stared at him.

"Pepper tells me you're visiting from Michigan, is that right?"

"Yes." His hands were enormous, the fingers long and slender. I loved the veins snaking across them, disappearing behind the cuff of his leather jacket. I always thought of veins as a sign of virility and strength.

"Business or pleasure?"

"Huh?" I mumbled, my head snapping back up to meet his eyes. "Uh, both, actually." Now I caught myself studying his whole face. He was almost *too* handsome with his sensual mouth, straight nose, and not-too-tan complexion. His lips looked soft and full, but not too much. I liked his ears, too, because they seemed a little small, but they were cute. I felt my face start to burn and I looked away. When I looked back at him, our eyes locked and it hit me.

"You look very familiar." I tilted my head to the side, looking at him through half-closed eyes. "I'm sure you hear something pitiful like this all the time, but where have I seen you before?"

Will shrugged and grinned in an "aw-shucks" manner. He leaned back in his chair, pushing the sleeves of his jacket up.

I recognized the cross and snake tattoo instantly.

Nodding my head, my memory restored, I grinned at him.

"Yes, now I know you. Thank God for iTunes, right?" He chuckled in response, looking very humble. "And *Good Day LA*. I caught your performance yesterday morning."

"I saw you leaving the green room, but I didn't catch your segment," Will admitted. "But I'm a fan of yours, too. Pepper told me you wrote *The Widow's Path*. I thought it was great."

Just when I was getting my bearings, the rug was pulled out from under me again. Admittedly, I didn't know Will Foster other than from songs on the radio and the TV show I'd heard about but never seen. But he didn't strike me as the type of person to read something like *The Widow's Path*. Then again, here I was in Los Angeles negotiating to get my book on the silver screen. Stranger things could happen.

"Thank you very much," I whispered, hoping he couldn't see my embarrassment in the dim lights. I picked at the lonely napkin on the table. "How did you come to read the book?" I couldn't help but ask.

Will grinned and lowered his eyes.

"My road manager's assistant was reading it and I stole it. I think we were in Germany at the time. One of our outdoor concerts got cancelled, so we were laying over for an extra day. I got so bored, I snatched it out of her bag and read it in a day."

"I'll take it as a compliment, then." I smirked.

"You should. It takes a lot to get me interested in a book. Yours had me from the first page."

"Thank you." My head kept dipping down because flattery was getting him *everywhere*.

"I'm sorry about what happened with the foundation. What a piece of shit." Will shook his head and frowned.

"Ah, so you've heard about my tragedy?"

"Who hasn't? It's been all over the news. I hope they catch that guy."

"Me too." I nodded glumly.

"I'll give you my number. If you ever need a band for a benefit or anything, I know the guys would be up for it. We played a couple of shows for the troops overseas last year."

My eyes widened at the very first high profile offer I'd ever gotten for the foundation, and one I had not begged for.

"Thank you! I will definitely let you know. I hope to take you up on that offer very soon. Things are a little, eh, up in the air right now."

Will gave me a sympathetic look and smiled, settling in to his chair a little more comfortably.

"Yeah, sounds like it. I can't believe what slime balls people can be."

I snorted. "Tell me about it."

As we chatted, waiting for Pepper's return, I realized why she had been away for so long before. Did she really "know him for years"? Or had she just finessed this rock star into coming by to flatter me? I didn't know, but I planned on finding out before things got any weirder.

Chapter 8

Pepper watched anxiously from the bar as Vivienne and Will talked. She gnawed on her thumb, eager to see what would happen between the two of them. Their body language looked a little stiff. She thought they were pausing too long before speaking.

"Definitely more alcohol," she murmured, signaling the bartender.

Balancing two beer bottles and a gin and tonic expertly, she crossed the room to Vivienne and Will.

"Tada!" she sang as she placed the beverages on the table without spilling a drop.

"Thanks." Will accepted the bottle a little too eagerly. Vivienne took her glass and frowned into it. Pepper grinned, showing a little too much tooth.

Will's cell phone jangled with alarming volume and he pulled it out of his pocket.

"'Scuse me ladies, I need to take this." He stepped away from the table to find a quieter spot.

Vivienne waited until he was out of earshot, then pounced.

"What the hell is going on?"

"What?" Pepper brought her beer to her lips coyly.

"Are you trying to set me up or what?" Vivienne's eyes flickered with accusation.

"Of course not!" Pepper lied.

"Pepper..."

Rolling her eyes, she sighed. *I should have gotten her drunker first.* "Oh, all right. I saw you looking at him at the bar earlier and since I knew him, I thought it would be fun to introduce you."

Vivienne glared at Pepper.

"Do you *really* know him?"

"Yes!" Pepper's eyes flew open. "Of course I do." She thought Vivienne looked unconvinced.

"I told you he was man candy, but that's *it*. Whatever made you think I'd be interested in actually *meeting* him?"

"Why *wouldn't* you be interested in meeting him? You won't be here that long. Why not have some fun while you are?"

Vivienne's mouth dropped open as she folded her arms across her chest.

"Just exactly what kind of fun are you referring to?"

Pepper sighed, leaning forward on her elbows.

"Give me a break, Viv. You know what I mean. Hook up with him for a night. It'll be great!"

Vivienne's mouth opened wider.

"Are you joking?"

Pepper tried not to laugh while she watched her friend's cheeks steam up.

"No." She took a swig of her beer.

"Patricia Evelyn Taylor! You know damn well I'm not that kind of a person."

Pepper cringed at the use of her given name, but recovered quickly.

"Oh please," she retorted. "You sound like an old lady. A *snooty* old lady. I distinctly remember a time when you were more than willing to hook up with a guy just for the hell of it." She gave Vivienne an irritated sneer and leaned back in her chair. "Do I have to remind you about Tom? Or how about Brian?"

Vivienne bristled with indignation.

"Stop! That was a long time ago. I'm not a teenager anymore."

"Pffft!" Pepper skipped the sip and took a healthy swallow of her drink. "A snooty old *prudey* lady."

"A woman with some *dignity*!" Vivienne looked away.

Pepper scowled.

"Okay, I'm not the most subtle person and I don't always have the most tact. I just thought you might want something to take home with you besides the memory of a shitty party, a bunch of boring meetings, and all the foundation stress. Live a little, Viv! *You're still young!*"

Vivienne groaned and reached for her friend's hand.

"Pep, I appreciate the thought. Really, I do. But I'm too old to be having one-night stands. Besides, I haven't been in a relationship in a long time and I've finally figured out that I'm okay with it. I don't even miss it." Vivienne squeezed Pepper's fingers, then let go to stare at her lap.

"I call bullshit!" Pepper shouted, sloshing beer onto the table causing nearby people to stare. She dipped her head into Vivienne's peripheral vision until she was forced to look up.

"Viv, I know losing Bruce was difficult." Vivienne glared. "Okay, *more* than difficult. I would never minimize your loss, you know that. But there's grieving and then there's hiding, and I think at some point one became the other. Here we are, almost two decades later and your instinct is to hide. If you don't want to hook up with Will, that's fine. I get it. But don't cop out just because you're afraid."

"I'm *not* afraid," Vivienne snarled.

Pepper smirked, admiring her friend's sudden passion.

"Okay, then don't hide because you're nervous. How long has it been since you've had sex?"

Rolling her eyes, Vivienne clucked her tongue.

"That's none of your business."

Pepper burst out laughing.

"Of *course* it is! When have we ever *not* talked about *anything*? Have you even *had* sex since Bruce died?"

The hesitation was there, but only for a moment.

"Of course I have!" Vivienne insisted.

"Once? Twice?"

"If you must know," Vivienne said haughtily, "I was in a relationship for six months."

"With a man?"

"Yes, with a *man*, you shit!" Vivienne couldn't hide her amusement.

Pepper shrugged.

"It wouldn't bother me if you came out, hun."

Vivienne continued to snort and laugh, trying to regain control.

"I'd probably do better with women, that's for sure."

Like a dog with a bone, Pepper wouldn't let go of the original question.

"When?"

"When what?"

"How long ago was this alleged affair?"

Vivienne squirmed in her chair.

"Four years ago," she whispered, her mirth extinguished.

"FOUR YEARS?" People once again turned to stare at them.

"All right, all right, calm down!" Vivienne exhaled noisily.

Pepper threw her hands up in the air.

"Fine, I won't push Will on you, but you definitely need to get laid, girl." Pepper snickered and finished off her drink.

"Please," Vivienne said softly. "Like he'd be interested in me, anyway. I'm old enough to be his mother."

"Hah! He's 32, you dolt. Last time I checked, seven-year-olds weren't giving birth anywhere on *this* planet. You only *act* like you're old enough to be his mother." Vivienne laughed then and Pepper felt the rest of the tension between them slip away. "Besides, he does think you're cute."

"Cute. That's a lovely word." Vivienne rolled her eyes. Peeking at Pepper, she asked, "Have you slept with him?"

Pepper's smile was genuine as she shook her head.

"No. There has never been anything physical between us. We moved in some of the same circles when he first got to California." Pepper didn't like the way Vivienne pursed her lips.

"You seem like exactly his type."

Pepper shrugged.

"Maybe physically, but our personalities did *not* mesh. It took a year before we even got to be friends."

Vivienne sat up in her chair a little straighter.

"Well that makes me feel a little better."

Pepper waggled her eyebrows.

"Are you changing your mind, then?"

"No!" Vivienne was emphatic. "But it's a nice fantasy. It'll give me some good inspiration when I get home."

"Bah!" Pepper scoffed. "You're making a *big* mistake, I'm telling you."

"How would *you* know if you haven't been with him?"

"I'm not speaking from personal experience." Pepper stuck her tongue out at Vivienne. "Just look at the man for Chrissake! He's hotter than hell! Don't tell me you wouldn't give your eye teeth to see him naked."

"Maybe," Vivienne admitted, grinning. The smile fell from her face almost immediately. "I could never hook up with some anonymous guy, though. You must know that."

"He's not anonymous. He's *famous*!"

The women laughed together and Will found them that way when he returned to the table.

"What's so funny?"

"Oh nothing, just girl stuff." Pepper gave him a cheesy grin.

"Well drink up, ladies. If you're interested, there's a party going on back at the house. Wanna come over?"

Pepper tried not to bounce in her chair and bobbed her head up and down. Vivienne inhaled and held her breath, then breathed out, smiled and nodded her head.

"Okay, sure."

"Excellent!" Pepper reached over and hugged Vivienne, almost knocking her over in the chair.

Chapter 9

Even though I'd only had four beers over the course of several hours, I didn't want to take the chance and drive. I'd probably blow drunk if I got stopped. Wouldn't the press have a field day with that? It had taken time to resuscitate my image after having been a party boy and womanizer in my twenties. Snagging a DUI wouldn't help, especially while in the company of a beleaguered author whose finances were in ruin. I might have slipped up by inviting them to a party at my house, but I had no intention of going back to *all* of my old habits. And I sure as hell didn't want to add to Vivienne's troubles.

"Where's your car?" Pepper asked, peering around. Full lots were on either side of the bar, and cars were lined along the street for several blocks.

"I think we'll get a cab." I crooked my finger and the girls followed me to the cabstand. "No sense taking a chance."

"I agree," Vivienne said quietly, giving me a reassuring look.

"Meh." Pepper shrugged noncommittally. "Not one of us is drunk, you know."

Vivienne scowled and I laughed.

"Maybe not, but I'm not in the mood for another tabloid run." I turned to Vivienne. "How about you?"

"No thanks, I'll pass." Her snort of derision made me laugh a little harder.

When the cab arrived, I opened the door for the girls and Pepper shoved Vivienne in first. Then she hopped inside and grabbed the door closed. It was my turn to scowl at her, but she grinned back in triumph. I walked around to the other side and opened the door. I eased myself in trying not rub up against Vivienne, who looked flustered. I gave the driver my address, then leaned back against the worn seat.

Vivienne fidgeted nervously next to me while Pepper talked on and on about nothing important. I was glad I had decided not to drive, even though the unexpected turn of events sobered me up pretty fast. I had gone to The Relic under totally different pretenses. Instead I reunited with an old pal and her pal, inviting them back to my place. After Pepper's ludicrous idea, I should have chatted Vivienne up and been on my way. But the rest of the guys I left at home had decided to ease their way back into life by throwing a fairly raucous party. If I'd known they were going to do that, I could have stayed there and none of this would be happening. I didn't think about what I was doing, I just went back to Pepper and Vivienne and asked them over like it was nothing, just like I would have when I was twenty-five. I probably should have thought about it first. I was pretty shocked at how easily I was slipping back into my old ways.

I stole glances at Vivienne from time to time. She looked on edge. She cracked her knuckles and her right knee bounced up and down faster than a hummingbird's wings.

"Why so nervous?" I asked, trying to sound calm and assuring, hoping she didn't catch me ogling.

"I'm not nervous." Her voice cracked with the fast answer. Pepper elbowed her and I turned to look out the window so they wouldn't see me grin. She just wasn't going to give up, that Pepper. When she dropped the idea of a hookup on me at the bar, it was shocking and I probably acted more offended than I had a right to. I was no saint, but now I was pretty amused by the thought. I had overheard the two of them talking about reliving their youth, acting young again, so I chalked the whole thing up to a couple of women playing a modern day version of Truth or Dare. But the truth was, I wasn't up for the dare.

In spite of what I told Pepper, I was still stinging over the whole Lucy thing. That girl took advantage of me in the worst way for a long time. I was still as angry with myself, as with her, for not facing it sooner. Deep down, I had known things were wrong with Lucy, but my ego didn't listen. How would I ever know if a woman liked me for me and not the money and fame? With my completely recognizable mug, how the hell was I supposed to meet nice, normal women? Lucy did a number on me and I didn't know when I would ever trust again.

I knew at some point I would, though. History dictated that I always did. But once I'd finally gotten rid of Lucy, I made a concerted effort to stay away from women. Even one-night stands. I couldn't admit that to Pepper, or else I'd have gotten the standard lecture from her, the one where she would badger me not to let one bad apple ruin the bunch and how I should get right back out there until I found "the one." So I told her that her friend was just cute, hoping she would back off.

The truth was I thought Vivienne was hot as hell. I usually went for the tall, anorexic blond because that's what guys in bands did. It was easy. There was no pressure. Vivienne was the polar opposite. Short and curvy with red hair, and the most incredible rack I'd ever seen. I noticed her at the bar because of it, and the chauvinist in me credited it for why I agreed to go talk to her. But there was so much more to her than her body. Vivienne was whip-smart, with a grace and sophistication I wasn't used to. She didn't stare at me with google eyes like most women did. She was more interested in me as a person than Will Foster of Static Neverland. As unwilling as I was to admit it, Vivienne intrigued me.

I mentally cursed myself *again* for even inviting them back to the house. I knew Pepper had gotten the wrong impression. But it was too late now. I couldn't exactly toss them out of the car by the side of the road.

I told myself, over and over, I was just going to be a good host and the perfect gentleman.

Chapter 10

Pepper tried to make me slam my almost untouched drink before leaving the bar. When she wasn't looking, I "accidentally" spilled it all over the table. She gave me the stink eye and I gave her my best innocent doe eyes. Shaking her head, Pepper pulled me from the bar as we followed Will outside.

He took us to a huge house in the Hollywood Hills, glowing with light from every window. Loud music was thumping from inside. I didn't recognize it, but it had a jazzy, bluesy feel and, somehow, it relaxed me. I even started to get a little excited.

"So this is the new place!" Pepper gazed out the window at the sprawling, ranch-style house in appreciation.

"Yep." Will paid for the cab in spite of my protests, and we eased out onto the sidewalk. The driveway was filled with cars and every spot was filled up along the street and down the block for as far as I could see. I was a little overwhelmed and very much impressed. It was well landscaped on the outside and reminded me of the homes along Lakeshore Drive back in Michigan, but not ostentatious and overdone like the mansion on Mulholland Drive earlier that night.

"It's *huge*!" I was unable to hide my awe. "All this for just one person?"

"Not exactly." Will led us up the front pathway paved with bluish-gray slate. "The whole band lives here. We bought it together because we're together all the time, anyway."

Before Will could open the wide, oak double doors for us, both doors swung inward and crashed against the walls of the entryway.

"Welcome! Welcome!" shouted the man who greeted us. A bottle of whiskey sloshed in his right hand as he gesticulated. He wore a pair of ratty cutoff jeans and nothing else. He had long, blond hair that was mussed up in all the right places to give him the look of a teenage boy throwing a house party while his parents were out of town.

"Easy, bud." Will chuckled. "I brought a couple of friends."

"I see this!" His words were slurred. "All beautiful ladies are welcome! Come on in and find yourself a drink!"

I grew uncomfortable and tried not to squirm when he stared at me for too long. Then his gaze was drawn to Pepper like a moth to flame.

"Hey, Billy," Pepper purred. "Don't you remember me?"

"Of course, baby!" His voice lowered to a sexy growl. His eyes brightened at the tall, sun-kissed blond. He reached to grab her around the waist, pulling her close. "Pepper, my love!" Planting a loud kiss on his cheek, Pepper laughed and put her arm around his waist. They led the way inside, perfectly in step.

"That was Billy Stern, the bass player." Will touched my elbow lightly and invited me in.

The first thing he did was introduce me to ten or fifteen people lining the entry way of the house. I nodded and smiled, saying my hellos. I don't think I caught a single name or heard anything more than "Hi," "How's it goin'," or "Hey," but the vibe I got back was friendly and warm. When we got past the vestibule, the house opened up into a huge living area with vaulted ceilings. There were five leather couches strategically placed around a giant glass and stone coffee table. At least thirty people were standing around and seated, drinking wine and beer, and comfortably enjoying their conversations, even if they had to speak over the music coming from the back of the house. What I noticed above all else was that the people in the room were of varying ages. It wasn't filled with only thirty-somethings. There were some guys who looked to be barely legal to drink, talking about guitars as they passed one back and forth amongst themselves. I noticed two couples in front of the fireplace who looked like they might have been in their fifties or sixties. The only evidence I had to go on was the lack of apparent plastic surgery and graying hair. Their conversation was animated and I think about politics, because one of the men made a disparaging remark about the current president and the other man smacked his forehead with his hand. The perfect mixture of laughter and easy dialogue was a kind of music of its own, competing with the sound coming from the other side of the house.

The song from the other room ended abruptly, giving Will the perfect opportunity to shout out to the crowd. The response was raised glasses and shouts of "Will!" I snickered inwardly, instantly reminded of the old TV show *Cheers*. He smirked down at me, and then the band revved up again. Once again, the house was filled with music.

"This is Vivienne!" he called out. "Vivienne, this is everyone!"

I grinned, then waived my hand in a sweeping motion. Glasses and bottles were raised, along with nods of recognition, from most. Will guided me toward the back of the room and into the kitchen. Billy may have been drunker than a skunk, but the rest of the partygoers I encountered seemed to be holding their liquor much better. This did wonders for my own mood of nervous excitement as I relaxed and let myself feel comfortable. Will excused Billy's behavior as decompression from getting off the road from the long tour. I accepted that without question, trying to imagine what a year away from home would be like. I couldn't. The couple of simple jaunts I'd made for book appearances wiped me out. Being on a bus or a plane for a year would have killed me. I wasn't the type to leave my own bed and pillow for any length of time.

"Sorry I had to introduce you like that." Will leaned down to speak into my right ear. "It's the only way into the kitchen and I didn't want to get stopped."

"No worries."

"Good. Come on!"

As we stepped into the obviously brand new, gourmet kitchen, with all its high-end appliances and finishes, I counted another dozen people. A couple of pretty, blond girls were perched on the counters. A few guys were surrounding them, hanging on their every word. Some people were leaning against the large island, peering into the family room, watching the band play.

Will led me to the stainless steel refrigerator, ignoring the people in the room. I wondered if he even knew any of them. They looked very young and nervous, as if they were wondering when they would be discovered as party crashers and asked to leave. I had a bit of sympathy for them, because Pepper and I had crashed our own fair share of parties. I'm sure we'd had the same expressions on our faces.

"Drink or beer?" Will half shouted. I mouthed the word beer and nodded for him to select one even though I had no intention of drinking it. It would make a good prop. I was astounded to notice the fridge not only contained a large stock of many brands of beer, but real food as well. It surprised me to think of a band of musicians living in a house and having actual food instead of all alcohol. I rolled my eyes mentally at the dowdy thought, but couldn't keep the real frown off my face. Pepper was right. When had I become such an old lady?

"You okay?" Will asked, peering at my face.

"Yes! I'm fine." Instantly, I replaced the sour look with a smile. I touched his elbow reassuringly.

Off the kitchen was a huge family room covering more square footage than my entire house in Michigan. In front of the marble-tiled fireplace, there were microphones, amplifiers, and a drum set and people were playing and singing. Comfy looking furniture in various shades of earth tones normally filled the room, I imagined, but now it was all pushed up against the walls. A massive modern glass chandelier hung from the ceiling, casting the whole room in warm light. It had a polished, chrome-plated steel rod and the arms extended out in wide swirls and curls. The bowls cradling the light bulbs were of the same chrome-plated steel. The floors were dark hardwood with an expansive area rug in the center of the room. It accented things perfectly with its color-blocked squares in red, brown, blue and green. At least fifty people filled the room, as though it were a small concert hall. Most had drinks in their hands and stood clumped together in small groups of three or four in front of the makeshift stage.

Will checked his watch, then waited for the song to end. When it did, he left me leaning against the island to weave in and out of the people in the room to the guys who had been having the impromptu jam session. I don't know what he said, but the volume of the music decreased dramatically. The general tone in the room relaxed and quieted down. He returned to my side and offered his beer bottle in a mock toast. Grinning, I clinked his with mine.

"We just moved in a few weeks ago. The guys and I try to make sure the music and partying doesn't go past midnight so we don't piss off the neighbors."

"Wise move. It didn't look like you have a lot of neighbors close by, though."

"No, but you have no idea how loud musicians can get when they're beered up."

I laughed, but disagreed.

"Oh, I think I do. Pepper and I hung out with all the bands when we were teenagers. I guess I thought that as musicians aged, they matured a little."

"Uh, no. Not always," Will admitted, shuffling his feet back and forth and turning his head. Just then, a man approached us and slung an arm around Will's shoulders.

"Who's your friend?" he drawled, the bangs of his long brown hair falling across his blue eyes. He was tall like Will, skinnier than Pepper, and eyed me like I was a tasty snack. I was flattered and discomfited at the same time.

"Tim, this is Vivienne Stark. Vivienne, this is Tim Walters, my oldest friend."

"How do you do," I whispered. He grasped my hand firmly, stepping closer. I tried to move backward, but the island held me prisoner. He was as handsome as the devil, but came on much too strong for me. Will put a hand on his chest and pushed him away so he could put out his fist for a bump. Tim's gaze left me and he stared at Will's fist for a half second before returning the bump.

"Nice to meetcha, Vivienne." Tim's eyes were fixed on mine again.

Will shuffled the slightest bit nearer to me. Tim cocked his head to the side, shaking his shaggy hair.

"Come sing with us, Will." He tried to pull Will toward a microphone across the room.

"Nah." Will shook his head in protest.

"Come on, man, just one song." Tim tugged a little harder.

Will looked at me for help, but I was none.

"Go ahead. It'll be like my own private concert." I nodded encouragement and Will exhaled, allowing Tim to lead him away. Waiting a moment or two, I zigzagged through the room and found the arm of a large chair vacant. The girl sitting in the chair encouraged me to share, so I did.

Will grabbed a guitar and his band mates launched into one of their radio hits I actually recognized. I started singing along and moving my shoulders to the beat. It was fun to see Will perform and watch all the people at the party enjoying themselves. I had to believe he put just as much effort into the performance in his home as he would have if on a big stage in front of thousands of people.

Pepper arrived beside me and she hugged me into her hip. Leaning down to speak, I turned my face to hers.

"Didn't I tell you this would be great?" I smelled pot and almost fell off the arm of the chair when laughter overtook me. Having no control, she joined me and we tried to hide our snickers behind our hands so that no one would notice. It didn't work. Will kept looking at us like we'd grown third eyes in our foreheads. When the first song ended and the next began, Pepper pulled me up toward a set of large French doors I hadn't noticed. They were half blocked off by one of the couches. The doors opened up to a spacious deck running along the entire backside of the house. The sound of crickets chirping and cicadas singing was peaceful and soothing. Their song seemed in tandem with the beat from the music inside, which was greatly muted by the closed doors.

"Isn't this gorgeous?" she said in wonderment, deeply breathing in the night air.

"Oh yeah." I was thinking maybe I was wrong to live so frugally. Maybe it would be nice to get a big fancy place with a view like this. Or of the ocean. Then I remembered the foundation and how much money I owed it. Fantasies of where I could live disappeared, replaced by a blanket of guilt. And the smell of pot again. Pepper bumped my arm holding out a lit joint to me.

I put my hands up.

"Uh-uh. You got me here, and you got two extra drinks in me. I can't."

"One drink, and a measly half a beer that you won't even finish. Come on, Viv. Just a couple of hits. It'll relax you," she coaxed.

I was suddenly assaulted by memories of all the parties we went to in high school and all the bands we'd been friends with. I recalled how free we were. How our lives seemed to stretch out before us. How we hadn't stopped to think of consequences, but lived for the moment. Now I was almost forty and my life was half over. I cringed with how *old* I felt inside.

Pepper grinned as I thrust my hand out to take the joint. Closing my lips around the tip, I sucked and inhaled deeply. Holding it for as long as I could, I finally exhaled in small bursts, shocked that I didn't cough up a lung.

"Ha! Old habits die hard, I see!" Pepper accused. "You haven't lost the touch. Have you been practicing on the sly?"

"It's a gift."

"Of which you have many," Pepper giggled.

After a little while, we noticed the live music had stopped, replaced by an iPod mix floating out of the speakers mounted on the side of the house. It was just loud enough to notice, but it didn't overwhelm the natural sounds outside. When Will sidled up beside Pepper, the smile I gave him was as warm as the sun had been on my face at the pool.

Good grief, was that really earlier today?

"Thanks for the concert. I enjoyed hearing you play very much." I hoped my voice sounded as normal to him as it did in my head.

"Then why did you leave?" He took a hit of pot and offered it back to me. I declined, allowing Pepper to finish it off.

"She needed some air." Pepper answered for me. I tried to laugh coyly, but what came barreling out was a donkey's bray. Then I snorted. Pepper blew smoke out in a choking sound and bent over, holding her stomach while she guffawed.

"I'm sorry, I'm sorry." There was a wheezy quality to my voice. "It's been a long time since I've smoked." My face burned with mortification, but I still had to fight the urge to start laughing again.

"No worries." Will looked amused and pushed us both over to a couple of metal lawn chairs. Before too long, Billy joined us, but there was no chair for him. Instead, Pepper stood and offered hers, then sat on his lap. I was buzzing quite nicely and was glad no one else came out to the deck to interrupt the intimacy the four of us shared. Our quiet chatter about nothing important was more stream of consciousness, and I was so glad I agreed to Will's invitation.

*****

Pepper watched Vivienne carefully. With each passing moment, she could feel her friend loosening up. The hookup still might not happen, but Vivienne seemed happy and was enjoying herself. Sure, it would have been better if she could have helped her friend get laid, but the idea had been so spur of the moment, it had been impossible to orchestrate it successfully.

I should have thought about it first, she thought as she watched Vivienne laugh at some story Will regaled her with. *The story of my life.*

Pepper wasn't blind to the fact that Will was warming to Vivienne in a way she hadn't expected. Billy was too drunk to join in too much of the conversation. He was simply holding her and zoning out while the insects serenaded them and voices murmured all around. But Will and Vivienne were engaged in a lively discussion, flitting from topic to topic like two kids with ADD. Pepper tried to follow it and participate for a while, but it felt too much like a mental tennis match to her. They talked about books and music she'd never heard of and movies she'd never seen. So she smiled dreamily and let the easy cadence of their voices soothe her and prolong her buzz.

Pepper started to shiver when the temperature dropped to near 60 degrees and the breeze blowing through the trees picked up. Her thin dress didn't offer much protection to the cooler night air. She asked Will if he had a sweater or hoodie she could borrow.

"Why don't we just go inside?" Will suggested. He helped Pepper off Billy's lap and then pulled Billy into a standing position. He listed to the side, then leaned against Pepper. Will then turned to Vivienne and offered her his hand, which she took right away, much to Pepper's delight.

"Where we goin'?" Billy slurred, causing Pepper to totter unstably on her stilettos.

Will reached for his arm and slung it around his shoulders.

"Inside, big guy." Arm in arm, they shuffled inside the house while Pepper and Vivienne followed.

Pepper was surprised to see the house had emptied considerably. The family room was completely empty. A couple of people were in the kitchen with Tim. Another couple of people were in the foyer, saying goodbye to the bass player, Dan. Looking at her watch, she saw it was almost one in the morning. As if on cue, a yawn yanked her mouth wide open and she struggled to hide it behind her hand.

"I saw that," Vivienne whispered.

"Heh, I guess I'm not much for stamina anymore." Pepper rubbed her eyes to keep them from drooping.

Vivienne's smile faded.

"We should call a cab, I guess."

"No, no. We can stay. I'm not ready to go, yawn or no yawn." Pepper waved her hands at Vivienne. *Shit*, she thought. *Damn yawn!*

"You can stay with me," Billy mumbled drunkenly as Will dropped him onto a soft leather couch.

"Thanks, Billy, but no thanks." Pepper patted his head affectionately.

"There's a guest room," Will offered. "Go crash if you want."

Pepper hesitated for a moment, unable to tell if Will wanted her to go so he could have Vivienne alone or if he was just being his usual kind self. She didn't take the chance, faking a second yawn.

"Show me the way. Come get me when you're ready to go, Viv."

"Not too much longer, I promise. Will was telling me about the shows they played for the troops." Vivienne's eyes were wide and bright with wakefulness, but missing any sort of lust, much to Pepper's disappointment. *Still, you never know what'll happen if I just get out of their hair.*

"Help me, Pepper." Will yanked Billy back into his arms. Pepper kicked off her shoes and picked them up in her right hand, then used her left to sling Billy's arm over her shoulders. Together, she and Will staggered with him over to the stairs and up each one slowly. The upper level looked out over the living room, and the hallway was lined with doors. Vivienne watched as Pepper opened the one Will pointed to, and they dragged Billy inside. When they came back out, Will closed the door and then led Pepper in the opposite direction. Pepper smiled, winked, and waved goodbye to Vivienne before disappearing from view.

Chapter 11

When Will came back, I was already comfortable on one of the leather couches with my legs curled up under me. My boots were on the floor and I had snagged a throw from the back of one of the leather chairs.

"Glad to see you're making yourself at home." Will had made a detour into the kitchen and returned with bottles of water. He tossed me one and winked, making me want to giggle like a teenager.

I gave him a cheesy grin and twisted the cap off.

"Thank you."

"You're welcome." Will tipped his water in my direction.

"Tell me about the tour." I leaned against the soft leather.

"Lord, do you have a month?" Will grinned, but launched into stories about the cities they'd seen and how exhausting it all was. He loved performing and didn't deny loving the crowds screaming and chanting for the band, but the business end of it all sucked. They needed to find a new manager, one that wouldn't book them for twelve months at a time and was more interested in the band members' wellbeing than the almighty dollar.

"I guess I never thought of it that way," I mused.

"What?"

"You're obviously doing what you love to do. You get to fly around in private jets and have every creature comfort possible. It never occurred to me that it could be exhausting or boring or a hassle." I suddenly felt bad for him. Maybe the grass *wasn't* always greener on the other side of the fence.

"It sucks, if you think about it too much." Will tilted his head from side to side as he considered it. "Then I think about what it's like to not have to worry about money. Helping out my family. Getting to see parts of the world I never thought I'd see. Having a job where I get to make *music*. It all becomes worth it, then."

"You're preaching to the choir." I gave him a thumbs up. "Before *The Widow's Path*, I was able to indie-publish pretty consistently. I wasn't wealthy, that's for sure, but it was enough to spend my life doing what I loved instead of tolerating what I had to."

Will grinned at me and I thought my heart would melt. I wanted to ask him how he could be so damn manly-slash-sexy and cute-slash-boyish all at the same time. I had to force myself to keep the conversation going, or else I'd have spent the rest of the night just staring at him, drinking in his good looks.

I must have asked him a hundred questions. I wanted to know all about Static Neverland, when he learned to love music, where he had grown up, what making a TV show was like. He answered them all with enthusiasm and a frankness I never would have expected. Will revealed his desire to get into acting and producing, and even admitted he had dabbled with short story writing a time or two.

"Really? I'd love to read your stuff sometime." *Yikes!* I couldn't believe I said that to him.

"Oh, no," Will demurred. "It's not that good. I just did it to see if I could."

I couldn't back out now, so I pressed him.

"Don't be silly. You've written some beautiful lyrics. Are the stories fiction?"

"Yeah."

"What genre?"

Will shrugged.

"One's kind of a sci-fi fantasy thing, but I don't have a real big science background, so I'm sure it sucks. And the other one's about a kid trying to decide what he wants to do with this life."

I nodded and gave him a warm smile.

"Well, if you change your mind, I'd be happy to take a look. I've been in a group for years and it's all about encouragement."

"Meh," Will said. "Maybe."

He changed the subject then and asked about *The Widow's Path*. He was shocked when I told him how it had been fifteen years in the writing. I was flattered because he really had read the book. He couldn't have asked some of the questions he did if he hadn't understood the story.

We talked about the foundation and my inspiration for starting it. I told him about the families who had been helped so far, and how excited I was to keep doing good work for those left behind. Will was adamant about the band helping out, and once again I was flabbergasted at the selflessness of the offer. I admit I was excited about having such a big name attached to the foundation. I knew it was selfish, but I couldn't help myself.

I opened up about my writing in a way I hadn't done with anyone but Pepper or my mom for such a long time. In spite of my own frankness, I could tell Will did not know the book was my own personal story. I didn't bother telling him that particular truth. It didn't seem important. He got the point of the story and had been moved by it, much like everyone else who read it, just like I had hoped when I published it. Besides, I didn't want him feeling sorry for me. The look on his face as I talked was one of interest and attention. I hated to watch peoples' faces morph with pity and discomfort when they found out I was a widow.

I was glad to get to know Will in a way Pepper never intended. He was much more easygoing than I would have thought, considering what little I knew about him before tonight. He seemed more normal than a celebrity should be. I was an avid magazine reader and I conceded with shame how often I just swallowed what was written about famous people without giving them the benefit of the doubt.

"Tell me about your family." Will's question caught me off guard. The array of topics we'd covered was so wide and varied, it never occurred to me that he'd be interested in family.

"Well, it's just me and my mom. My dad died seven years ago."

"Oh, man, I'm sorry." Will's bottom lip slipped forward in a slight pout. I almost passed out when I wondered what it would be like to bite it.

"Uh, yeah," I muttered, clearing my throat and studying a hangnail on my finger. "My dad was the best."

"What did he do?"

"He was a construction superintendent for a company that built commercial banks, and he built furniture in his spare time. He was really talented. Half the stuff in my house is from him." My eyes misted a little thinking about Dad. It didn't matter how long he'd been gone or how old I got, it was always painful to think about him not being around.

"That's really awesome. What about your mom? Is she creative, too?"

I cocked my head to the side. "Well, not in the typical sense. But she's scary smart."

"Scary?" Will laughed. "What the hell does that mean?"

I grinned.

"Some people are smart. Other people are really smart. And then there are the ones who know so much it scares you. That's scary smart." I groaned inwardly thinking how juvenile that sounded. It was a concept I'd developed when I was a teenager and never let go of, in spite of moving into my fourth decade of life.

Will chuckled and nodded at me.

"I like it. I know scary smart people, too. It sounds like you're pretty close with your mom."

"Yeah. She's as much my best friend as Pepper."

"Any brothers or sisters?"

"Nope. Just me. My folks were onlies too, so it's just the two of us."

"Wow," Will whispered. "You're so... *lucky*!" Astonishment filled his eyes. "It must have been so peaceful and quiet."

Laughing, I shook my head.

"I suppose. Sometimes it was lonely."

The Widow and the Rock Star

When I asked him about his family, he regaled me with stories about his two older sisters and two younger brothers and being the "middle child." I laughed until my sides ached listening to him relate countless exploits he'd had growing up. The time his sisters dressed him up in their clothes and carried him around like a baby doll. The practical joke competitions with his little brothers and how much blame he could lay at their door for his misdeeds. His parents were still married and living in the house where he grew up back home in Kansas City. I had to admit I was a bit jealous, having been an only child and having no frame of reference to relate to his experiences.

I concentrated on sipping my water when the laughter we shared died down. Will looked tired and I thought it was probably time to get Pepper and head back to the hotel. I was just about to open my mouth to voice my thoughts when he beat me to it with a question.

"Have you ever been married?"

All at once, my body tensed. I don't know why I thought it wouldn't come up. It was probably natural for him to wonder. After all, we'd talked about every other subject under the sun.

"Well, I was once," I said softly, staring at my hands, having a difficult time remembering what it was like to wear a wedding ring. The change in conversation made my stomach start to ache.

"Didn't work out?" he asked, not recognizing my discomfort. He was leaning forward in his chair, elbows resting on knees, looking at me intently.

"Not exactly." I leveled my gaze to his. "I'm a widow, actually."

Normally I took a perverse sort of pleasure at dropping that bomb on people when they asked about my marital status. At my age, being unmarried intimated there was something wrong with me. The shock and shame that would spread across the inquisitor's face made me feel vindicated, and I would soak in all the apologies to come. But the distress on Will's face and the stunned shock in his eyes made me feel sick with guilt.

"I'm so sorry." He looked away quickly. I didn't know what to say, so I didn't speak.

The misery on Will's face abruptly deepened and understanding bloomed as his cheeks paled.

"The book's about you, isn't it?" He sat back up and looked at me, his eyes full of anguish. Then he surprised me again by crossing the room to sit down beside me.

"Yes, it is." *No sense lying about it.*

"Oh, fuck." Will ran his fingers through his hair and leaned forward. "What a shitty thing. My God! I'm so sorry," he said again. "Why didn't you say anything?"

"It's okay, Will. It was my choice not to make it public. You don't have anything to be sorry about." I cracked my knuckles and avoided looking at him.

"Did you have any kids? I mean, *do* you have any kids?"

"No." An image of the last care package I ever sent flashed through my mind. I had written a letter to Bruce pouring my heart out about how much I loved him and how I couldn't wait to have a baby when he got home. "We thought we had plenty of time for them later."

"Well that's good." Realizing at once he'd said something insensitive, Will tried to backtrack. "Wait, I didn't mean that."

I touched his arm trying to make him feel better.

"I know what you meant." I didn't want what had turned out to be such a special night morphing into something he would be embarrassed to remember. I was used to sensitive people saying insensitive things without thinking.

He put his hand over mine and I thought he was just being supportive and grateful for my forgiveness. But his eyes came back to mine.

And then he was kissing me.

Chapter 12

And then I was kissing her.

Two thoughts ran simultaneously through my brain. *Man is this woman hot!* And *What the hell are you doing?* I was half on top of her, my mouth smashed against hers. I hadn't been with a woman in well over a year. I felt that year in my pants the instant my lips touched hers. I was embarrassed to hear a groan start in the back of my throat. I cut it off immediately.

I could tell she was shocked because, when I peeked, her eyes were wide open. I almost stopped, but she was pulling me closer. Her fingers were laced together behind my neck and I could feel the gentle pressure forcing me nearer. She was trying to kiss back, but she seemed unsure of herself. Then she closed her eyes.

My hands had started on her biceps. I moved my right arm around her to cradle her shoulders. My left hand shot into her hair to pull it out of the loose ponytail she wore all night. I pressed our chests together and cupped the back of her head in my hand. Oh, how I wanted her now. Her kisses were becoming more confident.

I let my tongue try to tease open her lips, waiting for any resistance. When I felt hers come out to meet mine, I knew it was going to be a very long night.

Chapter 13

Will was the best kisser I'd ever known. I tried hard not to compare him to Bruce, but when it first started it was difficult not to. Bruce had been pushy and aggressive with his kissing, and it hadn't lasted long before he would move on to other things, forgetting all about my lips. It wasn't that it was bad, but it was really the only real experience I had.

I didn't lie to Pepper when I said I'd been in a relationship with a man for six months four years ago. But that man had never touched me, which was why we broke up. I wasn't interested in a physical relationship, so he had moved on and, honestly, I couldn't blame him. But the truth was, I hadn't had sex since the last time with Bruce, when I was only 21 years old.

And now I was in the arms of a man seven years younger than me, sexier than *hell*, and he was kissing me! And it was *exciting*!

His one arm snaked around me, and a feeling of warmth and safety mingled with my racing hormones. His tongue touched my lips and I steeled myself not to freak out. A little voice popped into my head screaming, *What the hell are you doing?* But I managed to ignore it. I couldn't believe I was doing what I was doing, but some baser instinct took over.

Somehow we got up from the couch while still kissing. Some way, we made it up the stairs to a door. My arms were curled around Will's neck and my hands were buried in his hair as he reached behind us to open it. My neck was stretched to the limit so I could keep my mouth on his and yet we glided smoothly inside. He used his foot to nudge it closed, never once breaking the contact between us.

He pressed up against me, pinning my hands above my head, lacing his fingers with mine, against the door. We stayed like that for a long time, just kissing.

"I must be drunk," I half giggled, half murmured, trying to catch my breath.

"No, you aren't."

"Then *you're* drunk."

"No, I'm not."

I wanted more and I untangled my fingers from his to get my hands free. When he let go and I reached for his shirt, he said "no" against my lips. Pulling away from me, he whispered into my ear, "Let me. This is all about you."

"Me?"

"Yes." He kissed me again, slowly. "Stop thinking. Just feel."

"But—"

"No buts, shh."

After that, the way he kissed me, the way he undressed me, the way he led me to his bed, the things we did when we got there, it was all just one long stream of consciousness because I listened. I let go. I was utterly overwhelmed by the feel and smell and taste of his mouth and hands and skin on mine.

It became clear that all the desire inside me had never disappeared. I never got rid of it or expunged it, no matter how much I thought I had. It lay dormant in me like a virus waiting for the right moment to come alive.

It was as though one small vein of lava was still inside my heart somewhere and his kisses were a warm breeze blowing on it, making it glow bright orange. With each new touch and stroke, the lava spread farther through my veins and my body was heated through until it rose to the surface, pouring out of my skin. I stopped thinking and analyzing and trying to give a response that I thought he expected. The things he did to my body and the way his hands and tongue moved over every inch of it made me feel as though he was playing me like one of his guitars. All of my reactions to every kiss, every stroke, were as spontaneous and unplanned as breathing.

He was skillful at anticipating what would feel good and what I would like, but my last experience was so far in the past, it couldn't have been too difficult. Everything seemed to make me groan, sometimes in surprise and other times with simple pleasure. When I didn't respond the way he expected, Will made me tell him what I was feeling and what I needed. When words failed me, he used my own hands against me to show him the way.

He memorized everything that made me breathe faster and forgot anything that didn't.

Will found a path and followed it without hesitation to the center of my sexual core, allowing me to selfishly accept everything happening without worrying about giving in return. Again and again, he took me to places inside myself I hadn't been in decades and to new places I never knew were there.

*****

I don't remember falling asleep. I don't remember Will curling up next to me or pulling the covers up over us. But I do recall the sun beating through the windows and burning behind my eyes. I do remember his hand cupped around my breast and his body pressing against mine.

My eyes popped open and I groaned as the light pierced my eyeballs. I snapped them shut again and lay perfectly still. My mind tried to rev up like a car engine and race through the night before, but I took a deep breath and remembered the sound of Will's voice saying, "Let go." I listened to the husky message play over and over in my head until I fell asleep again.

When I woke up for the second time, I was alone in the bed. I opened my eyes and the light wasn't as harsh, but still plentiful. I sat up to look around, not finding Will. For the first time, I took note of the large room. No wonder the sun had brought me out of sleep. One whole side was nothing but windows overlooking the woods and mountains behind the house. The walls were painted in a warm, cream color and the ceiling was done in gorgeous terracotta. The floor was dark hardwood and the furniture was dark oak to match. It was a masculine room, but not overdone.

Images of the night before began to flash in my head. Will's hands on me, his mouth on me. I groaned, dropping my face into my hands. I couldn't believe it. Conflict roared through my body and brain; one reveling in the beauty of it, the other reviling it. As though I could still feel his touch, my body tingled all over. The smile spreading over my face couldn't be helped. But then I could hear that little voice in my head, that devil, shaming me for my promiscuity. From that, my mind conjured an image of Bruce. This was a conditioned response any time I let myself feel happy or excited about something. Most times, thinking of him brought a mixture of sadness and yearning for him to be with me, to enjoy whatever was happening. But this morning, his face inspired only horror. From as far back as I could remember, my mom had taught me that anyone who died was "always with us and watching over." I hoped to God he hadn't been spying last night.

"Yikes," I whispered, ashamed and aroused at the same time. Just then, Will leaned out of a doorway from across the room. He was completely naked. I yelped in surprise, pulling the sheet up over my bare chest.

"Hey, you're awake," he said companionably. "How are you doing?"

"Uh, okay." I couldn't meet his eyes, trying desperately to avoid looking at his naked body. The speed with which desire spread through me took my breath away. I knew what basic attraction felt like, but one slight glance at him sent me from zero to sixty in a heartbeat. Thoughts of Bruce vanished, but only for a split second, replaced with guilt.

"I'm going to hit the shower." He was trying to get me to look at him, leaning forward, moving his hands around. "You want to join me?"

"Uh, no thank you," I squeaked, then cleared my throat, running one hand through my mussed hair. "You go ahead."

"Okay." Will chuckled and disappeared, but he didn't shut the door.

I heard the water start running and waited until I was sure he had to be under the spray. My eyes darted around and I spotted a cell phone on the bedside table. I had no idea where my *own* phone was. Somewhere inside my purse, somewhere inside the house, so I yanked the sheet as hard as I could to free it from the bed. I jumped up, wrapped it around me and then grabbed what I supposed was Will's phone, quickly clicking it on. Thank God there was no password protection on it. It was an iPhone and I struggled to use it in my anxious state. I frantically dialed Pepper's number, hoping she would answer. When she didn't, I thought I would hyperventilate. Forcing myself to take slow, deep breaths through my nose and exhale out of my mouth, I redialed and almost wept when a groggy voice finally came back to me.

"Mmm, hullo?"

"Pepper! Where are you?" I whispered hysterically, wild eyes whizzing back toward the open bathroom door.

"Whosdis?" She was nowhere near awake.

"It's Vivienne, you twit! Where *are* you?" I demanded, trying to keep my voice quiet.

"Viv?" I could hear some muffled noises. "I don't know. Oh wait, I'm still at Will's. In the guest room. Where are you?"

I hesitated before answering.

"Wait a minute." She sounded more alert. "Whose number is this? Vivienne, where the hell are *you*?" Her voice was filled with concern.

"Um, I'm here."

"*Where* is *here?*" Pepper demanded.

"Uh, Will's room," I whispered.

Pepper's trill of laughter was so loud, I had to pull the phone away from my ear. Then I clapped it back against my head so she wouldn't be heard by the whole of Los Angeles.

"You did it! You did it!" she cawed. "I just *knew* you still had it in you!"

"Pepper, it's not funny," I moaned.

"Oh yes it is! You said you wouldn't hook up and look at you now!" She hooted with laughter and I could feel my frustration building. "Wait... where's Will?"

"He's in the shower."

"Well get in there with him!" she shouted.

"Pepper, I *can't*." My body was screaming, *Oh yes you can*!

"Don't go all Victorian on me now! If you spent the night with him, spend the morning, too. Or afternoon. I have no clue what time it is."

"No, I think it's best if I just get dressed and we get out of here."

"Vivienne," Pepper's voice warned. "You cannot just leave without saying goodbye. Make your manners, young lady." I was in no mood to be teased.

"We have to *go*," I insisted.

"Go where?" Will asked.

Shit!

Chapter 14

I climbed out of the shower and started to towel off when I caught my reflection in the mirror. I had this stupid, shit-eating grin on my face and I didn't even realize it. Scenes from the night before flicked in my brain like a slide show, and my smile got wider. But then I heard Pepper's voice in my head and the grin vanished. *Shit*. She was going to give me all kinds of hell when I saw her next. All that bullshit I spewed about not hooking up with Vivienne and look at what happened. Ah, well. It was *so* worth it.

I would never have hooked up with Vivienne if I hadn't spent most of the night talking to her. Yeah, I thought she was gorgeous, but it was her personality that really got me. She asked questions about my life like she was really interested, not like she was interviewing me. She made me feel like a real person, not a celebrity. All the time we talked, I felt like we could have been having the same conversation in a dive diner or a crappy studio apartment, and it wouldn't have made a difference to her. The money, the fame, the celebrity, it all fell away and we were just two people hanging out. That still might not have been enough to make me jump on her like I did, but the stuff about the book and her situation made me forget myself.

Sex with random girls because of my rock star status was pretty cut and dried. I knew how those women operated and I could handle the morning after with a fair degree of calm. But Vivienne wasn't a random one-night stand. She was a real person and I had started to *like* her. I needed to tread carefully.

I thought I heard her talking and I walked into the bedroom, still wiping water off my arms. I almost laughed out loud when she jumped like I'd pinched her. She threw my phone behind her back, and then just deflated onto the bed, slumping on the edge.

I wrapped the towel around my waist and padded across the room to sit beside her. She looked really upset and that worried me. Here I was grinning like an asshole, thinking about what a great night I'd just had, and Vivienne was clearly bothered. It confused me because I thought she had enjoyed herself.

"Hey." I pushed my shoulder against hers.

"Hey."

"What's wrong?" I bumped her a little harder to make her look at me.

"Oh, Will. I'm sorry, I just feel so stupid," she finally said, clasping her hands in her lap, but still refusing to meet my eyes.

"Why?" A guilty woman after a night in the sack was something I definitely didn't understand. Maybe that was just my arrogance talking.

"I'm not like this." Vivienne shook her head. "I don't sleep with someone I just met."

Oh that's all. I smirked. "Well, for the record, I don't usually do that, either." That got her attention. She raised her eyebrows at me in disbelief, and I caught myself laughing.

"Okay, maybe I did when I was in my twenties." I watched her left brow raise and the right one lower. She was giving me the "I call bullshit" look. "All right, I did it a lot. What can you expect? I was twenty-five and in a band and women threw themselves at me!"

Vivienne shrugged and rolled her eyes.

"The thing is, though, I stopped all that right around the time I turned thirty. Put someone in the public eye for a few years and their perspective changes. Sure, it was fun to sleep with hot chicks, but then they started talking to the tabloids. Or the ones who were actually cool started getting *stalked* by the tabloids. It wasn't really fair to them and it made me look like a douchebag. So I learned discretion and gained a little maturity."

"Then why did you sleep with me last night?" There was an edge of accusation in her tone.

I shrugged my shoulders. "I sure as hell wasn't planning on it."

"Thanks a lot," she muttered.

"That's not how I meant it," I said quickly. Turning to face her a little bit, I put my hands on her shoulders to make her face me. "Usually, if I meet someone new, I make up my mind pretty quickly whether or not I'm ever going to get physical with them. Still, it's not until we've been out a few times. When *we* met," my finger pointed back and forth between us, "I thought you were cute and funny, but I didn't even think about something more."

Vivienne waved her hand, but she looked offended.

"I get it. No worries." She smiled, and it was the first time I noticed she had dimple in her right cheek.

"What's *really* bothering you?" I frowned. "Are you worried I think you're easy or something?"

"Eh," she answered, shrugging. "There is that."

I didn't think that was totally it, but I couldn't make her say anything she didn't want to.

"Don't be silly." I rolled my eyes and squeezed her biceps. Only then I realized I'd never taken my hands off her. "If that's what I thought, I'd have gone back to your hotel room with you so I could sneak out. You're at my place, in my world. I can't just walk out of my own house and abandon you here." I was glad to see she could laugh at the thought.

"It's not you, Will, really. It's me. This is just so out of character, I think I'm still in shock." She looked absolutely miserable, like she was about to say something more.

"Maybe that's what you needed. A shock to your system." I patted her leg beneath the sheet. "Believe me, I'm pretty surprised myself. I didn't know I could be so spontaneous, either." I realized I was lying to her in a way. I could have just as easily told her that I liked her. I could have admitted that I enjoyed the way she treated me like a real person. But I couldn't bring myself to do it. The wall went up instinctively.

She was just so *different* than most of the women I spent time with. Vivienne told the truth and didn't sugarcoat shit. She didn't fawn over me. She turned me on in a way I hadn't been prepared for. It dawned on me she was turning me on again. I shouldn't have been shocked, after all I'm a horndog and she was naked beneath the sheet.

She leaned into me and put her head on my shoulder. I wrapped my arms around her and kissed her on the head. It was all so innocent and friendly when it could have been awkward. All I wanted to do was comfort her and make sure she knew I had enjoyed myself and I didn't think less of her in any way.

But then I was kissing her again.

Chapter 15

Will was kissing me again. The sexual monster in my gut wanted nothing more than to give in to his warm mouth and strong arms. The idiot in me said I couldn't, it wouldn't be right. Last night was a mistake I shouldn't repeat. I let myself enjoy the feel of his lips for another half second before I forced myself to put a stop to it. It was the hardest thing I'd done in a long time, especially because I didn't want him to stop. Ever. And that was probably the most difficult thing I'd had to admit to myself in a very long time.

"Oh, I don't think that's a good idea." I was breathless as I pressed my palms into his naked, still damp chest. I was momentarily mesmerized by the droplets of water that clung to the fuzzy hair covering his chest. The look on his face said he clearly disagreed with me. I tried harder to catch my breath because, even though he stopped the kissing, he didn't pull away and he didn't stop staring.

"Please don't look at me like that." I swear I could feel the lust shooting out of his eyes and into mine.

"I'm sorry." He couldn't have meant it, though, because he kept it up. The longer his green eyes pierced mine, the more lost I felt. My resistance was about to be futile. *Assimilate me into the Borg.*

"I thought we agreed this was a mistake." I pressed my lips together in a tight smile, trying to affect an air of propriety. *That was convincing, sure.*

"I don't know who *you've* been talking to, but I never said last night was a mistake." I thought I felt his arms tighten around me, but I could have imagined it.

"How *do* you feel?" My voice cracked the tiniest bit.

"I thought it was *great.*" Once again, that sexy lilt filled my ears, making my heart race and warmth spread through me.

"Awesome, actually. *Stupendous!*" This time his arms *did* tighten around me and I couldn't deny it. They were so strong and hot against the bare skin of my arms. "I'm ready to do it all again, just say the word." He waggled his eyebrows at me and grinned.

I thought about pushing him away again to force an end to the close contact we shared. I considered telling him it would be best to leave things where they were. I wondered if the shock of my foundation going broke had pitched me full bore into insanity and, right this minute, I was sitting in a padded room waiting for more medication. But I didn't say a word. For at least ten seconds, I sat where I was trying to figure out what to do.

In the end, I followed my gut.

As corny as it sounds, it's like a switch flipped inside me. One minute, I was ashamed and embarrassed about my wanton behavior, worrying whether or not my dead husband knew what I had done, unable to justify that I was an adult woman with long-denied needs. Logically, I… oh, fuck logic, no pun intended. I was on him like a cat on a mouse.

I wasn't about to let him have as much control this time. I didn't want it to be all about me. I flung the sheet away from my body and slung my leg over his lap, pushing him down on the bed with a wicked grin.

Chapter 16

"This time you're taking a shower with me," I insisted. Vivienne lay sprawled in the bed looking like she was about to fall asleep again. She opened her eyes slowly and then nodded. There was no doubt this time she was feeling good. She looked about as satisfied as a cat with a full stomach. "Besides, you have to check out this bathroom. It's the coolest thing I've ever seen. It might be the only reason I really wanted the house." In the back of my mind I knew I was taking a chance inviting her into what was normally a really private sanctuary for me, but she didn't know that.

As I pulled her to her feet, she grabbed the sheet from the bed and wrapped it around her body. We stood in the doorway and I waved my arm.

"This bathroom is probably half the size of most of the apartments I lived in when I first got to LA."

Vivienne's mouth dropped open as she looked inside.

"Wow!"

"The previous owners redid the whole thing and I didn't want to change it at all." I stepped inside and pointed to my feet, wiggling my toes. "The floor is heated."

She took a tentative step inside, then looked up at me and grinned. All of a sudden, she looked away and I could see her cheeks getting red. "That *is* nice," she whispered.

I cocked my head to the side.

"What's wrong?"

"Nothing," she insisted. "Wouldn't you like a towel?" Vivienne bit her bottom lip, refusing to meet my eyes.

I laughed and grabbed a towel from the bar on the wall and wrapped it around my waist.

"Better?"

Considering for a moment, she shrugged, still looking away.

"Yes and no."

"Anyway," I continued, "they put the toilet in that little closet back there. The tub is a top-of-the-line Jacuzzi tub and it's a double size." I pointed to the wall at the foot of the tub. "They even put a TV in the wall so you can watch while you soak."

"That's a little odd, isn't it?" Her brows were furrowed.

"I thought so at first, too. Until I got myself a beer and sat in it. I think I watched half a season of *Sons of Anarchy* before I stopped emptying and refilling the hot water and got out."

Vivienne laughed and stepped a little farther into the room. I watched as she ran her fingers along the vanity's granite countertops, taking in all the high-end finishes and details. She made a "hmm" sound when she looked up to admire the skylight in the ceiling. She finally looked to her right and caught sight of the shower, then gasped.

"Good Lord! The shower alone is bigger than my kitchen *and* bathroom at home!"

I nodded and took her by the hand to walk her toward the glass wall.

"I never would have thought I could love a bathroom as much as I love this one."

"You'd never get me out of the tub," Vivienne said, her eyes shining with amusement. "I'd be a prune forever."

"Would you rather have a soak?" I asked her. After the things she'd just done for me over the last two hours, I would have signed over the deed to the place if she asked.

"No, no. Like I said, you'd never get me out. Show me how the shower works."

I did more than show her. I gently tugged the sheet out of her fingers and let it pool around her feet. I took her hands in mine and stepped backward so I could take a nice long look at her naked body.

I wiggled my hips and the towel around my waist joined the sheet. She wouldn't look me in the eye, but I could tell she was sneaking a peek here and there. I pulled her inside the shower, then reached behind her to yank the door shut. I turned nozzles here and there, and hot water shot out, drenching us.

"Now I understand why these fixtures are so expensive," she murmured. "They're worth every penny."

"Don't I know it." I reached for some shampoo I hoped wasn't too manly for her. "May I?"

She opened her eyes and nodded her head. I washed her hair, massaging her scalp from front to back and side to side, including her neck and shoulders. When she was covered in suds, I pushed her under one of the showerheads to rinse. I was glad she kept her eyes closed because I was able to watch her without making her nervous.

While I worked the lather out of her hair, I wanted to tell her she was the first woman to ever share a shower with me. I doubt she would have believed it. I had been with my ex for almost two years before it ended, and I didn't even let her into the bathroom when I used it. I think it was because I never fully trusted Lucy.

But I didn't say anything. That was the thing about Vivienne, she had me thinking about things I hadn't before, or things I wouldn't have thought about sharing with anyone else. I stopped counting the number of times I opened my mouth to say something, only to shut it again when I realized I was about to reveal an ultra-personal fact to someone I hardly knew.

The thing is, I had this feeling I could trust Vivienne if I did slip up and say anything too personal. It wouldn't end up in the tabs the next day or on Facebook or Twitter. She didn't seem the type to divulge secrets about someone else. She didn't want anything from me. Still, I didn't want to embarrass her, either, by coming off as an over-sharer.

I knew I was taking a risk just like she took one to spend the night with me, and that was enough.

Chapter 17

Will's hands on my head were as proficient as any technician who'd washed my hair at the fancy salon I frequented back home. I almost made a joke about how he could have another career if he decided to give up music. But still, I worried about how relaxed I was. It all seemed too easy. I gave in to the temptation and thought of Bruce. Instead of the usual yearning, I felt... I don't know. Nostalgic? Peaceful? Not even trying, he disappeared from my mental TV screen and was replaced with Will. That was a nice surprise.

Will finished rinsing my hair, so I offered to give him the same treatment. I'd never washed another person's hair before, and I hoped I was able to make him feel as good as he did me. I stood behind him and filled my palm with shampoo, but when I reached up to put it into his hair he was too tall.

"I can't reach!"

"Here." He turned to me and bent down. I spread the soap into his hair and began massaging, but soon it started running down his cheeks and got into his eyes and mouth. He sputtered and I laughed as he stood up to clear his face under the spray.

"I'm sorry!" I tried to hide my giggling behind a soapy hand.

"That's all right. I have a better idea. Sit down."

I turned and noticed for the first time that there was a tiled bench along the wall. I hissed a little as my butt and back hit the cool tiles of the seat and wall. He pushed my legs apart and then turned his back to me to sit down between my thighs.

"Let's try this again."

I squirted a fresh dollop of shampoo into my hand and put it on the back of his head, which was now a couple of inches above my own. I rubbed in a circle, creating a thick lather that smelled like mint and spices. I inhaled deeply, recognizing the scent as part of the smell of him. I then began using both of my hands to rub his entire head and behind his ears, and then his neck and shoulders like he had done mine.

"Is this okay?" I asked after I was at it for a couple of minutes.

"Mmm. Now scratch. All over."

I grazed my nails across his scalp and I think he actually shivered a couple of times. I felt a sense of power when he did, because I'd never been in that position before. In control, in charge, taking the lead in a given situation. It was exciting to know my touch could inspire a good feeling in someone else. I had gotten married so young and Bruce had been the alpha in our relationship. I didn't know the first thing about power or control from a sexual standpoint.

But Will still held all the cards in many ways, even if he didn't know it. The feel of his wet skin against mine made me shudder inside. I could have gone on like that for an hour, but he finally leaned toward one of the jets in the wall to rinse away the foam. When he sat back up, I leaned into him to rest my cheek against his back and he leaned back into me until I was pressed against the wall. The pressure of the cool tile against my back and his warm skin on my chest and cheek was satisfying. I ran my hands along his arms and up to his shoulders to massage them and back down again. I felt his hands reach around to rest on my thighs. It all felt like an incredible dream and I did *not* want to wake up.

"This is one hell of a shower," I whispered.

"Oh yeah." His fingers moved smoothly up and down my upper legs. The feel of his thumbs on my inner thighs was making it difficult to breathe normally.

Any regrets I had about the whole night dripped off me and slipped down the drain. I let them. Any humiliation about my behavior followed along. I mentally waved goodbye. All the self-loathing with which I'd padded myself was cleansed. *Good riddance.* In that moment, feeling his strong fingers on my legs and his skin on mine, I didn't care anymore. I had been alone for seventeen years, at a time in my life when I should have had a husband and family. I think the universe owed me, and I gladly accepted the payment sitting in front of me. If I spent the next 117 years alone, it would be totally worth it. The memory of the last twelve hours would sustain me far into old age, I hoped.

I lifted my legs up to circle around Will's waist and squeezed. I stopped massaging his shoulders and reached around to spread my hands across his muscled chest. I kissed the small bumps of his spine and there was no doubt he trembled. I moved my hands as low as his stomach before he turned to reach for me.

I knew what I was starting in that shower and I happily told myself the third time was the charm.

*****

By the time we made it downstairs, Pepper was gone. She left a note saying Billy was going to drive her home and she would call me later. The faint smell of bacon was still in the air and it reminded me I was starving. I thought I would call a cab and head back to the hotel for some room service, or maybe Pepper would come by to hang out. But then I looked at Will. He was mousing around in the refrigerator. I couldn't see his head, only his denim-clad backside. I felt a rush of warmth explode in my stomach and shivered as it spread to my limbs. The words popped into my brain and out of my mouth like someone was speaking for me.

"Are you hungry?"

He peeked around the door with an apple. "Ravenous." He bit into it and started crunching away. "You?"

"Duh." I rolled my eyes. "Let me take you to lunch."

Will glanced at his watch.

"I think dinner's more in order." The clock on the stove read 4:12 p.m.

I gaped in disbelief.

"My God, it's that late?" Will grinned and tossed the half-finished apple into the trash.

"Yep. Let's go find some real food." He came close and I could smell the sweet scent of red delicious on his breath. I swallowed with some difficulty, lurching from the room ahead of him, wondering out loud where my purse was.

While pulling on my boots and finding my black clutch, Will made a phone call to his assistant, asking him to bring home his car from The Relic. I had to admit, I was surprised. Will didn't strike me as the kind of guy who'd have an assistant.

"I hope you pay that guy a lot," I teased, as he led me out of the house.

"We do, believe me." He stopped on the front porch to shove a pair of sunglasses onto his nose. "Finn is a good kid. We found him when he was eighteen and the band was about five years into fame. Been with us ever since." Together, we walked toward a silver Mercedes Benz that looked *very* expensive.

"Whose car is this?" I asked, as he opened the door for me.

"It's mine."

"I thought you left your car in LA last night."

"I did," Will said as he closed the door and then trotted around to ease into the driver's seat. "This one's mine, too." He grinned and gently pushed the key into the ignition and turned it. The engine roared to life, and he hit the gas pedal to rev it a couple of times. "What can I say? I like cars."

"How many others do you have?"

Will gave me his "aw-shucks" look.

"Five. The one in LA is a Porsche 911. This is a Mercedes-AMG. And in storage, I have a 1957 Chevy, a 1965 Buick LeSabre, and a 1940 Ford."

"Wow!" I considered what it would be like to indulge in something as expensive as classic cars. I suppose I could have, considering the amount of money I'd made from the book. Instead, I'd pumped most of it into the foundation.

As I put on my seatbelt, I noticed that one of the buttons on the shirt I wore was undone. It was a crisp, white oxford Will loaned to me to wear over my too fancy for daytime dress. Fortunately, I hadn't had any trouble finding my bra, but my panties had gone missing. I tried not to be embarrassed about it, but Will found it quite amusing. He told me to get over it and go commando, then handed me the button down. *Good grief*, was all that had run through my head when I donned the dress and his shirt. It was longer than the hem of my dress, so I had to tie the ends in a knot around my waist, *Pretty Woman* style.

Will spent a minute fiddling with the stereo to find music while the air conditioning cooled off the interior. The temperature outside hovered in the mid-eighties, and the sun was beating down without regret. When he put the car into gear and it started to move, my cell phone buzzed and vibrated inside my purse, making it walk off my lap. I grabbed it before it could land on the floor and took the phone out. Glancing at the unrecognizable number, I frowned, debating on whether to answer.

"That Pepper?" Will asked casually as he headed out of the driveway.

"I don't know who it is." While I waited for the call to go to voicemail, I checked my text messages and felt my stomach clench when I saw more than a dozen from Jake Rushmore and two from Pepper. Not bothering to read any of them, I dialed to check voicemail when the missed call icon stopped flashing. It was Jake inquiring about why I had missed the meeting at 2:00 p.m. along with seven other voicemails from him in the hour-and-a-half leading up to the meeting. There were also two voicemails from Pepper and my mom.

"Shit!"

"Uh oh," Will said.

"My agent. I missed a meeting at two. I totally forgot about it." I rubbed my forehead as guilt and shame rose from my toes up into my brain.

Will turned to look at me and smirked.

"You were indisposed."

"That's one way of putting it," I muttered, fighting the urge to scream at my recklessness. "I need to call him back." I dialed Jake's cell phone and waited for him to answer. My heart started beating again when I got *his* voicemail. I put on my most apologetic voice. "Hey, Jake! I'm so sorry about the meeting. I went out with friends and I lost track of time, then my phone died. I swear I will call you a little later. Bye!" I ended the call and powered down the phone before he could call me back.

"You're a kiss ass." Will teased, smacking my arm.

"No, I'm not!" I punched him back. "I'm normally a conscientious person who doesn't blow off appointments for hot sex." My hand clamped against my mouth in surprise at my poor choice of words.

"It *was* pretty hot, wasn't it?" Will wiggled his eyebrows at me.

"Good grief," I muttered.

Chapter 18

The restaurant I had in mind was at least a 20-minute drive away, and it took Vivienne that long to settle down about missing her meeting.

"You don't understand," she had said. "I don't miss things. I'm never late for anything. I'm a *responsible adult*, for Chrissake."

"Take it easy," I teased. "You're human, aren'tcha? You don't have to be perfect."

"I didn't say I was perfect," she muttered.

I raised an eyebrow at her. "Tomato, toe-mah-toe. Look, if you want to skip dinner, we can. I'll take you right back to the hotel or to your agent's office. I don't want you freaking out all night."

Vivienne got very quiet and I watched her bite and chew on her bottom lip as she gazed out the window. When she took a deep breath and exhaled, I thought she would agree and ask to go back to the hotel. Instead, she surprised me, and herself, I think.

"No. It's done and over with. Jake's waited this long, he can wait a little longer. I asked you to dinner because I wanted to."

"Don't lie, I heard your stomach growling."

Vivienne giggled softly.

"Well, there is that. What difference does it make if I get my ass chewed now or later?"

"Good point."

I took Vivienne to Café Gratitude, thinking it would be low key, but recognized my mistake immediately. The paparazzi had the place staked out. Someone more famous than me had to be inside. When we arrived, I climbed out of the car for the valet to park it and Vivienne slid out of her seat, clueless as to what was about to happen. As I hopped around the front of the car to get to her side, the sound of clicking cameras filled the air like machine gun fire. I was pretty practiced at ignoring it all, or throwing a smile and high sign to the photogs, but Vivienne froze like a deer in headlights. Feeling my presence, she sealed herself to my side and I wrapped an arm around her shoulders. She pressed against me and turned her face into my chest as I speed-walked her to the door of the restaurant.

Once we got inside, she seemed to relax because the shutter sounds disappeared and the people inside didn't pay any attention to us. The other patrons were used to seeing celebrities, so my mug didn't give them pause, if they even recognized me. Jennifer Skarsgaard and Luke Framingham were the reason the paparazzi were swarming the place. I asked for a quieter table in the back so she could forget about the scene on the way in.

"That was horrifying." Vivienne's lip wavered a little as she slipped into her seat.

The trembling I noticed in her hands made me frown.

"Does that happen all the time?" she asked.

"Pretty much. You actually get used to it." I opened my menu and leaned back casually, hoping my attitude of disinterest would spread to her. "They treat you as well as you treat them. If you get all pissed off and avoid them, they try harder. If you give them what they want, they usually click away and then leave you alone for the next victim."

"Ugh!" She shivered in disgust.

Blasé wasn't cutting it. I leaned forward and closer to her.

"You're a famous author now. Haven't you done any publicity?"

"Puh-leease!" She gave me a skeptical look. "I wrote a *book*. I'm not a *rock star*. I think there were two photographers when I had my tiny press conference at the local Barnes and Noble, and one was from the Shores Sentinel for Chrissake!" By now she was laughing a little, and I felt less worried by her reaction to the ruckus outside. "Before all this foundation crap, all the TV I did was pre-taped."

The waiter arrived with water glasses and a wine menu, but Vivienne snatched it from him and set it aside before I could touch it.

"Would the lady care for a drink?" he asked in a smooth, practiced tone.

"No, thank you. And neither would the gentleman." Her voice was genteel and her hands were folded primly in her lap.

"Of course." He backed away from the table without any expression on his face.

I raised my eyebrows at her. I actually didn't want a drink, but she had taken away my opportunity to decline. It was probably the first strong act I'd seen from Vivienne since meeting her. Well, outside the bedroom, anyway.

"I'm sorry." She reached for my arm and her fingers were cool on my skin. "I can tell you're unhappy with how I handled that. But I don't seem to have much control of myself around you, and I don't want any more alcohol to get in the way right now."

"Fair enough." I tilted my head to the side. "We are in public, though. It's not like I can throw you down on the table." I waggled my eyebrows at her and grinned.

"This is Hollywood, Will. I wouldn't be surprised by anything at this point."

I burst out laughing because she was half right. Stranger things had happened with the celebrity crowd, and she caught on fast to the antics.

"Okay. Let's have a nice, civilized dinner and then I will take you back to your hotel. Agreed?"

"Agreed." She put out her hand, expecting me to shake it, and instead I lifted it to my lips and kissed it. She shivered and the color in her cheeks I was getting used to appeared on cue. *What the hell was I doing?*

Chapter 19

I let the damn waiter talk me into a glass of wine to go with the fancy dinner I ordered. *You must have the red with it, ma'am*, he said. *It brings out the taste of the meat*, he said. *Blah, blah, blah.* That opened the door for Will to ask for the bottle. I was determined, though, to hold onto some modicum of control and not deteriorate into the wanton woman I was unwittingly trying to be. Yes, I'd come to grips with what had happened between Will and me over the course of the last twenty-four hours. But that didn't mean I was going to go completely down the rabbit hole. Our brief tête-à-tête was just that, brief but *over*. At least as far as the sex went. I would be going home to Michigan soon.

At first, I didn't know if Will was really as easygoing as he seemed, or if he was just a better actor than he claimed. But the longer we sat together, the more convinced I became that he really was a pretty good guy. I couldn't remember ever feeling as comfortable with another person, other than Pepper or my mom.

"Thank you for coming out with me," I said, as I placed my knife and fork across my plate, feeling full and satisfied by both the meal and the company. "You are excellent company."

Will dabbed his mouth with his napkin and then tossed it on the table beside his plate. "Thank you for inviting me. I don't get to go out to quiet dinners very often." His hands fidgeted with the end of the tablecloth for a moment or two, and then he placed them flat on the tabletop. He must have recognized my puzzled look.

"Sorry, I used to smoke. It's been about five years, but I still crave one after I finish eating."

I nodded in sympathy.

"I feel your pain. I quit seventeen years ago."

"Yeah? Still miss it?"

Shaking my head no, I said, "*Every single day.*" Sighing dramatically, I rolled my eyes. "I picked it up in college to help me stay awake when I would study. Bruce picked it up in the military and the two of us were fiends."

"I'm surprised you quit."

I shrugged.

"After Bruce died, I was so depressed I didn't eat and I fell out of the habit. When I finally started feeling better, I figured it was probably a good thing not to pick it up again."

Will reached across the table to put his hand over one of mine.

"That must have been really hard. You were so young."

The heat from his palm against the back of my hand felt nice and the warmth spread up my arm.

"It was." I could have said more. I could have told him about the sleepless nights and the crying jags. I could have said that the depression was something I still struggled with. I could have explained that depression led to fear and fear kept me from living a normal life like everyone else. But I didn't want to put a pall on an otherwise lovely evening so far.

Instead I asked him to make me laugh.

"Tell me something funny, Will. What's the silliest thing that's happened since you became a celebrity?"

The look of half-humor, half-grimace that crossed his face made me chuckle right away.

"Hell, I haven't said anything and you're cracking up." He leaned back in his chair and ran his fingers through his hair. "I wouldn't know where to start. A *lot* of crazy shit has happened in the last ten years. I've had girls try to break into my house. There have been a few paternity suits."

I raised my eyebrows in mock surprise.

"Oh really? Just how many?"

Will grinned.

"Three. All false." He crossed his heart with his index finger. "One time, Tim posted my number on Facebook as a joke. I think I got about a thousand calls in the first five minutes, not to mention tens of thousands of text messages."

That made me laugh out loud.

"Oh, that must have been horrible!"

"I couldn't get to the store fast enough to get a new number," Will admitted. "Most of the stuff that's happened has been harmless enough or amusing. Even the lawsuits were kind of funny, because the kids didn't even look anything *like* me. But there's been a lot of bad stuff, too. You just gotta deal with it. If you're going to put yourself out there to the world, it comes at a price."

While my experience was nowhere near the level of his, I commiserated nonetheless.

"I'm realizing that. Sure, I got a lot of attention when my book first came out, but after a while, things calmed down and life went back to normal, such as it was. But all this foundation business has the attention at a hundred times worse. I hate the idea that the media will feast on the tragedies, but only nibble on the successes."

"You're right." Will shrugged his shoulders, but the strain on his face was clear. "I get more publicity for hookups and breakups and stupid shit than I do for the music I make. But I get to do what I want, when I want, and if I choose to do something stupid and it gets in the papers, I take the lumps for it. If I really wanted it all to go away, it would."

I was about to ask about the paternity foolishness when the waiter interrupted to ask if we wanted dessert. Will went ahead and ordered tiramisu and two forks. I wasn't about to turn that down. By the time the dessert arrived, one glass of wine turned into two and a half. I was laughing coyly and even flirting with him a little. Inwardly convinced I was a burgeoning alcoholic, I no longer recognized myself. To the casual observer, it must have looked like we were on a date. Wine or no wine, I was still coherent enough to know it wasn't. I liked Will and I was enjoying his company, but we were different people with wholly different existences. I knew it was wrong to flirt, even just a little, but it was so much fun. Something I hadn't done in so very long.

When the tiramisu was finished and our forks lay crossed on the plate, the waiter discreetly left the check on the table and I reached for it to pay, feeling obligated because I had invited him out. When Will snagged it before I could, I grabbed his hand. He laced his fingers in mine and I felt a vibration go up my arm.

I cleared my throat and squeezed his hand.

"Oh, no. My treat. Hand it over."

"Nope." He pulled his wallet from his pocket.

"Will," I said in a warning tone. "Is it William?"

"Yeah."

"William what?"

"William Rowan."

"Oh, that's nice." Momentarily distracted by the way his name rolled off my tongue, I snapped myself back to the present. Sitting up straight, I glared at him without too much ferocity. "William Rowan Foster, you hand over that check. *I* invited you."

Will shook his head and covered our intertwined hands with his free one.

"You are something else, Vivienne."

"Oh, I'm something else, all right. Now cough it up."

"Only if you let me get the tip."

"Agreed."

He handed me the bill, and I was surprised at the reasonable total, given the fancy air of the restaurant. I slapped my American Express down with it onto the table, telling Will to leave twenty percent or so. The waiter, who lurked nearby, swooped in and carried it away. When he returned, I scribbled my name on the scrap of paper and stuffed my copy into my purse along with the credit card. I scooted my chair back to stand up, as Will tossed a hundred dollar bill on the table. My mouth dropped open and I gaped at him, blown away by his generosity.

"Close your mouth, please. We are not a codfish," he whispered, leaning in close to my ear. I giggled. "Most of these guys are trying to make it in show business. They need all the help they can get. I'm just a schmuck who happened to get there."

"Paying it forward?" I murmured, enjoying the feel of his warm breath on my neck.

"In a way."

Will linked his arm in mine and he walked me out of the restaurant. Standing on the curb, we waited for the valet to bring his car around. The paparazzi had thinned considerably, and only two or three photographers remained. They snapped a few pictures of us, but it was nothing like when we arrived, and the wine in my blood kept me relaxed. I was not impervious enough to mug for their shots, and turned my face away from them and toward Will. Will was gracious, though, and smiled for the pictures, giving a wave to the photographers. My forehead rested almost into his armpit and I was suddenly struck by how tall he was in spite of the four-inch heels I wore. I looked up at him and my neck tilted quite far back.

"Thank you for dinner." His chin turned down.

"You're welcome." I could feel my neck muscles straining. "You're awfully tall."

He snickered.

"You're just now noticing?"

"Well, we've spent most of our time together sitting down—"

"Or lying down." There went the eyebrows again.

"Yes, there is that." I sneered. "I guess I didn't realize how tall you were." Bruce was six-foot-four and I always loved how he towered over me, making me feel petite. "How tall *are* you?"

"Six-four."

Oh boy.

"Are you sure you're all right to drive?" I asked.

"Of course." He mimicked my earlier sneer. "You're the one who drank all the wine."

Dammit. "And whose fault is that? You ordered the bottle."

He looked away and pretended to scan the street, watching for the car.

"You didn't have to drink it."

Dammit! He was right. I threw my hands up in the air and told him so.

"I don't know what is wrong with me."

The Widow and the Rock Star

The car arrived then, and Will opened my door for me. When I was settled, he took my chin in his hand and looked me in the eye.

"Vivienne, there is *nothing* wrong with you."

Sappy fool that I am, I could feel my eyes start to tear up. I yanked my chin away as smoothly as I could and forced a laugh.

"Thank you, Will." It meant nothing, but it was the nicest thing he could have said to me right then. He closed my door, then jogged around to climb into the driver's seat, expertly slipping a tip into the valet's hand.

As he pulled out into traffic, I decided to check my phone. Another five voicemails from Jake, two more texts from Pepper and a missed call from Mom. I sighed.

"Do you mind if I make a quick call?" I asked.

"Go for it." Will waved his right hand at me. "Going to take your ass chewing now?"

"I hope not," I murmured as I tapped the speed dial icon for my mom. "I need to call my Mom."

Will snorted and gave me an amused look.

"Hey now. I haven't spoken with her since I got to LA and I don't want her to worry, that's all." It was a little after ten, but I knew she would still be awake. She answered by the third ring. "Hey, Mom!"

"Vivienne! I thought you'd died or something," Mom said with a hint of sarcasm.

"No, Mom, I haven't died. I've just been, uh, really busy." My cheeks flamed as Will watched me and grinned lasciviously.

"I know," Mom admitted, but she sounded relieved nonetheless. "I was wondering if you'd heard anything about the thief."

"No, unfortunately not. But they're working on it. I had a meeting with a movie studio today," I lied, "but it was pretty boring. Nothing you'd want to hear about. And yesterday I hung out with Pepper all day."

"Oh, how is she? Give her my love!"

"She's awesome. And I already did. How are things with you? You all right?"

"Oh, things are fine. Same old, same old."

I nattered on with her for another few minutes before I was finally able to segue into a goodbye pattern of conversation.

"I'm not sure what's on my agenda for the next couple of days, Mom, so if I don't check in, don't freak out, okay? Email me, if you want, and I can always sneak my phone out during a meeting to write back."

"All right, dear. You sound awfully tired. Try to get some rest."

You'll never know, I thought.

"I will, Mom. I love you."

"I love you, too."

"Bye."

"Goodbye, dear."

I tapped the "end" button and my mom was gone.

"Sorry about that." I tried not to look embarrassed to be almost forty and still checking in with my mom.

"No worries. I think it's cool that you check up on your mom."

I smiled with relief. Will got it. I wasn't checking *in*, I was checking *up*. Mom was seventy-eight and I was the only relative she had. I would always be her daughter, but as we got older, we were becoming more and more like friends. I liked it that way.

"Thanks. She's pretty cool, and I owe the good life I've had to her. Most people I know don't get along with their folks as well as I get along with mine."

"True enough." Will nodded. "Sounds like how I get along with my parents. My brothers and sisters are closer to them, though. They still live in same town and all, with regular lives and jobs and families of their own. I'm the black sheep who ran away."

I leaned back against the seat and smiled. Will was turning out to be a very sweet and thoughtful soul, much more than his public image gave him credit for. He seemed normal and sane in a world thriving on the abnormal and insane. When I'd accepted the glass of wine at dinner, I thought I knew exactly what I was doing. Will's simple charm and easy manner at dinner had convinced me that I wanted to spend one more night with him. The rest of my time in California was going to be taken up with meetings and lawyers and Jake. *I deserved one more night of fun, didn't I?*

At the same time, I was getting confused. I thought maybe Will was starting to care a little bit too much of what I thought. I could see the struggle on his face to always find the right thing to say whenever I expressed a doubt or some uncertainty. Was I was reading more into things than I had a right to? I didn't know. I was having second thoughts, because I didn't want to be unfair and lead Will on. If he was becoming more attached, I didn't want him to get hurt. I decided I would just let him drive me back to the hotel and say a heartfelt goodbye there.

The rest of the ride back to the hotel was peaceful and quiet.

Chapter 20

The drive back to the hotel was silent and awkward. After she talked to her mother and responded to a couple of texts, Vivienne sat in the passenger seat staring out the window, not talking or looking at me. I felt like an idiot because whatever I said to her didn't seem to help. Leaving the restaurant, I only wanted to make sure she knew she was a normal person and instead I almost made her cry.

Dinner had been great up until the end. We laughed and talked and I found out a lot more about her. Our creative sides were a lot alike, and she was getting a taste of celebrity, so I felt like I gave her some good advice about it. Only, she started to get pretty flirty just before the bill came. Normally I would have liked that. And given the time we'd spent together in bed, I thought it gave me the green light to keep going.

But then she'd gotten upset when I was closing her door and now I didn't know what the hell to think. I didn't want her to feel like I was using her or anything. I only wanted to sleep with her again because I liked her so damn much, not just because I *could*. I would never pressure her about it. It was funny how she could be really honest about her past and things that had happened to her, but she wasn't real up front or clear about what was going on in her head in the present. Could she be falling in love with me? Shit, that's all I needed.

What the fuck was wrong with me? Why did I even care so much about reassuring someone I had no intention of sticking with? I liked Vivienne, but she would go back to Michigan and resume her life and I was staying in California to go on with mine. Was I losing sight of the fact that this was only a hookup that had gone on a little longer than expected? *Double shit.* That's all I *really* needed, to lose my heart to someone who had no intention of sticking around, either.

It was probably best if I just dropped her off at the hotel before things got any weirder or more confusing. Maybe a bit of distance was what I needed to figure things out. Me and my impulses. If I'd only told Pepper no last night, all this wouldn't be happening. I glanced over at Vivienne, and she was still staring out the window. Well, even if things got messy, I wouldn't regret it. She was hot and smart and we'd had a great time together.

When I pulled into the driveway of the hotel, I waved the valet off. I swiveled to face Vivienne, opening my mouth to speak, but she beat me to it.

"Is this not the most beautiful hotel you've ever seen? I can hardly believe they put me up here."

"Yeah, it's great. I stayed here for a while before I found my first place," I said. "My mortgage payments were cheaper, that's for sure!" She laughed and clapped her hands together.

"I hear you. All I know is that the bill is going somewhere else and I have no desire to see it."

"Hit the mini bar. Take everything," I encouraged her.

"I checked it out, and let Pepper raid it. But it doesn't have ice cream. That's *my* one passion." She had a cheeky little smile on her face. "I'd probably give up a hotel this nice for some *really* good ice cream."

We sat for a moment and I struggled with how to say goodbye to her. I wanted to be gracious without sounding stupid.

"I should give you your shirt back," she offered, looking unsure, fingering the buttons on her chest.

"Uh," I stuttered. "That's okay, you can keep it." She frowned and looked down at her lap. *Shit!*

"Okay." She picked at her fingernails a little bit. "Well, thanks." She grabbed her purse and reached to unbuckle her seatbelt.

I threw the car in park and jumped out to run around and open her door before the doorman could approach. She reached for my hand and I grasped her slender fingers to naturally help her out of the car.

Smoothing the skirt of her dress, she looked up to me. I couldn't read the expression on her face until she smiled.

"Thank you, Will. I've had a really nice couple of days. I'm so glad I got to know you."

I couldn't believe it, but I felt my face getting warm.

"You're welcome," I stammered. "If you get bored before you go home, give me a call or something."

"Okay." She cocked her head to the side and her smile wilted a little. *Shit.*

"Maybe you and Pepper can come hang out with me or something." I sounded like an idiot, which was what I wanted to avoid. *Shit.*

"Sure," she said softly. She leaned up and pecked me on the cheek and then walked toward the wide glass entrance to the hotel. The doorman pulled open the heavy door and waited for her to go through. She turned one last time and waved at me. "Bye."

Shit, shit, shit.

Chapter 21

I rode the elevator up to my room on the twelfth floor feeling lonesome. The parting hadn't gone as I planned. I wanted it to be filled with easy laughter to show Will I didn't regret anything. Instead it felt clumsy and tense. I decided I'd write him a letter, and give it to Pepper to deliver. I could always put my thoughts on paper much more easily than I could speak. That way, I could tell him everything he needed to know about our encounter without having to really face him.

When the metal doors slid open, I turned right and walked slowly to the door of my suite. I struggled with the credit card key a couple of times before finally letting myself in. Just like the day I arrived, I was bowled over by the sumptuousness of the rooms — expensive furniture and fixtures, plush carpeting, and pristine linens on the bed.

"I could get used to this," I said out loud to no one.

I noticed the light was flashing on the telephone and figured it must be a message from Pepper or Jake. I decided to check it later, not yet ready to answer questions and give details about the last thirty-six hours of my life to anyone, friend or agent.

I dropped my purse on the bed and stared at the piles of bags from the shopping excursion the day before. I sat down in a comfortable leather chair near the table where I stacked them all and started to go through them. I removed tags and pulled off stickers and made separate piles for shirts and skirts and pants, deliberately trying not to think about Will. Pepper certainly did have a good eye for fashion most of the time, and I found myself imagining wearing the new clothes back home in my little city.

Suddenly, returning to St. Clair Shores seemed sad. I loved it there, but I worried it would feel claustrophobic after having spent time in such a pulsing city like Los Angeles. Shaking my head, I knew I'd never be able to write in a place holding far too many distractions, least of which was Will. Whether or not I *could* feel more for him than lust was beside the point, I *desired* him beyond reason. Until I'd had my fill, I wouldn't be able to put a word on the page. And Pepper, Lord, she would keep me busy with parties and bars and who knew what else, just to make up for all the years we hadn't been together. Then, of course, there was Mom. Even though she was still as active and capable as someone thirty years younger, I knew I wouldn't consider leaving her alone. We were all we had. There weren't any aunts or uncles or cousins, just us two. I could daydream about staying in California, but that's all it could be. Just a fantasy.

No, I knew I'd go home and resume my life there. I would let Jake help me find someone trustworthy to run the foundation, and I would throw myself back into writing. It was really the only thing I knew how to do well, and hopefully it would bring me the peace I'd been searching for since Bruce died. Finishing *The Widow's Path* would have to be the door opening to a new life. I'd already wasted seventeen years of my life being stupid, I wasn't going to waste any more being selfish and goofy.

I pulled off my boots, my feet screaming with relief. Tiptoeing my way into the bathroom, I started the water. A nice, long bath would ease the returning exhaustion I felt. I pulled my hair into a ponytail and pinned it up on top. My head was still buzzing weakly from the wine, and I looked forward to a good night's sleep. I'd call Jake and Pepper in the morning.

Carrying a large, white, fluffy bathrobe, I left the tub to fill with steaming water. I plugged my cell phone in to charge and clicked a button on the room's phone to get rid of the annoying red light still blinking with accusation. I went to my suitcase and pulled out a pair of yoga pants and tank top to change into.

I unbuttoned the white shirt, easing it off my shoulders, bringing it around in front of me. I decided I would have it cleaned and sent back to Will with the letter. What would I do with a man's button-down

Oxford shirt? He should have it back. I then reached around to unzip my dress and shimmy out of it, leaving it in a pile on the floor.

Standing there, I was struck with sadness.

"I know I'm not in love with him," I said to the empty room. "But dammit, I *like* him."

There was no one there to answer me or argue with me about Will's merits or faults. I heard no voice telling me I was wrong to think about going home. The room was as quiet as a morgue. Sighing dejectedly, I slipped into the bathrobe and tied it tightly around my waist. Digging through my carry on for my iPod, the heavy knock that made the door vibrate in its frame made me yelp in surprise.

I walked slowly to the door, worried some psycho might be outside, or maybe even a photographer who followed Will and me from the restaurant.

"Who is it?" I called nervously.

"It's Will."

I lunged for the handle and whipped it open so fast that it banged on the wall, making me cringe.

In his hands, he held a pint of ice cream.

"I thought you looked like a cherry cordial kind of girl."

Chapter 22

The ice cream was a brilliant idea, I thought. I must have sat in my car outside the hotel for ten minutes mentally kicking myself in the ass for how awkward the whole goodbye thing had gone. Just because Vivienne had wanted to give me the shirt back didn't mean she wanted me to jump into bed again. Or did she? I couldn't stop second-guessing myself.

Did it really matter? I wasn't falling in love with Vivienne Stark, but if I did, it was going to take a lot longer than just a few hours together and some wild time in bed. I wasn't going to give up my heart that easily, especially after what Lucy had done to me. But I really *liked* Vivienne. She was easy to talk to and interesting. She had a brain and coherent thoughts about a million different things. It occurred to me I was starving for some real conversation and a genuine person to hang out with, someone *not* in my band. Someone who didn't talk to me like they were conducting an interview. Someone I didn't feel I had to impress with witty repartee.

To hell with it! I drove to the nearest drugstore and raced inside to the coolers. The first flavor I saw was cherry cordial and it struck a chord in me so fierce, I knew it was the right choice. Paying for it, I didn't even wait for my change before racing out and back to the hotel.

It took a little convincing to get the receptionist at the front desk to give up Vivienne's room number, but having my face splashed all over the media as "one of the hottest rock stars in the world" went a long way. That, an autograph, and a selfie on her cell phone.

Praying the ice cream wouldn't melt too much while I rode up in the elevator, I cleared my throat and shook the tension out of my shoulders. I was more nervous than before I went on stage for a show.

I stood outside the door to Vivienne's room for all of ten seconds before I made a fist and banged on it.

"Who is it?" she called out. I could hear the nervousness in her voice.

"It's Will."

I thought the door was going to come off the hinges, she opened it so fast. Vivienne looked adorable in the oversized hotel robe and her hair piled high on top of her head in a messy kind of bun.

"I thought you looked like a cherry cordial kind of girl."

Chapter 23

My first instinct was to jump on Will, but that would have been abusive to the ice cream. Instead, I stepped aside and let him come in first.

"Thank you. Cherry cordial happens to be my favorite." Taking it from him, I forced it into the tiny freezer space inside the minibar's fridge.

Then I jumped on him. Kissing him was so familiar and comfortable now and all the internal conversation from earlier dissipated like a puff of smoke. Will juggled me a little to more comfortably place his arms under my butt, while I wrapped my legs around his waist. He kissed back with a fierceness that surprised me.

"Shit, the tub." I broke the kiss, panting a little. "I forgot it was running." Thinking he would put me down, Will instead carried me to the bathroom. He sat down on the edge of the tub, not letting me go, and reached one hand for the faucet to turn off the water.

"Looks nice," he said, nuzzling my neck. "Not as big as mine, though."

I snorted, the mind-numbing haze of passion broken for the moment. I continued to sit on his lap, enjoying the feel of his arms around me.

"Want to join me for a soak?"

"Yes." There was no hesitation on his part.

Will stood and placed me on my feet. I untied the robe and it fell to the floor, then I slipped into the almost scalding water, while he took off his clothes. I pretended not to look, but couldn't help myself. Watching his jeans pile up next to my robe was almost as exciting as scanning up his long, lean legs and beyond. Having a writer's imagination was probably a good thing. When he was naked, he stepped into the tub and lowered himself to sit at the opposite end. He hissed through his teeth as the water hit his butt, sloshing over the sides.

"Damn, that's freakin' hot!"

"I like it this way," I said coyly, batting my eyelashes at him with exaggeration. Beneath the surface of the water, I put my hands on his calves as they stretched out beside my thighs and massaged them lightly. He took my right foot between his hands and did the same.

"I'm glad I came back." He stared at my toes.

"I'm glad you did, too." I studied the hair on his legs.

"I'm also a little bit worried." His tone was cautious as he spoke. He switched to my left foot, pressing his thumb into the arch.

"What about?"

"I'm worried that all this means too much or too little."

I nodded my head. He put it just the way I felt.

"Me too."

"I think we've gone beyond just a hook up."

"Me too."

"But I'm not exactly ready to run off to Vegas and marry your ass, either."

I brayed with laughter, yanking on the hairs of his legs and he yelped.

"I do *not* accept your inept proposal, William."

He pretended to nip my toe and when I tried to pull away he kissed it instead.

"I don't expect you to blow off your meetings and spend all the rest of your time with me while you're here. But I didn't like how we said goodbye. It didn't seem right."

I nodded and slid down a little further until the water was up to my chin.

"I didn't like it, either."

"If we want to hang out, we do it and not worry about whether or not it means anything. Yeah?"

I sighed with pleasure as he pressed his thumb into the ball of my foot.

"Yeah." He switched to my other foot and I was grateful. "No pressure. We both know I'm going home in a couple of weeks and you're going back to your rock star thing."

"Agreed. Friends?" he asked.

"Of course!" I sat up straight.

"Good." Will nodded his head and looked visibly more relaxed. The tension in his face disappeared, and he lowered himself down below the surface until he was completely submerged. When he came back up, he reached for me.

"Now, come here."

I crawled through the water to stretch out on top of him, my cheek resting on his chest.

"Mmm, this is nice. I think I'm going to have to remodel my bathroom at home so I can get one of these suckers."

"Nothing beats a big bathtub," Will murmured into my hair. He moved his hands through the water, making waves of the hot liquid wash over my back.

I wanted to close my eyes, but my attention was taken by the tattoos on his arm. The sleeve of black ink on his left arm was mostly abstract shapes and swirls, but I noticed in the center of his inner forearm the strangest thing. I ran my finger over the face of a brown-and-black striped tabby cat. The eyes were a vibrant green and it was done so well, I thought it might start purring at me.

"I love your cat," I whispered.

"Mmm, thanks. That's Smudge." Will tilted his head to look down at the tattoo. "I had that cat for nineteen years."

"He's adorable." I liked cats, just not the responsibility of taking care of one. "How long has he been gone?"

"Couple years. He got old and went to sleep one night and never woke up. I miss him every day."

I kissed Will's chest, making sympathetic noises.

"He was pretty cool. Liked people, liked riding in cars. I could walk him on a leash. I even took him on the road with me a few times."

"Will you get another one someday?"

"Oh yeah. I'm a total cat guy. But I'm not ready. Shit, I still tear up when I think about him," Will chuckled. "I got this tat about six months after he died."

"It's a beautiful tribute." I rubbed the little face like he was real. "I thought about getting a tattoo after my dad died, something in his honor. But I chickened out at the last minute. I didn't think I could handle the pain."

Will rubbed my head and I could feel a laugh rumble up in his chest. "It's not as bad as you think."

The water was cooling off, but I was so comfortable in Will's arms I didn't want to move. I think I could have fallen asleep that way, until his hands started roaming more freely. The skin not covered by water became chilled and goose bumps broke out on my neck and arms.

"I'm starting to get cold," I whispered.

"Well then let me warm you up."

Chapter 24

We shared the ice cream in bed, but I let Vivienne have most of it. Cherry cordial really was her favorite because she dipped her finger into the empty carton to capture a last lump of chocolate her spoon couldn't reach. We were swaddled in the hotel robes and wrapped up in the down comforter on the bed, a tangle of arms and legs. Her damp hair smelled like cherries from her shampoo and I tried to smooth the wrinkles from her pruned up fingertips as we held hands.

I felt a lot better with where we were mentally after talking in the bath, but I still kept my guard up in case she didn't believe me about the "just friends" thing. Trusting women was not in my frame of reference. Every time I did, I got my heart busted into pieces. My last girlfriend had been the worst. Lucy proclaimed a love for me so deep and pure, and I bought it hook, line, and sinker. It took a year before I let myself see she was just using me for money, fame and to further her nonexistent career. It took another six months after that to get rid of her. I wasn't about to jump into another relationship, no matter how honest the woman seemed to be, especially Vivienne. I didn't think she was capable of lying to anyone. Well, maybe just herself.

She acted like a strong, confident woman with her keen brain and thoughtful opinions, but then she'd say the meanest things about herself. It was starting to drive me crazy. In between bites of ice cream she panned her own ability to write and that's when I let her have it.

"You gotta knock that shit off, woman." I clipped the back of her head lightly.

"What?"

"Don't talk about yourself like you're stupid or incapable of putting a sentence together. If you're fishing for compliments, don't bother."

"I'm *not* fishing for compliments," she snapped.

"Could have fooled me. Why else would someone who is up for the National Book Award—"

"How'd you know about that?" She pulled out of the clutch we were in to stare at me.

Pulling her down and forcing her back into the crook of my arm, I ignored her question.

"Never mind how I know. You're up for the award and yet you talk about yourself like you're a moron with the IQ of a gnat. It's *not* attractive."

Vivienne harrumphed but didn't move away. After a while, I felt her sigh.

"I don't do it on purpose. I swear I don't."

I kissed the top of her forehead and squeezed her tight.

"I didn't think you did. I bet when you were a kid and had no confidence, you got into the habit and never broke it."

"Sort of, yeah." She took in a deep, shuddering breath and I changed my tone.

"Break it now, Viv," I admonished her gently, stealing Pepper's pet name. "Sounds like you had the status quo going for a long time, but now you could have a really successful career ahead of you, if you want it badly enough. But you have to believe in yourself. You *have* to know how talented and smart you are. *You are*. If you don't get over it, you'll go back to the mediocre, just-getting-by writer."

I stopped talking and lifted her chin so she could see my eyes and that I meant what I said.

"If that's what you want, cool. But I get the feeling there's a lot more in you."

"There is." Her voice was so faint I could barely hear her.

"Atta girl." I closed my eyes while I rested my head on the pillow behind me, content to hold her and listen to silence and peace. I thought I would fall asleep that way, but I think she took my speech to heart when I felt her hands begin to pry open my robe so she could work on her confidence.

Chapter 25

In spite of the several hours of enormously satisfying sex, I had a difficult time sleeping. When I did, it was filled with weird dreams starring Bruce, several children we'd never had, my dad, and a strange apocalyptic feeling of doom. When I didn't sleep, I was content to listen to Will's breathing as he slept beside me until my brain wound itself up with thoughts and feelings I didn't want to consider.

As I lay there, I recalled the conversation from the bathtub. We both agreed there was no pressure. We both admitted there would be no strings attached. In reality, we had the perfect situation going. Neither one of us had any responsibility to the other and we could behave as hedonistically as we wanted. *That* thought alone made me shiver pleasantly and I huddled a little deeper beneath the comforter.

But that wasn't really reality. At least not for me. I didn't have enough experience with men to know what I was doing. I could speak the words I thought Will wanted to hear, but I had no way of knowing if my heart would follow the rules. Relationships with men and intimacy frightened me. I'd only ever had *one* of them in my almost forty years of life. I met Bruce in the first semester of the first year of college. He was the first man who paid attention to me as a woman. It was a heady, addictive feeling and I fancied myself in love with him from the very first minute. We'd had three years together total from the day we met to the day he died. That was all. I had met, married and lost the only person I'd ever loved in the span of three short years.

But had I really loved Bruce? That was the question I never said out loud, *ever*, to *anyone*. Nineteen was so young. I was so idealistic and full of piss and vinegar then. I thought I was going to have a completely different life. Instead, I ended up married to a soldier, traveling around the country, following him from base to base until he'd been shipped overseas. In many ways, it was the perfect relationship. He was gone doing his military thing so much that I spent a great deal of time alone writing passionate stories and romanticizing our marriage. When Bruce was home, he was the perfect prince charming. It was easy to convince myself I was really in love.

Truthfully, I think I was more relieved I would never have to date again. Sex with Bruce was new and exciting and as satisfying as I could have expected it to be, not knowing anything about it beyond what I read or saw in the movies. It was enough. He wanted to be with me, take care of me, have a life and family with me. He was handsome, smart, and treated me with respect. At nineteen, I'd breathed a huge sigh of relief thinking I'd gotten it "right" on the first try and wouldn't have to worry about it ever again.

And then he died.

I was obviously devastated because the perfect life I thought I had ended as abruptly as Bruce's life. I had no contingency plan. I hadn't finished college, I didn't have a job. I was living in Lacey, Washington, while Bruce was stationed at Fort Lewis. My parents came out to get me and bring me home, all the while helping me deal with the military red tape. In the end, my three-year adventure came to a halt and I found myself right back where I started: living with my folks, going to college, trying to become a writer.

How had I gone from that to lying naked beside a hot, famous rock star? I didn't have a clue. For most of the last seventeen years I hid myself in the same little 'burb where I was born and raised. I pumped out the average chick-lit novel a couple of times a year to supplement the small pension I got from the government and Bruce's life insurance. I hung out with nice, safe girlfriends and my parents. I volunteered at the local animal shelter from time to time, and helped out at a local senior center once in a while. I had even consented to a few dates here and there over the years, but they rarely panned out. Honestly, I knew I gave off a "not interested" vibe whether I was or not, because the effort to get to know another man was too much work for my wounded and terrified soul.

Turning my journals into a story and then putting that story out there for the world was what got me next to such a handsome man, in this bed, in this hotel. No, my husband *dying* was what got me to this point. That was the catalyst. Had it not happened, my whole life would have been different, traveling a different path. I'd spent the last seventeen years lamenting that fact instead of learning to accept it and following a new road.

What a waste of time. I could have been doing *this* kind of thing all along. I could have found some other love and learned so much more. I groaned inwardly, flipping onto my back to stare up at the ceiling. I wished I could talk to Pepper about it all, but as much as I loved her and as close as we were, I was too ashamed. These were the thoughts and feelings I didn't share with anyone. They stayed locked inside. If anyone on the planet ever figured out that I regretted the last twenty years of my life, I'd never be able to leave the house again. I much preferred being viewed as the saddened widow who never got over the love of her life. It was way more romantic and understandable than consciously choosing to hide away and avoid life. My mother would beat the crap out of me if I told her the truth. Pepper would hold me down while she did it. I'd never be able to live with their disappointment.

I wasn't stupid. I knew that it didn't really matter *what* circumstances got me to this point. What mattered was how I proceeded. A door had opened and I was being given an opportunity to change how my future would be. I knew it couldn't possibly include Will, after our conversation the night before. He didn't want any attachments or complications. I couldn't blame him. Why would he want to be involved with an older, boring woman like me when he could have his pick of the most beautiful women on Earth? I tried to tell myself it didn't matter. What I learned from Will already would stay with me forever. Surely there had to be other handsome, intelligent men in the world who could be as passionate and interesting as him. Even someone who would support me in my writing.

The Widow and the Rock Star

As I watched the night sky outside gradually lighten to an orange-yellow glow, Will sighed and moved closer to me. I didn't know if he was awake or not, but he threw his arm over my waist and buried his face into the back of my neck. It was as warm and cozy a feeling as the sunrise filling the room. I tried to block out my thoughts and enjoy the intimacy, hoping it would lull me back to sleep. It didn't. I kept staring out the window, thinking about the last twenty years and the next twenty. I was obsessing and I knew it wasn't a good thing.

I shifted away from Will and he groaned a little before flipping onto his back, leaving me free to climb carefully out of the bed. With my arms wrapped around me in a protective hug, I watched him for more than a minute. In spite of the stubble on his face, he looked so young while asleep. His skin was smooth and unlined, and I envied the complete relaxation of his body. His breathing was deep and even and his arms jutted out to the sides, leaving him spread eagle on the soft mattress. Part of me wanted to hop right back into the bed and snuggle up with him, maybe even wake him up with some sort of surprise move I'd only read about in books but never tried. But a larger part of me wanted more time to myself to think.

I jumped into the shower, hoping it wouldn't wake him *and* hoping it would. It didn't. I was able to shampoo and condition my hair and wash my body thoroughly for the first time in two days. Luxuriating under the spray, I stretched my arms and legs, listening to the muscles and tendons pop and crack. It occurred to me that, except for last night, I'd slept better in the last couple of nights than I had in years, the repose of the satisfied. Had I gotten the rest I needed last night, I might not be standing in the shower obsessing over the past and worrying about the future.

When the water began to run cold in spite of my cranking the faucet all the way to hot, I admitted defeat and climbed out. I put on my yoga pants and tank top, abandoned from the night before, and brushed my teeth for five minutes. Moisturized, deodorized, and hair brushed, I tiptoed out of the bathroom to find Will still in bed, but back on his stomach and buried deep beneath the blanket. I could only see the top of his head and a little of his forehead because he pulled the blanket up so far.

I sat on the corner of the bed to pull on a pair of socks. In spite of the warm glow of sunshine, my toes felt like ice. As I yanked them on, I watched him sleep some more, fascinated once again by how at ease he was. I reached out and put my hand on his leg and rubbed it gently, glad the blanket was between his flesh and my hand. Feeling his skin directly might have been my undoing. He never moved, not even a twitch. I squeezed and then drew my hand back and smiled.

Reluctantly, I stood up and reached for my cell phone on the bedside table, then headed out to the large balcony off my room. The view was even more gorgeous from up close instead of from the bed, and I could see the ocean glinting in the distance. I chose a chair and sat cross legged while my phone powered up. Another four missed calls from Jake filled the screen. I listened to the irritated voicemails instructing me where and when the next meeting was, then texted him my most repentant apologies swearing on my father's grave that I would be there. I probably should have called him, but it was only 7:30 a.m. and I couldn't face the admonishments so early.

I decided to call Pepper instead.

"Hello? Is this my long lost friend from Michigan who's abandoned me for good sex?" came a cheery, caffeinated voice.

"You're up?!"

"You bet. I've been sitting here enjoying my second pot of coffee waiting for your call." Pepper sounded a little miffed.

"I know and I'm sorry. Things got a little, er, out of hand." I nibbled on my fingernail, grateful she couldn't see me.

"Ya think?" she snorted. "Don't worry about it. Where are you now?"

"I'm at the hotel. Will's with me, still sleeping."

"Hot damn!" she yelled and I heard some commotion in the background. I imagined she was spilling coffee. "Hold on a sec, I spilled my coffee." It was my turn to snort as I waited, and when she returned, she demanded details.

"Well, you know what happened at the house, and by the time we got up the next day you were already gone." I stared out into the sky watching seagulls dip and swoop and the clouds float lazily in the fresh sun.

"I don't give a shit about that," she snapped. "How was the *sex?*"

"Pepper," I demurred.

"Tell!" she insisted.

"Very, very, very good." I giggled like a teenager. "The best I've ever had in my entire life. Probably in *any* lifetime."

Pepper cackled and hooted with delight. "Is he—"

"Stop!" I held up a hand I knew she couldn't see. "Don't ask. I will tell you as much as I am willing to, but I will *not* gossip about his size."

"That's not what I was going to ask!" she protested. I imagined her bottom lip jutting out in a classic Pepper pout.

"It wasn't?"

"All right, all right. Fine, don't tell me. Besides, I've already read the tabloid gossip."

I shook my head and grinned, but then got serious. "Pepper, I'm sorry if I fought you about the hookup and I apologize for anything I might have said to hurt your feelings. You were right. I needed the last two nights."

"That's okay Viv," Pepper sighed. "I'm just glad it happened. You both are such dear people to me."

For the next half hour, I answered her questions, amazed at how easily I reverted to sounding like a sixteen-year-old. I told her about the terrible goodbye we'd had and how he came back with the pint of ice cream. Brilliant, she called it. I didn't bother to tell her about the conversation in the tub because it didn't really matter in the end. Feeling better with some girl talk under my belt, I looked forward to when she and I would be together again. "I have a meeting at the Gleaming Bee offices, so I'm going to have to get going soon. Let's do lunch after."

"Viv," Pepper said and I could hear the hesitation in her voice. "I appreciate you calling to let me know you're okay and I loved hearing all the juicy details. But the one thing I'm not hearing is how you really feel about Will."

"What do you mean?" I was dreading this.

"Do you like him?"

"Of course!"

"No, I mean, *really like* him."

I closed my eyes and rubbed them. "What is this? Middle school? Are you asking me if I 'like-like' him? Sheesh." I thought by making light of her question, it would throw her off track. Duh, I really must have been exhausted to think that would work.

"Knock it off," Pepper growled. "You know what I mean."

I knew it was a make-it-or-break-it moment, so I went with what would be the safest route. Even it wasn't too soon to consider, even if Will wanted to be with me, even if I wasn't too scared to be with him, it just wasn't a possibility. We were too different.

"No, Pep. He's a beautiful, wonderful guy. He's funny and smart and a *lot* of fun to be with, in *and* out of the sack. But we're really different kinds of people."

"Is that so bad?"

"No, of course not. There's nothing *wrong* with him, it's just that I couldn't live the kind of life he does. I'm a homebody and I like my privacy. He's a major celebrity and everyone wants a piece of him."

That was really what it was about, now wasn't it? I never could stand to have any attention placed on me and, starting with my friendship with Pepper, I'd always chosen people to take that attention away. She was beautiful and vivacious, I was not. People looked at her when she spoke, not at me. I could still be a part of the world when in her company, but I could hide in the shadows and observe, not participate. Granted, the foundation scandal had put me into the limelight, but that would eventually fade and I would find someone else to run it and interference with the world.

"Piffle," Pepper said. "If you wanted to make it work, you could. Sounds to me like you're too afraid to try."

"No." I shook my head. "After everything I've been through in the last three days, I don't think I'll be afraid of anything anymore. But I do know I don't want to jump into some pseudo relationship with the first guy I've slept with since my husband died."

Pepper gasped. "Say that again?"

"Shit." I slapped my forehead with my hand and mentally kicked myself in the ass about a thousand times.

"I thought you said—"

I cut her off. "I know what I said—"

"But you told me—"

"*I lied, okay?!*" I shouted.

"Okay!"

"Don't give me grief about it," I warned.

"I won't," Pepper promised. "I'm surprised you *aren't* already in love with Will then. Seventeen years is pretty damn long time to go without."

The tension relieved, I guffawed and stood up to stretch my numbing legs.

"Yeah, you'd think I'd be clinging to him like Saran Wrap on leftovers. But I'm smarter than that. And older now. I don't want to confuse things."

"With him?"

"With *me*! My whole life is starting over at this point and I don't want to waste any more time making bad decisions."

"I wouldn't call Will a bad decision." There was a peevish tone in her voice.

"I didn't mean it that way."

"If you stopped and thought about it, you might realize he could be a very *good* decision for you."

I glared at the screen, not wanting the voice of reason pushing aside all of my warm, gushy feelings from the last couple of days.

"Not now, Pep."

"All right," Pepper said softly. "Go get ready for your meeting and call me when you get back."

"I'll do it."

As soon as I hung up with her, my phone vibrated with another incoming call. I contritely listened to Jake Rushmore as he shamed me for disappearing for two days, nodding my head even though I knew he couldn't see. He was on his way to pick me up and would arrive at the hotel in fifteen minutes. Giving him a solemn oath, yet again, that I would be waiting, I hung up and rushed back inside the room to change clothes. Will still hadn't moved and I could hear him snoring softly, which gave me a pleasant feeling in the pit of my stomach. I scrawled a quick note telling him where I'd gone and that I hoped to see him when I got back.

My entire body tingled as I stared at him while pulling on a pretty little scoop-neck dress with a flower print and black wedge sandals. I was glad he didn't wake up because I would have surely broken my promise to Jake. How embarrassing would that be to have him pounding at the door while I attacked the lead singer of Static Neverland? On second thought, my agent would probably be thrilled.

Chapter 26

Pepper yanked on a pair of jeans, plain white tee-shirt, and her favorite pair of worn, holey purple Converse high tops. Pulling her long blond hair into a ponytail, she looked around for her cell phone, purse and keys. Juggling all three, she left her apartment and managed to drop the phone into her purse before it could crash to the pavement and shatter, like her last three phones.

She hopped into her beat-up, old Jeep Wrangler and took the quickest route to the Ritz Carlton Hotel, which was only about twenty minutes away under normal circumstances. Rush hour traffic was something she had planned for and, forty-five minutes later, she pulled into the driveway, allowing the valet guy to drive it away.

"You don't have to bring it back," she shouted after him.

The doorman chuckled when he held the door open for her. Breezing her way through the lobby, she saluted the staff at the desk with confidence, just like she belonged there. Impatiently tapping her toe, she rode the elevator to the 12th floor then strode to the room, banging on the door loudly. It only took about 30 seconds before Will swung open the door wearing only boxers and messy hair.

"Good morning, sunshine!" Pepper said cheerily, inviting herself into the room.

"Good morning to you, too. Where's Vivienne?" he mumbled, following her in and rubbing his eyes with the palms of his hands.

"She's at her meeting. She must not have woken you up." Pepper scanned the room, spying the note left by Viv. She picked it up and read it aloud, then took a seat in one of the soft leather chairs. She reached for the phone on the table and snatched it up, dialing room service.

"Hello, this is Vivienne Stark in room 1223. Could you please be so kind as to send up an extraordinary amount of coffee? No, nothing to eat right now. Just coffee. Yes, thank you."

"Stealing identities now, are we?" Will asked as he plopped down on the couch across from her.

Pepper smiled cheekily.

"So, I think someone owes me an apology, don't you?" She wiggled her eyebrows up and down as she peered at him.

"Fuck off." There was no malice in Will's voice to Pepper's amusement. He grinned as he said it, then yawned.

"I thought you weren't going to hook up with Viv. I thought you said you didn't *do* that anymore." She shook a finger at him in jest and then jumped up to cross the room, flinging herself on the couch beside him.

"God, it's too early for this. Can't we wait for the coffee?" He closed his eyes and he threw his arm over them.

"Pffft," she spat. "Come on, Will, talk to me. I know you're more awake than you're pretending." She poked him in the ribs with her finger, making him flinch. Will had stayed with her more than a dozen years ago, for a short period of time, while he figured out where he wanted to live. It was back when the band signed their first contract and he finally had money to spend on a home. Even though it had been so long ago, Pepper remembered all of his habits and quirks.

Uncovering his face, he opened one eye.

"Yeah, you're right. I'm awake. I was lying in bed wondering where Vivienne was when you so politely rapped upon the door." He pulled is legs up and swung them around her into a sitting position. "I apologize, Pepper. I know I said I wasn't going to hook up with Vivienne, but I changed my mind." He didn't sound the least bit sorry to Pepper.

She slapped her hands on her knees and whistled.

"I knew you wouldn't be able to resist her. Apology accepted."

"It's weird, though. I swear to you, I had no intention of sleeping with her. Even after you left to crash, we just talked. I wasn't turned on, I wasn't drunk, and I wasn't stoned. I was yammering on with her like she was one of my buddies." Will clasped his hands and leaned on his knees. "Then she told me about her husband."

"Oh no," Pepper breathed. "It wasn't pity sex was it? Viv would be mortified."

"No, it wasn't even that. It was just like…" he stopped. "It's like when I plug my guitar into the amplifier and I hear that first humming and feel that first vibration as the juice runs through the wires. She was looking at me, I was looking at her, and I felt that vibration, so I just kind of jumped on her." His face was strained with the admission.

Pepper rubbed Will's arm and leaned into his line of sight.

"It's okay, Will. You make it sound like a bad thing." She put on a light and airy tone of voice to inspire him to find the humor and fun in the situation.

"I know. It's not bad. It *could* have been bad, but it turned out okay. She really beat herself up about it the next day, though."

"I knew she would," Pepper admitted. "But in the end it was worth it. I think it was something she had to go through."

"You make it sound like I was therapy for her."

Pepper sighed.

"Well, to be honest, it probably was. How much did she tell you about her husband?"

"Not a whole lot. They met in college, married young and he was killed."

"Did she tell you she hasn't had sex since he died?"

Will's head whipped around.

"*What?*"

"Whoops! I guess not." Pepper grimaced. "It's true. She hasn't been with anyone since Bruce was killed. Now she'll kill *me* for telling you that, but I think it's important for you to know."

Will stood up and paced around the room, running his fingers through his hair. "Dammit, I wish I'd known that before now. I *never* would have slept with her."

"Why not?" Pepper demanded.

"Because now she's going to—I mean, I bet she'll—aw, fuck!" Will sat back down heavily beside Pepper.

"How does this change anything?" Pepper kept her voice calm.

"I said some stuff last night…" Will stopped and Pepper frowned.

"Go on." Just then, room service arrived with the coffee. "Hold that thought," she told him, and then rushed to let in the waiter.

While she poured and he drank, Will told Pepper about the awkward parting at the hotel and how he had come back. He told her about the bathtub conversation, and his half-assed way of confronting Vivienne about the whole affair meaning too much or too little.

"I don't know if I should see her again. Maybe I should get the hell out of here and let it go."

"You most certainly will *not!*" Pepper hollered. Never had she seen two people who were on the exact same page, but had mistakenly found themselves in totally different books. "If you're worried Viv is going to become obsessed with you, become your newest stalker, don't. She's not like that."

"No, but, shit," Will swallowed more coffee. "I guess it's like she was a virgin again and I took that."

Pepper gawped at Will and then burst into laughter. She held her stomach and flopped onto the couch, tears squirting out of her eyes. Will glared at her but remained silent. When Pepper was finally able to get control, she continued to giggle as she wiped her eyes.

"You have *got* to be kidding me," she spluttered. "Are you *serious?*"

"Well—"

"Get *over* yourself. I might not know from personal experience, but you are *not* God's gift in the sack, Will."

Will hung his head at the rebuke.

"I'm sorry. I didn't think about how that would sound."

"Don't even *think* it, Will. You're not that kind of guy."

"Well, not anymore, I hope," he admitted. "I fall off the wagon now and then."

"Yeah, and that was a hell of a fall you just took." Pepper scowled at him and shook a finger to let him know she wasn't really that angry.

"You both have been agonizing over what you *think* the other one is thinking and you haven't even bothered to ask each other!" She sat up straight. Unable to help herself, she went on. "You're worried she's too vulnerable and is falling in love with you. She's worried you're falling in love with *her*. *Neither one of you is in love with the other!*"

Secretly, Pepper wasn't so sure about that. She knew if they weren't in love with one another yet, it was only a short matter of time before they were, if they would just let themselves fall. But she preferred to deal with the present.

Pepper sighed. "Viv only feels guilty about what she's done because she waited so long to get over Bruce. She doesn't want you to feel used. She likes you a lot, but doesn't want to hurt your feelings."

Will looked like he was considering her words, so she continued.

"And listening to you, it sounds like you think the same thing. You're worried that she'll feel used and discarded. You like *her* a lot, but don't want to hurt *her* feelings. Am I right?"

"Exactly."

"I think you were on your way to getting there in the conversation last night, but you got a little sidetracked." Pepper leered at him.

Will had the good graces to blush and nod his head.

"Yeah. I was too uncomfortable to go farther than the 'let's be friends' thing."

"That's your problem, Will. You've never been able to take that next step. And when you did once, with Lucy, you got burned. Don't go back to the way you used to be when you were twenty-five and all the little chickies were throwing themselves at you," Pepper warned. "That's not who you really are."

"No, it isn't."

"And don't worry about Vivienne. She'll find her way. She'll go back to Michigan and her life. She'll figure out what she needs and wants and now she'll finally be free to go out and get it. Be glad you're the inspiration for that."

Will grinned.

"Now do I get to smack you in the face because you're the one who told the truth?"

Pepper grinned right back.

"Try it."

Chapter 27

I got back to the hotel around 2:30 in the afternoon and Will was gone. I was disappointed because I hoped he would still be asleep, or at least lounging around the room watching TV. He left his number, though, and I was anxious to call him to make sure we were still okay. I controlled myself with a fair amount of effort, calling Pepper first.

"What's up?" she asked casually.

"Will's gone."

"And that surprises you?"

"No. Well, kind of. I don't know." I stared around me at the empty suite.

"Did you really think he'd hang around all day waiting for you to get back? He's got other obligations, too." Pepper's tone was more flippant than I expected.

"Of course he does," I snapped. "I'm sorry. The meeting didn't go well and I was looking forward to seeing him because he has a way of cheering me up."

"Orgasms will do that," Pepper chided.

"D'oh!"

"You still do the best Homer Simpson." She tittered. "Did he leave his number?"

"Yes."

"Then call him."

"No, I'll wait. I haven't seen you in a while. Want to come over for a swim?"

"Oh, so I'm second fiddle to the swingin' dick?" she teased.

"Stop that!" But I couldn't help laughing. Pepper was always the same and I knew I could count on her for it.

"Actually, I'm right in the area so I'll meet you by the pool. I've got a suit with me, just give me fifteen minutes."

"Great! I'll save us a couple of seats."

Feeling better, I changed into my bathing suit and what Pepper called my "granny cover-up." It was a black-cotton, knitted jacket thing that tied in front. I was a whirling dervish of activity, slipping on some flip-flops, grabbing my sun hat and throwing the sunscreen, my phone, the iPod, a notebook and pen into my bag. I rushed from the room to get to the pool before Pepper.

When I walked out into the bright sunshine from the dimly lit hotel, I had to shield my eyes, having forgotten my sunglasses. I looked around for a good spot close to the bar and I almost dropped my bag when I saw Pepper sprawled out on a chaise lounge holding a drink. Beside her, in the next chair, was Will. He wore a pair of black swim trunks with red, orange and yellow flames along the side and dark aviator sunglasses. They were both doing a Queen Elizabeth wave at me. I almost tripped in my cheap dollar store flip-flops, but managed to save myself from looking like too much of an idiot, I hoped.

"What are you guys doing here?" I tossed my bag onto the lounge on Will's other side, which happened to be perfectly positioned beneath a large umbrella.

"I called Will to check on him," Pepper said, "and he told me he was here. I came by to wait for you with him."

I couldn't help but smile and I sat down with that dopey grin on my face.

"I'm so glad to see *both* of you."

Will leaned toward me and it took me a second to realize he was waiting for a kiss. I obliged, but kept it chaste.

"Welcome home," he said.

"How rude, Will! Get this woman a cocktail! She looks like she could use one." Pepper whacked him on the arm.

Will gave a two-fingered salute, then obediently rose and trotted off to the bar.

"You're awful." I shook my finger at her.

"Yeah, so they tell me." Pepper rolled her eyes. "So what happened at this meeting?"

"Ugh," I spat. "It too was awful. They went on and on about their vision for the film, but they changed so much it wasn't even remotely close to the story I wrote."

"Jake warned you about that."

"Yes, I know. But they changed my age, they gave me two kids, and they changed the end. They wanted my mother to be dead but my father alive. They added about four subplots that didn't even relate to the theme." I threw my hands up in exasperation. "If they wanted something so different, why not just write their own independent script? Why waste all the cash they're offering to buy my book?"

"So go with EJR, then." Pepper shrugged.

"Then they brought up the foundation scandal, making me feel like a jackass. Jake handled it beautifully, but he was *not* happy."

"All the more reason to go with EJR."

"I s'pose."

Will returned and handed me a gin and tonic with extra lime.

"There you go. I made sure they didn't use too much ice. No sense letting all that frozen water soak up the gin."

"Thank you." I sipped until a third of the liquid was gone then smacked my lips.

"Viv was just telling me about her bust of a meeting."

"Yeah?" Will tried to look interested but it was impossible to tell behind those dark glasses.

"It sucked." Another third of my cocktail disappeared down my throat.

"Oh." He stopped trying to look interested and put his glasses up on his forehead. "That's Hollywood for ya."

"Indeed." I yanked my sunscreen out of the bag and began to liberally slather my pale skin. "What about you? Don't you have anything better to do than hang out here? No big rock star crap to manage?"

Will laughed and settled himself more definitely in the chair.

"You're looking at it. I'm having a beer while sandwiched between two gorgeous women. That's all we celebrities do, don'tcha know?" Will emphasized the point by taking a deep swig of his beer and resting it on his stomach.

Pepper snorted and dipped her fingers into her drink, flicking it at him. I swatted him with my sun hat. The afternoon was definitely looking to go better than my morning.

*****

A few hours, a swim and a couple of cocktails later, Pepper was tapping and swiping along on her iPad when she felt her stomach flip flop. *Here we go*, she thought. Pictures of Will and Vivienne's evening out were all over the Internet. OMG, Inside Edition, TMZ— they all had various shots and blurbs to match.

"It's official," Pepper said. "You're really famous now, Viv." She nudged Will's arm and he lifted his head off of his crossed arms. He was sprawled on his stomach on the chaise and had been snoring. She passed the device to him and he squinted at it.

"Yeah, that's us," he mumbled, handing the iPad to Vivienne. He put his head back down.

"What?" Vivienne's face grew paler, if that was possible, and her mouth opened wider and wider. "'Will Foster was spotted on the town with hot new novelist Vivienne Stark yesterday evening. Stark wrote— blah, blah, blah—Is this Will's latest conquest in a long line of celebrity babes? If so, Miss Stark is a far cry from the luscious bombshells of Foster's long history.' Oh my God! Pepper, this is terrible!"

"No it's not," Pepper and Will said in unison.

"I look like a deer in headlights! And I'm a 'far cry' from your usual bimbos. Fuck!" Vivienne seethed. "Jake is going to *kill* me."

Will groaned and flipped onto his back to sit up. He elevated the chaise and looked irritated.

"Stop it, Vivienne. It's okay."

Pepper glared at him and kicked his shin, not appreciating his blasé attitude.

"It's not okay!" Vivienne wailed. "I look like a troll!"

"Calm down," Pepper hissed when other people in the vicinity glanced over at them. "Don't make a scene." She got up to sit beside Vivienne. "So what if you had a few pictures taken? Will's a pretty big celebrity. What did you think was going to happen?"

Vivienne's mouth snapped shut.

"I don't know," she finally muttered. "I just wasn't thinking. Jake is *really* going to murder me."

"No he won't," Pepper snapped. "Here, give me that." She took the iPad back and put it under her towel.

"They refer to you as the 'hot new novelist'," Will pointed out. "They hardly mentioned the foundation."

"Ugh." Vivienne buried her face in her hands. "Is this what I'm in for?" she asked through her fingers. "Are the paparazzi going to stalk me just because I had one dinner with a famous rock star?"

"Probably," Will admitted. Pepper kicked him again more sharply. "Ow!"

"No, you aren't going to be stalked. You'll go home in a few days and no one will follow you to Michigan." Pepper hugged her in assurance. She regretted having brought any of it to Vivienne's attention. *She probably would have never known or at least not found out until she got home. Dammit.*

"Oh God," Vivienne moaned. "A far cry…" she sounded close to tears and that got Will's attention. He sat up straighter and leaned his elbows on his knees.

"Vivienne, please don't. Do *not* take a word of that shit seriously. The vipers spew venom just to get a rise. This is really *no big deal*. All I have to do is have my publicist release a statement saying you're just a friend and that I took you out to dinner while you were visiting LA. Or, better yet, we can tell the press you were talking to me about the foundation and how the band could help out or something."

He looked around for his phone and picked it up.

"I can tweet something right now, post on Facebook. Would that make you feel better?"

Pepper rubbed her back, trying to get her to relax. Vivienne peeked through her hands, which she kept cupped around her eyes. "But it looks like we were on a date. No one's going to believe that."

"No, it looks like he's shielding you from the photographers. I swear." Pepper tried to show her the iPad again, but Vivienne refused to look. "He's right, Viv." Pepper leaned into her line of sight to nod.

Shaking her head, Vivienne covered her eyes again.

"I'm going to cancel the rest of my meetings and appearances. I'm not leaving this hotel again until it's time to go to the airport."

"Don't be ridiculous." Pepper hoped she didn't sound too harsh. *But that's Vivvy. The first sign of trouble and down the rabbit hole she runs.*

"Best thing you could do is go out again," Will said matter-of-factly. "I told you before, the harder you try to hide, the harder they work to find you. Give them what they want and they get bored."

"Exactly!" Pepper's eyes flashed.

Still shaking her head, Vivienne jumped up and reached for her bag to dig out her cell phone.

"I need to call Jake." She stalked off and Pepper watched intently as her friend had a very animated conversation with her agent. She could only catch snippets of the conversation, but judging by the slump of Vivienne's shoulders, she was hearing the same advice from Jake that Will had just given.

Not more than two minutes later, Vivienne returned, none too pleased. She flopped onto her chair, looking frightened and ill. Pepper waited for her to speak, staring at her silently, willing her to spit out the details of what she'd been told.

Finally, Vivienne sighed.

"Jake knew all about it. He won't let me cancel anything."

"Told ya," Will whispered. Vivienne glared at him, her eyes crackling with fury.

"I bet he told you this is a *good* thing." Pepper looked up at the sky when Vivienne turned the stink eye her way.

"As a matter of fact, smarty pants, he *did* say that." Vivienne tossed her phone back into the bag and groaned loudly. "Don't worry about tweeting, Will. Jake's going to put out a statement for me."

"Cool." Will was busy on his own phone, typing something. "But I already posted on Facebook. How's this? 'Had dinner last night with the coolest writer ever, check out *The Widow's Path Foundation*. Totally worthy cause.'"

Vivienne's face softened and she gave him a strained smile.

"Thanks, Will."

"It's settled, then." Pepper stood up and put her hands on her hips. "We'll all go out tonight. The three of us. Somewhere fancy and obvious. We'll dress to the nines and shove that 'a far cry' shit right down their throats!"

Vivienne's mouth dropped open again.

"You're joking, right?" She shook her head vehemently. "You can't be serious."

"I am!" Pepper grabbed Vivienne's hands. "Then you can have your revenge. You can be seen out on the town and look like a billion bucks."

"Not just a million." Will pointed his finger at her.

"You could cash in on your *own* growing celebrity, Viv. Maybe if you're seen out, it'll help your negotiations or the foundation."

"No way. I can't cancel all the stuff Jake set up, but I don't have to leave the hotel until I have to."

"Oh yes, you do," Pepper insisted, glaring at her friend. She sighed knowing she was going to have to fight tooth and nail to get Viv to give in.

"You know…" Will pursed his lips in thought. "I had an invitation to some red carpet thing tonight, but I blew it off. I bet I could get us back on the list."

"Yes!" Pepper shouted, as Vivienne yelled, "No!"

"It was just a thought." Will shrugged.

"Make the call." Pepper pointed her finger at Will. He raised his eyebrows in question and she nodded her head and waggled her finger.

"No one is going to be able to convince me to leave." Vivienne sounded adamant.

Except me, Pepper thought.

Chapter 28

"Read me the statement again," I demanded. I was upstairs in my room talking to Jake while Pepper and Will went in search of suitable "costumes" for the evening out they thought I'd participate in. I was relieved when they left because then I could talk to Jake again and work on damage control.

"I'm not reading it to you again. I already did twice, *and* I sent it by email. It's out and there's nothing you can do about it." Jake was getting irritated with me but I couldn't help it. I was beside myself with worry thinking all publicity was bad and the foundation would continue to suffer in spite of all my attempts to protect it.

"I'm sorry, Jake," I sighed. "I just feel awful about this. I'm glad it was just a dinner that got caught on film and nothing else."

"*Is* there something else I should know?"

My hesitation confirmed what I wouldn't say out loud.

"Where *were* you last night, Vivienne?"

"That's none of your business," I snapped, waiting for Jake to explode. Instead he belly laughed.

"You don't have to answer, I know all I need to know."

"Don't you *dare* breathe a word of this—"

"Don't worry, Vivienne, I won't release anything more. But I suggest you be more discreet if you don't want the press making up stories of their own."

I sat on the edge of the bed and rubbed my eyes, trying not to regret every single action since the moment I left The Relic the previous night.

"I just don't want to make any more mistakes that could hurt the foundation. Have you heard anything from the police?"

"Nothing yet, but I called the detectives with the new information you gave me."

Earlier, when we had been together, Jake and I discussed Tony Lyleson and everything I could possibly think of from the one meeting and multiple phone calls we'd had after I'd put him in charge of the foundation.

"Tell me more about where you're going tonight."

"*If* I go," I reminded him. "I don't have the slightest idea. Something about a premiere for a television show."

"Which one?"

"I don't know! Does it matter? I can't believe you're supporting this cockamamie idea!" I yelled.

"When are you going to get it through your thick skull?" Jake hollered right back. "Nothing you've done is wrong or bad for the foundation. It is all working to your benefit. It just looks like you're developing relationships and connections to help the foundation recover from what amounts to nothing more than a robbery."

I grimaced as he chastised me, logically understanding every word he said, unable to take it to heart.

"You'll go tonight. You'll smile when you need to smile and if you're asked any questions, you'll answer them. You're probably the *only* one of my clients I completely trust to speak coherently and intelligently."

"Thank you, Jake," I whispered, stunned by his supportive tone.

"Seriously, Vivienne. You're every agent's dream client. You don't create drama or scandal, but if it happens, you can handle it with dignity and grace. It leaves me able to focus on the real issue without having to handle you at the same time. Most of my other clients could take lessons from you."

I knew all along Jake was the best agent I could have chosen, but his words instantly lifted my spirits.

"I appreciate that, Jake."

"You should."

There he is, back to his usual self. I laughed. I wanted to say more, but another call was coming through. I checked the display on my phone, seeing Pepper's name and face on the screen.

"Pepper's beeping in, Jake. I'll let you go and call if anything else comes up." I started to say goodbye, but changed my mind. "Thank you again for everything you're doing. I'm sorry I've turned in to such a pain in the ass."

Jake chuckled.

"It's okay, Vivienne. This is my job. You just have to trust me when I tell you everything will be okay."

"All right. I'll talk to you later."

"Bye."

I clicked over to catch Pepper, but she'd already gone to voicemail. Not bothering to listen to it, I dialed her number and wasn't surprised when she answered before the first ring was finished. She was with Will at his house getting his clothes and would be back in less than half an hour. I could detect the surprise in her voice when I told her I would still be here waiting because I knew she expected another round of protestations.

"Tell me what size shoe you wear again," Pepper commanded.

"Six-and-a-half."

"Okay, great. I'll be bringing shoes too. You're lucky I know so many people in Hollywood, my friend." Then she hung up on me before I could say another word.

I tossed my phone onto the bed and walked to the windows to peer out over the Los Angeles skyline. I couldn't believe how much had happened and how much things had changed in less than a week. It was one thing to publish a book and gain a certain amount of notoriety for it, but this was way beyond what even my imagination could have come up with.

I cursed Tony Lyleson with every ounce of my heart for the scoundrel he was. I knew this type of scandal wasn't new. Hell, lots of charities and organizations had gotten ripped off for way more money than mine had, causes just as vital and meaningful as the widows and widowers of fallen soldiers. But I still couldn't help feeling a certain amount of righteous indignation because *I* was one of those widows. *My* husband was a fallen soldier. I started the foundation, wanting to help without wanting *anything* for myself, and this dirty rotten bastard had ruined it all. I couldn't give a rat's ass about paying the money back out of my own funds, if I had to, but he had effectively cheated hundreds of people out of the opportunity to begin their lives anew. If not for him, I might not have been in California at all. Oh sure, there were the negotiations for the movie rights going on, but I probably could have stayed home in Michigan for those and allowed Jake to handle it all.

Wanting some fresh air, I went to the balcony door and stepped outside. I could hear the traffic below and took quite a few deep breaths to try and begin gearing myself up for the festivities later in the evening. From a quiet existence in suburban Detroit to the noise and constant activity of Los Angeles was a huge leap for me.

I was lucky I even heard it, but my phone ringing brought me back to the moment and I walked back to the bed to see who could be calling now. The display said "unknown" and I hesitated before answering. Praying it wasn't some reporter or more bad news, I tapped the screen to answer.

"Hello?"

"Hello, Vivienne."

I recognized Tony Lyleson's voice instantly, wondering if all my evil thoughts about him had actually tempted him into calling me.

"You bastard!" I hissed. "I don't suppose you'd like to tell me where the hell you are and where all the money is?"

"Don't be silly! I'd never do that." His tone was syrupy and patronizing, making my blood boil. I stomped my foot, grateful for the deep-pile carpeting.

"How dare you call and gloat!" I was losing control and I knew it's what he wanted, but I couldn't stop the anger from overflowing out of my mouth any more than I could have held back vomit during a bout of food poisoning.

"Oh, I'm not gloating. I just wanted to tell you to drop the investigation. You'll never find me, so don't waste your time." His oily voice was filled with confidence. "And if you *don't* stop, I may just have to hack into your *personal* accounts as well."

"*You sorry son of a bitch!*" I hissed.

"Ta-ta for now, dear!" he chortled and then hung up on me.

And that's when I *really* lost it. I threw the phone across the room and it crashed against the door just as Will came through it.

Chapter 29

"That guy has balls," I said, completely shocked at what Vivienne related to us after I almost got beaned with her phone.

"And I'll cut 'em off myself if I ever get my hands on him," Vivienne spat. Her eyes were crackling with rage and her face was flushed. I was embarrassed to find her exquisitely beautiful in that moment, so I found something else to look at. Angry Vivienne was hotter than hell.

"Down, girl." Pepper grabbed her by the arms and made her sit down. "Have you called the police?" She sat down beside her and clasped hands with her.

"No, I was too busy throwing a fit." Vivienne's flush grew deeper with her shame and I glanced at her in the mirror so she couldn't see me.

"Well you better call them or Jake." Pepper stood and went to the minibar. She retrieved a tiny bottle of brandy and cracked it open, handing it to her friend. "Have a drink. It'll calm your nerves."

Vivienne snatched the bottle and tipped it up, downing the entire thing in four large gulps.

Tossing the bottle into the trash, Vivienne stomped over to where her phone was still on the floor. Grabbing it, she rolled her eyes. "Thank goodness for a good case, eh?" Then she marched out to the balcony leaving me alone with Pepper.

"Remind me never to piss her off," I said softly, craning to see her through the window.

Pepper laughed and smacked me in the arm.

"I've known her all my life and, I have to say, I don't think I've ever seen her this mad before."

I nodded and flopped onto the bed, throwing my arms above my head. Pepper had dropped the four dresses she'd been carrying when we arrived and she began picking them up off the floor. Hanging them on the back of the bathroom door, she took the plastic off each one.

"You think this is still a good idea? Going out tonight?"

"Yes," Pepper insisted. "We need to keep her busy and active. Distracted from all this bullshit, as much as possible."

"She's pretty nervous about it."

"Viv thinks too much," Pepper sniffed. "When she stops thinking and just goes with the flow, she has a great time." She winked at Will and smirked. "Look at the other night. You got a taste of the *real* Vivienne."

I snorted.

"Pun intended?"

"Of course!"

Pepper was still laughing as she arranged the shoes when Vivienne came back into the room.

"Well?" we asked in unison.

Vivienne sighed and stretched out beside me on the bed. She laced the fingers of her hands together and rested them on her stomach.

"Jake said he would call the police. I don't know if they can trace the call through phone records or not, but I sure as hell hope so."

I brought my arms down to put one around her shoulders. She instinctively raised her head so I could get it under there. I squeezed her in support and she snuggled up next to me. Pepper tried not to show her pleasure, but I caught the grin spreading across her face as she turned around to continue her busy work.

"So are we still on for tonight?" I asked quietly.

"Yeah. Jake wouldn't let me bow out. He said I probably looked quite fetching in my pique and I would photograph better that way."

Pepper and I both burst out laughing at that, and Vivienne muttered her favorite phrase. "Good grief."

Chapter 30

Pepper emerged from the bathroom. Feeling like a Greek Goddess, she was wearing a floor-length, silver, toga-style gown and black, strappy, high-heel sandals. Her hair was piled high onto her head, held up with crystal-encrusted bobby pins. She knew she looked good.

"Wow!" Will whistled as she grinned and rummaged through her purse, frowning when her favorite lipstick played hide and seek.

"Thanks love," Pepper said, grasping the tube at last. "But I'm not the one who will need the compliments." She jerked her head back in the direction of the closed bathroom door.

Will gave her two thumbs up and turned to the mirror to continue working on his tie. Pepper playfully nudged him out of the way. She didn't notice when Vivienne came out, but knew she had by the stunned look on Will's face. It made her smile because she could see his eyes smolder in the mirror's reflection.

"Holy cow," he breathed.

Pepper watched him cross the room to take Vivienne's hands and twirl her around; she was pleased by the electricity between them.

Pepper had called in a favor to one of her costumer friends to find a dress for Viv. Of all the choices offered, Pepper knew the forest green dress was the perfect one. Her eyes almost filled with tears at the sight of her friend in the silk, sleeveless sheath with the sweetheart neckline and ruched bodice. The hem of the dress stopped at the knee in the front and floated out in back with a long train. Vivienne looked as beautiful on the outside as Pepper knew she was on the inside.

"Ravishing!" Will was saying. "Gorgeous! Extraordinary!"

"Stop," Vivienne protested, blushing furiously. She turned her face to Pepper. "Is it okay? It feels a little tight."

The Widow and the Rock Star

"Good, good, good! If you can breathe, it isn't tight enough!" Pepper did her best impression of Auntie Mame and took note of Vivienne's amusement.

"Looks *perfect.*" Will's eyes were fixed on her body.

Maybe I ought to leave them alone for a while, Pepper thought, holding her cackle inside.

"Viv, it's great. I swear." Pepper crossed her heart.

"I feel silly," Vivienne murmured. "Like I'm playing dress up in my mother's clothes."

"Your mom never had a dress like that." Pepper grabbed her hand. "Come here and sit down."

Vivienne obeyed and took a seat at the vanity so Pepper could work on her hair and makeup.

"Not too much."

"Nope, I promise."

Only minutes later, Pepper urged her to open her eyes.

"Look in the mirror, girl! You look awesome!"

"I can't believe I'm doing this," Vivienne whispered, not recognizing herself.

Pepper had applied light foundation, mascara and light-pink lip gloss. It was all Vivienne needed to enhance the natural beauty of her face. Her long, red hair flowed down her back in large waves. Pepper slipped in a jeweled barrette to pin it off of her face.

Will stepped behind her and put his hands on Vivienne's bare shoulders.

"Stunning." Leaning down, he kissed her on the cheek. "Really stunning."

Pepper shivered with goose bumps as she watched Vivienne blossom from the compliments. *If ever two people had potential, it's them*, she thought. But she was finished interfering. She said her piece to each of them and they were going to have to find their way on their own, whether together or apart. *I just hope it's together.*

"What time will the car be here?" Pepper turned back toward the mirror to check her hair one more time.

"Ari said it would be here at five." Vivienne slipped into the borrowed Manolo Blahnik shoes and grew four inches instantly. Pepper thought the bronze-metallic-stamped heels accentuated Vivienne's outfit perfectly.

"Jake wants to hire the two of you, he's so impressed. He thinks you convinced me to go out when it was really him."

"Tell him I don't need dental." Will grinned with his perfect teeth and then linked his hand with Vivienne's.

"Viv, I'm telling you, when you fall off the horse, you get right back on. You're going out there like nothing's wrong and make them eat crow." Pepper crossed the room to take her friend's other hand. Glancing at the clock on the wall, it read 4:55 p.m. "Let's go. By the time we float down the elevator, the car will be waiting."

In a cloud of Arden Beauty perfume and high hopes, Pepper led them out of the suite.

Chapter 31

Will and Pepper looked perfect together as I followed them to the waiting limousine. The driver held the door and Will helped Pepper inside. He turned to take my hand next and I stalled.

"Don't quit on me now." He took my hand gently, pulling me toward the car. In spite of his outward confidence, Will's eyes looked worried and I realized it was for me.

"I'm so nervous." My knees were knocking and I reached to smooth the soft material on my hips.

"And an hour ago you were all rage and wrath. Just pretend you're someone else for the night. Have fun with it!"

I bit my lip and started to shake my head.

"You two should go without me. Pepper has that red carpet look. Not me."

"I call bullshit!" Pepper roared from inside.

"I call bullshit, too." Will pretended to glare at me. "You look good enough for the Grammys or the Oscars, not some rinky dink TV show premiere. Now get in the car, beautiful!"

Taking a deep breath, I slipped inside of the black stretch limo, wanting his words to be true. I wanted just a drop of Pepper's confidence.

Twenty minutes later, the limo took its place in a long line of cars beside the venue.

"We can wait our turn or climb out now and walk the gauntlet." Will peered out the window taking in the scene.

"Let's wait." Pepper nodded to me. She clutched my hand to steady the trembling, which got worse as we got closer.

I reached into my purse and took out my cell phone, trying to take my mind off what was coming. I opened up the web browser and started searching for any other news about mine and Will's "date" from the evening before. All the pictures and stories were the same, thank God, but there were thousands more comments from readers and fans of the stories, which made my skin crawl. If anything seemed remotely derogatory about me, I skipped it to avoid taking any further hits to my confidence and self-esteem. Pepper got annoyed with my obsession and snatched the phone away from me, throwing it into the front seat with the driver.

"Don't let her have that back," Pepper commanded. I smiled and then actually chuckled a little bit.

"Will, dear?" My voice was sugary sweet, an octave above normal.

"Yeah?"

"May I borrow your phone?"

He didn't even think, just reached into his coat for it.

Pepper kicked him sharply with the toe of her sandal and threatened his life.

"Don't you dare give her that phone!"

I hid my giggles behind my hand, but she caught me anyway and then gave me a kick, too, only more gently. With some of the tension relieved, I sat back against the soft leather of the seat and tried to relax. Taking Will's advice, I tried to channel my earlier anger from Tony's phone call, but I couldn't. Instead, my teenage insecurities surged back from the moment I read the comment about me being a far cry from Will's usual choices, making my stomach churn. It took years to get over not being tall and thin and gorgeous like Pepper and, in one afternoon, I let an Internet tabloid threaten it.

The flashbulbs lighting up the sky made the blood in my veins icy. I was nauseous with the thought of facing them. I wanted so much to have the kind of confidence Pepper had, but it did not come naturally to me. The words of my therapist from years ago popped into my head: "Fake it till you make it, Vivienne."

Will leaned over to nuzzle my neck.

"Exactly."

"God, did I say that out loud?" I whispered, enjoying his warm breath on my skin.

"Yes, you did. And it's true."

"It is," Pepper agreed. She blew me an air kiss. "Remember when we were kids and we dreamed about being rich and famous? You always wanted to be Stephen King or Toni Morrison. I always wanted to be Julia Roberts or Sandra Bullock. It's all just an act, Viv. Give 'em the performance of your life!"

Pepper almost had me convinced. I was feeling nostalgic for our childhood and teenage years, hopeful that being on a red carpet would be a fun game to play. But then I saw the more than a hundred photographers clustered behind wooden sawhorses, vying for positions and the best shot. I gulped hard and tried to smile.

"You'll have to do better than that," Pepper laughed. "Come on. I'll get out first, then Will and you last. That way we can shield you from the first wave."

She knocked on the glass and the driver pulled open the door. I could hear the shutter sounds beginning already as Pepper gracefully lifted herself out.

Will turned to me and took my face in his hands. He kissed me softly and then grabbed my hand before I could change my mind. Getting out of the limo, I bobbed up like a buoy in the ocean and the bright flashes made gold spots explode in my vision.

"Smile," Will said into my ear as he linked his arm through mine. Pepper appeared on his other side and then we were gliding to the door. I focused my returning vision on the TV network symbol a hundred yards away, a stiff smile pasted on my face.

I could hear the photographers yelling for Will to look this way and that way and he obliged every request. I felt his pace slow and took a step ahead of him, nearly stumbling. They were yelling questions at him and he was answering, giving smiles and poses, only inching progress being made to our escape. My smile disappeared but Pepper's became more brilliant if that was possible. She posed and spun for the photogs as naturally as if she were at a photo shoot. They shouted for her name and she gave it willingly. They ate her up, calling her name over and over.

"Smile," Will reminded me. He unlinked arms so he could circle my waist instead and pull me closer. My stilted smile returned and then I heard my own name added to the chorus.

"Vivienne Stark! Over here!"

Conditioned like Pavlov's dogs, I turned when spoken to. The flashes quickened, the shutter clicks became deafening. It never occurred to me they would know who I was, but wasn't I a bestselling author and the head of a broke foundation now? Wasn't I all over the Internet because of last night? The realizations made my urge to vomit stronger, but I fought it as hard as I could for Will's and Pepper's sakes.

I didn't even notice Pepper had fallen behind until we were a few steps from safety. I whirled around to look for her and stopped short to see her still posing and strutting for the cameras. She looked like a movie star from times gone by, all glitz and glamour and love for the camera. In that moment, I forgot I was still being captured on film as well, and clapped my hands together for her. Happiness surged through me to see Pepper so alive and in her element. Will rooted her on and she blew kisses to us and to the photographers. Lifting the hem of her dress, she ran on tip-toe to catch up with us.

Back together, we ran inside once again linked at the arms, out of the prying eyes of the press, and I fell into Pepper's arms, squeezing until she squealed.

"That wasn't so bad now, was it?" Pepper asked, filled with glee, her adrenaline pumping.

"Not for you! You're a natural!" I hugged her again and felt myself relax the slightest bit.

"She's right." Will nodded in agreement. "From now on, you're my red carpet stand-in."

"You got it!" Pepper wiggled her hips. "I need all the exposure I can get. This gal ain't gettin' any younger."

We milled around the backstage area until one of the production assistants told us it was our turn to enter the main area. When we had gotten ten feet away, but were still camouflaged by black curtains and huge cardboard advertisements, I skidded to a halt.

"Wait, I see more flashes."

"Yeah, there's one more gauntlet to get through." Will avoided my eyes.

"Oh no, I've had enough." I crossed my arms against my chest, refusing to take another step. "There has to be another way in without that."

"I'm afraid there isn't," Will admitted. He grabbed a passing production assistant and made him confirm it.

"Shit."

"You did fine before," Pepper assured me. She patted my hair and rubbed a thumb against my check to smooth my makeup.

"How do you do this?" I cringed at how whiny I sounded. "I could never do it on a regular basis."

"You get used to it." Will shrugged. "The first time is the worst."

"I *don't* plan on having a second time," I muttered as we were ushered forward.

"Pepper, you go on." Will pushed her a little. Giving us two thumbs up, she sauntered from behind the black curtains to a less raucous roar from the smaller crowd sequestered behind red velvet ropes. She revived her brilliant smile and pose from before, and performed for several moments, completely at ease with her surroundings. I watched her, filled with jealousy, wishing I could be so carefree. Where had that girl gone, the one I'd been at 14, 15, 16, wishing I could be rich and famous? Why wasn't this a dream come true for me? *Get a grip, Viv.*

I buried my face into Will's chest for one last moment and then we were walking forward. Because we were inside and there were large, bright lights set up at the edge of the walkway, the flashes weren't as blinding and I was able to see more clearly.

"We have to stop here for just a minute," Will whispered. "Smile."

I tried to look natural and prayed I wasn't failing or making him look ridiculous. To my horror, a very tall brunette with a microphone approached us as if she were on roller skates instead of five-inch stilettos. She thrust the microphone into Will's face and began speaking as if she were trying to win a Guinness World record for speed talking. I never even caught her name. Ignoring me, she congratulated Will on the tour and his TV show and then peppered him with the usual inane questions. The whole while, I tried to pull away so I could run as far away as possible, but Will's grip on my waist was vice-tight. It turned out to be a good thing, because then she turned her attention to me and I felt my legs begin to weaken. If not for his clutch, I might have gone to my knees.

"Vivienne Stark! Congratulations on your wonderful novel, *The Widow's Path*. What a surprise to see you here tonight *and* with Will Foster. Is there some news you'd like to share with us?" Her tone was cheeky, perhaps thinking she came across as charming and amusing.

Irritation coursed through me and I glared at her while keeping a chilly smile on my face.

"Will is a good friend of my best friend and we were introduced this week. He's offered to help promote The Widow's Path Foundation in its efforts to help the families of fallen soldiers."

Unbothered by my icy response or attempt to shame her, she cooed appreciatively.

"How wonderful for the foundation. Do you have any comment on the current investigation into the embezzlement of its funds?"

Before I could answer, Will squeezed me to his side and leaned in.

"There isn't any comment to be made other than Tony Lyleson is the scum of the Earth, stealing money from the families whose loved ones made the ultimate sacrifice for their country. They'll catch him and throw his butt in jail."

I smiled up at him gratefully and turned back to the reporter.

"My sentiments exactly."

The reporter gave a suspicious smirk and moved the microphone back in front of me.

"What a lovely gown. Who are you wearing tonight?"

"I haven't a clue," I said nonchalantly. "It's borrowed." With that, Will whisked me back into obscurity and the darkness behind the stage.

Chapter 32

Pepper threw back the rest of her martini and scanned the crowd for Will and Vivienne. They sat beside one another in a booth at the back of Chateau Marmont Restaurant. She watched them laugh and talk, this time more pleased at their easy body language.

Vivienne appeared relaxed, toying with the unfinished glass of champagne in front of her. Will's right arm rested on the back of the booth and only slightly on her shoulders. Pepper sighed when they touched foreheads for a second and then laughed about something.

She didn't give one whit about all of Viv's protestations. Her best friend had looked lovely tonight, on the red carpet and while watching the premiere. She knew Viv was quaking on the inside, but her outward appearance had been flawless. Pepper had always thought Vivienne would have made the better actress. No one ever knew what was going on inside her head because her face was always calm and serene.

Setting her glass on passing waiter's tray, Pepper reached into her bag for her phone to send Vivienne a text saying she would grab a cab. She felt a tap on her shoulder.

"Pepper Taylor?"

"Yes?" She turned and her eyes opened wide in surprise. There before her stood one of the most powerful men in Hollywood and the president of EJR Productions.

"I'm Gabriel Seigal."

"Yes, I know." Pepper extended her hand. "It's a pleasure to meet you."

"It's nice to meet you, too." Gabriel squeezed her hand.

Pepper liked his wavy, brown hair with the flecks of gray shooting through it. He had kind, blue eyes. His hand was rough but warm, and he smelled of cigar smoke, scotch and leather. His best feature was that he was actually taller than she, even with her four-inch heels.

"I see you're a friend of Vivienne Stark." His cultured British accent made her shiver.

"Yes." Pepper's shoulders deflated the tiniest bit. All night she had been approached by various members of the Hollywood crowd inquiring about Vivienne. Pepper wasn't jealous, but frustrated because Vivienne had no interest in the contacts she could make, and Pepper would give her eye teeth to have the ear of any one of them.

"She's a lovely woman."

"Yes, I know. We've been friends since we were kids."

"Really?" Gabriel looked surprised. "I hope she goes with EJR Productions. I'm dying to get my hands on the project."

"I'm afraid I can't help you there." Pepper stared at her hands clutching her purse. "We're pals, but she doesn't talk business with me."

"No, that's not what I mean," Gabriel said quickly. He shuffled from foot to foot. "I suppose I'm going to sound foolish, but I wanted an excuse to speak with you, and your association with Ms. Stark seemed to be my way in."

Pepper was startled by his honesty.

"Why would you need an excuse to talk to me? I've been here all night."

Gabriel looked abashed.

"It's taken me all evening just to approach you. You see, I'm not used to being in the company of such a beautiful woman."

Pepper laughed heartily.

"Come on! You've directed some of the hottest women in the world!"

"Directed, yes. Worked with, yes. *Conversed with*, no." Pepper could see a deep flush creep up his neck and she felt at once he was genuine.

She looked at him, tossed her head and grinned. Touching his arm, she said, "Well, you can talk to me. I'm just a regular person in better packaging today. You should see me after cleaning my apartment or a night without sleep."

Gabriel's flushed cheeks cooled.

"Would you care for a drink?"

Pepper hesitated and tilted her head downward.

"I was just about to leave, actually. Grab a cab, head home." She threw her thumb back toward the door behind her.

The dejection in his voice was unmistakable and he pulled away.

"Oh. Another time, then."

"Would you like to get a bite to eat?" Pepper reached for his arm again. "Someplace a little less crowded?"

Gabriel's eyes lit up.

"Yes! I have a car. I'll go get it." He turned to leave, and Pepper squeezed his arm.

"Wait! Let me go say goodbye to Viv. Would you like to come with me?"

"No, no, you go ahead. I said hello to her earlier and I don't wish her to think me a pest. I'll get the car and meet you around front." Gabriel grinned and then raced from the restaurant.

Tittering, Pepper hurried to Will and Vivienne's table.

"I'm outta here, guys."

"What? Where are you going?" Vivienne demanded.

"I just scored myself a date."

"With whom?" Vivienne leaned forward.

"Someone nice, I think. You wouldn't know him." Pepper reached across the table and kissed each of them on the cheek. "I'll call you tomorrow."

"Have fun!" Will raised his glass to her.

"Be good!" Vivienne called out.

"If I can't be good, I'll be careful!" Pepper winked and then dashed away.

Chapter 33

Between kisses, Will forced me to admit I'd had a good time. When we left the party and got into the limo, he pulled me onto his lap to press his lips against mine. I tried to protest, but he was insistent and my heart fluttered. He was exquisitely adept at making me lose all willpower to resist.

"I don't—"

Kiss!

"—think—"

Kiss!

"—we should—"

Kiss!

"—be doing—"

Kiss!

And then I did that letting go thing again. No alcohol for an excuse this time, I just decided to live in the moment.

When the car pulled up in front of the hotel, we stopped kissing long enough for me to straighten my dress and hair and for Will to adjust his tie and jacket. Ever the gentleman, he helped me out and then tipped an imaginary hat to the doorman as he held the door for us. I grinned at the ridiculousness of it. My heels clacked loudly on the marble floor of the lobby as Will guided me to the elevators.

When the doors opened, I stepped inside alone. Will remained outside. I looked at him with a confused expression.

"Well, I think I'll say goodnight."

"What?" My eyes flew open, locking onto his.

"I wouldn't want to take advantage or anything—"

I grabbed his tie and yanked him inside just before the doors slid shut.

Chapter 34

Pepper didn't get home until the sun began its rise. She replayed in her mind parts of her nine-hour date with Gabriel Seigal, as she unlocked the door and stepped inside. Her cell phone vibrated unexpectedly and she fought to get it out of her purse and close the door at the same time.

"Hello?" She didn't bother to check the number.

"I wanted to hear your voice one more time."

"Gabe, that's sweet," Pepper said. "But this isn't my voice anymore. After nine hours, I'm hoarse."

"Very well. Ring me when your voice returns."

"I will."

"Do you think it will be back in an hour?"

Pepper barked out a partial laugh.

"Probably not. I *will* call you later, though, I promise."

"All right then. Goodbye."

"Bye."

Pepper ended the call and tossed the phone on the couch. She felt luckier than a lottery winner as she eased her tired body down. Stripping off her sandals, Pepper shivered with the memory of Gabriel's brief, chaste, goodnight kiss.

He had whisked her away from the party to a quiet little all-night diner thirty minutes outside of LA. After his initial nervousness vanished, they ate and talked for five hours about the movie business, how they'd each gotten into it, family history.

You name it and we talked about it, she thought fondly.

They interrupted each other whenever a new opinion or memory or story popped into their heads. They finished each other's sentences when they found something they agreed on. It had been the kind of date Pepper could never have dreamed up.

Fearing they would be asked to pay rent, Gabriel took her to the beach, where they sat and walked and talked for four more hours. When she finally thought she would collapse with exhaustion, Pepper begged him to take her home. He was sweetly apologetic and honored her wishes.

Hugging herself, Pepper smiled, hopeful that the evening hadn't been a dream but could actually mean something.

Pulling herself up to finally go to bed, her phone rang again. Giggling, she grabbed it and flipped it open.

"Gabriel, I said I'd call you later."

"It's Will. I fucked up."

Pepper was fired back into wakefulness like a gunshot.

"What are you talking about? Where's Vivienne?"

"I left her at the hotel sleeping."

Pepper exhaled with relief.

"How did you fuck up?" She walked to her fridge and grabbed a bottle of water to offer some relief to her parched throat.

"I *left*."

"So what?"

"I shouldn't have." Will voice was watery and weak, like he had just vomited.

Pepper sighed.

"Then why did you?"

"I don't know!"

"All right, calm down." Pepper took a swallow. "Where are you now?"

"Home."

"Have you slept?"

"No."

"Well, I suggest you do. Unless you plan on driving back to the hotel right now, there's nothing else you *can* do."

"I can't sleep," Will groaned.

"Look, I'm not coming over to read you a bedtime story," Pepper snapped. Rubbing her eyes, she apologized. "I haven't been to bed myself and I'm exhausted."

Juggling the water and the phone, she tried to get undressed, only spilling a little bit of the water and leaving her dress in a heap on the floor.

"Will, be honest with me and tell me what's really going on."

She could hear him opening his mouth and closing it again.

Finally, he said, "I did it again."

"What?"

"I ran. I chickened out. The old Will popped into my head and I bailed."

"But tell me why. What made you do it?" Pepper pinned the phone between her ear and shoulder as she wrestled off her bra and panties.

"That's the hell of it," Will sighed. "I can't. It felt almost like a reflex. It's what I normally do, so it's what I needed to do. Does that make any sense?"

Pepper smirked.

"Makes perfect sense."

"But I got home," he continued, "and I can smell her perfume on the sheets. It's like she's right *here*."

Pepper stifled a chuckle by taking another drink of water. As she crawled into bed, she whispered, "Aw, Will, you've got it bad."

"That's what I'm afraid of." His voice was barely audible.

"Nothing to do about it now." Pepper yawned. "Either go back to the hotel and face her or wait till you're both awake and coherent." When he didn't say anything, Pepper's brows furrowed. "Do you love her?"

"I don't know."

"I think you need to figure that out first, don't you?" Pepper said the words softly, not wanting him to feel any worse than he obviously did.

"I've been trying."

"Well you aren't going to at six in the morning on no sleep." Pepper frowned and rubbed her eyes again.

"You aren't helping me." Will was getting peevish.

"I can't give you answers I don't have, Will."

"She doesn't love me, Pep."

"Maybe not yet. But that doesn't mean she can't."

"What if she *chooses* not to?"

Pepper was saddened by the despondent tone of his voice.

"Then you deal with it." She hated saying that to him, but Pepper knew how stubborn Vivienne could be. If Viv wasn't willing to stay in California, she wanted Will to be prepared for that. She wouldn't lie to him or Vivienne.

"That does *not* help." The churlishness returned.

"I'm sorry, Will. I can only bully Viv so far. Getting her to go out partying or shopping or even walking the red carpet is one thing. Making her fall in love is out of my control."

"Shit."

"Exactly. Try to get some sleep. If I know Viv, she'll call you later."

Chapter 35

When I woke up around nine, Will was gone. I was mostly disappointed, but a tiny bit relieved, too. I needed some time to myself. But I did snuggle back into the comforter and pillows to get another nose full of his cologne. I had no idea what it was. It reminded me of the ocean and clean sheets, and I was stunned to find myself missing him. I didn't expect him to leave without waking me or saying goodbye. Reluctantly, I let go of the covers and crawled out of bed. I spied the note he wrote and grabbed it up, happy he had taken the time to leave it. He said he'd call later and I trusted that he would.

My stomach growled loudly and I couldn't remember the last time I'd had anything decent to eat. I ordered a huge breakfast from room service and then took a hot shower. When the food arrived, I rolled the cart out to the balcony so I could enjoy my meal outside. I sat in my bathrobe, hair wrapped in a thick white towel and contemplated the food before me. Suddenly I found myself lonesome. I didn't mind eating alone, preferred it, in fact, but something was missing. I hated admitting it, even if just to myself, but I wished Will was with me.

Trying to put him out of my mind, I proceeded to stuff myself with eggs, pancakes and coffee until I thought I would either throw up or go into a carb coma. It didn't work. The whole time I ate, I went over every moment together since we met.

I tossed my napkin onto my empty plate and flopped back in the chair. The towel unraveled from my head and dropped to the floor, allowing my still damp hair to cascade behind me in a wave of tangles. I put my hands into it and rubbed vigorously giving it a crazy, snarled look. The now-hot sunshine baked my face and I could almost taste the salty ocean as the smell filled my nose.

"You're such an idiot," I said out loud. Then I laughed, but it sounded bitter to my ears. How had I gotten myself into this mess? I never should have come to California, no matter the circumstances. Had I stayed home, I would not have met Will and I wouldn't be so conflicted about what to do with the rest of my life. I'd have stayed ignorantly buried in my safe little cave in Michigan.

Instead, I was swimming in a sea of smarts. Knowledge of things I hadn't had in years, stuff I wasn't sure I wanted to know about. What it felt like to sleep beside someone all night long and then wake up with him. What it was like to have a best friend to do things with whenever the whim struck. What it meant to have a fulfilling life instead of just an existence. But now that it was all in my head, I couldn't turn it off or run away from it. I was going to have to force myself to face it all.

With no one to see or hear or know, I admitted the things that were hardest for me. I wanted to stay in California. I wanted to play with Pepper. I wanted to leave Bruce and Michigan behind. I wanted to write more books and spend my life doing the things I wanted to do without being afraid or worried about what other people thought. I wanted to be irresponsible and spontaneous. I wanted to live the next twenty years of my life like I wished I'd lived the last twenty. I wanted a do-over.

The thing is, I couldn't do all of that. I had a home and responsibilities in Michigan that I couldn't just walk away from. The economy was in the toilet and I'd never sell my house. My mom was damn near 80 years old, and I couldn't leave her all alone. Pepper would poo-poo them as trivial matters, problems easily solved just to get me out to the West Coast. It would be easy for her to say, she wouldn't have to deal with the repercussions of the hasty decisions my libido wanted me to make.

I knew there was nothing wrong with wanting to stay in California. I also accepted that there was no problem with wanting Will in my life on a more permanent basis. But what was difficult was dealing with the fact that I couldn't have those things now that I knew I wanted them. I felt like a child who couldn't have the toy she demanded.

I was going to have to face facts. I would be going home, probably sooner than later, so as not to prolong the agony. I was going to have to break this news to Pepper and she was not going to be happy. Last, I would have to talk to Will. I know we had promised not to get attached, but I needed to be honest with him. I wanted him to know how important he was to me and how much I appreciated all he'd taught me.

I thought I was completely resigned to my fate, but then my cell phone rang. *Ahh, Mom.* Julie Andrews' "My Favorite Things" floated out of the phone and into the air.

"Good morning!" I chirped, after I answered it.

"Well good morning to you, too! But it's afternoon here." I loved how I could always hear Mom's smile in her voice.

"Well, whatever. How the heck are ya?"

"I'm okay. Just doing my thing. I saw something interesting on television last night."

"Oh?" My eyebrows raised. And then my breakfast whipped around like a tornado in my stomach. *The premiere!*

"I was watching channel four and they were talking about a local celebrity being on the red carpet."

I stopped thinking about losing my breakfast when I heard Mom's muffled laughter.

"Uh, oh. You saw that, huh?"

"Yes, young lady, I did."

"I was going to call you—"

"You looked *wonderful!*" Mom said, her voice breathless with excitement. "I wish you *had* called me so I could have been prepared. I would have recorded it on the DVR. Wherever did you get that gorgeous dress?"

I took in a deep breath and let it out slowly, relieved that Mom sounded happy.

"Pepper had a costumer friend who loaned it to me. It was a last-minute thing that came up and we decided to go."

"It was the perfect choice for you, dear. I don't recall you ever looking quite that beautiful," Mom whispered. *Was she crying?*

"Thank you, Mom. I appreciate that. I was really nervous, though. I've never been in a situation like that. Did I look scared?"

"No!" Mom said with a little irritation. "I'm telling you, you looked absolutely great. But who was that handsome young man you were with? Not another loan from Pepper?" She laughed at her own joke.

"Heh, not at all. His name is Will and he *is* Pepper's friend, but technically I guess you could call him my date for the evening."

"I see."

I couldn't tell what she meant by that.

"He's just a friend, though. A new friend."

"Well, I'll take your word for it, but he certainly seemed like more than just a friend."

I choked on the sip of coffee I had been taking.

"What do you mean?"

"What do you think? Vivienne, he looks at you like he's madly in love with you. It's the same look your father gave me for forty-four years."

Tears instantly filled my eyes and dripped down my cheeks. I knew the look she meant. I'd seen it myself all my life up until the day Dad died. It was the look I had always wanted from Bruce.

"You're just imagining things, Mom."

"Bet me and lose," Mom muttered.

"What was that?" I was trying to wipe my face on the sleeve of my robe and hadn't caught what she said.

"Never mind. Where did you meet Will?"

"Pepper introduced us a few nights ago when we went to a bar to hear a few bands play. I guess they met when he came out to LA a few years after she did. He's a really nice guy." Leaving out the more intimate details, I told her we'd spent some time together and with Pepper. "The premiere was really more for publicity than anything else."

"For the foundation?"

Damn, Mom caught on fast.

"Yes. You see, Will and I went to dinner the other night and a bunch of our pictures turned up in the tabloids and on the Internet. My agent thought it would be a good idea to go out again so it would look like I was trying to cultivate a relationship with Will for the foundation."

"The news said he's a musician."

"Yep. He's the lead singer for a band called Static Neverland."

"Never heard of them," Mom admitted, then laughed. "But I suppose you know that already."

"Yeah, that's why I didn't really tell you about any of this. I didn't think it would matter to you." That was the thing, though, everything that happened to me always mattered to my mom. She loved me and was proud of me.

"Of course it does! I would have been furious with you if I hadn't gotten to see you in that dress on the red carpet. I know I'm not much of a Hollywood celebrity watcher or anything, but of course I would be where my own daughter is concerned!"

It was good to talk to Mom about the event. I told her about how nervous I'd been and how angry I was to have to do it in the first place. As if I was there all over again, I remembered the night at the restaurant when all the photographers converged on us. Mom clucked and "for shamed" the paparazzi for interfering with our privacy. I recounted the party at Will's house and how the band had played for the people there that night. I described how we had bumped into each other at the bar and how Pepper had used that as an opportunity to introduce us. When I finally stopped talking, it occurred to me that I had worked my whole timeline with Will back to the beginning for Mom. Such a short period of time, but we had bonded so much.

"I have to say, Vivienne, you sound much happier than you have in years. *Years*."

I didn't know how to respond, so I said nothing.

"When do you think you'll be coming home?" Mom asked suddenly. The question surprised me.

"Oh, soon, I'm sure. Jake and I are having lunch today to make some final decisions about the movie deal and what's going to happen with the foundation. I think he might have a couple more interviews set up for me, but I'd like to get home before the middle of the week." As the words left my mouth, I knew they weren't true. "There's really no reason for me to stay."

"Hmm," Mom murmured. "Maybe you should stay for a little while longer? You haven't seen Pepper in so many years. I think the time with her would do you good."

I stood up then to lean on the railing of the balcony. Mom had no idea how much she had hit the nail on the head. "Well, I can't mooch off the movie studio forever. Once I make my offer, they're going to want me to get out of this hoity-toity hotel."

"So stay with Pepper for a while."

"Mom, I can't—"

"Why *not?*" she demanded.

I held the phone away from my face to stare in surprise at her profile picture on the screen. The conversation was turning weird, like she was reading my mind.

"No, Mom. I need to get back home. I've got my house to take care of, and—"

"Don't you dare say me. Don't even *think* about coming home just to take care of me." The edge in her voice was the same one she used on me when I was a kid and was hinting at doing something stupid.

"I wasn't going to say that," I said meekly.

"I would hope not. I am perfectly capable of seeing to my own welfare." Mom sniffed, clearly offended.

"Of course you are!" I assured her. "I need to get home so I can get back to work. I'm going to need to pump out a book a week if I plan on paying back the foundation." It was the only valid reason I could give her.

"Hmm." I could hear the doubt in her voice. "I don't think you're being honest with me."

Dammit. She could always tell when I wasn't telling the truth.

"Look, Mom, I will be honest. I *am* tempted to stay for a while. I've had a lot of fun with Pepper and the weather is awesome."

"What about Will?"

Dammit! How was I supposed to answer that?

"What about Will?" I answered her question with one of my own.

Mom sighed and I knew she was frustrated with me.

"Vivienne Astrid Stark, you make my brain itch."

I burst out laughing in spite of her anger.

"I'm sorry, Mom. I don't mean to."

"I know you don't *mean* to. But you do. I told you I could see how Will looks at you. I was hoping not to have to say I could see *you* looking at *him* the same way."

I groaned and closed my eyes. A picture of Will floated in my mind's eye. Handsome as ever.

"Mom, I don't want to talk about this."

"I know that. But I think you should. It sounds like the two of you have become quite close in these last few days. Tell the truth now."

"Yes," I whispered. "I like him very much."

"Honey, that's *great*! Then why don't you stay? I can look after your house and make sure things are okay. You have your laptop, so do your writing out there. I heard you say there was no reason for you to stay, but I think you have lots of reasons. You only have one reason to come home. I don't want to be it, please, I don't."

I could feel the tears threatening again. "Mom, it's not *just* you, but you are a big reason for me to stay in Michigan. There's only us. You don't have anyone else, if you need anything."

"Piffle! I have plenty of friends and neighbors I can rely on. If you come home and throw away your chances at having a normal life, I'd never be able to live with myself. I'd feel guilty forever."

"Stop! You wouldn't have anything to feel guilty about. I'm a big girl and I can make my own decisions. There are lots of things going on in my head right now that I can't begin to explain to you. But no matter what I decide, promise me you won't blame yourself. I'm looking at every angle right now, not just the mom angle."

"Do *you* promise I'm not your sole reason for coming home?"

"I promise, Mom."

"Then I promise not to feel responsible if you make any unwise choices."

"Mom—"

"No, I'm going to have my say. You can look at all your angles and make all kinds of excuses, but you can't turn your back on happiness." She hesitated ever so slightly, then started talking faster. "This is my fault. I've always babied you, kept you too close. When Bruce died, I should have kicked you to the curb and forced you to make a new life for yourself. Instead, I let you wallow around here for too long and by the time you did leave, you were too mired down in your guilt and depression to live like a normal person."

I was stunned by her words. I couldn't have disagreed more. My mother, and Dad to some degree, had been my biggest supporters in the darkest days after I lost Bruce. In my view, she was the one who kept me from going off the deep end. I had lived with her and Dad for six years after becoming a widow before finally deciding to buy my own house and that was only because I'd been able to save a down payment in those years. She hadn't coddled me. She had given me the time I needed to get some strength back. Maybe not strength enough to find another relationship, but certainly the fortitude to live, period.

"You're nuts," I said with feigned petulance.

Chuckling, she continued, "Think what you want, Vivienne, but you need to consider the rest of your life very carefully. I won't be around forever, and you can't use me as an excuse to keep from moving forward. You'd only be a phone call or plane ride away."

How did this all get started? I had thought we were going to chit chat about nothing and somehow we'd gotten embroiled in a weird conversation I'd had no intention of having.

"That's enough for now, Mom."

"Yes, you're right. I've said my piece and now it's up to you. Think carefully and make the right choice for *yourself*, Vivienne. You need to be the priority now."

Smiling, I made a kissing sound at the phone.
"Thanks, Mom. I love you and I'll talk to you later."

Chapter 36

Pepper was dreaming about Gabriel and walking on the beach. The dream was so real. She thought she could feel the sand scratching between her toes and hear her favorite song playing. When the music stopped, Pepper felt sad, but then it began again.

That's my phone, Pepper's conscious mind said within the dream and she clawed her way to wakefulness. On the nightstand beside her bed, the cell phone frolicked and bounced, blaring "Merry Go Round" by the Jane Dear Girls. Before she could grasp it, the music cut off and "missed call" filled the display. Pepper groaned and let her head fall back onto her pillow, but within seconds the phone repeated its serenade.

"Hello?" she muttered, answering the call with her eyes closed and no clue who it could be.

"Good morning, sleepyhead!" Vivienne sang.

"What time is it?" Pepper snuggled deeper beneath her blanket, tilting her head to balance the phone on her cheek and ear so she didn't have to hold on to it.

"Actually, it's afternoon now. It's quarter to one. Are you still in bed?"

Pepper yawned.

"Uh huh."

"What time did you get in?"

"Dunno."

"*Wake up!*" Vivienne called out, laughing as she did so. "I want you to come have lunch with Jake and me."

Pepper groaned inwardly, wanting only to stay where she was and hopefully return to the pleasant dream she'd been having. What would she do at a lunch with Vivienne and her agent, besides listen and be bored?

"Nah," she croaked, her voice still wounded from the night before.

"Are you coming down with something?" Vivienne asked.

"No, I'm just really tired."

"Oh, poo. Come on, I really want you to be there."

"Why?" Pepper's eyes fluttered open against her will. Sighing, she reached up to catch the phone as it slid off her face when she sat up. She threw the covers off, then swung her legs over the side, surprised at the soreness she felt from all the walking last night.

"Because! I've got a lot of decisions to make and you're a really good voice of reason for me. Please, won't you come?" Vivienne pleaded. "Plus, I had a really long conversation with my mom this morning and I want to talk to you about that, too."

Pepper smiled as she walked to the bathroom.

"Okay, Viv. Anything for you. Is Mom okay?"

"Oh yeah, she's great. Feisty as ever."

"What time is lunch?"

"Well, it was supposed to be here at the hotel at one-ish. But I'll push it back and we'll come pick you up. I'll have Jake make reservations at a restaurant. How's that?"

"Perfect."

"Thank you!" Vivienne sounded relieved and excited at the same time.

"Don't thank me yet. I'm starving and you're paying, right?"

"Of course!" Vivienne laughed. "Pick you up about two?"

"I'll see you then." Pepper hung up and chuckled as she started the water to the shower. While she shampooed and conditioned her hair, she went over her date with Gabriel in her mind, alternately praising herself for some witty repartee and kicking herself over a dorky remark. All in all, she felt good about the time she spent with him and was confident there would be a second date in the near future.

She really wanted to tell Vivienne about Gabriel, but didn't dare. It was obvious to Pepper that Vivienne should and probably would go with Gabriel's company, EJR Productions, for the movie rights, but Pepper didn't want to exercise any undue influence.

Climbing out of the tub, she cursed herself for forgetting a towel and walked naked and dripping to the bedroom where she picked one out of the dirty clothes pile in the corner. It didn't smell bad, so she used it to bundle her blond locks and then dried her body with a tee-shirt from a couple of days before. Standing in her walk-in closet, she pulled on fresh panties and a bra. While she was choosing her clothes, she heard the phone go off again and hurried to pick it up. It was Will and Pepper frowned.

"Hey, what's up?" she asked.

"Nothing. I called Vivienne this morning but she didn't answer." Will sounded as though he had not slept a wink and he confirmed it when Pepper asked.

"I know she's busy today. She's got a lunch with her agent at two and then I don't know what else afterward." Pepper contemplated inviting him along, but then decided against it. Vivienne had sounded so happy earlier, she didn't want to chance ruining her good mood with another surprise. But then again, she liked Will. A lot. *What the hell?* Pepper thought.

"She invited me to go with her at lunch. Maybe you should come, too?"

"No, I don't think so."

"You *obviously* want to see her. Why not tag along? How fast can you get to my place?" Pepper pulled her phone away to check the time. It was only 1:15 p.m. Shoving the phone back to her ear and holding it in place with her shoulder, she continued to flip through the clothes hanging in her closet.

"I think that might piss her off." Will sounded skeptical but excited at the same time.

"So what? If it does, it does. Then you have your answer. And if it doesn't, then you can keep wooing her." Pepper giggled, then snorted, then giggled some more.

"Easy for *you* to say," Will growled. "You aren't the one who'll look like an asshole for showing up uninvited."

"No, I'll be the asshole who invited you."

Waiting for Will to think it over and respond, Pepper clicked the speaker button and put the phone on the bed while she donned a pair of royal purple Capri pants and a plain black tee-shirt. She slipped her feet into a comfortable pair of black flip flops decorated with fake rhinestones. Grabbing the phone she moved back into the bathroom to work on hair and makeup.

"Make up your mind pal. You gonna do this thing or not?"

Will sighed.

"Okay. I can be there in about twenty minutes."

"Good, because they're picking me up at two. Get your ass in gear."

Pepper ended the call before he could respond, then worked on drying and styling her hair and putting on a fresh face of makeup.

Twenty minutes later, she sat on the steps outside her apartment, waiting to see who would show up first: Will or Vivienne. Luckily it was he, rather than she, and Pepper gave him a winning smile and firm hug for support.

"I still don't know about this, Pep." He was as nervous as a groom on his wedding day, hands sweaty and anxiety written all over his face. But he was freshly shaved and showered, looking incredibly hot in motorcycle boots, jeans, and a plain white tee-shirt with a dark blue chambray shirt over top.

"It's too late to back out now," Pepper said, pointing for him to turn around. Marvin the driver pulled up in his black Lincoln Town Car and hopped out to help them in. The look on Vivienne's face when she saw Will was all pleasure at first, then surprise, and lastly confused and a little irritated. Pepper was relieved that happiness was the first reaction.

"Viv, I hope you don't mind, I invited Will along. He stopped by to see me and I couldn't very well leave him out in the cold." Pepper grinned her signature toothy grin, waiting for the controlled response she knew Vivienne would give.

"Of course not!" Vivienne surprised them all by leaning over and kissing Will full on the lips and grabbing his hands. Pepper had pushed him in first, so he had scooted across the seat to be across from Viv, and Pepper now faced Jake Rushmore who looked amused as hell.

"Jake, this is my very best friend Pepper Taylor," Vivienne pointed left, and then to the right, "and Will Foster."

"Pleasure," Jake answered, shaking both their hands. "I'm glad you're both joining us today. Vivienne needs to make some decisions and I can't get her to do it."

"Heh," Pepper snorted and Vivienne kicked her in the shin.

"You two seem to have gotten her to do more in the last few days than I've ever been able to. I'll lay out her options and then she can bounce all her doubts off you." Jake smirked and nodded his head at Vivienne, who returned his haughty look of derision with her own.

When they arrived at Fig & Olive, they were seated immediately in spite of the reservation having been made for only two. Jake assured them it happened all the time when celebrities showed up with a bigger entourage than intended, and didn't give a hoot how much of a pain in the ass it was to rearrange everything. Vivienne apologized profusely to the person who seated them, and Pepper thanked them at least three times for their efforts.

As they perused the menus, Pepper and Vivienne chattered with one another while Jake and Will talked about the band and other business. While her answers about her date from the night before were fairly vague, they satisfied Vivienne's curiosity, and Pepper changed the subject. She caught some of what Will and Jake were talking about, and it sounded like Jake was fishing for Will's business for representation.

"Hey now, if you're looking for new clients, I'm available," she teased, giving Vivienne a wink.

"That's not a bad idea, actually," Jake said as he sipped a glass of wine. "Given your friendship with Vivienne, I could probably find you some decent opportunities."

Pepper's face looked pinched and she rolled her eyes.

"Uh, thanks. I think."

Vivienne glared at Jake, but he didn't seem to notice he had screwed up. Will saved him by changing the subject to The Widow's Path Foundation. Eventually, the talk of business subsided somewhat as their meals arrived and the delicious food served as a silencer.

Halfway through lunch, Jake stopped eating and commandeered Vivienne's attention.

"Regarding the movie rights, I think your decision is clear. Gleaming Bee is offering the most money."

Pepper watched Vivienne shake her head and finish chewing and swallowing a bite of her salmon before answering.

"I don't care about the money. Their vision for the script is too far off track from the book. EJR is willing to stay more true to the story, and I would feel better letting them have it, even if they aren't offering the same amount."

Atta girl! Pepper cheered silently.

"I think you're being foolish," Jake countered. "You keep saying you want to repay the foundation and you could almost do it in one fell swoop if you take Gleaming Bee's offer."

Shut up, you idiot! Pepper raved in her head.

Vivienne sat back in her chair and raised her water to her lips, clearly thinking it over by the furrow of her brows and look of intense concentration.

"May I say something?" Will raised his right hand a couple of inches off the table. He looked directly at Vivienne, waiting for her approval. She nodded enthusiastically, waving her hand for him to go ahead. "Are you asking for a percentage of the profits when the movie comes out?" He looked to Jake for the answer.

"EJR is offering a percentage and a lower cash payment. Gleaming Bee just wants to buy the rights flat out for about a third more." Jake glanced at Vivienne. "I'm not comfortable speaking exact numbers in mixed company. No offense, of course."

"None taken," Will replied, while Pepper only nodded. "Then I think if you want to go with EJR, you should, Vivienne. If the movie is a hit, you can pay back the foundation not only with the upfront payment, but also with the proceeds that come in from movie sales. It might take a little longer if the movie doesn't do well, but I'm thinking it'll be a hit if the public likes it as much as the book. The only way they'll do that is if you go with a company who sticks to the story."

Jake glowered at Will, clearly irritated with the musician's opinion on the matter. Seeing this, Pepper smirked and spoke up.

"Yeah," she threw a thumb in Will's direction, "what he said."

Vivienne laughed and reached to take each one of their hands.

"Thank you very much, both of you, for your input. I have to say, Will, your insight is amazing because I was thinking the exact same thing." Turning to Jake and his unhappy face, she firmed up her posture and voice. "Make the call, Jake. Do the deal with EJR."

Jake sighed and his shoulders deflated a little.

"All right, if that's really what you want. Can I at least try to work the numbers more in your favor?"

"Go ahead, but don't piss them off. I want them." Pepper was trembling in her seat, trying not to shout with glee, and Vivienne could see her excitement.

"Geeze, Pep, you're almost more excited than me!"

"Oh, that's my usual state," Pepper breathed. "You know me, over the top all the time." She brayed a fake laugh and then followed it with a real one.

"Let's have a toast," Will suggested. He signaled for the waiter and asked for a bottle of champagne. While they waited for it, Jake's cell jangled obnoxiously and he whipped it out of his jacket breast pocket. Excusing himself, he left the table to walk through the restaurant, talking loudly the whole way.

Will fiddled with his hands, avoiding eye contact with Vivienne, but he spoke to her, anyway.

"I hope you don't mind me busting in on your party here." His voice was soft and he sounded embarrassed.

"Well, I was a little surprised to see you," Vivienne admitted. "But it was a nice surprise. I missed you this morning."

"Should I leave?" Pepper waved her hands to remind them of her presence.

Will smirked and flipped her off, causing both women to laugh out loud.

"Besides, I know it was Pepper's idea to bring you along. She orchestrates everything." Vivienne waggled her eyebrows at Pepper, who pretended to whistle and look around the restaurant.

"I'm sorry I left—"

"That's okay." Vivienne placed a hand over one of his. "I was able to have a nice long chat with my Mom. That's why I didn't call you back."

Pepper watched relief wash over Will's face and was glad to see him visibly relax, but thought Vivienne jumped to assure him a little too quickly. *What's going on with her?* she wondered.

The waiter returned with the champagne and four flutes, and Will took it from him, saying he would pour when their fourth returned. Nodding, the waiter left with a nod and a smile. Will passed the glasses around and then set the bottle on the table. Pepper was about to ask Vivienne what her plans for the rest of the day were, when *her* cell phone went off rather unexpectedly.

I'm with all the important people, she thought. "Now who could that be?" she wondered aloud as she reached inside her purse. Her face instantly flushed red when she saw Gabriel Seigal's name on the display.

"Shit! I have to take this! I'll be right back." Jumping up, her knees struck the edge of the table causing silverware and dishes to tinkle and crash against each other as she rushed away.

Chapter 37

As Will and I watched Pepper bolt from the restaurant, Jake returned and was nearly bowled over by the departing blond.

"Where's Pepper going?" he asked.

"Not sure," I said. "She got a phone call, too."

"Well, you can fill her in later." Jake sat back down and scooted closer to the table to place his elbows on the surface, his fingers laced beneath his chin. "I have some very interesting news."

I raised my eyebrows and then glanced over at Will, who shrugged and turned his attention back to Jake.

"That was the police."

We both leaned forward with twin expressions of shock.

"They think they know where Tony is."

"Did they trace the phone call?" Will asked. "Is he under arrest?"

"Where's the money?" I growled.

"Hold on!" Jake laughed in spite of himself. "No, they didn't trace the phone call. They didn't have to. It turns out, one Lyle Anthony opened a credit card in his real name as an officer of the foundation and the police have tracked him to Amsterdam."

"What a fucking moron!" I yelled causing other patrons to glare at me. "His real name is Lyle Anthony?" Jake nodded. "And he opened up a credit card in his *real name*?" Jake nodded again. "I cannot believe anyone smart enough to get away with cashing a forged check would be so damn stupid!"

Jake shook his head.

"He didn't act alone, either. His sister, Lola Anthony, was the teller at the bank the day he cashed the check. That's why the forged signature went through."

"Good grief." I sighed, lowering my face into my hands.

"So what happens now?" Will asked.

"LAPD is working with the Netherlands to apprehend him and extradite him back to the States for prosecution."

"Where's the money?" I raised my head and peered at Jake hopefully. I thought the happy ending might not be so happy if Tony/Lyle had been able to hide the money.

"They're still looking into that, but if he was dumb enough to use his real name and his sister as an accomplice, he probably didn't hide the money very well. But it doesn't really matter because the bank's at fault. They're on the hook and will have to return the money, tout suite."

All at once, laughter began to bubble up from my throat and soon I was roaring with it, covering my mouth in a vain attempt to quiet myself. The thought of Tony, or Lyle, or whoever the hell he was, being brought back to the United States to stand trial was satisfying enough, but knowing all those dollars would be back in the foundation's accounts regardless was icing on the cake.

"Pour that champagne, Will!" I demanded, grabbing a glass and holding it out for him. Giving me a salute, he uncorked the bottle expertly and the frothing liquid squirted out, falling right into my glass. Raising it for a toast, I smiled at them.

"This is truly a good day. I'm surrounded by people who do their best to take good care of me. Thank you for everything you've done."

"And here's to negotiating more money!" Jake added, drawing mirthless looks from Will and me.

Will put his glass into the cluster and stared at me.

"Here's to a long and happy future full of storytelling for you, Vivienne."

My heart beat a little faster at that, and I clasped his free hand with my own.

Chapter 38

"All it says is, 'I'm so sorry, something's come up. I promise I'll call you later.'" Vivienne read me the text message from Pepper with a growing look of concern on her face. "That is *not* like Pepper."

"Sure it is," I scoffed. "She's flighty as hell. Maybe she got a call for a job or audition or something."

"I don't think so, Will. If I wasn't here, *maybe*, but we haven't seen each other in seventeen years. I wouldn't think she'd blow me off like this."

We stood outside the restaurant waiting for the car to come around. Jake stood about five feet away, jawing into his phone again. I scanned the streets, just in case Pepper was still in the vicinity, spying on us. This definitely seemed like a stunt she would pull so that Vivienne and I would be left alone together again.

"She knew I was here. It's not like she abandoned you completely." I grinned at her and slung a friendly arm around her shoulders. She wore a pair Levi's that hugged her curves perfectly and made her legs look longer, a yellow shirt and black, leather blazer. She seemed shorter and I noticed she had on flat shoes instead of the heels I had gotten used to in the last few days. Vivienne didn't seem convinced because she kept staring at her phone.

"Just call her then."

"I *did*," she snapped, then looked up at me and frowned. "I'm sorry. I did call her when you were in the men's room. I got her voicemail, then I got this text."

"So text her back and tell her you're worried."

Marvin appeared at the curb and he leaped out to open the door for us. Vivienne climbed in and scooted across the seat, making room for me. Jake jogged up and got inside behind us to sit across, still arguing with whomever he was on the phone with. Settling herself into the seat, Vivienne tapped out a text and I watched her hit the send button.

"I told her to call me to let me know she's okay, and if I don't hear from her, I'm calling the police."

"That's a little drastic, don't you think?" I tried not to laugh at Vivienne's paranoia. She scowled at me, continuing to stare at the phone like she was trying to will it to ring. It must have worked, because it did.

"Pepper?" she said breathlessly. I could hear Pepper's voice on the other end, but I couldn't make out what she was saying. When Vivienne relaxed and smiled, I smiled, too, and looked out the window into the bright, cloudless day.

"Okay, just call me when you get home. I don't care what time. Bye."

I turned to look back at Vivienne and she was already gazing at me.

"Well?"

"She got a call from her date from last night and he asked her out again."

"So she dumped you for a guy." I nodded, pushing out my bottom lip in an understanding pout.

She reached over and punched me in the arm while giggling like a teenager.

"Technically, I guess you're right, but I'm not offended."

Jake finally ended his call and looked at us with confusion.

"Where's Pepper?"

"She had another engagement," Vivienne told him. "Marvin? Can you take us back to Pepper's apartment so Will can get his car?"

"Of course." Marvin winked at us from the rear-view mirror.

When I had hung up with Pepper in the dawn hours, I had not felt better at all. But I never did feel good when people told me the truth. I could be the worst kind of dumbass when I didn't get what I wanted, especially if I didn't even *know* what I wanted. So I'd made some strong coffee and sat out on my balcony drinking it, hoping I could have an honest conversation with myself. What I came up with was that I really liked Vivienne. I loved the sex, but it wasn't the only reason I liked her. It actually made the liking better. I thought she was a smart, funny, caring person whose take on life was so different from mine, I wanted to spend time with her and learn from her. None of my past girlfriends ever inspired me to learn anything except their bra size or what position in bed they liked best. Vivienne made me want to use my brain, which thrilled me more than anything else. I was nervous when Pepper spontaneously invited me on the lunch outing, but I agreed because I knew I wanted to follow where this thing with Vivienne led.

When we got to Pepper's complex, Marvin pulled the car right up next to my Beamer, but I wouldn't let him get out and open my door. I grabbed Vivienne's hand and pulled her out with me.

"What are you doing for the rest of the afternoon?" I noticed Jake move away to the far end of the seat and I was grateful for some privacy.

Vivienne frowned.

"Jake said he has a couple of magazine interviews for me."

"No I don't!" Jake called from inside the car. Vivienne whipped around to stare at him with her mouth open.

"But you said—"

"Never mind what I said. Take the afternoon off." Jake smiled and turned to speak to Marvin, then he reached over and grabbed the door handle. "I'll talk to you later." He pulled the door closed and Marvin gunned the engine, pulling back into traffic and narrowly missing a red Smart Car whizzing by.

Vivienne feigned anger, placing her hands on her hips.

"*Now* I've been abandoned. I guess you'll have to take me home."

"I have a better idea." I gave her my best sly wink.

Chapter 39

Will was driving his BMW, maneuvering through the traffic in LA with impressive expertise.

"Where are we going?" I asked for the tenth time.

"You'll see."

"Come on! I don't like surprises. Tell me!"

Will laughed and grinned at me as he turned left onto Ventura Boulevard.

"We'll be there in a just a few minutes."

True to his word, about ten minutes later, he turned right into a parking lot and I craned my neck to see what was in the area. It seemed like a normal city block with drugstores and gas stations and the standard 7-11. He parked the car and then came around to open my door to help me out. I kept looking around for what might be our destination, but I wasn't able to figure it out.

Not until he walked me to the front door of Studio City Tattoo.

"What on Earth are we doing here?" I asked, stopping short of going inside.

"I thought it might be a good time for that tattoo."

My mouth dropped open and I took a step backward.

"Oh Will, I can't."

He touched my arm gently and pulled me to his side.

"You don't have to if you really don't want to, Viv. But I'm in the mood for a little ink. How about you watch and see, yeah?"

I looked up into Will's face and was calmed by the patient look in his eyes.

"Okay. We'll see how it goes."

Opening the door for me, Will put his hand on the small of my back to guide me through. I was struck by the display of artwork on every wall and surface. A heavily tattooed girl stood behind the counter running the length of the shop.

"Hi! What can we do for you today?" she asked, not looking up. She was placing a ring display beneath the glass. When she did make eye contact, her mouth opened wide and then she smiled.

"You're Will Foster!"

"Yes, indeed." Will reached to shake her hand. "And you are?"

"I'm Max," she said nervously. "How can we help you?"

"Well, Max, I'm looking to get a piece for this arm." Will shook off his jacket and pushed up the right sleeve of his shirt. "Right here."

"Okay," she stammered. "Did you have an appointment? Uh, I mean, no, of course you don't. You're not on the books. But we can fit you in!"

Will lowered his head slightly and gave her the sexy smile I knew all too well. I turned away so they wouldn't catch my amusement. I busied myself looking at the display racks of various tattoos, while he and Max made arrangements for his piece. I liked flipping through the artwork, remembering how much I had wanted a tattoo of my own when I was younger. Pepper and I had talked about it a lot when we were sixteen and too young to get them, knowing our parents would kill us. She had wanted roses and flowers and butterflies. I had wanted Bugs Bunny. When she left for LA all those years ago, I knew eventually she would have her girly tattoo, and she did. But I'd never gotten my Bugs Bunny. My desire for ink was renewed when my dad died. I thought about getting a tribute piece with his initials and birthdate, but once again I had stalled.

"Viv?"

I turned to Will's voice coming from the other end of the counter.

"They're going to take me right now." He beckoned me over. He stood in front of a black leather chair. I walked toward him, but Max stopped me a few feet before I got there.

"Are you his girlfriend?" The adoration mixed with jealousy in her eyes was disconcerting.

"Uh, no, just a friend."

"Oh, okay!" The envy disappeared, replaced with determination. I backed away from the counter and continued to Will's side.

Placing a hand on his chest, I nodded for him to come close. "I think you have an admirer," I whispered. Will chuckled and rolled his eyes.

"Could you hold on to this for me?" He handed me his coat and shirt, standing before me in his plain white tee. He rolled up the sleeve, exposing his muscular bicep and pale, smooth skin.

"What are you getting?"

"A pinup girl. Right here." He tapped the inner part of his arm. Then he grabbed a piece of paper from the tray beside the chair. On it was a tracing of what the tattoo would look like. It was much smaller than I thought. The girl was seen from the back, looking over her shoulder, with her hands on her hips. She had long, wavy hair and wore a vintage, polka dotted, two-piece bathing suit.

"Very cute. What color will her hair be?"

"I haven't decided yet."

The tattoo artist appeared from behind a long beaded curtain, holding a piece of transfer paper with the pinup girl. "You ready, man?"

"Absolutely," Will said excitedly. He sat down in the chair and held out his arm. "Joe, this is Vivienne. Viv, this is Joe."

"Pleasure." Joe nodded in my direction and then turned his attention back to Will.

"Nice to meet you," I mumbled as I watched him prepare Will's arm. Within minutes, the noise of the tattoo machine filled the air. I was fascinated at first, watching the ink shoot into Will's skin. After a while, the buzzing started to give me a headache, so I decided to get some fresh air.

"You okay?" Will asked, concern furrowing his brow. I was amazed at his pain tolerance. He hadn't flinched once that I could see.

"I'm fine. Just going to get a little air. I'll be right back." When I stepped outside, the sun was still shining and the temperature hovered in the mid-eighties. Max stood outside on the sidewalk smoking a cigarette.

"So how do you know Will?" she asked, tilting her head and blowing smoke into the sky.

"Friend of a friend." I really didn't want to be standing here talking to her, but I had no choice. I didn't have it in me to be rude and walk away.

"Is he single?" Her eyes sparkled with excitement.

"Uh, I'm not sure." That was a question I was not prepared for. Of course he was, but I was overcome with a rush of jealousy. Mentally, I rolled my eyes.

"Think I should ask him out?" Max tossed her cigarette to the pavement and crushed it with the heel of her spiked stiletto. She wore a short, tight skirt, fishnet stockings, and a thin, spaghetti-strap tank top, all in black. Most of her tattoos were black and white, with a few color pieces scattered here and there, but all very tastefully done. Her platinum blond hair was long and pulled up in a messy ponytail on the top of her head. I could see dark roots at her hairline, but that seemed to be the style she was going for. Her makeup was heavy and in line with the Goth style, with thick, black eyeliner and blood red lips.

"Uh, I guess." My voice lacked any enthusiasm, but she didn't seem to notice. She squealed with delight and rushed into the shop.

Shaking my head, I took a deep breath and smiled. In spite of my general lack of confidence in most situations, I was pretty positive her request for a date would be turned down. Regardless of whether or not Will and I were any sort of item, I didn't think he would accept an invitation from someone else until I was long gone back to Michigan.

Although, I was beginning to wonder if I would be going home any time soon. The conversation with my mom that morning had really planted a seed of doubt in my mind. Mom was so insistent that I stay and I knew she only had my best interests at heart. Maybe I could stay for a while, then go home to check on things for a while. I imagined dividing my time between the West Coast and the Midwest. *Could it work?*

Tired of thinking about it all and realizing I'd been gone quite a while, I went back inside the shop. The buzzing noise had stopped. As I moved toward the back, I had to pass Max, who was behind the counter once again. She glared at me like I'd just murdered her kitten. I looked away quickly in my pursuit of Will.

"You're not finished yet, are you?"

"Almost. It's pretty small, so it's not taking that long." Will smiled at me, but turned his arm so I couldn't see the progress. "Don't look yet. I want to wait until it's done."

"All right."

"Have you thought about one for yourself?"

I scrunched up my face.

"Not really. I've been thinking of other things." I glanced around at the hundreds of tattoos on the walls. "I'll keep looking."

"Joe here said he'd do ya," Will waggled his eyebrows, "so don't think too long."

"Heh, right." I snorted and walked away to keep browsing. I liked the idea of an inkpot and quill to signify my writing, but it didn't really have much to do with Dad. I was too old to consider Bugs Bunny anymore. And I really wasn't the flower, dolphin, and butterfly kind of girl.

And then I saw it. It was on the wall, about level with my waist. I might not have noticed it at all if I hadn't reached down to scratch an itch on my knee. It was a feathered quill pen standing up amongst a beautiful swirl of black lines. The background was variant shades of purples and blues outlining the black lines. I knew without a doubt that if I were to get a tattoo, this was it. Squatting down, I leaned in closer to look at the wild, curly black lines. It reminded me of my thought processes when writing. All over the place at first, but when you backed away, it was a tightly woven labyrinth of words.

"I think I found something," I called out over my shoulder in Will's direction. The buzzing of the tattoo gun stopped.

"Just in time," Will answered. I stepped back over to him to watch Joe spray something on his arm. The hint of alcohol told me it had to be an antiseptic. Then he slathered Will's arm with petroleum jelly to protect the fresh piece.

"What do you think?" He leaned close so I could see it better.

I didn't know what to think. The pinup girl now had long, red flowing hair exactly the shade of my own. Her bathing suit was no longer a two-piece but a sexier one piece that reminded me of my own suit. And instead of her one hand resting on her hip, it was now jutting out, and between her fingers was an old-fashioned fountain pen. She was winking at me.

"Wow," was all I could manage.

Will frowned.

"You don't like it?"

I did like it. The line work was phenomenal and the colors popped like the girl was going to jump right off his bicep and into his arms. It was wonderful. But it was *me*.

"It's beautiful, Will," I stammered. "It doesn't look like the sketch you showed me."

He pulled himself out of the chair and stepped to my side.

"It evolved." That's all he said, and then he leaned down to kiss me in a slow and gentle way.

"Which one did you want?" Joe appeared behind Will, drying his hands with a towel.

I shook my head a little to clear my brain and then I froze. Was I really going to do this nutty thing?

"Well, it's over here." I pulled Will with me to show him the picture.

"That's perfect!" Will grinned. "It's totally you."

"Yes, it is," I admitted. "I'm not sure I'm ready for it yet."

Joe looked impatient and it made me cringe.

"I'm sorry if I've wasted your time." I looked to Will for support. His understanding smile calmed me down.

"It's okay." Joe shrugged and retreated behind the beaded curtain. He returned with some medical tape and a roll of paper towel. He covered Will's bicep and then gave him all the instructions to care for the new tattoo. They shook hands and Will thanked him.

"Let me pay for this and we'll get out of here, okay?"

I nodded and started walking to the door as Will went to the counter. When he was finished, he joined me and held the door as we left. Once in the car, he turned to me.

"That Max girl asked me out."

I snorted.

"Yeah, she asked me outside if it would be okay."

"I said no. Immediately." Will shook his head. "I think she might not have taken the hint until she saw the tattoo."

I raised my eyebrows.

"Oh?"

"Yeah. When she saw how much it was like you, she got *real* cold, *real* fast." We both laughed out loud. "I hope you aren't upset about it. I thought you'd be flattered."

"Oh, I am!" I reached to squeeze his hand. "It just shocked me a little bit. I've never been immortalized in ink before."

He laughed and leaned over to give me a quick kiss.

"You hungry yet? It's after seven."

"Eh, not really. Are you?"

"Hell, I can always eat." Will rubbed is stomach. "I'll hold off, though. Want to head back to my place? We could hang out, watch a movie?"

That was intriguing. I wouldn't have thought a quiet evening at home was something Will would want.

"That sounds nice." I settled back in the seat as he put the car into gear and headed back to his house.

Chapter 40

I knew I was crushing hard on Vivienne, but it was clear she wasn't feeling the same. She was distracted the whole way home and didn't talk much. Making the tattoo look so much like her was probably a mistake. *I gotta stop being so damn impulsive.*

I did manage to nail her down before we got to the house and we stopped to pick up some pizza. While we waited for it, I ran next door to 7-11 and got ice cream for dessert. That seemed to perk up her spirits when she checked to make sure I'd gotten cherry cordial. Shit, that was an easy one.

When we got home, we ran into Billy and Tim as they were leaving to go bar hopping.

"Hey, do you guys want to come along?" Billy asked, taking Vivienne's hands in his and doing a little dance with her. It made me feel good to see her laugh and let him twirl her around.

"Nah, we just got some pizza and we're gonna hang." I held up the box.

"Suit yourself." Billy released Vivienne and gave her a deep bow. Tim nodded to her and slugged me in the arm.

"Don't do anything I wouldn't do," Tim muttered, a grin spreading across his face.

Vivienne blushed and I flipped Tim off while ushering her inside.

We made our way to the kitchen so she could put the ice cream in the freezer. I put the pizza on the counter and moved around her easily to get plates from the cupboard.

"Beer?" she asked, opening the fridge.

"You bet."

"Any preference?"

"Nope, it's all cold."

I grabbed some napkins from the top of the fridge as she closed the door and then scooted under my arm.

"Where shall we eat?" Vivienne held a beer in each hand. She pointed to the living room with one and the family room with the other.

"TV's in there." I waved the napkins in the direction of the family room. "Let's get comfy."

She took one end of the sofa and I took the other, placing the pizza box between us. I tore off a slice for her and put it on a plate, then handed it to her. I did the same for myself and we sat back to eat. I annihilated mine while Vivienne only picked at hers. I downed another slice and half my beer before she got near the crust of her own.

"Viv, are you sure everything is all right?" I put my beer down on the end table and stared at her.

"Yes, of course." Her hands fluttered to her neck to fiddle with the silver necklace she wore.

I felt a little better because she looked conflicted, not angry. Taking a chance, I was honest with her.

"It seems like maybe you don't want to be here."

The look she gave me was filled with anxiety.

Chapter 41

Here was my opportunity. Will had opened the door for me to be honest about my feelings, but as usual, I was stalling. I wished I had my laptop with me so I could write out what I wanted to say before I spoke. How frustrating to be almost forty and not be able to articulate my feelings in a mature and rational manner.

"First, I want you to know, it has nothing to do with you," I began. He looked puzzled.

"Okay. What's what got to do with what?"

I smiled and sighed.

"An awful lot has happened to me this week, Will. I think I've experienced more in the last five days than I did in the last fifteen years." I stared down at the unfinished slice of pizza on my plate. I leaned over and carefully put the plate on the coffee table. I wiped my hands with a paper napkin and crumpled it up, nervously working it between my fingers.

"I can understand that, Viv." Will nudged my leg with his knee. "You can be honest with me. Did I do something to upset you?"

"Oh, no!"

I wanted to scream. I was messing this up and I put my hands into my hair and pulled.

"I'm super confused right now. I have a lot of feelings boiling up inside me I didn't think I'd ever have. I didn't realize how much I missed Pepper until I saw her again. I never expected to meet someone, *you*, who could make me feel so good. I'm beginning to realize that a lot of great things are going on, in spite of Tony wiping me out. Too much... *awesomeness* all at once, I guess."

Will grinned and took a swig of beer.

"Now you're talkin' my language. I was only twenty-two when Static got signed, and within a year, things exploded for us. I always think it must have been like what the Beetles or the Stones felt when they got so hot."

I chuckled and peeked at him beneath my lashes.

"Well, I wouldn't go so far as to compare myself with the Beetles or the Rolling Stones."

"Stephen King, then."

"Pffft, as *if*!" I shook my head. "You're right, though. That's a little how I feel. It's like I'm waiting for the other shoe to drop."

Will reached for my hand and I let him take it.

"That is no way to live."

"I know." I liked how our fingers looked together, his nicely tanned hands against the paleness of mine. "I wish I could explain to you what the last twenty years have been like for me, but you wouldn't believe it, anyway."

"Just talk, Viv." Will looked at me and I liked how his eyes shone in the dim lighting of the room.

And the floodgates opened.

I talked about Bruce and our marriage. I told him about how much writing meant to me. I recalled how Pepper and I first met and how our friendship was forged out of a mutual desire to be accepted as we were. I summarized the last seventeen years and how I'd hidden myself away so I didn't have to face reality. He listened without interrupting. He was quiet and attentive. There was no judgment in his eyes or manner, and that alone gave me the confidence to keep going.

"I spent a lot of time being angry at God and the universe for taking Bruce away from me. It was wasted time, and now I'm turning that anger inside. I'm furious with myself for giving away so many years. I can't stand that I'm weak and have no confidence. No matter how much positive reinforcement I get, I still refuse to accept the good things in my life. Why do I *do* that?"

Will did not offer any answers. I didn't want him to. I needed to find the answers within me.

"I tell everyone all the lies they want to hear. I agree when people tell me I'm smart or talented or attractive, but I never believe it inside. In my head, I'm saying, 'Yeah, right, if you only knew the truth.' It's been so long, I don't even know what the truth about anything is."

What was it about this man that I could lay my psyche bare before him? I couldn't remember ever having been so forthcoming with Bruce. I could do it with Pepper, sure, but she would always smack me and tell me I was being an idiot. Of course, I expected that from her. And my mom. But Will was inspiring me to levels I didn't know where there.

"You have got to be sick of listening to me by now," I sighed. I had no idea how late it was or how long I'd been blathering at him.

"Not at all." Will reached across the couch for me and pulled me into his arms. "You can talk as long as you want. We're friends, right? That's what friends do."

I appreciated his words and believed him. But I still hadn't told him *everything*. I'd butted up to my feelings about him and staying in California a couple of times, never quite making the leap to say them out loud. As much as I needed someone to listen, I knew I wasn't quite ready to go that far. As I lay in his arms, not speaking, my head was whirling with all the secrets I'd told him. Instead of feeling unburdened or lighter, I was weighted down with anxiety about what he was feeling or thinking about all of my baggage. *You're such an idiot, Viv.*

We stayed silent and still for a while, until I felt Will kiss the top of my head.

"Better?"

"Eh. I guess."

"Want to know what I think now?" His voice was calm and soft.

"No." I smiled into his chest. "I don't think I'd like it."

"You might be surprised."

"O-okay." I snuggled in closer against his chest, so I wouldn't have to look at him as he spoke.

"I think you're way more normal than you think you are."

That was a good opening. I almost pulled away to stare at him.

"Most people do the same things to themselves. They put on a face for the world that says 'I'm confident, I'm smart, I can do this.' But inside, they're just as scared and doubtful as you are. The difference is, you've had some extraordinarily bad shit happen to you. Most people don't marry at nineteen anymore and lose their spouse at twenty-two."

"No." I never thought of my experience as any worse than anyone else's.

"You had every right to take it hard and give up a little. Sounds to me like you were pretty idealistic and had the confidence to believe all your dreams and plans would come true. You had no reason *not* to believe. When everything crashed, it had to have been a pretty bad blow."

"Yeah," I whispered. I could feel tears filling my eyes and hoped I could blink them back before he noticed his shirt getting wet.

"Could you have handled it differently? Probably. Could you have made some different choices going forward? Sure. But you didn't. You did the best you could with what you had, and there's no sense regretting it all now. Water under the bridge. Spilled milk. Whatever. I'm thinking you've finally figured that out. Now you get to go forward with whatever you damn well want, and it scares you."

"Yup." I swiped at my face, glad it wasn't as wet as it could have been.

"Shit, I'd be scared too. I think we all get to be about eighteen and then we stop. Oh sure, our bodies get older and the birthdays go by, we learn lessons as we go. But, emotionally and mentally, we never stop being the people we are when we're young and full of hope and desire."

Will pulled his arms away and put his hands on mine. He pulled me up to look at him.

"I would never tell you to forget your husband or the time you spent with him. Far be it from me to tell you how to deal with your mom or Pepper or any other relationships you have. But if you want to know the truth, I think you're pretty damn lucky. It might be a scary spot to be in, but you can make any choice you want at this point, and even if it's a bad choice, you don't have anything holding you back. You've got freedom *most* people don't have. Just stop being so hard on yourself. Give yourself permission to live and laugh and love. I think once you do that, you'll be just fine."

That did it. The waterworks opened up and I couldn't stop, even if I wanted to. Will handed me some napkins to mop at my face, grinning at me with an impish gleam in his eye.

"I don't know why you're crying. Unless those are tears of joy."

I snorted and laughed, then hiccupped like a toddler getting over a tantrum.

"No, I'm just an overly emotional doofus at this moment."

He shrugged and wrapped me back into a tight hug.

"That's okay. I like doofuses." He reached behind me for the TV remote resting on the coffee table. "What do you say we watch a movie now? Lighten the mood?"

We cuddled together on the couch while he brought up the movie menu on the TV. "What's your pleasure? Drama? Action/adventure? Romance? Classic black and white?"

"*Fight Club*!" I shouted, pointing at the screen. "I love that movie!"

"Well, it's not exactly a lighthearted flick, but it's one of my favorites, too," Will agreed.

As the movie ended, I felt myself getting sleepy. I closed my eyes and nestled closer to Will, leaning my head on his shoulder. From far away, I thought I heard Bruce Springsteen's voice singing. After a few seconds, I recognized my phone ringing and jumped up. I banged my knees on the coffee table. "Shit!"

"What's wrong?" Will's eyes shot open. He had been dozing too.

"That's my phone. I'm sorry!" I moved around the edge of the table and strode toward the living room to find my bag. As I reached inside, it stopped ringing and the screen went black. I palmed the device and swiped my thumb to the right, bringing it back to life. The missed call was from Jake. I saw the time was 10:30 p.m. and thought it was way too late for a call from my agent. Given the circumstances, I thought it important to call him back. There might be news about Tony. He picked up on the first ring.

"Good news, kiddo!" he shouted, probably knowing it was me from the caller ID. I could hear loud music and many voices in the background.

"Where are you?"

"I'm at a club with another client, but I just got a call from the police. They got him!"

"What?" I broke out in a cold sweat.

"Tony was apprehended about an hour ago trying to fly out of Amsterdam."

"YES!" I pumped my fist in the air. "What happens next?"

"They'll process him over there and then shuttle his ass back on the first flight available. He will be met by representatives of the Los Angeles Police Department." Jake cackled—I think he'd had one too many cocktails.

"That is the best news I've heard all night!" I wiggled my hips and did a little dance.

"Oh no, it's not!" Jake crowed. "The *best* news is they found the money! Not all of it, but about ninety percent!"

I screamed with joy, causing Will to rush into the room, a look of stark terror on his face. He could tell I was happy about something, so he just smiled at me and leaned against the door frame, waiting for me to get off the phone.

No curse word or euphemism would do, I simply screeched out my happiness as if I'd just been told I won the lottery. In a manner of speaking, I had. No longer would I be burdened with three-quarters of a million dollar debt or the pressure to produce in order to repay it. I couldn't remember having felt so good in... well, ever.

"Jake, thank you so much for calling!"

"You got it, kid. I'm going to have a whole new round of appearances and interviews for you to do now."

"Hah! Go celebrate and we'll talk about *that* later."

I ended the call and crumpled to the floor, overwhelmed by the adrenaline dump. My arms and legs felt like Jell-O.

"Well?" Will held up his hands in front of him. "Don't leave me on tender hooks! What's going on?"

"Tony's in custody *and* they found the money!" I squealed, jumping back up to my feet with a renewed sense of energy.

"Fuckin' A!" He crossed the room to sweep me up and swing me around as we both whooped with joy.

"I have to call Pepper!" Will released me and I grabbed my phone from where it had landed on the floor. I tapped her speed dial icon. When I got her voicemail, I was a bit perturbed, but then remembered she was probably still on her date.

I shouldn't be the only one to get lucky, I thought cheekily. Grinning until I thought my face would split, I left her a breathless voicemail and told her to call me at her first opportunity, knowing full well it might not be until tomorrow.

"Now I need to call my mom!"

"It's 1:30 a.m.," Will reminded me.

"Doesn't matter," I whispered. I'd already dialed and it was ringing. "If I didn't call her right away, she'd kill— Hi Mom!"

Mom was scared to death something was wrong because it was so late. It took a good five minutes for her to wake up somewhat and comprehend that nothing bad had happened, and that I was okay.

Will watched me talk and I had a difficult time keeping my focus on the conversation. As Mom rapid-fired questions, I answered just as fast. Movement caught my eye and I noticed Will taking off his tee-shirt.

"I'm sorry, Mom, what did you say?" I couldn't look away.

Will unbuttoned his jeans and slowly pulled the zipper down.

"N-no, I'm not sure when I'll be home."

He took a step toward me and eased his pants a little lower on his naked hips.

"Yes, I'm fine. I-it's late, Mom. I should let you get back to sleep."

Will pushed a little harder and I caught a glimpse of dark, curly hair before I quickly pivoted away.

"Oh, I'm grateful they found any of the money. But it's awesome to know they got most of it." I gasped when I heard the denim hit the floor.

"I'm fine, just got a shock when I touched the metal lamp next to the bed." I only just managed to stifle a hiss of breath when I felt Will press up against me and his lips land on my neck.

"O-okay, Mom. You get back to sleep. I'll call you again tomorrow when I know more." I was barely able to hang up the phone when I felt Will's hands reach around to my midsection.

"You're *bad*," I panted.

"Yes, I am."

Chapter 42

Having no idea of what was up with Vivienne, Pepper slipped her key into her apartment door and opened it nervously. She prayed Gabriel would not be shocked or offended at its simplicity. She turned to allow him in, surprised when he grabbed her and pulled her close for a passionate kiss.

Not surprised enough, Pepper dropped her keys and purse and wrapped her arms around Gabriel's neck, returning the kiss with just as much intensity. They remained locked in the embrace for several minutes before Pepper finally had to come up for air.

"Wow!" She felt breathless and lightheaded with arousal. Gabriel grinned, squeezing her closer, trying to move in for another kiss.

"Wait," Pepper laughed. She extricated herself from his arms and shut the apartment door, throwing the deadbolt. "No need to give the neighbors a show, for cryin' out loud."

"I suppose not." Gabriel grinned, but the moment seemed stalled. "I apologize, dear. Having stared at you all evening, I couldn't help myself. I was overcome."

Pepper stepped back next to him, putting her arms around his waist and smiled.

"You have nothing to apologize for. This may only be date number two, but since both of them have been multiple hours long, I think we're probably more on number four or five at this point."

Gabriel put his hands on her elbows and rubbed, while pressing his forehead against hers. His blue eyes sparkled and a smile so genuine spread over his face that Pepper was overcome with a warm sensation, making her heart beat faster.

"I have so enjoyed spending time with you, Pepper."

"It's been fun!" She nodded her head against his. "I can't remember the last time I had this much fun with a man."

Pulling away from her, Gabriel took her hand and led her to the couch to sit down. When she tried to sit a respectable distance away, he pulled her by the waist until she was pressed up against him. Pepper wondered if he planned it that way so he wouldn't have to face her as he spoke.

"I have never been comfortable with women my entire life, but our two dates have given me the ability to be as close to myself as possible. There's something about you that inspires me not to hide."

Pepper was honored by his admission, but was still too afraid to make any of her own. She wasn't prepared to tell him about her past experiences with love and how awful they'd been. The alcoholic abuser who had put her in the hospital for a month, causing her to almost end up living out of her car when she couldn't get work because of the bruises and scars to her face. The pedophile who'd been hauled off to jail for preying on preteen girls in the apartment complex where they lived. It had taken a fair amount of bribing to keep her name out of the papers on that one, otherwise her entire career *and* life would have been destroyed. The long line of jobless, aimless, pretty bums who claimed they were going to make it big and take care of her for the rest of her life, while she was the one out earning the paycheck and paying the bills. What would Gabriel think of her, knowing how poorly she had chosen up to that point? Instead of revealing any of her shame, she encouraged and praised him for his disclosure.

"I'm so glad you feel comfortable with me," Pepper said as she rested her cheek against his chest. "I don't know why you're so worried. You're funny and charming and intelligent. I've probably learned more from you in our time together than I would have learned if I went to college."

Gabriel chuckled and squeezed her, making her giggle too.

"I rather doubt that. You aren't like the other women I've come into contact with. You're absolutely gorgeous. You never judge me or anyone else that I've noticed. And it seems as though you are always attempting to make others feel at ease, never once thinking of yourself."

Pepper's eyebrows raised as she considered how Gabriel viewed her. It certainly wasn't the way she saw herself.

I'm the loud, crazy one, she thought. *Always looking for attention.*

"I don't think of you as loud or crazy or seeking attention. You're vivacious and happy and interesting."

Pepper gasped, sitting up to look at him in shock. "I swear, I was just thinking that. Freaky!"

Laughing, he stroked her head. "I don't think you're that difficult to understand."

Pepper wanted to kick herself in the ass when she felt tears threaten to fill her eyes. No one but Vivienne had said anything so kind to her and actually meant it. Sure, the idiots she'd been with all her life had spewed flowery sentiments all the time, but Pepper had known they meant none of it. Gabriel's words were true and honest, coming directly from his heart.

"Thank you," she whispered. She kissed him then, softly and gently.

*****

Pepper breezed into Starbucks, looking as gorgeous as ever, full of energy and with a gleam in her eye. She squinted and scanned around until she saw Vivienne sitting by the windows, staring out into the hot California sunshine. *Uh-oh, she looks like she's been thinking too much.*

Earlier that morning, after seeing Gabriel off, Pepper had finally gotten around to checking her phone to see the missed call and numerous texts from Viv. Feeling guilty, she had texted back immediately saying she was okay and glad about Tony. A response came back within a minute asking her to meet at the coffee shop a block from the hotel to talk. Agreeing, Pepper had gotten ready and headed over.

"So how's my almost-millionaire writer bestie?" she bubbled, taking a seat across from Vivienne.

Vivienne laughed.

"I'm great. Obviously, very relieved and elated that I no longer have to worry about paying back all that money."

"I bet!" Pepper reached into her pocket to pull out some bills. "I'm going to get my coffee. You need anything?"

"Nope, I'm all set." Vivienne tapped the venti cup on the table.

When Pepper returned, she carried an iced coffee and two blueberry muffins.

"Here. You look like you need a nosh."

"Where have you *been*?" Vivienne demanded, ignoring the food.

Pepper gave a wicked smile and shook her head.

"Not tellin'. Not yet, anyway."

"But—"

"No buts. I'll give you all the details when I'm ready. Suffice it to say, I've spent some time with a very nice man and I'm worried about jinxing it by talking about him too soon."

Vivienne held up her hands in defeat.

"Fair enough."

"What about you? What's all the news?"

Vivienne's shoulders tensed and her toe began to bounce.

"Well, I'm thinking about staying in California a little longer."

Pepper's eyes nearly bugged out of her head.

"*What?!*"

"Calm down!" Vivienne snorted. "I'm only *thinking* about it."

"Why the change of heart?"

Vivienne paused to take a sip of her latte.

"I can't really give you a defining moment. But I keep wondering to myself about things."

"Like what?"

"Well, what it would be like to wake up beside someone every day. How it would feel to go to the beach every day. How nice it would be to see you all the time instead of once every two decades."

Pepper laughed and grabbed Vivienne's hand, squeezing tightly.

"Those are wonderful things to wonder about."

"I'm scared, though."

Pepper nodded slowly.

"I know you are."

"Things are happening way too fast."

"With Will?"

"With *everything!*" Vivienne threw her hands up in exasperation. "Ever since I published the book, it seems like life has gone crazy. First with Sunny Pen snatching it up and all the publicity over that. Then starting the foundation and traveling around all over the place trying to get money. Just when I thought things had finally calmed down and I could go back to my quiet existence, Tony pulls his shit."

Pepper tried not to roll her eyes and snicker.

"That's life, hun. You've just managed to avoid living a real one since Bruce died."

Vivienne sighed.

"Just because I chose a path less flamboyant than yours, doesn't mean it's less valid."

"Touché." Pepper took another long sip from her straw. "But you can't avoid the fact that things *have* changed."

"No. That's why I've been thinking about it so much." Vivienne wrung her hands in frustration. "But I'm afraid I'll take on too much all at once. I'm not used to having to switch gears like this."

"Well, one thing at a time, then. Stay just a few weeks and camp out with me." Pepper grinned, bobbing her head up and down, thinking it the perfect solution.

"I could. But I would still have to figure out a way to write. Figure out what to do with the foundation. Figure out a way to keep Jake from taking over my whole life." Vivienne stopped and looked away.

"Figure out a way to deal with Will," Pepper said for her.

"There is that," Vivienne admitted, chewing on her bottom lip. "I think that would have to be the *first* thing on the list if I decided to stay."

"Why do you have to 'deal' with it at all? Why not just let things happen naturally?" Pepper was beginning to get frustrated with how complicated Vivienne was making things out to be.

"Because it's scary, Pep. Let's face facts here," she held up her right hand, closing each finger as she ticked things off. "If I stay, I'm staying because of Will and you, not because of any other reason. If I admit that, then I have to admit Will means more to me than is reasonable for having known him less than a week. If it doesn't work out with him, I'm crushed emotionally and will probably resort to old habits and run home to Michigan. If you think I've been a hermit the last seventeen years, can you imagine what I'd do with the next seventeen?"

Pepper chuckled as she listened to Vivienne come up with excuse after excuse. When she couldn't take any more, she shushed her friend.

"Look, enough is enough. I know you're afraid, but you have to take a chance somewhere, sometime. If love isn't a good enough risk to bet on, what will be?"

"I'm not in love with him!" Vivienne's look was horrified.

Are you sure about that? Pepper replied silently. She decided not to push the issue. *Getting her to stay, period, is the goal.*

"I'm also worried that I won't be able to write if I stay out here. Between you and Will and what the two of you would cook up, I'll probably never get a thing done."

"Bah, you're making more excuses."

"No I'm not," Vivienne insisted. "I'm trying to be honest with myself *and* you. I'm a pretty screwed up person in a lot of ways and it's not fair to lay waste to our friendship or whatever is developing with Will just because I can't figure shit out."

Pepper sighed.

"What am I going to do with you? Do you want me to tell you to go home? Give up? Walk away? Fine. Go. But don't blame me when you become a crazy cat lady."

Chapter 43

Pepper just didn't get it. I was trying to explain to her what I was feeling, but she just glossed over all of it like it was no big deal. Why couldn't she see how monumental a decision this was for me? Well, that was unfair. She'd never been widowed. How could I possibly expect her to understand what it would be like to lose a husband and then mourn for seventeen years?

"What if I stay out here and try to follow this thing with Will. What if it doesn't end up working out because of *me* or *my* issues?" I asked her. I squirmed in my seat, hating how weak I sounded.

"He's a big boy. He can handle it."

"No, that just makes him collateral damage because I'm an idiot. I would never want that to happen."

"Of course you wouldn't," Pepper agreed. She gave me a sympathetic look. "But it's not *going* to happen."

"How can you be so sure?" I dared her. "I've got a lot of baggage to deal with. I don't think it's fair to ask him to wait around while I deal with it. And it's definitely not fair to be involved with him *while* I deal with it."

Pepper sat back and her brows knitted while she thought. Maybe *now* she was finally seeing things from my point of view.

"It would seem to me," she began, "that it's all about balance. And boundaries. If you're up front and honest with Will about things, he should be the one to decide whether or not he wants to hang with you."

Dammit. Pepper always knew what to say.

"You're right. But what if, after a while, he decides it's not what he signed on for? What if I have so much shit on my plate that he decides to bail? Where does that leave me?" I grabbed my coffee and took a swallow.

"You need to stop obsessing." Pepper shook her head. "You're worrying about stuff that isn't going to happen." Her confidence never ceased to amaze me.

I groaned and dropped my head into my hands.

"That is so easy for you to say. What if I'm confusing sex with love?" There. I'd said it out loud.

Pepper laughed and handed me a napkin.

"Look, Viv. You're going to have to talk to him. You can't just stick around for no reason and then stalk him. I'm telling you the truth, and that's all you've ever asked me for."

"Couldn't you sugarcoat things from time to time?" I tossed the crumpled napkin at her.

"No." She tossed it back.

"Well, how about some regular truth instead of the *brutal* honesty?" I stared at my hands resting in my lap, trying to accept reality.

"Never," Pepper teased. She flipped her hair back, giving the radiant smile that always melted anyone's resolve. "You already know you want to be here. You already know it's going to be difficult. You already know you're stronger now than you've ever been. Just make up your mind and do it."

When I didn't say anything, she reached across to hug me close.

*****

Pepper knew she was right, and she watched the truth wash across Vivienne's face as her friend pulled out of their embrace. She remembered having to talk Vivienne into things when they were kids, but Pepper didn't recall it ever being this difficult. Vivienne had gotten a lot more set in her ways and stubborn over the years.

"When are you going to see Will next?" *Soon, I hope.*

"Later tonight. I want to go walking on the beach at sunset." Vivienne's cheeks got pinker as she spoke.

"Hmm, sounds pretty romantic to me. You sure you aren't just a *little* in love with him?" Pepper pinched her thumb and forefinger together.

"No!" Vivienne insisted, but she couldn't quite stifle the smile fighting its way onto her face.

"Well, if you aren't now, you will be soon." Pepper smirked. "I want you to say the words out loud. *I am staying in California.* Come on. Say it."

Vivienne hesitated until Pepper shook a finger at her. When she opened her mouth to speak, her phone rang. "Restricted" washed across the display, making her frown.

"Who could that be?"

Pepper picked at her cuticles while Vivienne took the call. Her head whipped up when she heard a gasp. She watched as her friend's face lost all of its color and felt her own heart speed up to double time. Pepper reached out to steady Vivienne's trembling arm.

"Viv? *Vivvy, what's <u>wrong</u>?*"

"Thank you, I'll be there as soon as I can!" Vivienne whispered. Her phone fell out of her hand and clattered to the table.

"Vivienne, what's wrong?" Pepper's guts clenched and beads of sweat popped out above her upper lip.

"It's my mother. She's had a stroke."

Chapter 44

The cab had barely stopped in front of the hospital entrance as I threw some twenty dollar bills at the driver and leaped out. I sprinted inside to the desk, breathlessly demanding to know where I could find my mom's room. The look of terror on my face surely kept visiting hours from applying to me. I was given the room number and directions and I bolted for the elevators, snatching my visitor's pass. It was after one in the morning.

The pungent odor of hospital disinfectant assaulted me the second the elevator doors opened. My nose burned with it as I hesitated long enough to scan the signs for which direction Room 402 was in. No one was at the nurses' station to stop me and I ran as fast as I could to get to Mom.

I skidded to a halt at the door of her private room. Three giant steps took me to her bedside. I stared at my mother, lying unconscious and paralyzed in a hospital bed, barely breathing while I tried desperately to catch mine. I flinched every time the machines surrounding her beeped, disturbing the otherwise silent room. There was an IV in both of her arms, wires attached to her chest and a large tube snaking down her throat, forcing her to breathe. Her skin was ashen, seeming to stretch across her bones. Oxygen flowed from little pieces of plastic inserted into her nostrils. Her eyes were closed and had been since she'd gone unconscious. This was the first time I'd ever seen my mother sick with more than a cold or the flu. My stomach roiled with acid and I clasped a clammy hand over my mouth to keep from throwing up.

Getting as much of a grip on myself as I could, I sat down and took her cool left hand in mine, struggling to find the words I wanted to say. I had already spoken with her ER doctor and he'd told me there was no hope she would recover. How could this be? I'd *just* spoken to her that morning! She was *fine*! What the hell was going on?

"Hi Mom," I whispered. I got no reaction. Tears welled up in my eyes and poured down my cheeks. My heart had been convinced she would sit up and talk back when she realized I was there.

I pressed her thin, motionless fingers to my cheek and cried. My pounding head and heart sent bolts of emotional pain through my soul. I found my voice after a few minutes and began begging for her forgiveness.

"I'm so sorry, Mom. I shouldn't have gone to California. Jake could have handled all of that shit, I didn't need to be there. I'm so sorry I wasn't here for you."

I lifted my head to the ceiling.

"Please God, please, not now. I won't go back. I won't leave her. Just help her. Please, help her God."

Nothing happened. Logically I knew it wouldn't. Never having been a religious person or a church attendee, I had no reason to expect God, if one existed, would answer any prayers I threw out there. I didn't deserve it. I hadn't earned it.

My heart felt like a lead weight inside my chest, each beat making it sink a little closer to my gut. Memories of our lives together flashed in my brain, making me cry a little harder with each one. Sitting on her lap while Dad drove us to some vacation destination spot, the rumbly feeling of her chest as she talked or sang. Shopping for a prom dress my senior year of high school. The day Bruce and I got married and she gave me a handkerchief that had belonged to her mother and grandmother. The day Dad died. When I signed the publishing contract and she cried with joy for me.

I was glad there was no one else in the room to see me lose it. The pain filling me up was worse than anything I'd ever experienced, even when Bruce died. I hadn't seen or spoken to Bruce in months when I found out he'd been killed. He was almost a dream to me, and the shock I felt kept me insulated from too much pain.

Sitting with Mom, all I could think was how I'd taken her for granted, believing she'd be around forever. I was childish and foolish to think so, but the idea of losing her was one I avoided at all costs. She wasn't supposed to be in this position. She was a good person with a full life, lots of friends and things to do. How could this have happened? I moaned and squeezed her hand harder, hoping it would garner some response, *any* response from her.

Just then a nurse came in to change one of Mom's IVs. I mopped my face on the edge of Mom's sheet. She gave me a kind smile and went about her chore as quickly as she could. Before she left, she touched me on the shoulder. "I'm so very sorry. My name is April. Is there anything I can get for you?"

I shook my head, unable to speak. Her kindness brought on a fresh batch of tears. I squeezed the fingers resting on my shoulder, mouthing the words, "thank you."

Dawn began creeping its way into the room through the cracks in the dull gray blinds covering the window. April had come and gone throughout the night to take Mom's vital signs and change IVs, always offering to get me anything I needed. Each time I declined, thanking her just the same. Not once had I closed my eyes and slept. As horrifying as the situation was, and as much as I hated seeing Mom this way, I didn't want to miss a moment of it. I had always been told the last thing to go when someone was dying was their hearing. I was desperate to make sure Mom knew how much I loved her. I swallowed my fear and anger to focus on giving her all my love and devotion.

A little after seven a.m., a crowd of doctors came pouring into the room. I only knew Dr. Naber, who was our family doctor. He'd been with Dad at the end, too. The neurologist, anesthesiologist, and some other "ologist" introduced themselves, but I was in no shape to remember their names.

"Hello, Vivienne," Dr. Naber said quietly, pulling me out of the chair to give me a firm hug. "I'm so sorry."

"Thank you," I whispered.

"You shouldn't be alone. Isn't there someone we can call to be with you?" His hands were planted firmly on my upper arms. "A friend, maybe?"

"No," I said. "I'll be okay."

I wanted to be by myself with Mom and my grief. I wasn't ready for the well-meaning but awkward sentiments and platitudes offered by people not feeling what I was feeling.

I tried to listen as the doctors explained Mom's condition. Medical terms floated into my ears, things like cerebrovascular accident, hemorrhagic stroke, and ruptured cerebral aneurysm. I had an abstract ability to understand what they were saying, but my heart blocked all of their words. My mom was brain dead, that was the long and the short of it. They could keep her on life support for as long as I wanted, but it wouldn't help. She wasn't coming back. I asked about whether or not she might be "locked in," a condition I'd heard about when stroke victims were fully aware of their surroundings but unable to respond.

Dr. Naber quickly disavowed me of that notion, assuring me every test had been run to detect any brain function. There was none. Hope leaked out of me through new tears.

Dr. Naber asked me if I had any questions. What was there to ask? He couldn't tell me why this had happened, or what I was going to do without her.

I hugged myself, shaking my head at the gaggle of medical professionals. I couldn't speak. I was exhausted from the flight and being up all night; I just wanted them all to leave. Dr. Naber must have sensed I was reaching my breaking point because he ushered them all out of the room. Before he closed the door, he offered me one more sad, sympathetic smile.

"I'll come back to see you later, okay?"

All I could do was nod and wave goodbye. I sat back down to hold Mom's hand again. I never felt so helpless in all my life. When Bruce died, I was a child. As sad and mournful as I was then, and for the next seventeen years, it was nothing, *nothing* compared to this. Even when

Dad died, Mom was there to hold me up. But now I was going to be alone, truly alone, for the rest of my life. I had no one.

I laid my head down on the bed beside her and lifted Mom's hand to rest on my head, pretending for the last time that she was comforting me.

*****

When Nurse April was clocking out from her shift, she came in to say goodbye.

"You should go home for a while. There's nothing you can do."

"I can't leave her." I hiccupped, and then clasped my hand over my mouth with embarrassment.

April stood beside me and smiled.

"She knows you're here. She knows you stayed all night. Tell her you'll be back."

I wanted to protest, but exhaustion was weighing me down. I needed a shower, my deodorant and perfume having worn away hours ago. My hair was a tangled mess and my clothes reeked. I still wore the light tee-shirt and shorts I'd put on two days before to meet Pepper.

"Maybe you're right."

"I am," April said. She put her hand on my back and encouraged me to stand up. "Go home and get some sleep. Then a shower and some food. She'll be here waiting for you, I promise."

"All right."

The first step away from the bed was the hardest, but once I got going, forward motion took over. April stayed with me as we rode down the elevator from the third floor. Then she walked me out to the cab stand in front of the hospital. The sun shone brightly and was hot as it bore down on me. She gave me another hug.

"I'll see you tonight."

"Thank you." I gave her a weak smile. It was all I could do. I fumbled inside my purse for my sunglasses to block the yellow rays from my bloodshot eyes.

The Widow and the Rock Star

I was too tired to think as the Yellow Cab sped along I-94 toward St. Clair Shores. I must have zoned out, because it seemed like the ride only took a few moments. I paid the fare with the last of my cash and the cab sped away.

I was trudging to the front porch of my shotgun ranch, knees wobbly, head throbbing with fatigue and heartbreak. Squinting, in spite of my dark glasses, I reached a hand into the pocket of my pants, thoroughly convinced my keys would be there so I could get inside.

"Dammit." I remembered then that Pepper had rushed me straight to the airport from Starbucks so I could fly home. I hadn't gone back for my luggage. I'd had my driver's license and credit cards with me, so my suitcase was not a necessity in my haste to leave California.

Turning around, I stepped back onto the driveway, around my car, and then headed through the gate toward the back door, stumbling into the garbage can.

"Dammit!" The stink of week-old garbage swirled around me. I wanted to kick the shit out of the mess surrounding me, but somehow managed to control the urge. Pushing the bag back inside with my foot, I replaced the lid and righted it.

Turning around, the concrete step was loose and I'd hidden a key behind it. Jiggling it away from the house, I could see the silver metal shining right where I left it. I bent down to reach for it and my knees gave out. I crashed down, skinning both of them and the palms of my hands as well, as I sprawled flat on my stomach.

"*Motherfucker!*"

I lay prone for several minutes trying to find the strength to get up. I didn't want to have to crawl up the step and try to fiddle with the key on my already injured knees.

"Come on Vivienne," I hissed. "Get the fuck *up!*"

By sheer force of will, I lunged myself up and barely stayed on my unsteady feet. Using the side of the house for support, I leaned against the cool steel of the door. I got the key in the lock on the first try and let myself in.

I flung the door open and it banged against the wall, trying to come back to hit me. Reflexively, I stopped the onslaught of metal and gently propped it open. Stepping up from the landing and into the kitchen, I was slammed by the sight of my home. While I was gone, Mom had come by to clean the place up.

There were no dirty dishes in the sink and the dishcloth was neatly hanging over the faucet, instead of lying in a damp lump like I usually left it. There was no trash in the garbage can and a fresh bag lined the inside, where I would have probably forgotten to put one in. All the counters were spotless and clean. The scent of Mom's product of choice, Clorox Cleanup, hung in the air. Walking through the kitchen and into the living and dining room, I could see the rug was freshly vacuumed and all the furniture surfaces were dust free. There was even a bunch of fairly fresh lilacs in a vase on the dining room table. Mom's favorite flowers.

I crumpled to the floor and covered my face with my hands. Knowing that one of the last things my mother did was clean my house crushed me. Clutching at my chest and throat, I tried to fill my lungs, but the air wouldn't come. It couldn't push past the sobs.

The gentle tears I'd shed in the quiet of the hospital turned into wailing like a wounded animal that knows it's caught in a trap and is going to die. With no one there to help me calm down, I howled and moaned until I passed out.

When I finally came to, my eyes were crusted shut from crying and I had to force them open with my fingers. Gazing at the wall clock, I saw that it was past one in the afternoon. I'd been on the floor for more than four hours.

I got up stiffly, massaging my knees and back, willing my body to move again. I tried not to look around, afraid I would notice more things Mom had done. I couldn't fall back into another fit like before. I needed to get myself cleaned up and back to the hospital.

I had turned my phone off when I boarded the plane at LAX. When I powered it up, I thought it was going to spontaneously combust with all the missed texts and voicemails. Both Pepper and

Will had blown up my phone. My vision blurred as I realized I had two people who cared about me that much. I slumped onto the couch with the phone in my hand. As much as it offered me some comfort to think of them, the morbid thoughts came hand in hand. Two more people who would eventually leave me. People get sick. People die. I couldn't call them. Watching and waiting for Mom to die was enough.

*****

I scalded myself with the hottest shower I could stand. I bandaged my knees and dressed in the first pair of shorts and tee-shirt I could find. I threw my dripping hair into a ponytail. My phone was on fire again with more texts and missed calls. I checked to make sure none were from the hospital. Not wanting to, but knowing it was what I had to do, I shot off a quick text to Pepper.

`Mom had a massive stroke. In ICU. Not sure what's going to happen. Will be in touch soon.`

Then I copied the text and send the same message to Will.

I turned off the phone before I could receive any replies or be forced to ignore any incoming calls from them. I could barely take care of myself at this point, how could I be expected to reassure them or accept their comfort?

I plucked my spare car key from the rack hanging in the kitchen and headed out to my trusty Ford pickup. Fortunately, the hospital was only twenty minutes from my house, as long as I did eighty miles per hour, and soon I was seated beside my mom once more.

Dr. Naber came and went twice a day for the next two days as I kept vigil. On the third, when he showed up for his morning rounds, I only had to nod my head and he understood. I asked him if he would be there, and he said yes. He would come right after he finished his rounds.

I sat with Mom that long morning and talked to her. I came clean and told her the entire truth about everything that happened in California. I had given her the Cliffs' Notes the day after the premiere, but this time I held nothing back. I started with my chance meeting with Will at the television studio, though I hadn't really known who he was at the time.

"If I'd known then what was going to happen, I might have run away right then," I told her, wishing she would laugh with me.

"Pepper took me to this awful party, Mom. Everyone was so beautiful and perfect. I felt like the class nerd."

I waited for Mom's hand to snake out and biff me on the head, but it didn't. So I went ahead and described every detail about the beautiful mansion I walked through and the people at the party.

"So we decided to blow that popsicle stand for something more fun. The bar was called The Relic, and it reminded me of the places Pepper and I used to hang out."

I found myself smiling as I told her about my official introduction to Will. I spared her the more intimate details, but I told her everything I could about him and our love affair. I spun a tale about how we had fallen in love and were going to be together. I said he loved me with all of his heart and was going to take good care of me. I told her about how Pepper had gotten us together. I described Pepper in vivid detail, making sure to say her "second daughter" loved her very much. I reminded her that Tony had been caught and that the foundation would, once again, go on to help all of those families that had suffered the loss of a loved one.

I asked her to give Dad a hug for me and tell him how much I missed him. I told her to give him all the news about the book and Pepper and Will. I wanted her to make sure he didn't worry about me either. I reminded her that I would miss her more than I could ever express. If ever I put another word on the page, it would be because of her support and love, which had been unconditional my entire life.

I thanked her for everything she'd ever done. Even though the words were guilt-ridden daggers stabbing me in the guts, I thanked her for cleaning my house one last time and managed a little laugh. I thought she would get a kick out of that.

When I finally exhausted my vault of words, I cried some more.

"I'm sorry, Mom. I know you wouldn't want me to cry, but I can't help it." I was losing her, and there was no way it wasn't going to hurt or not make me sad. "It is what it is, right, Mom?" I used our favorite catchphrase.

Time seemed to crawl while I waited for Dr. Naber to return, but when he walked into the room, I struggled not to scream at him to leave.

"Are you ready, Vivienne?"

Like I could ever be ready for this. Taking a deep breath and exhaling, I nodded. "Yes. She would hate being like this."

"You're right." Dr. Naber stepped to the bedside and patted Mom's hand. "Goodbye, Olivia."

A moment later, two nurses, one of them April, filed into the room. Each took a place on either side of Mom's bed and they began removing IVs and tubes. When it was time to stop the respirator, Dr. Naber did that himself. He'd been Mom's doctor for more than forty years. I would have done it myself, but it was against hospital policy.

Everyone respectfully left the room, while I sat beside my mother, holding her hand. It only took a few seconds for her breathing to slow.

"I love you, Mom. I'll see you again someday."

And then her breathing stopped altogether.

*****

This time, the details of death did not tread softly on me. When Bruce died, I had no idea what a Casualty Notification Officer was until one showed up at my apartment door. He was dressed in his Class A uniform and wasn't alone. An Army Chaplin was with him. They were calm and kind, delivering the news that my husband was dead in the forced casualness that was required of them. Everything after that was a blur. I remember holding hands with one of them while I dialed my parents, and the other one getting a glass of water for me to sip. I had one of them get my neighbor, an older woman who collected stuffed cats, because the building allowed no animals. Upon

Evelyn's arrival, the CNO and Chaplin left and I just kind of zoned out until my parents arrived. They handled everything, from all the contact with the Army, to the calls back and forth to Bruce's family. When I wrote the book, anything I couldn't remember, I made up and filled in with what I thought happened.

Now, I was numbly standing at the nurse's station being presented with forms and decisions to make, having no one to hand the responsibility off to. Who knew there was so much paperwork to sign? I gritted my teeth and scribbled on form after form, furious. Was I doing everything right? Was I making the right choices and checking off the right boxes? I had no way of knowing.

When Dad died, Mom had been so strong. I knew how devastated she was because we had talked about the day it would finally happen. But she managed to hold her head high and complete the task. I was the one sitting in the corner crying, my heart in pieces on the floor, along with the remnants of the doctors' last efforts to save Dad. A wave of guilt and shame crashed down on me as I realized it should have been *me* taking care of *her* that day. *I* should have been the one to comfort her and take care of the particulars. Once again, someone else had done the dirty work for me. I sent another apology skyward to where I hoped Mom's spirit was whirling about.

When the random nurse handing me the paperwork asked what funeral home I intended to use, I stared at her dumbly for more than a minute. She had the brass tacks to look irritated with me.

"I beg your pardon?" I slammed the pen down on the countertop.

"You'll need to contact a funeral home to collect the body."

I half expected her to add "Duh" to the end of the sentence. I shifted the pen in my hand so I could stab her in the forehead with it.

"Van Lerberghe in St. Clair Shores."

"I don't know that one," she sighed.

"*Look it up, then*," I growled, my teeth clenched as tightly together as possible.

Just then, Nurse April appeared at my side and I felt her cool fingertips on my arm.

"Is everything okay?" Her tone was gentle and kind.

"Yes," I breathed in deeply. "Yes, fine. Am I finished yet?"

"Of course." April nodded and took the clipboard away from me, shoving it across the counter to the other nurse. "If anything else needs to be signed, we'll send it to you." She wrapped her arm around my shoulders and led me away from what could have been a justifiable homicide.

Thanking April, I gave her a hug and then went back to Mom's room for one more goodbye before I left the hospital for the last time. I had to admit, she looked at peace, lying there. But the longer I stood staring, the more agitated I became. My skin began to itch. I wanted to give her one last kiss, hold her hand one last time. But that wasn't my mother anymore. Mom was somewhere in the universe with my Dad. The body on the bed was just a shell. I was filled with a deep sense of shame because it was beginning to freak me out.

From the foot of her bed, I put my fingers to my lips and blew her a kiss.

"Goodbye, Mom. I love you."

I rushed out of the room.

*****

Sitting in the car, I couldn't find the strength to lift the key to the ignition, much less the inclination to drive home. Instead, I let the tears roll down my face, gravity pulling them off my chin to soak the front of my shirt. The finality of the moment when mom's breathing stopped was like a dream. Something I wished I could pretend wasn't real and could avoid, like so many other things in my stupid, coddled life. Slumped behind the wheel of my pickup, I was pulverized with the feeling of aloneness. There would be no brothers or sisters to help shoulder the burden of the funeral arrangements. No aunts or uncles or cousins supporting me and hugging me close while I grieved. I was alone in my responsibilities, in my mourning. I wasn't prepared for this.

My parents and Bruce's family had taken care of his arrangements. I had been kept in beds or chairs or on couches to "rest" until the day I had to sit in the front of a funeral parlor, gazing at a flag-draped casket. With my Mom on my right and Bruce's mother on my left, I'd listed from one side to the other, as the minister droned on. Numbness had been the predominant feeling. Disbelief, confusion, and fear were the petals on my flowering stupor.

A frown inched over my face as I realized how babied I'd been. Instead of facing the devastation of Bruce's death, I'd been overprotected, considered too young and fragile to manage the wretchedness of death.

Hiding in my car, I was ashamed and grateful at the same time that I wouldn't have to plan a public service for Mom. After the stress and strain of Dad's, Mom declared she did not want one for herself. She considered them barbaric and unnecessary. Even though I tried to explain to her that funerals were more for the people left behind than the actual deceased person, she would have none of it.

"Don't you dare have a funeral for me, Vivienne. I don't want you to have to go through it alone and I *certainly* don't want a bunch of people wandering around crying over my corpse. It's sick. Throw a party instead!"

Even in death, Mom was trying to protect me. Did she not want a funeral because she really believed that nonsense of them being barbaric, or was she just trying to keep me from having to deal with it all?

Using the last few crumpled up napkins in my glove box to clean up my wet, snotty face, I willed myself to start the car and drive home. My brain was pulsing with thoughts as my car auto-piloted its way down the freeway. I would have to disregard Mom's wishes about not publishing anything in the paper. She had too many people who loved her not to let them know. I'd write something up for the *Free Press* and tell people to make donations in her name.

The Widow and the Rock Star

Without realizing what I was doing, I found myself pulling into the driveway of Mom's house. I hadn't bothered to check on it since I'd gotten back from California because I'd spent all my time with her.

As expected, her front door was closed but unlocked. So was the back door. And none of her windows were secured, most of them still wide open in the hot summer weather. I stood in the living room feeling completely empty. We'd never sit together on the couch again. We'd never again argue over what to watch on television. Never again would I see the annual Christmas cards draped across the mantel above the fireplace. I wanted to cry, but for the moment, there just weren't any tears left.

I plodded through the saltbox colonial, closing all of the windows and locking them tight. I pulled the curtains on each of them. I went up the stairs and did the same for the eight windows on the second floor. When I got to Mom's bedroom, I found myself laughing, even though that was the last thing I thought I could have ever done.

Mom had taken the time to tidy my house, but there was her bed, rumpled and unmade. A paperback lay open, but face down on the bed, about halfway through. A basket of laundry stood in the corner, waiting to be toted downstairs. The closet door was open, and Mom's slippers were on the floor, tossed haphazardly inside. I left it all as it was. I didn't have the nerve to change what she had last touched. I went to each window and shut them, trying not to look at anything specific, afraid I would scream out loud.

Backing out of the room, I pulled the door closed. I hurried down the stairs to stand in the hallway by the front door. I forced myself to take several deep breaths, and then moved from the foyer to the kitchen. Mom's laptop sat open on the kitchen table, the screen dark. It drew me in. I tapped the space bar and the screen came to life. I entered the password I'd created for her, and several web pages woke up, including Mom's favorite crossword puzzle site, Facebook, and some news pages.

I closed the news and puzzle pages, but left Facebook open. The words from Mom's last post were seared into my brain and memory.

"So proud of my daughter! Got to see her on the red carpet, on the arm of a handsome young man. Her foundation caught the dirty bastard thief who tried to steal all the money. And she sounds happier than she has in years. Yay for Vivienne!"

That was what threw me over the edge. I ran from the house like my ass was on fire, hitching in great gulps of air. I jumped into my truck and screeched the tires obnoxiously as I sped away, making the mile-and-a-half drive in under three minutes. I slammed the breaks as hard as I could, hitting my own driveway at a reckless speed leaving long, black tire-marks. I ignored the odd looks from the neighbors as I dashed inside.

I tore through the whole house, shutting every window and drawing all the curtains to keep out the light. Mom had loved summer and the sunshine, basking in the glow, getting a nice, deep tan. I did not want to see the sun at all. I did not want the reminder of her favorite season. I made my house a tomb.

I went to my bedroom and stripped off my clothes, leaving them in a heap on the floor. I crawled into bed, on top of the covers and hugged one of my four pillows tight to my chest and wept. I let all the memories of my life run through my mind, not trying to hide from them or squash them. It was like slowly pressing a knife into my heart. I thought if I pushed the blade down hard enough, causing myself enough pain, I would push past it and come out on the other side. I crushed a corner of the pillow deep inside my mouth and screamed until my throat was on fire.

I began to feel nauseous and had to sprint to the bathroom to throw up. I'd barely eaten in almost four days and was wracked with dry heaves. I moaned like I was being murdered with each and every one.

After who knows how many hours of wailing and heaving, I lay prone on the freezing, hard tile floor. My back was jammed against the vanity and my butt rested on the cold base of the toilet. I closed my eyes and watched my mother's smiling face float around in my mind, taunting me.

*****

When had I crawled to bed? I didn't know. How had I gotten dressed? I fingered the plain white tee-shirt and yoga pants on my body. Was it the middle of the night? Morning? Maybe afternoon? I couldn't tell. The drapes in my room kept the knowledge from me. It didn't matter. Whether my eyes were open or closed, all I could see was Mom's last Facebook post.

There was a high-pitched keening, even more nightmarish in that it was coming from me. Torture victims couldn't produce the sounds I was making. Had it not been for all the closed and sealed windows, the neighbors might have called the police.

Unintelligible gibberish flew from my lips as I screamed and cursed God, the universe, whatever came to mind. Half words, half-formed sentences. No one could have known I was a writer with a flair for language. I kept at it for more than an hour, until I couldn't breathe. My nose was clogged and my face was drenched with the tears pouring out of my eyes. I contemplated killing myself. If there had been any prescription drugs in the house or any other painless way to do myself in, I think I would have taken it.

Exhausted amidst the emotional wreckage of my breakdown, I reached for the phone by the bed. It seemed an eternity and an instant for it to power on. Instinctively I dialed Pepper. Four rings later, a male voice I didn't recognize answered her phone. "Hello?"

"Pepper?"

"A moment, please."

I heard the sounds of shuffling and muffled voices.

"Hello?" Pepper sounded slightly out of breath.

"It's Viv."

"Vivvy! Finally! How are you? How's Mom? I miss you!" she cried. "Wait. *What's wrong?*"

"Uh--"

"It's three in the morning here. Are you okay?"

My lower lip trembled and I almost hung up. "Mom," was all I could manage. I couldn't say another word. I moaned and snuffled, knowing I was scaring the shit out of her, but nothing would come out of my mouth.

"Viv, calm down," Pepper commanded. "It's going to be okay. Where are you?"

"H-h-home," I stammered. "Mom—" I choked down bile rising in my raw throat.

I could hear her moving around.

"I'll be there tomorrow! I'll grab the first flight I can!"

"N-n-uhng." Language completely failed me.

"Shh. I'm on my way. I should have come sooner," she soothed, but I could hear the tears in her voice, too. "I'm so sorry Viv, I'm so sorry. Just hold on. Don't do anything at all. *I'm coming!*"

Chapter 45

Gripping her silent phone, Pepper jumped out of bed, searching frantically for her bra and panties, swiping at her cheeks sticky with tears. Gabriel lay sprawled on the bed watching, his eyes intense with growing concern. They had just finished making love when Pepper's phone rang. He tried to grab it as a joke, teasing her that her other boyfriend was calling.

"I need to go, Gabe." Pepper found her pants and jerked them on, forgetting about the underwear. She snatched her tee-shirt from the back of a chair and yanked it over her head.

"What's wrong, love?"

"Viv's having a breakdown. She couldn't even *speak*. I think her mother must have died. How fast do you think I could get a flight to Detroit?"

"Wait a minute." Gabriel sat up. "You can't just run off to the airport in the middle of the night." He grabbed her hand and forced her to sit.

"I'm sorry, Gabe." Pepper kissed him. "You don't understand. She's my best friend and I can tell she's in trouble. I won't be able to sit here for the rest of the night waiting for morning."

Gabriel climbed out of bed naked and padded to the closet in the master bedroom of his Hollywood Hills mansion. He emerged a moment later holding boxers, jeans and a shirt.

"Finish getting dressed, love. We'll take my jet."

Chapter 46

Bleary eyed from crying and lack of, or too much, sleep, I wandered through the dim house wondering if I really called Pepper the night before or if it had been a nightmare. My grimy bathrobe hung off me and I couldn't figure out where the horrible smell filling my nose was coming from.

I stopped by the bathroom to pee and then struggled to raise myself from the seat when I was finished. I stared at the bathtub wondering if I should fill it.

"Fuck it." My language was back. I schlepped toward the bedroom.

Before I could crawl back into bed, a loud pounding at my front door made me shriek. I didn't know what time it was. Clutching my robe tight to my chest, I tiptoed down the hall toward the door. Irrational fear of the unknown kept me from opening it. Then I heard Pepper shouting and banging again.

"Vivienne! Let me in!"

When I clicked the lock, she heard it and came barreling in, sweeping me into a tight hug. Fresh tears burst from my eyes as relief spread over me.

It was true, I did call her! And she was here, she was *here*! Slamming the door shut with her foot, she practically carried me to the couch.

"I'm here now Viv, I'm here," she said into my hair over and over, stroking my head rocking me back and forth. She was crying, too, and I could feel the wetness on my scalp.

"Mom's gone!" I wailed.

She hushed me.

"I'm here now."

*****

The Widow and the Rock Star

Pepper felt her arms go numb as she held Vivienne for more than an hour, unable to do anything but whisper soothing words. It took that long for Vivienne to relax and stop weeping, but Pepper waited her out. She wrinkled her nose, wondering when Vivienne had last taken a shower.

When she finally went limp, Pepper pulled away to see if maybe she had fallen asleep, but Vivienne's green eyes were open and her face was drenched.

"Come on, hun. Let's get you into the tub." Pepper hoisted her up and guided her down the hallway to the bathroom, setting her down on the toilet. She ran the water as hot as she dared, then helped Vivienne out of the filthy robe sticking to her skin. Pepper eased her in, and Vivienne drew up her knees to her chest.

Masking her disgust, Pepper took the dirty robe and carried it out to the kitchen, dropping it in the garbage can. She opened doors along the hallway until she found the linen closet. She pulled out the last two clean towels and hurried back to the bathroom. Vivienne remained in the same position, hugging her knees with her face buried in them. She was crying again, and Pepper tried not to join her. Instead, she dropped to her knees and picked up a bright pink, netted sponge out of the water and covered it with cherry-scented body wash from a bottle on the edge of the tub. She tried handing it to Vivienne, who still hadn't looked up, so Pepper washed her dearest friend's arms and back as lovingly as she would have cleansed her own child. The fragrance of the soap began to replace Vivienne's funk and, finally, she lifted her head from her knees but still didn't meet Pepper's gaze.

She'll look at me when she's ready, Pepper thought. Progress was made when Vivienne reached for the sponge to continue washing herself, so Pepper fumbled for the shampoo.

"Don't," Vivienne whispered. "I can finish."

"Okay. Do you want me to leave?"

"Yes, please."

"You got it. I'll just be outside if you need me." Pepper got up and left the bathroom, closing the door behind her.

While Vivienne was in the bathroom, Pepper surveyed the house. There weren't any dishes or garbage in the kitchen, which gave her the impression that Vivienne hadn't been eating, or at least not at home. There was a beginning layer of dust everywhere and everything smelled dank and stale. She thought she detected the faint lingering odor of something else more vile.

Starting in the living room, she threw open the front door and propped it open with a shoe. She then opened all of the curtains and lifted the windows wide. A warm summer breeze filled the room right away, helping to whisk some of the staleness away.

Pepper located Lysol and garbage bags under the kitchen sink and took them to the bedroom. Opening the door, she was smacked in the face by the stench of body odor, urine, and vomit.

"Oh God," she whispered, cupping her hands over her mouth and nose. She went quickly to the windows and got them open as fast as she could. Leaning close to the screen, she took in a breath of fresh air before turning back around.

Wishing she had gloves, Pepper stripped the sheets off the bed and stuffed them into a garbage bag, not bothering to consider laundering them. She peered next to the bed into the wastebasket beside it.

"*Oh God*," she hissed, shocked at the gelatinous muck congealed at the bottom. She grabbed it and threw it into the bag with the sheets, then dragged it out of the house to stuff it into a garbage can in the back yard. Returning to the bedroom, Pepper sprayed the bare mattress liberally with almost half the can of Lysol and then struggled to flip it over. She sprayed that side too, just in case. Then she found fresh sheets to remake the bed. She was relieved that the smell in the room was much improved. When she smoothed the last corner of the bedspread, Pepper heard the water running in the shower so she checked on Vivienne's progress.

"You okay in there?"

"Yes, thank you." Vivienne's voice was muffled by the door and the water, but it sounded strong, if a bit hoarse.

Pepper smiled and heaved a sigh of relief. Knowing it couldn't be put off, she wandered down the stairs to the basement, feeling along the wall for any light switches. The only light was coming through small glass block windows, which probably hadn't been washed or cleaned since Viv bought the place. Eventually she found what she was looking for and flipped the switch to fill the rooms with fake fluorescent light. The door to the laundry room was closed, so Pepper grabbed the knob and threw it open. The mountain of clothing piled up beneath the laundry chute from the bathroom was almost as tall as she was. Sighing and shaking her head, Pepper began sorting through the pile, separating the colors and whites and towels. She started with all of Vivienne's yoga pants, dark tee-shirts and black underwear, knowing she would need something to wear and that Pepper's clothes wouldn't fit her.

With the first load agitating, Pepper went back upstairs. Pulling her phone out of her pocket, she opened a map on the GPS and searched the local restaurants to see what she could order in. Chinese food sounded good and she called the only restaurant that delivered to bring a boatload of food, everything from sweet and sour pork to General Tso's chicken, fried rice, egg rolls, soup, pot stickers and crab rangoon.

While she waited for the food, she searched through closets and the two spare bedrooms for a vacuum cleaner, but couldn't find one. Returning to the living room, Pepper looked around for something to do next. Vivienne appeared in the doorway, her body and hair wrapped in the separate mismatched towels.

"I'm going to get dressed now," she announced.

"You do that, hun. I'll be right here waiting."

"Okay." Vivienne disappeared down the hall back to her bedroom and Pepper sat down on the couch to wait. She took her phone from her pocket once more and dialed Gabriel. The familiar sound of his voice soothed her frayed nerves.

"Darling," he answered.

"Hey, Gabe."

"How is she?"

"Alive. Worse than I thought, but getting better already, I hope." Pepper's voice trembled. "She sure scared me."

"I know. And you scared me. Shall I come by?"

"Oh no, not now. In fact, I'm not sure when I'll be back in touch. You should probably go back to LA, because I think I'm going to be here for a while." Pepper sighed and pinched the bridge of her nose between two fingers.

"Don't be ridiculous," Gabriel said. "I will make myself comfortable at the hotel until I hear from you again. I have my computer and phone. I can work quite nicely from here. You just take care of that lovely girl."

"Thank you, Gabriel." Pepper's voice cracked with gratitude. "You can't know how much I appreciate this."

Gabriel gave a soft laugh.

"Of course I do. Ring me when you're able, love."

"I'll do it."

She tapped the end button on her phone and leaned back to wait for Vivienne to return.

Chapter 47

I stood in my bedroom staring at the fresh bedding and tidied room, trying with great difficulty not to cry. While I always considered Pepper to be my very best friend, she had really outdone herself this time, hauling her cookies back to Michigan at the drop of a hat to take care of me. She had cleaned my room, too.

I tried to think what day it was and could not fathom a guess. That frightened me. How long had I been home before I called Pepper? I didn't even know what time it was. I searched my dresser for clean clothes, but the only thing left was a pair of striped flannel pajamas. I pulled them on and left the bedroom to go face Pepper and all the questions I knew would be coming.

But she surprised me once again. She only smiled when I found her still in the living room, lounging on the couch.

"Nice jammies."

"Thanks." I plopped onto the couch beside her.

"No, thank you for changing. And showering." Pepper pinched her nose shut and winked at me.

"Yeah, yeah. I was pretty rank." I wasn't ready to laugh about it, but I did give her a minute smile. I glanced at the clock on the wall. *Two-thirty? Good grief!*

"That's an understatement," she muttered, giving me a toothy grin. She was trying way too hard to get me to laugh. I wanted to please her but I couldn't do it.

"I get it." I picked at my now clean cuticles. "Thanks for cleaning up. You didn't have to do that."

"Nope, I didn't. I wanted to. And you're welcome." Pepper lifted her long legs onto the couch and poked at me with her toes. "I ordered food and it'll be here any minute. You *will* eat."

"Okay." I didn't argue with her, but I wasn't sure I was ready for food any more than laughter yet.

Pepper sat with her hands folded in her lap, glancing around the room and saying nothing. I needed to talk, was ready to talk, but I didn't know how to. I was so ashamed. I was wracked with guilt even while feeling so much relief that Pepper had come. Worst of all was knowing I would have to admit to Pepper that I'd wanted to die. That if there had been a means available to me, I probably would have taken it.

Pepper was at the ready when the food arrived, paying for it and then spreading it out on the dining room table. I chose a seat, waiting for her to do the same.

"That reminds me of something. I'll be right back." She bolted down the stairs to the basement, and I heard the familiar sounds of laundry being transferred from washer to dryer. When she returned, she gave me a bright smile. "I did all your comfies in one load, including some underwear."

"Thank you," I whispered, barely able to keep from crying again. She waved her hands in dismissal, and motioned for me to start eating.

I struggled with the chopsticks, thinking I could use that as an excuse for not eating, but soon the smell of the food made my stomach growl. Within moments, I devoured an eggroll in three bites.

"Easy, girl. I don't want you getting sick on me."

"No worries." My mouth was full and the words were garbled. She chuckled and tucked in to the sweet and sour pork.

"Out with it. Start at the beginning." Pepper reached for a pot sticker.

"I don't know if I can." I put down my chopsticks and pushed the carton of fried rice in front of me to the middle of the table. "There's so much."

"Start slow, then."

I hugged myself and shrugged. Losing Mom had apparently caused my knack for speaking to abandon me as well. As long as I kept shoveling food into my mouth, Pepper didn't push the issue. She knew

I would fill up eventually. When I did, I laid the sticks down and sighed. I picked a single piece up between two fingers and rolled it around before flicking it halfway across the table.

"Gross." Pepper retrieved it and placed it daintily on her own plate. "If you aren't ready to talk, don't. But you don't have to make a mess." She shook a finger at me.

My bottom lip trembled and I opened my mouth and closed it several times.

"My mom is dead."

"I know." Pepper's bottom lip trembled, too.

Snuffling, I sucked in a shuddering breath.

"She's gone, Pep. And she's never coming back."

Pepper reached over and laid a hand on mine.

"I know, Viv. And I'm so sorry." She was crying too.

And then the words came.

Pepper never interrupted and let me talk until my voice was nearly gone and my butt went numb. She listened with a patience I didn't know she had. Her normally frenetic energy was reigned in, leaving her calm and attentive. Every detail of every moment from the time I walked into Mom's hospital room, to the point when I called Pepper came pouring out as fast as coffee from a pot. The more I talked, the faster the haze around me dissipated. The less foggy I got, the more I talked. I started to feel more normal again. Well, as normal as possible with the emptiness I felt inside.

Pepper listened and never judged me. She didn't offer advice or opinions, didn't jump into the conversation or interrupt. She let me get it all out until well after the sun went down.

"Why didn't you call sooner, Viv?" Pepper asked sadly. "I wanted to be here with you, *for* you."

"I just couldn't, Pep. I can't explain it. The pain was so bad, but I wanted it to hurt worse. I thought if it got bad enough I'd just die right along with Mom." I rubbed my eyes, willing the tears back inside. "I guess I went crazy."

"You were bad when Bruce died, but not like *this*," Pepper said quietly. She had that look someone has while they're getting over a very bad scare, pale and strained. "From this day forward, I am *never* listening to you again when you say you don't need anything."

"You shouldn't," I admitted. "I am not to be trusted when depressed."

I could tell she wasn't satisfied with my agreement. The state in which she found me was far beyond anything I was explaining away while the food got cold and the plum sauce congealed.

Glancing at her watch, Pepper finally made me go to bed. I was so grateful to have her there; I couldn't believe the calm and peace she brought, in spite of her vivaciousness and general nervous energy. As I shuffled down the hall, her hands on my shoulders, I tried to ask her questions. How she had gotten home so fast, how was she going to afford it, but she wouldn't answer. She shushed me every time. She promised me she would be there when I woke up and that we would talk more then.

I slept all night, the next whole day and night as well. Pepper had arrived around noon on a Sunday and I did not crawl out of bed again until Tuesday, just after eight in the morning. When I opened my eyes and saw her beside me, snoring softly, I sighed, just as relieved as when she burst through the door.

Trying not to disturb her, I eased myself off the bed and out of the room. I took another long, hot shower and conditioned my hair. I cried again a little and my tears mixed with the water swirling down the drain. I felt ashamed and guilty for scaring Pepper and for letting myself go crazy. As the water turned icy on my skin, I tried to stop feeling sorry for myself. I beat myself up pretty good mentally while the frigid spray stabbed at my body.

When my teeth started to chatter, I turned off the faucet and stood shivering in the tub, punishing myself a little more before finally grabbing a towel to dry off. Standing in front of the mirror, I looked at my face long and hard. I was shocked to see how gaunt it looked, how haunted my eyes were.

"What a waste," I said to the reflection. "First you waste seventeen years over a dead husband and now you're trying to throw away the next seventeen because your Mom died. What a dumbass!" In a fit of petulance, I stuck my tongue out. "Nyaaaaah!"

I thought the gurgling in my throat was vomit until I realized I was snickering, which then turned into full-blown laughter. I stumbled backwards, my back thumping against the bathroom wall. I slid down onto my butt, still cackling into my fists so I wouldn't wake up Pepper. What a fool I'd been. *Pepper's going to kick my ass for sure*, I thought.

I pulled myself up and was much more satisfied by the face meeting me in the mirror. The eyes were bright and clear and the frown lines were far less prominent. I brushed my teeth and surprised myself by humming a tune while I did it.

When I opened the bathroom door, I was smacked in the face by the heavenly smell of strong coffee. I guess I hadn't been as quiet as I thought. Pepper must have gotten up. I tiptoed to the kitchen, wrapped only in a towel, and screamed bloody murder when I saw a man I didn't know in my kitchen pouring himself a cup of the steaming, dark liquid.

"Wait! Wait!" he yelled over my screaming. Pepper stumbled in, trying to make sense of the chaos she confronted.

"Viv! Stop! He's with me!"

Hiding behind Pepper, I squinted my eyes, finally recognizing the stranger in my kitchen.

"Gabriel? Gabriel Seigal?"

"Yes," he wheezed, his hands trembling around the coffee cup he still grasped.

"What are you doing here?" I demanded.

"He's with me, Viv," Pepper explained. "We've been dating since you left California."

My mouth dropped open and I stared at her.

"What? Why didn't you tell me?"

Pepper grinned and shuffled over to Gabriel. She leaned against him and put her head on his shoulder, then snagged the cup out of his hand to take a deep swallow.

"We've been taking things slow. Keeping it quiet."

"O-okay." I tried to process what I was seeing. Gabriel Seigal in my house. Dating my best friend. *What the hell?* I realized then I was still in my towel and jumped back out of the doorway, leaving only my head visible. "I'm going to go get dressed. I'll be back in a minute."

"Please do." Gabriel pointed a finger at me and winked.

Chapter 48

"I'm so sorry." Gabriel poured himself another cup of coffee and stood in the tiny kitchen with Pepper. "I had no idea she would wake up."

"It's okay, Gabe. No harm done." Pepper smiled lovingly, but she was trying her best not to laugh. Gabriel was always so eager to please, and it usually went awry, though not as loudly as it had a few moments ago. Pepper loved him all the more for it. They took their coffee to the living room and made themselves comfortable on the couch while they waited.

Before they'd left California, Pepper had called Jake Rushmore to fill him in on Vivienne's sudden disappearance. Properly sympathetic and contrite after having bitched Pepper out for calling at such an unholy hour, he'd actually gotten out of bed at 4 a.m. and hauled his ass over to the Ritz. Using his considerable influence to gain entrance to her room, Jake had retrieved Vivienne's luggage and then passed it off to Pepper and Gabriel as their limo pulled up to the hotel. Pepper gave him her promise that she would keep in contact as soon as she knew what was going on herself.

While Vivienne slept for two days, Pepper made it a point to finish all the laundry and put it away. Gabriel had brought Vivienne's suitcases over from the hotel and spent time keeping vigil with Pepper. The first twenty-four hours were quiet as Vivienne slept the sleep of one truly exhausted from her ordeal. But as she moved into the next phase of her slumber, Pepper got worried. She watched as her best friend thrashed around in the throes of what surely were vicious nightmares. Whispering soothing words and stroking her back was all she could do to try and pacify Vivienne. Gabriel agreed to stay the second night, camping out in the spare bedroom while Pepper got up every hour to check on Viv. The fits had finally abated around three in the morning. Pepper was too exhausted to go back to Gabriel and had fallen asleep beside Vivienne.

Pepper rubbed her eyes and sipped more coffee as Vivienne walked into the living room, carrying her own cup. She curled up in the only spot left on the couch.

"You look good." Pepper eyed her closely. "Your eyes are clear."

"I feel a lot better. I owe it all to you." She drank some coffee. "Thanks for bringing up the clean clothes."

"Pffft, twarn't nuttin'." Pepper flipped her a salute.

"It's your turn." Vivienne sipped her coffee. "Tell me everything. How did you get here so fast?"

Pepper swiveled her head back at Gabriel and then to Vivienne.

"Who has two thumbs and is dating a guy with his own private jet?" Pepper asked, turning her eyes up to the ceiling. "This girl. We met the night of the premiere Will took us to. He was the date I left for."

Vivienne sighed and smiled genuinely for the first time in days, Pepper felt sure.

"That's wonderful! Why didn't you tell me before?"

"That was my doing," Gabriel interrupted. "We were still in negotiations and Pepper was forbidden from saying anything to you so that your decision would not be influenced in any way."

"Bah! I already knew I was going with EJR," Vivienne admitted.

"*We* didn't know that." Pepper shook her head indignantly. "Our first date that night was about nine hours of conversation. It was a wonder I had a voice the next day because he barely said a word." Pepper jacked her thumb at him. Gabriel grinned. "And the rest, as they say, is history. We've been dating since then."

Vivienne sat expectantly waiting for more, then thunked herself in the forehead with her fist.

"Duh. I'll get the details when Gabriel's not around." Pepper winked at her, and Gabriel looked up at the ceiling and around the room.

"Besides, I'm more worried about you." The concern was beginning to settle in Pepper's eyes again. "You scared the hell out of me."

"I scared the hell out of me, too."

"You not only look better today, you're acting more like yourself. Are you hungry? There's leftover Chinese or I can fix you something to eat. I went to the store yesterday while you were sleeping and got a couple of things. You still need a hell of a lot more." Pepper started to get up, but Gabriel held her back. He stood up and gave a little bow.

"Allow me. If you have eggs, I can whip something up."

"There are eggs, bacon and more coffee. I also got some orange juice and bottled water, but that's about it." Pepper ticked off the shopping list on her fingers.

"I shall return." Gabriel wandered out to the kitchen to leave them alone.

When he was out of earshot, Vivienne leaned closer to Pepper.

"Well?"

"He's really the best," Pepper sighed, her eyes softening and a natural smile crossing her face, instead of her usual, cynical smirk. "I couldn't be happier."

"I'm so glad!"

Pepper shrugged her shoulders, but they were quivering with excitement as she did so.

"I don't know where it's going, but we're happy where we are, and that's all that counts." She leaned back and slurped from her cup. "Seriously, though, I'm here for *you*."

"Well, don't worry. You came right when I needed you, and I feel like my old self again already."

Pepper frowned.

"Yeah, right. And what happens when I leave?"

Vivienne blanched.

"I don't know, but I had a long talk with myself in the shower this morning. I can promise you I won't go nuts like that again."

Setting her coffee cup on the side table, Pepper stared hard at Vivienne.

"Viv, I don't know how you could be so *stupid*. You lost your mother for Chrissake. How could you even *think* you could handle that all by yourself?"

Vivienne shook her head.

"I don't know. I feel, *felt*, so guilty for not being here when she had the stroke. I should have been home, with her. She was in her seventies and I shouldn't have left her alone." Tears were dangerously close to falling from her eyes again. Pepper felt awash with pity as she watched Vivienne struggle to blink them back.

"Vivvy, it was *not* your fault. Mom didn't have the stroke because you weren't here. You *have* to know that."

"But I don't!" Vivienne cried. "She cleaned my house the day before she fucking died! How do I know she didn't overdo it?"

Pepper said nothing, just took the coffee cup out of her hands to set it on the coffee table. She pulled Vivienne into her arms and held on.

"It's not your fault, hun. *It is not your fault.*"

Vivienne sobbed uncontrollably, clutching at Pepper.

Gabriel entered the room with two plates in his hands, but Pepper waved him away, shaking her head. He nodded and slowly backed out.

A half an hour later, Vivienne was spent and Pepper was wiping the tears off her face with a tissue.

"Feel a little better?" she asked.

"No." Vivienne pouted. "I want my mom."

"I know you do. Hell, *I* want your mom, too."

That made Vivienne smile a little and Pepper's heart soared.

"You'll adjust, hun. It's going to take a long time, but you'll get there."

"I know." She didn't sound convincing to Pepper. Not in the least.

"Let's go see what Gabe fixed for us to eat. I'm starved." Pepper stood up and pulled Vivienne into a standing position. With their arms around one another's waists, they went into the kitchen for breakfast.

*****

I wish I could have warned Pepper that things wouldn't stay so calm or upbeat. I should have told her that I would spiral just as quickly as I flew, but my emotions swung one way and then the other too fast. We all ate breakfast at the table, banal chit chat filling the silences in between chewing. The rationality I'd found in the bathroom earlier disappeared.

I watched Pepper and Gabriel touch each other. On the hand, the face, the shoulder, the knee. I don't think they were even aware of it. Their intimacy should have made me feel happy for them and glad that Pepper finally had someone worthy of her love. Instead, it drove home that I would not have that kind of intimacy again. Had I been in my right mind, I could have thought of Will. But I didn't. I only thought of my mom. She was my biggest supporter, shoulder to cry on, and font of inspiration since Bruce died. Pepper might be my best *peer* friend, but Mom had become my best friend in everyday life. The concept of no more Mom was making the eggs in my stomach churn. Nausea shot through me faster than the vomit, which would surely follow.

I didn't excuse myself, but ran to the bathroom, knocking my chair over in the process. Once again, I found myself emptying the contents of my guts into the toilet for nearly an hour. I was mortified that Gabriel could hear me, and it made me sicker. Pepper came in to hold my hair back and wipe a cool washcloth on my forehead, but her kindness only hurt more. It seemed like the nicer she was to me, the harder I cried and the more upset I got. When there was nothing left to vomit, and the heaving abated, Pepper helped me back to bed. I could hear her talking to Gabriel.

"You okay, hun?" Pepper whispered from the doorway of my room.

Of course I wasn't okay. "I'm sorry," I whimpered, the covers pulled up to my chin. I kept my eyes shut so I couldn't see the sympathy on her face and the pity in her eyes.

"Don't be." She perched on the edge of the bed. "It's going to take time. I'm here."

*****

Pepper closed the door with a gentle click. Gabriel stood at the end of the hallway waiting for her. Her pace quickened and she lunged at him, needing to feel his arms around her. She clutched him tightly and breathed in the familiar scent of his cologne, sending a prayer of thanks out to the universe for his presence.

"I'm sorry you had to see that." Her voice was muffled against his chest.

"No worries, love." He guided her into the living room and together they sat down on the couch. "Are you all right?"

"Me? I'm fine. It's my best friend coming apart at the seams." Pepper's bottom lip quivered the tiniest bit and she chomped down on it with her teeth to keep him from seeing. "I know everything will be okay, but it breaks my heart to see her in so much pain."

"It just takes time." Gabriel stroked her hair and kissed her on the forehead.

"Patience is not one of my virtues," Pepper muttered. Snuggling against him, she allowed herself to enjoy the comfort and calm he offered. The knock on the door jangled her nerves and sent her straight back into a state of anxiety.

"Are you expecting anyone?"

"No." Pepper jumped up and ran to the door. When she opened it, a delivery man stood holding a huge arrangements of flowers.

"Vivienne Stark?" he asked.

"Yes," Pepper lied. She opened the screen door and took the flowers, surprised at the weight of them. Gabriel appeared directly behind her to take them out of her hands. He set them on the table while Pepper signed her acceptance.

"Thank you."

Closing the door, she went to the table to search for the card in the flowers. Opening it, she smiled brightly. "Aw, look at this!" She held the card out for Gabriel to read.

"I'm so sorry about your mom. Missing you and hoping to see you soon. Love, Will," he read aloud. "It would seem he's quite smitten with her."

"Yes, indeed." Pepper leaned over to examine the flowers more closely. There were red, yellow and white roses, along with peach colored tulips, daisies, white lilies, and two or three other flowers she couldn't identify. "These are gorgeous and they smell wonderful!" Pepper lifted the heavy, green glass vase and placed it in the middle of the dining room table. Gabriel took the empty cardboard box and put it on the floor. Putting her nose directly into a rose, Pepper inhaled deeply.

"It's a lovely arrangement," Gabriel agreed. "Those are snap dragons." He pointed to some orange and purple blossoms. "And the greenery is ruscus, very nice filler."

"Wow, movie mogul *and* a horticulturist. I'm a lucky gal," Pepper laughed. She stood for another minute admiring the flowers, but her smile disintegrated. "We can't let Vivienne see these."

"What? Why ever not?"

"If she gets back on the edge, these will send her right on over." Pepper frowned, no longer excited by the beautiful gift from Will.

"You can't be certain of that, Pepper. If she knows they're from Will, it might be just the thing to perk up her spirits."

Pepper shook her head.

"I don't know. I think it might be too much of a risk."

"Tell you what," Gabriel said as he reached for the vase. "Put them in the corner by the couch so that she won't notice them straight off. Then, if she does, you can give her the card."

He walked the flowers over to the end table in the corner of the room, setting them carefully down beside the lamp so that they shared the space.

"There. Not quite so noticeable now, yeah?"

Pepper put her hands on her hips and tilted her head from side to side.

"Okay. Not bad. I better call Will and let him know they got here."

"All right, love. I think I'll go back to the hotel and get a little work done. My phone has been buzzing in my pocket for quite some time. Sure you'll be all right?"

"Yes, of course. Go on. I'll call you later."

Pepper walked Gabriel out to the rental car and kissed him goodbye. When he'd driven off, she went back inside to find her phone. She plopped on the couch and crossed her legs while she listened to the ringing.

"Hello?"

"Hey, Will."

"How is she?" His voice was anxious and tense.

"Up and down," Pepper admitted, pinching the bridge of her nose. "I thought she was doing better this morning, but then she had a bit of a setback. She's sleeping now."

"Has she gotten the flowers I sent?"

"They just arrived. Absolutely gorgeous. Did you pick them out yourself?"

"Yeah."

Pepper stifled a giggle at how pleased with himself he sounded.

"Very nice job. She'll love them."

"I really want to be there."

"I know. But she's a basket case, Will. When she broke down a little while ago, I could tell she was embarrassed as hell that Gabe was here. I don't think she could bear for you to see her like this."

"I love her, Pepper, I don't give a shit."

The admission itself was a shock, but the exasperation in his voice hit Pepper like a slap in the face.

"I realize that. But Vivienne hadn't come to grips with her feelings for you, yet, before all this happened. She has enough to deal with without having those feelings thrown at her, too. Can you understand that?"

Pepper waited for his response and didn't like when it took so long to come.

"Yeah, I get that," Will finally said, his tone sad and resigned. "Tell me the truth. Do you think I still have a shot with her?"

Pepper honestly didn't know, but she wasn't about to admit that to him.

"Of course. But it will take some time. You're going to have to be patient."

"Shit."

"Yeah, I hear ya. Believe me, I'm struggling as much as you are, just in a different way." Pepper hated how stressed she sounded, especially when she was trying so hard to put him at ease. "I'll keep in touch. Just sit tight and I promise as soon as I think it's okay for a call, I'll let you know. All right?"

"Yes. Please. Text if you can't call. Just keep me posted."

"I promise."

*****

In my dream, I was standing in the hospital room beside Mom's bed. She was sitting up and smiling, laughing at something. There was a dinner tray in front of her and I was trying to convince her to eat a little something. She was arguing with me that she'd rather eat bugs and ground glass before touching hospital food. I laughed with her and the feeling of relief that she was alive was so overwhelming, I had to sit down on the edge of the bed.

"I'm so glad you're not dead," I whispered to her. Mom cocked her head to the side and gave me a puzzled look. I mirrored her confusion.

"What?"

I waited for her to speak, but she just tilted her head to the side and looked at me with pity and sadness on her face.

And then I woke up, sweat coating my face and neck, as though I were running a fever of a hundred and four. My breath was coming in fast pants. It was so real, the dream, if I could have, I would never have woken up. I would have stayed there forever with my mom.

I covered my face with my hands and cried, a harsh hacking sound coming from my throat. What a cruel and senseless dream to let me believe Mom was still alive. What kind of a God or higher power would let me feel that relief and then snatch it away? I cursed the universe as I rocked back and forth in my bed, the skin on my cheeks slick with tears. I couldn't take any more. I didn't know how I was going to survive this.

Chapter 49

Sitting alone on the front porch, Pepper tore at blades of grass, scattering the remnants on the bottom step. She wasn't sure how to handle Vivienne and the grief paralyzing her best friend. She knew all people grieved differently, but Pepper was as unfamiliar with death as a nun with a husband. There had been all kinds of tragedies and strife throughout her life, but Pepper had yet to deal with someone she truly loved dying. She'd cut all ties with her family when she left Michigan twenty-three years ago. She didn't even know if her parents were still kicking around, or her brother and sister, much less any of the numerous other relatives. Frankly, she didn't care. None of them had attempted to reach out to her in any way since her departure, so she figured they didn't care any more than she did.

Olivia Forest had been more of a mother to her just by sending a Christmas card every year, and Pepper was going to miss her desperately. Not nearly as much as her daughter would, but Pepper loved Olivia, too. Pepper knew she would have to tread carefully with her own mourning, making sure never to compare it to Vivienne's. No matter how many cards came in the mail, her sadness would never equal a daughter's.

Sighing, Pepper let a few tears fall in honor of Olivia.

"I'm going to miss you, lady. Besides your kid, you were the only other person who cared that I actually walked the Earth." Laughing a little, Pepper wiped her face with the hem of her tank top. "Be at peace, old girl. You deserve it. And don't worry about your daughter. I've got this."

Chapter 50

The room was completely dark when I woke up. It took me a minute to realize it was partly because I had the covers over my head. When I tossed them off, sweet, fresh air filled my nose. It was still dark, though, because Pepper had closed the windows and drapes. I could hear the faint humming of the air conditioning unit outside my window. The green glow of the clock radio on the bedside table told me it was 7:23 p.m.

I needed to pee and wished I didn't have to get up to do it. I laid still for another few minutes before I got to the point where I might actually have an accident. Struggling out of the covers, I rolled off the side of the bed, landing on my knees. Groaning, I stood up. My body ached all over and my joints felt stiff and sore. My head pounded steadily and I could barely lift it. I shuffled to the door and opened it. I could hear quiet voices and they stopped. Ignoring them, I made my way to the bathroom.

When I came out, I debated on whether or not to go straight back to bed or investigate what was going on in the living room. The smell of pizza made my stomach lurch with both hunger and disgust. I dragged myself down the hall and into kitchen. Gabriel stood at the counter, filling a plate with a hot, cheesy slice.

"Hello, Vivienne," he said when he saw me. There on his face was the pity I so desperately wanted to avoid.

"Hi." My voice sounded scratchy and flat.

"Would you care for a bite?" He offered the plate he held to me.

I wrinkled my nose and stepped back as though he were offering me poison.

"No thanks."

"All right. Well, come and sit with us for a few minutes, then, yeah?" He stretched out his hand for me to take. I didn't have the strength to lift my arm so I just stumbled next to him and then into the dining room. Pepper was sitting at the table, nibbling at the crust of her finished piece of pizza.

"Hey, Vivvy." She smiled, but she knew me better than anyone and managed to keep her face bland and her tone even.

"Hey." I slumped into the chair on one side of her, while Gabriel took the other.

"Want anything?"

I shook my head, not wanting to speak. *Why did I come out here? Why don't I just go back to bed?*

The silence between us was tense. Whatever Gabriel and Pepper had been discussing was obviously not something they wanted to continue in front of me. I looked at the empty chair at the table. Mom would have loved to be here, meeting Pepper's boyfriend, glad that her "second daughter" had found someone. Sighing, I wondered if I would *ever* be able to look at an empty chair or space without wishing my mother was in it.

"I spoke to Jake today," Pepper said slowly.

I just sat there, not really caring. *Jake? Oh yeah, my agent. Whatever.*

"He says everything is handled and you don't have to worry about a thing."

"'K." *So what?*

I saw Pepper give Gabriel a worried look.

"I know you don't want to hear this, but do I need to be doing anything about a funeral?"

I shook my head.

"No funeral. Mom didn't want one." *No I don't want to hear this.*

Pepper laughed a little.

"That sounds like your mom. Okay. What about her house? Do I need to go over there and check on anything?"

Shrugging, I hugged myself tightly.

"Dunno. Probably not." *Why does she keep asking questions?*

Nodding, Pepper leaned away from the table. "Did she—"

"*What?*" I hissed. "Just leave it, Pepper. What the fuck does it matter anyway?" Finding energy in my anger, I stood up and shoved my chair back. I stomped back down the hallway and into my room, slamming the door behind me.

*****

"Well, that was interesting," Gabriel whispered when Vivienne had gone. Pepper sighed and shook her head sadly. She reached over and righted the upturned chair.

"Yeah, well, that's what happens when you lose the only thing you have in life. What about your parents? You still have them?"

Gabriel looked abashed.

"Yes, actually. They're both still in England. Well into their nineties, but doing smashingly."

"Are you close with them?" Pepper asked.

"Well, not as much as I should be, I suppose. But I see that they have the very best of everything."

Pepper snorted.

"Wait till they die, Gabe. Then you'll know what Vivienne's going through." Pushing her plate away, she sighed and rubbed her forehead. "I'm sorry. That wasn't fair."

"Quite all right, my dear." He reached across the table to put his hand over hers.

"I'm not sure what to be doing right now," Pepper admitted. "I know I should leave her be, but she worries me. How long do I let this go on before I try to get her to snap out of it?" She didn't appreciate the confused and unsure look Gabriel gave her.

"I really couldn't say, darling."

"Well, you're no help." Pepper winked, when she really felt like weeping. He bit into his pizza, and Pepper watched him, her heart aching with love. She wasn't only worried about Viv, but about Gabriel, too. He had a billion dollar company to manage; he didn't need to be sitting around while she cared for Vivienne. It scared her to think maybe he would get irritated after a while and dump her. Her heart knew better, but her experience with men reminded her that they could turn at a moment's notice. One minute they were kissing you, the next they were trying to kill you. Pepper knew she needed to talk to him about going back to California, but was reluctant to bring it up. She liked having him near, especially when she was struggling so hard to help Vivienne. But she knew it wasn't fair to ask him to put his life on hold for her, especially when it was so much more important than her own.

"I think you should go back to California." She said it quickly before she could chicken out.

"What?" Gabriel's mouth was full and he snatched at a napkin to cover it.

"You heard me. I don't have a clue how long I'm going to be here and you have a business to run. And don't give me that song and dance about having a phone and a laptop. You need to be in the office."

Gabriel gave her a kind and patient look, and Pepper's racing heart calmed immediately. *He wouldn't look like that if he was thinking about leaving me, right?*

"Pepper, darling, don't be ridiculous. I'm the head of the company. I can do as I please. And right now, it pleases me to stay with you."

Pepper looked away so he wouldn't see the tears forming in her eyes. Grateful wasn't the word she felt. There was no one single word to describe her relief. That solace gave her the courage to go on.

"I appreciate that, Gabe, more than I can say. But I can tell it's going to get pretty messy around here. Vivienne wouldn't want you here to see it all."

"Then I'll stay in the hotel and you can visit me at your leisure."

"*Now* who's being ridiculous?" She leaned toward him to place her hand on his face. "Really. Stay a couple more days if you want, but it makes more sense for you to go home. I can call and we can text."

Sighing, Gabriel threw his napkin on the table.

"I loathe the idea of leaving you here all alone to deal with this. I want to help."

"I know, but there's nothing you can do." Pepper leaned to give him a tender kiss. "This is a job strictly for the best friend."

"Vivienne is extraordinarily lucky. I hope one day she realizes it."

"Believe me, she does. You don't get to be best friends without hitting a few bumps in the road. She'll be fine, eventually." Glad the mood of the moment was lightening, Pepper grinned. "Besides, she has to be. You guys have a movie to make."

*****

Shivering beneath the covers once more, I felt like a coward and a piece of shit. I had no right to attack Pepper the way I had. All she did was try to help and I lashed out at her. My shame kept me from going out to apologize to both her and Gabriel for my bad behavior. Guilt at what my mother would think of my conduct ate away at my heart, making me burrow farther beneath the blankets.

In just a little over a week, my life had turned completely upside down. Days ago, I had been sitting in a posh hotel with my best friend, contemplating a move to California to maybe develop a relationship with the first man I'd dated since my husband died. Now I was trapped in bed, trying to wrap my head around the fact that I'd lost my only living relative and the most beloved person in my life. I was also doing my best to drive away the best friend I ever had.

I drowsed for a while, thoughts swirling through my brain. I wondered if Nurse April was being as kind and considerate to her next dying patient's family. I thought about my mother's house and what I was going to do with it. I wondered if her car was still in good shape. Should I sell it or keep it? I needed to call her lawyer and find out if she'd ever updated her last will and testament. I thought sadly about her neighbors. Grace, the lady who lived on the right side, was the one who saw Mom drop in the driveway. If she hadn't been getting her mail out of the box, she wouldn't have seen it and called 911. How long would Mom have lain on the hard concrete before someone noticed her? I wondered if Mom had known anything was wrong. Did she have any symptoms? Had she been anywhere or seen anyone and just not said anything, not wanting to bother someone else with what she believed was nothing?

Too many thoughts, too much information. Too much pain and too many unanswered questions. And the most galling thing was that none of it *mattered*.

Chapter 51

Vivienne hardly came out of the bedroom, unless it was to use the bathroom or get a glass of water. She did not eat and she did not speak, and it was obvious to Pepper that she tried to make her forays out when Pepper wasn't around. This went on for several days.

Pepper busied herself by keeping the house tidy and puttering around in Vivienne's yard. Never having been one for outdoor work (she'd never had a yard in California), she was comforted with pulling weeds out of the flower beds, hoping what she yanked out of the ground were, in fact, weeds, and sweeping the concrete patio. She enjoyed sitting outside, relishing the warm sunshine and summer breeze while she waited for Vivienne to get to the next level.

Gabe stayed at the hotel for the most part and only came to the house to pick her up for meals out. Pepper told him every day to go home, but he refused to leave her. He said he wasn't comfortable going back until he knew Vivienne was on the mend. He took her shopping for groceries, and then one morning presented her with a brand new, top of the line Apple laptop so they could Skype when he did go.

Pepper kept in touch with Jake with texts, saying there was no progress and that he should continue to handle things as he saw fit. It was a good thing he had a financial durable power of attorney so he could conduct certain business on Vivienne's behalf. Pepper also kept Will posted through texts and emails.

Every day, the mail brought more sympathy cards. Pepper wondered how word had gotten out about Olivia, and Gabriel suggested to her that Vivienne might have published a notice in the paper. Pepper verified this when she went online and found the obituary. She took the cards and placed them in a box in the spare bedroom closet, not knowing if Vivienne would ever be able to look at them.

Pepper found herself on a Friday morning mousing in the kitchen for something to eat without having to cook. Gabriel wasn't coming by until later, as he had been up late working and was sleeping in. She nearly wet her pants when Vivienne's house phone jangled loudly in the silence of the house. The thing had hardly rung, and the couple of times it had, the calls were from solicitors. Pepper dove for the receiver mounted on the wall in the kitchen, praying the sound hadn't disturbed Vivienne.

"Hello?" she was breathless and cleared her throat to hide it.

"Uh, hello. May I speak with Vivienne, please?" The female voice was smooth and calm.

"She's not available. Is there something I can help you with?"

"Well, are you a family member?" The voice remained even, but there was a hesitancy to it.

Pepper frowned and her whole body went stiff with fear.

"No. Can I ask who's calling?"

"This is Van Lerberghe Funeral Home."

Shit. Pepper groaned inwardly. "Vivienne isn't able to come to the phone just now. I'm her best friend, Pepper Taylor. Is there a message I can give her?"

"Hi, Pepper. My name is Karen Howell. I'm the Director here. I was calling to let Vivienne know that her mother's ashes are ready to be picked up. Forgive me, but I was startled when someone other than Vivienne answered the phone. How is she doing?"

Pepper's knees went watery with relief.

"Frankly, Karen, not well. But what else can you expect? Her mother was her only family."

"Yes, I know. We handled her father's funeral several years ago. When I got the call about Olivia, I was very sad. Please let her know she can take all the time she needs. We'll keep her mother safe and sound until she's ready to come by."

"Thank you Karen, I'll let her know."

Pepper hung up the phone and leaned against it, her forehead resting on her arm. *Shit, just what I want to do.*

"Who was that?"

Pepper whipped around to find Vivienne standing in the hallway, swallowed by her robe. Her hair was wild and tangled, pitching out at odd angles from her head. There were deep, dark circles beneath her listless eyes. Her skin was almost gray. Pepper gasped at the sight of her.

"You scared the *crap* out of me!" She tried a smile, but Vivienne did not return it.

"Who was that?" Vivienne repeated.

Letting go of the phone like it was burning her, it clattered on the countertop. Pepper shoved her hands into the pocket of her shorts.

"That was the funeral home." She watched as a look of anguish spread across Vivienne's face. "Mom's ready to be picked up."

*****

"Mom's ready to be picked up."

Pepper's words slammed into me like a dodge ball from elementary school gym class and I heard myself groan. My knees went weak and I lost the ability to remain standing. I crumpled to the floor and started to hyperventilate.

Pepper rushed to me and wrapped her arms around my shoulders, telling me to breathe slowly. My first instinct was to push her away, hit her, slap her, make her feel as bad as I did. But she was too strong and she smashed me to her chest. Something deep within me recognized the comfort she offered and I leaned into her.

"*Why?*" I screamed, my throat cracking with the force of my voice. "*Why?!*"

"I don't know!" Pepper was crying with me.

"Fucking God! I hate you!" My hands gripped Pepper's arms and squeezed. "You rotten, motherfucking piece of shit!"

"That's it, Vivvy, let it out," Pepper whispered into my ear.

"First my husband and then my dad and now my mom! *Why does everyone fucking die on me?*"

"I'm here, I'm here." Pepper's voice was like a knife cutting through my madness. I clutched her more tightly.

"But you'll die, too!" I wailed, mucus flowing out of my nose. Spit flew out of my mouth and I watched it drop to the floor.

"I'm not going anywhere." Pepper's words were a promise I couldn't believe.

"It hurts, Pepper. It hurts so much." I snuffled and wiped my face on her bare arm. "I want to die, I just want to be dead. Please, God, just let me die!" Pepper's gasp of shock did nothing to ease my desire to be dead.

"It's going to hurt forever, Viv, but you have to fight. You gotta fight that pain as hard as you can. I need you here with me. Now *you're* all *I* have left. Don't leave *me*."

*****

Pepper sat on the floor in the hallway with Vivienne for close to an hour before she was able to get her friend up and to the couch. By then, her legs were tingly and her back was stiff, but she didn't care. Vivienne was all that mattered and Pepper would do anything for her. She hadn't stuck around after Bruce died, knowing that Viv's parents would be there to pick up the pieces. She couldn't help but wonder if this is what Olivia and Daniel Forest had dealt with all those years ago. Somehow, Pepper didn't think so. She knew Viv had loved Bruce and all, but that was only three short years out of her life. Surely, Vivienne couldn't have reacted this badly.

This has to be normal, right? She sat on the couch, still holding Vivienne like a mother holding a child. Never having experienced the kind of love and devotion from her parents, Pepper could only pretend to know what Vivienne was going through. *One moment at a time*, she told herself.

*****

A voice in my head told me to keep holding on to Pepper. She was going to get me through this, whether I wanted to survive or not. All I had to do was hang on tight, and soon things would get better. Months later, I would come to believe it was the sound of my mom's voice. But in the moment, I didn't care who it was. I listened.

"You know what?" My head was pressed against Pepper's chest and I could feel her heart beating very fast.

"What?" she murmured as she stroked my hair. It reminded me of my mom and when I would sit on her lap as a small child.

"I think I feel better."

Pepper laughed and it helped me to smile.

"I hope so." She ruffled my head with affection. "You gotta quit scaring me, Vivvy."

"I'm so sorry." I sniffled and then sat up, away from her. I stared into her bright blue eyes, which were still fearful. "I'm going to do better, I promise."

"Pffft. Don't make promises you can't keep right now. It's okay."

Sighing, I pulled my legs up on the couch and hugged my knees to my chest.

"I think it hurt this bad when Dad died, but I can't remember. I can't feel anything but Mom right now."

"Makes sense." Pepper nodded. "I can't say I know what it's like, Viv. I probably won't ever know how bad you feel. All I do know is that I won't go anywhere."

I reached out to hold her hand.

"Thank you."

We sat still, holding hands for a long time. I couldn't tell what she was thinking, but there was an aura of strength flowing from her fingers into mine.

"I feel awful that I can't be stronger. I'm ashamed of myself for falling apart like this. I wish I had inherited my mom's strength for situations like these."

Pepper shrugged.

"There's nothing to be ashamed of. Everyone is different. Just because you aren't a rock, doesn't make you less of a person. You'll get it together when you're ready."

"Let's hope it doesn't take me another seventeen years," I muttered.

Pepper snorted and squeezed my fingers.

"It won't. You learned your lesson."

"Did I?" I wasn't so sure. Look at me, I was a mess. I couldn't just weep gentle tears and dab my eyes with a tissue, while wishing for my mom to be alive. No, I had to lose all my marbles and dive headfirst into the deep end of the crazy pool. "I don't see anyone else turning into a basket case the way I do."

Pepper released my hands to shake both fists at me.

"Stop or I'm going to clock you! You've always been so damn hard on yourself. Just give yourself permission to be a mess for a while, and then you'll pull yourself out of it, when you're ready."

"When am I going to be ready?" I wondered out loud.

"For Christ's sakes, Viv, it's only been a couple of weeks. Give yourself time and don't ask how much. Your heart will tell you when." Pepper gave me an overly dramatic scowl and punched me in the arm for good measure. It made me laugh a little.

Suddenly, words from my last conversation with mom rung in my ears. She'd told me she'd babied me and I had scoffed at the thought. It occurred to me then that maybe Mom *should* have taken the tough love stance with me all those years ago when Bruce died. If she'd just gotten tough with me and told me to stop being so critical of myself, maybe I would have gotten my act together sooner and not wasted seventeen years hiding away. It felt like a betrayal to even have those thoughts, but my logical brain was stirring. Pepper was giving me the space I needed to paddle around in the waters of grief, but she also had the life preserver at the ready to toss when I wanted it. She wasn't worried I would drown.

I knew then I would have my leaky moments, times when I wouldn't be able to face the world. But that would be okay. I could stay in bed all day and use up a box of tissues if I wanted. I could eat a gallon of ice cream if I wanted. I could yell and scream and bitch all of my frustrations into my pillow if I wanted. And it would all be okay. In time, I would come back to reality and life and go on with it. I was responsible for myself now, and I could make whatever choices I needed to make when I was prepared to make them.

Chapter 52

Wishing she could stay under the hot spray for another week, Pepper reluctantly climbed out of the shower. She wrapped her hair up in a fluffy towel and then used another one to rub her body all over. She shivered in spite of the humidity in the bathroom. Standing on the bathmat, she shifted from side to side while droplets of water trickled down her legs, dreading the task she was preparing for. In just a little while, she and Vivienne would be going to pick up Olivia Forest's ashes. After a moment, she tiptoed to the door and pulled it open. A cloud of steam puffed out into the hallway. Pepper yelped in surprise to be confronted with a large vase of flowers in her vision.

"Who sent these?" Vivienne demanded. Her head was obscured behind the huge bouquet of blossoms.

"Uh," Pepper stammered. *Shit, I forgot about those.* "They came from Will." She watched the vase lower slowly, as though Vivienne was losing the strength to hold it up. Pepper reached to help her, but Vivienne shook her head. The look on her face was one of stunned confusion.

"Did you call him?"

"No," Pepper lied. "But I've texted him." *Okay, I only half lied.*

"Oh." Vivienne turned away and carried the flowers down the hall. Not caring she was only in a towel, Pepper followed closely behind.

"They're beautiful, aren't they?"

"Yes," Vivienne admitted. "It was the smell."

"What?"

"It was the smell I noticed. At first, I thought it was your shampoo or something coming from the bathroom while you showered. But then I figured you wouldn't use something that smelled like roses."

Pepper cocked her head to the side and watched her friend closely. She couldn't tell if this was bothering Vivienne or if it was making her happy. She waited patiently to see what Viv's next reaction would be.

"I'll have to write him a thank you note."

Wistful was not the emotion Pepper expected to see in Vivienne's eyes.

"Maybe you could call him."

Vivienne shook her head.

"No, it's too late for that. He probably had his assistant send these."

"I don't think so," Pepper argued. "The arrangement feels too personal."

"Still," Vivienne argued back, "he's probably forgotten all about me."

Pepper's jaw dropped in surprise. Her first instinct was to face off with Vivienne about how absolutely ludicrous that notion was, but she controlled herself. She closed her mouth with a snap and looked away, so as not to be tempted into a squabble just yet. *One thing at a time.* There was still too much stuff to deal with about Viv's mom before tackling the issue of Will.

"I'm going to get dressed. Are you going to shower?"

Vivienne was still staring at the flowers she'd placed on the table. After a long moment, she nodded. "Yes. We need to bring Mom home."

"All right. Then let's get this done, okay?" Pepper waited for eye contact. Vivienne looked up and smiled.

"Yes. I'll be ready in a half hour."

"Cool."

While Pepper finished drying off and choosing an outfit to wear, Vivienne was in the shower. By the time Pepper had her clothes on and her hair and face ready, Vivienne was exiting the bathroom and twisting her hair into a wet, tangled-messy bun on her head. "What does one wear to collect one's mother's ashes from the funeral home?"

Pepper laughed out loud, boosted by her friend's wry humor.

"Well, I don't know. A ball gown is out of the question. Perhaps a simple cocktail dress?"

Vivienne laughed too and went to her room. When she emerged, she wore a pair of simple white shorts and a red tee-shirt. She carried a pair of red, open-toed espadrilles. "Too casual?" she asked, winking at Pepper.

"Nope, just perfect." Pepper swept her hands down the length of her body. She wore red shorts and a black tee-shirt, with black, flat sandals on her feet. "I'd say we're of a like mind."

As they collected their purses and the keys to the truck, Pepper made sure to tuck a travel packet of tissues into her pocket. She had no idea what might occur on the way to the funeral home or when they were there. She hopped into the passenger side and Vivienne slid into the driver's seat. Never having been big on prayer, Pepper sent one or two out to the universe that Vivienne would be able to hold it together as they went to collect Olivia Forest's ashes.

*****

I made the trip to Van Lerberghe on auto pilot. Pepper sat beside me, wisely saying nothing. I thought she might chatter on about how much her hometown had changed since she left, but she didn't, and I was grateful. While I drove, I repeated the same phrase over and over in my head: *You can do this. You can do this.*

When we got there, the parking lot was filled with cars. I laughed out loud, startling Pepper.

"What's so funny?" she asked.

"Mom used to say the funniest thing," I whispered. "It's really wicked. Extremely irreverent."

"What? Tell me!" Pepper poked me in the arm.

"'Obviously, Karen has been passing out bad mushrooms again. Business is booming.'"

Pepper stared at me for a moment and then burst into gales of laughter, holding her stomach. My heart wanted me to cry because I'd never hear my mom's voice again with one of her totally scandalous comments. But my brain took over instead, and I laughed with abandon beside Pepper. There were people crossing the parking lot to enter the funeral home, and they probably thought we were completely insane as we giggled and snorted, tears streaming down our faces.

"Oh man," Pepper gasped. "That is the best line I've ever heard! Your mom was a *hoot*!"

"Yeah, I know." I rubbed the moisture from beneath my eyes and tried to stop chuckling. "That *was* one of her better ones." I had to admit, laughing that hard felt *good*.

Once we calmed down enough, we got out of the vehicle to make the walk to the door. Pepper reached for my hand and I took it gladly. The hilarity from moments before gave me the strength to move steadily toward the entrance, but I wasn't sure how long it would last. Pepper opened the door for me, and I stepped into the dim coolness.

We were greeted immediately by one of the employees who was directing traffic to the three viewings taking place.

"Good afternoon. Which family are you here to see today?"

I opened my mouth to speak, but words wouldn't come. My tongue felt swollen and thick inside my dried up mouth. Pepper stepped up immediately.

"We aren't here for a viewing. We're here to pick up Olivia Forest's ashes, please."

"Of course. Karen's in her office. It's right down the hall." The thirty-something man in his crisp, unwrinkled suit pointed to the right and Pepper gently guided me down the hall. When we reached Karen's office, she was inside, sitting behind her large oak desk.

"Vivienne!" She stood up and glided from behind the desk as if on an invisible conveyor belt. I was in her arms and being squeezed before I could say a word. "How are you?"

"Fine," I croaked.

"Do you have some water?" Pepper asked. "I think she needs a sip of something."

"Of course." Karen turned to the water cooler behind her, and I stared at the bubbles gurgling up in the bottle as she got me a cup. I sipped it and reveled in the cold moisture revitalizing my mouth.

"Thank you," I said in a voice closer to my normal one. "Karen, this is my best friend, Pepper Taylor."

"Of course, we spoke on the phone earlier." Karen extended a perfectly manicured hand and Pepper took it. "Why don't you both have a seat?" She pointed to the expensive upholstered chairs in front of the desk.

As we sat, Karen did, too. She was discreet as she pulled a plain, white box from a drawer in her desk and placed it in front of me.

"I'm so sorry for your loss, Vivienne. Your mother was a lovely woman and I know you'll miss her very much."

"Thank you," I murmured as I reached for the box. I held it on my lap and caressed it, trying not to think of it as the remnants of my mom's body, but instead as a piece of her spirit for me to keep. Looking up, I gave Karen the best smile I could muster. "Thank you for all you've done, Karen. I do appreciate it."

"You're welcome." She said it so kindly and simply. She really was good at her job, well-matched for dealing with people in their grief.

Not wanting to prolong things, I stood up, cradling the box in my left arm and reaching to shake Karen's hand with my right.

"Hopefully, I'll never see you again." I winked at her and she grinned.

"Let's hope not."

Pepper guided me out of the office and back to the exit. As we walked back out into the bright sunshine, I squinted and took a huge shuddery breath.

"I'm going to need you to drive."

"No problem, hun." Pepper took the keys from me.

All the way home, I hugged the box to my chest, talking to Mom inside my head.

I know you can't hear me, but I just want you to know I love you. Everything's going to be okay. You just keep on flying around the universe with Dad. Don't worry about me. I'll be fine.

I wasn't sure I believed what I was saying, but it sounded good in my mind.

I was beginning to recognize the signs of a breakdown coming on. My body felt heavier and heavier as Pepper navigated the few miles to the house. My head started to pound and my chest was hurting. I blinked faster and faster, hoping I could stave off the tears, but it only squeezed them out and they wetted my cheeks. When we pulled into the driveway, I didn't move right away. Pepper jumped out and came to my side, opening the door. She waited for me to undo my seatbelt, and then put an arm around my shoulder to ease me from the truck. We stumbled to the front door and she unlocked it to let me inside.

I took the box with me, whimpering as I slugged down the hallway to my room. I went inside and closed the door on Pepper, not bothering to apologize. I knew she knew I wasn't trying to be mean. I put Mom on the bedside table and crawled into bed to mourn.

Chapter 53

Pepper scribbled a note to Vivienne and then left the house as quietly as she could. Gabriel waited outside in the car to take her to dinner. As they drove to a quaint diner they had discovered, Pepper told him about the days' events, culminating in bringing Olivia home.

"She's ensconced in her room once again, is she?"

"Yeah, but it'll be okay." Pepper took a deep breath and nodded with confidence. "I'm sure that was the hardest thing she's ever done in her life. Nothing compared to losing Bruce or her dad. If she wants to hide out again for a couple of days, more power to her."

"You certainly know her better than I do," Gabriel said as he maneuvered into a parking spot. "But I will say Vivienne is about the luckiest woman on Earth to have a friend such as you."

Pepper grinned and leaned over to kiss him. They got out of the car and walked hand in hand into the restaurant. After being seated, and while they perused the menu, Pepper caught him looking at his watch a couple of times. Worry made her heart beat a little faster. It wasn't like Gabe to do that. When he pulled his cell phone out of his pocket and started texting, Pepper frowned.

"What's up, babe?" She closed her menu and set it on the table. "Is everything okay?"

"Oh yes, yes." Gabriel set the phone face down. "Just a lot of business."

Pepper let the matter drop as the waitress arrived to take their orders, but knew she was going to have to drag it out of him when he fidgeted while they waited for their food.

"Gabe, you're as nervous as a cat. Tell me what's going on," Pepper demanded.

"I'm sorry, darling." Gabe sighed and ran his fingers through his thick, wavy hair. "I've just been putting out a few fires today." Leaning back in his seat, he tried to smile. "Tell me the truth, love, are you certain Vivienne is on the mend?"

Cocking her head to the side, Pepper's frown grew deeper.

"Well, as best as I can tell. I know she's going to have her moments here and there, but I think she turned a corner today, for sure. Why?"

Gabriel looked nervous, taking a deep breath before he spoke.

"Well, I have two projects that are set to begin filming within the next several days. I also had three sets of contracts messengered to me that need to be gone over. And then there's the starlet, who shall remain nameless, being squired off to rehab as we speak."

Pepper chuckled. Reaching across the table, she put her hands on his, hoping to reassure him.

"In other words, all hell is breaking loose and you need to get home." Squeezing, she gave him a long, hard look. "I understand. In fact, I'm surprised you haven't gone before now. I kept telling you to go."

"I did not think it right to leave you alone until Vivienne was a tad more stable." Gabriel repeated what he'd been saying all along. "But if you think she's doing well enough and I needn't worry, then yes, I must return to LA tomorrow."

"Of course." Pepper scooted out of her side of the booth to slide in beside him. "I understand, Gabe." Laying her head on his shoulder, Pepper couldn't deny the disappointment she felt squeezing her heart. But she knew better than to try and hold on to him when he had so many other things to worry about. If she wasn't one of them, then that would be a good thing.

"Thank you, darling." Gabriel kissed the top of her blond head and slung his arm around her shoulders. "Let's spend this evening together and then tomorrow you can send me off."

"You bet." Pepper tilted her head to look up at him and gave him the most loving smile she could manage. "I'm going to miss the hell out of you, though."

"And I shall miss you. But I have no doubt you'll return to California in due course. Perhaps with your dearest friend in tow?"

Pepper's bottom lip pooched out as she considered the possibility.

"I can't lie. It's been in the back of my mind. I just haven't wanted to really think about it until I got Viv stable again."

"I suggest you begin planting your seeds, love. In spite of all the things left to do, time will pass quickly. The time will come for Vivienne to make some choices, and I certainly hope she makes the right ones."

"Hmm," Pepper murmured. "I hope she does, too."

*****

The next morning, Gabriel dropped Pepper back off at Vivienne's house. Pepper tried to keep from tearing up, but didn't quite make it. Gabriel offered her a handkerchief from his pocket and assured her that he would call and text often.

"Keep your computer at the ready, darling. We will Skype tonight, yeah?"

"Y-yes," Pepper stammered as she dabbed at her eyes.

After many kisses and several long embraces, Pepper finally let him go. She stood on the porch of the house and watched him drive away until the rental car disappeared down the long block and she couldn't see it anymore.

"Shit," she muttered, swiping angrily at the wetness in her eyes. While Pepper had no qualms at all about staying with Vivienne and helping her through any tough times, she knew it was going to be a lot harder without having Gabe at hand for her own support.

Letting herself inside, Pepper knew immediately something was different. Even though it was very faint, she could hear the sound of typing coming from somewhere in the house. Going down the hall toward Vivienne's bedroom, she could see that the door was open and her friend was not in bed. The only other place in the small home she could be was the basement.

Pepper hesitated at the top of the stairs, debating on whether or not she should interrupt. Vivienne could be in the middle of something good, and Pepper didn't want to ruin it. Surely her footsteps and the creaking floors had alerted Vivienne to her presence. Just as she lifted her foot to take the first step down, the typing stopped.

"I know you're home," came Vivienne's voice, floating up the stairs.

"Can I come down?" Pepper called back.

"Maybe later. I don't want to break my stride."

"Okay. Do you want anything? Something to eat?"

"No!"

Pepper frowned at the snarky tone, but abided by Vivienne's wishes. She would wait this phase out, just like all the others.

Chapter 54

I could feel Pepper's presence in the house, but I wouldn't be lured away from the keyboard. When she'd left the night before, I had thought I would stay in bed and wallow some more until I fell asleep. But, lying there, I kept thinking about things I'd done with my mother. Or things she had said to me. Stories and memories from my childhood. *I should write this stuff down*, I'd thought and then I felt like the world's biggest idiot.

I was a writer, and instead of putting all my thoughts and feelings down on paper, I'd been floundering around in my grief like a turtle on its back. I'd started out with my laptop in bed, but I couldn't get comfortable and my hands kept bumping the touch pad causing whole paragraphs to get deleted. I found myself hitting control Z to undo more than I was writing and that pissed me off. So I headed to the basement writing nook, where my dinosaur of a desktop waited.

It hadn't taken long to get into the zone. Hours sped by as I poured out all the stories jumbling around in my brain. No detail went unrecorded. No feeling went unexplored. I never once bothered to wipe away the tears when they came. I didn't stop, except to go to the bathroom, but not until I thought I would wet myself if I didn't.

The fluorescent lighting in the basement and lack of true windows kept me from keeping track of time. I had no idea night had come and gone. I didn't see the sun rise or care. I just kept chipping away at the rock of grief that had settled in my heart. And all the words and stories didn't just focus on Mom. I rehashed Dad's illness and Bruce's death. I compared the grief and levels of depression, experiencing it all over again.

And as all of the memories and thoughts and emotions burst out of my brain and onto the page, self-awareness bloomed like the daisies in my backyard, each petal a new level of understanding of myself and my life.

My early childhood was idyllic, with my parents spoiling me to some degree, as an only child. They managed to teach me right from wrong, and kept me from being too much of a brat. My teenage years had the requisite amount of angst as I tested their patience by staying out late and using my wardrobe and music choices to rebel. They remained patient and understanding, treating me with a more adult respect, expecting me to make the right choices and decisions. I always did because I didn't want to disappoint them. Mom and Dad gave me an intellectual understanding of the world, but I was definitely protected from a lot of harsh realities. Even though I loved my parents desperately, I couldn't help but feel they'd done me a huge disservice.

The first time I ever did venture out of my comfort zone was when I married Bruce. Our meeting was by chance at a sorority party (he didn't even go to Michigan State University) and our romance was stereotypically whirlwind. When he told me he was enlisting and proposed to me, I accepted on the spot. It was the stuff romantic dreams are made of. My writer's heart could never have said no.

Mom and Dad were devastated, and even tried to forbid me from doing it, but that was a farce. I was their only child and nothing I did could make them not be there for me. In typical fashion, they helped to make the small, fast wedding a beautiful affair. They organized and paid the expenses every time I moved to be with Bruce at a new post. They took care of me as much as they had when I was living with them. I was torn between feeling grateful at the memory of not having to struggle and feeling angry that I hadn't had to stand on my own two feet.

After Bruce died and Mom and Dad had rescued me, yet again, I lived with them for six years. I went back and finished college. I wanted to get my degree in English with a master's in creative writing, but I allowed them to convince me to get a teaching certificate so I would have something to "fall back on." I couldn't remember getting angry at the time, thinking they were trying to squash my dreams or demonstrate their lack of confidence in my writing. *But I was angry now.* Why couldn't they have shown the littlest bit of faith in me? It seemed pointless to be mad about it, considering I'd proven them wrong. I wasn't wealthy, but I earned enough to buy a small house and live on my own. I just couldn't help myself. The bitterness I was feeling as I punched on the keys was probably a product of grief. Because they weren't here to defend themselves, I was able to make them the scapegoats.

The longer I wrote, the more energized I felt. I should have been exhausted and yearning to give myself over to sleep, but I wasn't. I could have gone to one of the couches and snatched a catnap. I should have been starving, since I couldn't remember the last time I ate. Pepper was waiting for me, and I could have gone upstairs to be with her.

Instead, I stayed where I was, typing faster and faster as the anguish inside splashed onto the screen like a cocktail thrown in my face. All my life, things came easily to me. Sometimes it was because I was smart and capable, but mostly it boiled down to the machinations of my parents and friends. I was weak and incapable of managing difficult situations. I was emotionally unprepared for life's tragedies and pitfalls. Even now, my best friend waited upstairs for me, probably nervous as a fly caught in a spider's web. Pepper was probably waiting for the other shoe to drop, wondering what kind of a shape I would be in when I came up, and what kind of a mess she would have to deal with.

How could I face her now that I truly understood who I was?

Well, I was going to have to. The only person left in my life who was going to help me was *me*. I wasn't going to rely on anyone else again.

Chapter 55

Pepper brushed off her knees, flipping away bits of dirt and grass. Pulling weeds while Vivienne wrote gave her a sense of accomplishment for herself. It also gave her time to think. She had no idea what to expect when Viv finally drug herself up from the basement. Would she be exhausted and go straight to bed? Pepper was sure she'd been up all night writing. Would there be another messy breakdown to walk her through?

"God, I hope not," she said aloud to no one but the birds in the trees and the bugs buzzing around. Immediately, she felt guilty for thinking that. What else was she here for but to walk Vivienne through the gauntlets of her grief? Cutting herself a little slack, Pepper knew it wasn't wrong to not want another breakdown.

Looking around, Pepper decided the lawn needed actual mowing. She didn't know the first thing about using a lawnmower, but figured now was as good a time as any to figure it out. She wandered through the grass to the shed in the back of the yard, but found it locked up tight. She poked her toe at a couple of pavers that looked loose, wondering if maybe Vivienne had hidden a key.

"You won't find a key."

Pepper turned around at the sound of Vivienne's voice, surprised at the strength in it. Her best friend stood at the end of the patio holding a tray with a pitcher of lemonade and two glasses on it.

"Gardening is thirsty work. Come have a seat with me."

"That's a good idea," Pepper said with a smile. She trotted across the yard to the patio table conveniently hiding beneath a large umbrella. Throwing herself into one of the chairs, she wiped the back of her hand across her forehead. "It's pretty hot out here."

"Yes, it is. That shouldn't be a problem for a girl from California, though." Vivienne grinned and poured glasses for each of them, then sat down, too. "Thank you for tending to the weeds. It could have become a jungle out here."

"My pleasure. It's nice to fiddle with a patch of grass." Pepper swigged down half of the lemony, sweet liquid in one gulp. She felt refreshed already, boosted by the calm mood coming from Vivienne. "You look really tired."

"Thank you. That's always a kind way of telling someone they look like shit."

Pepper snorted.

"Now, you know that's not true. If I thought you looked like shit, I'd say it straight out."

Vivienne nodded.

"Yeah, you're right. No pulled punches from you. It's a shame everyone in my life hasn't been as honest as you."

"What do you mean?" Pepper's brows furrowed and her stomach tightened with anxiety.

"Oh I'm just feeling pissed off right now." Vivienne slouched down in her chair and leaned her head back. "I'm going to be forty in a couple of months and I'm no better prepared for life than a four-year-old."

Pepper opened her mouth to argue, but thought better of it. She sensed a rant coming on, and didn't think it would be a good idea to stop it. When Vivienne wanted to rant, it was like trying to stop a runaway train on the rails. So Pepper threw open the switch as the locomotive picked up steam.

"How so?"

"Just look at me. I'm a mess," Vivienne sighed. "I won't minimize the situation. Losing my mom is hard and it sucks. I'm angry and sad and depressed. I feel like I've lost one of the last things in my life that was worth sticking around for. But Jesus Christ, people die all the time. I'm not the first person to lose her parents and I won't be the last. Most people cry and grieve and then pull themselves up by their bootstraps to get on with life. Oh, but not *me*. I break down and hide under the covers. I collapse into a pile of goo. I let everyone else pick up the pieces and take care of me like I was a child."

Vivienne yanked herself up to sit straight in the chair. Slamming her elbow down on the table, she pointed at Pepper with her index finger.

"My parents kept me sheltered and protected all of my life, whenever anything bad happened. Instead of telling me to get my head out of my ass, they just stepped in and handled whatever situation needed to be dealt with. Not once did they ever say 'Vivienne, buck up.' Why did they *do* that?"

Pepper hoped the question was rhetorical, because she had no valid answer. Once, she was jealous of how loving and caring Vivienne's parents were, wishing she'd had the same. But listening to Vivienne, it occurred to her that her own upbringing had given her the backbone to go out and achieve everything she'd ever set out to.

"I'll tell you why they did it," Vivienne snarled. "Because I was the only kid they had and they loved me. They loved me *too* much. They didn't want me to struggle like they did. They wanted only the best for me all the time. And that's great. *Awesome*! But they didn't think about what it was going to be like for me one day when they were gone. They forgot to teach me how to deal with life's crappiest situations so that I could pick up my *own* pieces and move on."

Vivienne stood up and began to pace around the patio.

"I feel bad about it, but I'm so fucking pissed right now I can hardly see straight! My mom was my best friend besides you. But you don't *do* that to your kid. Especially when it's your only kid. Because if you *die*, your kid is left alone and unable to handle shit. People have kids for all kinds of reasons but, in the end, when they get old, the kid is supposed to be able to take care of herself. The kid is supposed to step up to the plate and take over, so that the parent doesn't have to deal with it alone *and* deal with a kid who can't survive.

"I'm hating myself right now, even though I *know* I'm not a bad person. I know I'm a good person, in spite of all my shortcomings. I did a lot of things right in my life and made my folks proud in a lot of ways. I made something of myself *in spite* of them. But I don't think I could look at myself in the mirror right now without throwing up. All I'd see is the fragile, uncertain, waste of skin I've been."

Pepper watched with pride as Vivienne strode back and forth. Vivienne was coming into her own, in a way, and Pepper was grateful to be there as a witness. She felt confident that Olivia and Daniel Forest were smiling down on their daughter.

*****

Oh, I was in the thick of it now. I raved and carried on like an evangelical preacher on Sunday while Pepper gazed at me in awe.

"I don't care how bad it makes me sound. I'm mad at my mom and dad for not teaching me to be stronger! I've been weak and sniveling and oh so willing to let others take care of me and my life, *all of my life*! Well no more! From this day forward, I'm in charge of myself. And I'm not going to let anyone else be responsible."

Suddenly, my knees began to tremble. My limbs got that shaky feeling when your blood sugar takes a nose dive. I slumped into my chair and took a deep, shuddery breath. I grabbed my glass of lemonade and shot-gunned the last inch of liquid.

"You finished?" Pepper asked, her tone soft and gentle, without any hint of reproach.

"For the moment." I winked at her and she grinned.

"You want my opinion?"

"Absolutely!"

Pepper reached over and placed her hand on mine.

"I am so proud of you right now. It's not an easy thing to admit things, and I think you just opened a door that's been slammed shut for a long time."

I leaned over and put my other hand on top of hers, squeezing.

"Thank you."

"I love you, Vivvy. I know you're going through a lot right now, but I want you to know that you're the only person who's ever stuck with me, my whole life. No matter what's happened to you and how you wish you'd done things differently, you've always been there for *me*."

I could feel tears prickling my eyes and I breathed in deep the scent of summer sun and flowers from my backyard.

"And you have been there for me much, much more, Pep."

Pepper shrugged.

"This is what friends do. I'm happy to be here and I'll do anything I can to help you. It doesn't matter how messy it gets or how much leaning you need to do."

"Well, I'm hoping the whole leaning thing is over," I said in all seriousness. "If you want to stick around and pat me on the back from time to time, I won't kick you to the curb. But I'd much rather you stand beside me from now on, instead of holding me up."

Pepper grinned wickedly.

"What? You mean I don't have to wipe your boogey nose anymore?"

I laughed so hard my stomach hurt. I was still wheezy as I said, "Nope. No more snot rags for you."

"Whew! That's a relief. Can we get something to eat now?"

"You bet!"

Chapter 56

"She did it again."

"What?" Pepper asked. She was sitting at the kitchen table, her Mac open to Facebook.

Only a couple of days had passed since I'd had my shouting session in the backyard. I sat down across from her and rested my chin in the palms of my hands.

"I just got off the phone with Mom's lawyer. Apparently, she didn't have a Last Will and Testament. She did something called a Lady Bird Deed on the house so it would transfer directly to me upon her death." My head was spinning with all the information I'd gotten from the attorney.

"That's a good thing, right?"

"Well, yeah. I was already on her checking and savings accounts. And I'm her beneficiary for her life insurance and retirement stuff. I won't have to go through probate to sell the house or her car." I was torn between feeling relief and anger that, once again, Mom had taken care of me. Pepper watched me closely, and I could tell she was waiting to see what I would do before she offered any opinion. I decided to be grateful. There was one less hassle for me to deal with. "This is a good thing."

"Damn straight." Pepper banged her hand on the table. "So you're free to do whatever you like and you don't have to wait around to do it."

"Yep."

"But at the same time, you won't have to hurry up and make any big decisions right away, either."

"Yep."

Pepper nodded and leaned back in her chair. She was quiet and I didn't say anything, either. After a while, she began to fidget.

"Well?" she said. "What do we do now?"

I had to laugh. I had overheard Pepper skyping with Gabriel and he had asked her when she would be coming back to California. She said she didn't know, but that she hoped soon. I felt bad for eavesdropping and then worse because she was only staying to be with me. I knew I was going to have to let her go home sooner or later, so now seemed to be the right time to broach the subject.

"Well, *you* don't do anything. *I* will figure out what to do with the house and everything in it." I got up and went into the kitchen to grab a bottle of water from the fridge. Leaning against the counter, I twisted open the cap and flipped it into the trash. After a long swallow, I wiped my mouth on the back of my hand. "Pep, I think it's time for you to go home."

She was up and out of that chair like someone had stuck her with a pin. She stood in the doorway of the kitchen and glared at me.

"Now why on Earth would I go back when you still have so much to do?"

"Because I can handle it myself now. You've done everything you're supposed to. You need to be with Gabriel." I chugged some more water and avoided looking her in the eye. I knew she didn't trust me just yet, but she couldn't hang around forever watching over me. I loved her with all my heart, but I couldn't ask her to stay any longer now that the worst, I hoped, was over.

"I call bullshit." Pepper slammed her hands on her hips and flounced over to me. "There are still tough times ahead, and I don't plan on leaving until it's *all* done." She poked me in the chest with her index finger and I looked up into her crystal blue eyes. She wasn't done with me yet. I could sense she was going to say something else. I had a sinking feeling I knew what it was.

*****

"Besides," Pepper continued, "I fully expect you to come with me." She watched with a combination of excitement and fear as realization spread over Vivienne's face.

"I knew you were going to say that." Vivienne raised her water for another sip, but stopped at the last minute and put the bottle on the counter. "You know I can't do that."

"I don't know anything of the kind," Pepper huffed, angry that her friend's response was immediate, and therefore reeked of forethought. *Dammit, she's been thinking about this already. I'm in for a fight.*

Pepper didn't care how much of an argument Vivienne intended to put up. Come hell or high water, she wasn't leaving her best friend alone in Michigan without family and no true friends.

"You made a promise to me. You swore you were going to give California a try. And now that you don't have anything tying you down, you have no valid excuse to break that promise." Pepper felt triumphant that she got her point across first before Vivienne could.

"I have plenty tying me down. I have to go through Mom's things. I need to sell the house, her car. I have to find someone to get the foundation back up and running. All of that is going to take months."

"And after that?" Pepper waited only a moment for an answer before plunging ahead. "When all that's finished, what excuse will you have?"

Vivienne floundered, opening and closing her mouth, trying to form some words. Pepper kept her from doing it.

"You won't have one. But by then, you'll be back to your hermit ways and I won't be able to blow your ass out of here with a stick of dynamite. Is that it?"

Vivienne's shoulders slumped in defeat.

"This is my home," she whispered. "I belong here."

"Why? If your parents are gone, what's to keep you?" Pepper demanded, her heart jumping around in her chest like a jackrabbit. "You don't even have to stay for all that other bullshit. You get an estate sale company to empty the house. You get a real estate agent to sell the house. And you sure as hell can find someone out in California to run your damn foundation!"

Vivienne shrunk away from Pepper, but Pepper didn't feel bad about it.

"I think you don't want to go because then you wouldn't have to face Will."

"That's not true!" Vivienne objected, but not as strongly as Pepper expected.

"I think it is. If you wait long enough, he'll move on and then you can say, 'Oh well, he dumped me, just like I knew he would.' And then you'll mourn the loss of the only *other* man you've ever loved and spend the rest of your life hiding *again*! Well I'm not going to let you do that. If I have to stay here for the next five years hounding your ass, I will do it!"

Pepper stormed out of the kitchen before she said anything more she would regret. She knew she was taking a huge risk pushing Vivienne so hard so soon after her breakthrough. But, instinctively, she felt time growing short. Will wasn't responding to her texts as quickly anymore, and he'd stopped asking to come to Michigan for a visit. Pepper naturally assumed Will was getting over Vivienne and if she didn't act quickly to bring them back together, he would go back to his blonde Barbie bimbos. Why else would he be pulling away?

Pacing in the spare bedroom, Pepper gnawed on her thumb, trying to decide what to do. Finally, she grabbed her cell phone off the nightstand and shot a text to Will.

Hey... u there?

She set the phone back down so she wouldn't stare at it, trying to will a response. *Heh, no pun intended*, she thought.

"Maybe I could have Gabriel lure her out there under some pretense for the movie," Pepper muttered under her breath. "Jake might be able to badger her out there."

Pepper continued to pace and talk to herself, avoiding what was really bothering her the most. The fact that *she*, Vivienne's best friend, wasn't the one who could talk the redhead into going back to

The Widow and the Rock Star

California. It hurt inside to think Vivienne didn't want to be with her. *Well, so be it.* If she had to resort to using trickery and underhandedness, she would do it. In the end, Pepper knew that Vivienne would forgive her anything, especially if Vivienne ended up happy.

As she was striding in the opposite direction of her phone, it vibrated on the table and she dashed back to it. Will had texted her back.

`Whats up`

Pepper's thumbs were a blur.

`Havent heard back from u in a bit. Everything okay?`

She waited patiently as she could, staring at the phone.

`Yep. Hows V`

"Yes!" Pepper pumped her fist in the air joyfully.

`A lot better.`

`Excellent!`

Pepper bounced up and down on the bed, giddy with hope.

`I think she misses you.`

Pepper held her breath, praying she was doing the right thing. She stared at the screen, hoping he would respond quickly.

`Yeah?`

Pepper's stomach clenched with anxiety. *That's not good.* She was hoping he would have said he missed her too, or asked if he could come for a visit. She felt herself getting more and more pissed off and worried by his lack of enthusiasm, when her phone vibrated in her hand. Reading the message, her whole body relaxed and a wave of happiness washed over her.

`Miss her 2`

Pepper jumped up and did a little dance around the room.

`Working on getting her back to LA. Keep you posted`

`Do that,` came back within seconds.

She needed to think about how next to proceed. This wasn't a situation where she could just come up with a plan on the fly, like the night she introduced Will and Vivienne at The Relic. Pepper knew she needed a clear-cut strategy with no room for error. Her thumb automatically found its way to her mouth and she chewed on the edges while she contemplated how she could convince Vivienne to go back to California. Now that she knew Will was still waiting for her, Pepper's mind was racing with the possibilities.

The knock on her door completely derailed her train of thought.

Chapter 57

I stood outside the bedroom door for a good three minutes before I finally knocked. Part of me was furious with Pepper for pushing me so hard, but my logical brain knew it was the right thing for her to do. She was totally right in all of her assumptions. I was using mom's death as an excuse to stay in Michigan and avoid Will. I had been on the verge of making some huge changes in my life before I had to rush back home. Now, I was back in my safe zone and struggling to decide whether to stay there or jump back out. I was disappointed with myself for finding it so easy to resort to old habits. But I also knew I was stronger and feeling more capable of breaking them.

I threw my shoulders back and rapped on the door.

"Come in."

I opened the door and stepped into the room. Pepper was sitting on the bed, her cell phone in hand.

"Can we talk?" I gave her a hopeful smile. When she smiled back, I knew it was all going to be okay, no matter what we said.

"Of course." Pepper tossed her phone onto the table. "I'm sorry I was so harsh, Vivvy."

I walked over to the bed and sat down beside her.

"It's okay. I'm not mad. You had every right to say the things you said. They're all true. I'm the one who owes you an apology. I should know better than to even *try* to lie to you."

Pepper chuckled and threw her arm around my shoulders and I completed the hug.

"Yes. You should know better," she said into my ear. Pulling away, she gave me the stink eye. "But I get it. Old habits die hard."

"Yes. They do." I nodded my head. "So I had an idea on how we might be able to kill them off."

"Yeah?"

"Let's start with Mom's ashes."

Pepper's look of shock made me laugh out loud.

"What do you mean?"

"I want to take Mom's ashes to the park and scatter them in the lake, like we did with Dad." I could remember, clearly, the nasty cold day Mom and I had walked to the park near our houses with Dad's ashes in the black plastic box. Fighting the wind coming off Lake St. Clair, we'd trudged along the walking path to the edge of the lake. We'd said a few words, wiped our eyes and noses, and then dumped the box into the lake. Dad had loved fishing and boating, and it was what we thought he would want. Now, I wanted to do the same thing with Mom. Maybe she might have wanted to be sprinkled in London (one of her favorite spots) or maybe she might have wanted to be with her parents in Minnesota, but I wasn't sure. We'd never talked about it. But in my heart, I felt she belonged with Dad.

"Are you sure you're ready to do that?" Pepper asked gently.

I nodded.

"Yes. I've been thinking about it since yesterday."

Pepper reached for my hand and held it tight.

"If you're sure, then I'd like to be there with you."

"Of course!" I wanted to cry, but I laughed instead. "Mom always called you her second daughter. You should be there."

"I'd be honored." Pepper brought her free hand up to dab at her eyes. "When?"

"How about now?" I know that shocked her. I was making decisions quickly these days, and I was finding that it felt good. Instead of obsessing over things and looking at every angle of every situation, I was going with my gut for the first time in years. I liked it. I planned to keep doing it.

"Okay!"

"I'll meet you on the porch in a couple of minutes." I got up and left her room for mine. I took the box with Mom's ashes off the table and held it to my chest for a moment.

"I hope this is the right thing, Mom. Don't haunt me if it's not, okay?" I grinned and then went to meet Pepper on the porch.

Chapter 58

Vivienne wanted to walk to the park instead of drive, and that suited Pepper just fine. Except for the light gardening, she hadn't had any exercise since leaving California. She wanted the workout and knew it would do her pal some good as well. Pepper was feeling hopeful that Viv was going to change her mind about going to California. She put aside her coup planning thoughts to wait and see how things would shake out.

"I'd forgotten how pretty this park is," Pepper sighed as they reached the entrance. Vivienne flashed her pass and they walked through. The park wasn't overly large, only a few acres, but Pepper gawped at the perfectly manicured grass and expanse of large, tall trees offering plenty of shade. It was fairly packed with families having barbeques; the smell of grilling food was thick in the air. Groups of old men were playing shuffleboard, horseshoes and bocce ball. The playground area was jammed with kids running, yelling and playing on the swings and climbing equipment. Pepper noticed the heavily populated splash pad and lamented the fact it hadn't existed when she was a kid growing up in St. Clair Shores. The walking path was filled with people strolling along at a leisurely pace, as well as the more serious exercise hounds with quick steps and arms pumping.

"Yeah, I like it. Sometimes I would bring my laptop and sit and write by the water." Vivienne side-stepped a couple of old ladies standing in the middle of the walking path. She kept the box she carried tucked under her arm and close to her body.

"Isn't this illegal?" Pepper whispered. Vivienne turned her head to look at her. "Throwing ashes into the lake, I mean."

"You bet," Vivienne said. "But I dare anyone to stop me."

Pepper snorted and grinned.

"I'd like to see *that* fight."

"If I get caught, I'll deal with it. I don't care. My mom belongs with my dad." Vivienne held her head high and Pepper linked arms with her.

"I agree. Let's do this thing."

The walking path wended its way around the perimeter of the park and, within a few minutes, they stood at the edge overlooking Lake St. Clair. Pepper glanced around, wondering if the crowd was too heavy for them to scatter the ashes discreetly. Every bench facing the lake was occupied and the foot traffic was steady.

"Come on," Vivienne said. She pointed a few yards away to a dirt path leading down toward the rocks at the lake's edge. Pepper followed her, hoping no one would catch on to what they were doing.

Vivienne stepped lightly down the path and then directly onto the rocks. They looked wet and slippery to Pepper, who had worn only flip-flops for their trek.

"Be careful, Viv."

"I will. You don't have to come down here if you don't want to."

"I'll be right there." Pepper stepped out of her flip-flops and followed Vivienne, picking her way among the flat, gray rocks carefully, her arms flung out for balance. When they both got as close to the water as they could, without pitching in headfirst, they crouched down and Vivienne placed the box in front of her. She pried open the top, and inside was a plastic bag with Olivia Forest's cremains. Vivienne pulled the bag out and opened the twisty tie that sealed the bag.

Holding it carefully, Pepper heard her friend sniff. That got her eyes to watering, too, as she watched Vivienne struggle for the right words.

"I know you're already with Dad," Vivienne said, after a few silent moments, "but now you can be fish food, too."

Pepper clasped her hand over her mouth to stifle the bark of laughter trying to burst out.

"Vivienne!"

"*Well?* That's what Mom always said after we turned Dad loose." Vivienne's face was slick with tears, but she was grinning and there was a gleam in her eye. "Come on, help me."

Pepper reached over and, together, they upended the bag and let the ashes dump out into the waves lapping against the rocks. Vivienne crumpled the empty plastic back into the box and replaced the top. They stayed where they were for a long time, watching the water carry the remnants of Olivia's body out into the lake.

Chapter 59

The day after I scattered Mom's ashes, Pepper and I went to her house to begin the process of clearing things out. I'd decided to take Pepper's advice and hire an estate sale company to handle selling anything I didn't want to keep and when that was done, I would find a real estate agent who could manage the sale of the house itself.

"So how do we do this?" Pepper asked, standing in the foyer of Mom's home. "How much are you keeping?"

I chewed on my bottom lip and looked around. "I don't know, really. It's kind of hard because I feel guilty letting stuff go, but we had totally different tastes. I'm not sure I want to keep much of it."

"Where will you put anything? Your house is pretty small. Maybe you should think about keeping this place and selling your house?" Pepper suggested.

I shook my head.

"No. This house is too big for just me." I took a few steps into the living room to glance around. A knot of sadness twisted around my heart, knowing Mom wasn't going to be sitting in her favorite chair again.

"Besides," I called back to Pepper and turned around to look her in the eye. "I don't know how big of a place I'll be able to afford in California, after all."

Pepper screeched with delight and barreled into me like a freight train, hugging me tight and lifting me in the air a couple of inches.

"You're going to do it? *Really?*"

Grinning like a buffoon, I nodded. "Eventually. I might divide my time between states until this place sells. Then, I'll come back and deal with my own house."

I couldn't have been more stunned by anything else when Pepper burst into tears.

"Hey! I'm the crier, here, what's wrong?" I grabbed her hands and pulled her close. She leaned down to press her forehead against mine for a second.

"I'm just so damn happy, Viv. Not only for you, but for *me*. I'll finally have a *real* friend in California!"

We hugged again and then she danced me around in circles.

"Just think of all the shopping we'll do and the places I'll show you. You're going to love it. I can help you house hunt and help you decorate." On and on she blathered, and it was the perfect balm to the grief still singeing my soul.

Chapter 60

Three weeks later, a six-pack of beer weighted down my right hand and a bag of munchies hung from the wrist on my left arm. Reaching up to knock, I took a deep breath, then exhaled slowly. I rapped my knuckles on the oak surface with force and confidence, hoping the sweat forming under my arms wouldn't turn into a river. I had not been this nervous in a long time.

When Will opened the door, I'll never forget the look on his face as long as I live. The mixture of elation, relief, shock and lust in his green eyes was more precious to me than any material thing I could have been given. He looked tremendously handsome in a pair of jeans and nothing else, the familiar five o'clock shadow stark on his cheeks, and his dark brown hair a rumpled mess. I wanted to rush him because, until I saw his face, I hadn't realized how much I missed him. But I held back and tried to start the conversation off right.

"Hi," I said, flipping my hair back. I thrust out the beer and snacks. "I'm your new neighbor, and I thought I'd introduce myself."

His smile was all the welcome I needed.

THE END

ABOUT THE AUTHOR

J. Thomas-Like is a writer born and raised in St. Clair Shores, Michigan. She lives with her doting husband, brilliant son, a passel of cats and a dog. This is her first novel, but definitely not her last. She started writing at a very young age, and is making her dreams come true, one story at a time.

NOTE FROM THE AUTHOR

I hope you enjoyed this story!

Please take a few minutes to leave an honest, constructive review at Amazon or on my Facebook page. Reviews are just tips for writers, like a gratuity for the waitperson who brought your meal the last time you dined out. It gives us encouragement for bad days when we think we'd be better off taking up poking badgers with spoons for a living.

Cover Art by James, GoOnWrite.com

Author Photo by Chasing Light Photography

Made in the USA
Charleston, SC
15 September 2015